MARJORY BASSETT is chair of the literary committee of the National Arts Club in New York. Originally from Kansas, she is a graduate of the University of Iowa, where she performed in theatrical productions and on the air. She has worked in broadcasting and international public relations and has published features in *Newsday* and the *Philadelphia Inquirer.* She lives in New York City.

Never Say Stark Naked

Never Say Stark Naked

A Novel

Marjory Bassett

WELCOME RAIN PUBLISHERS
NEW YORK

Excerpt from "Recuerdo" by Edna St.Vincent Millay. From *Collected Poems*,
HarperCollins. Copyright 1922, 1950 by Edna St.Vincent Millay.

The first chapter of this novel appeared in *Confrontation*,
published by Long Island University, No. 66/67 Fall 1998/Winter 1999.

Library of Congress CIP data available from the publisher.

Direct any inquiries to
Welcome Rain Publishers LLC

ISBN 1-56649-246-7

Printed in the United States of America by
HAMILTON PRINTING COMPANY

Interior design and composition by
MULBERRY TREE PRESS, INC.
(www.mulberrytreepress.com)

First Edition: June 2002
1 3 5 7 9 10 8 6 4 2

For Sally and Helen

Acknowledgments

THANK YOU to Katerina Czarnecki for generously giving me the advantage of her extensive knowledge. To Jean Ayer, Susan Jackson, Katie Meister, Elizabeth "Buffy" Morgan, Holly Peppe, Cherry Provost, and Wanda Smith for cheerful and informed suggestions. I'm grateful to readers of various versions of the manuscript, including Lisa Dickler Awano, John Baker, Bruce Bauman, Nancy Dougherty, Mary Page Evans, Audrey Fecht, Mary Campbell Gallagher, Deb Galyan, James Greene, Shirley Homer, Frances Maclean, Marilyn Marx, Audrey Nichols, Rachel Pollack, Margaret Ritter, Ellen Stone, Rebecca Stowe, Madeleine Thompson, Martin Tucker, Ann Van Saun, and Margaret Willey. My gratitude to the literary committee of the beautiful National Arts Club, to idyllic Ragdale, and to that paradise called the Virginia Center for the Creative Arts. To Josephine Hildyard Smith for musical advice and lifelong friendship. To Alana Jelinek for her international vision. To Jeffry Fry for his astonishing wit. To my neices and nephews. To Monty Leech for describing the work of an ambulance driver. To the visual artist Robert Kostka for information on color. To Mary Lou Waters at whose house on Long Island parts of the novel were written. To J.D. Dolan and Kelly Morgan for persuasive pep talks about computers. To Michael and Dary Derchin for years of understanding. To the portrait painter Everett Raymond Kinstler for sharing insights. To John Seinoski for his expertise. I especially thank John Weber, Chuck Kim, Charles Defanti, Mara Lurie, Christian Dierig, and Michele Ann Lamorte of Welcome Rain Publishers.

Never Say Stark Naked

One

SHE WAS, OF COURSE, known as Phoebe Stanhope in those days in Harkenstown, there on the plains in the middle of Kansas. That was essential information in recalling the moments of that New Year's Eve. She had been in the kitchen and managed to finish whipping the cream. Then with potholders she took the baking pan containing four apple turnovers from the oven and placed it on the kitchen counter. She was aware of her husband, Niles, standing there, watching her. She tried to hold on to that fact because it was as if she were wearing someone else's life.

"You're taking it a lot better than I'd expected," she heard him say.

She arranged the turnovers on four dessert plates and with a tablespoon she piled whipped cream on each one. "I can't believe it, that's why. It hasn't sunk in yet."

"What are you going to do?" he asked her.

What am I going to do? she asked herself silently. She felt as if she were living in slow motion. Her dreamlike inclination was to take this apple turnover in her hand and place it on his face so that he would be covered in whipped cream, like a scene from an old movie. That felt like the thing to do, but somehow she was not doing it. She was arranging the dishes neatly on the tray, as if spacing them evenly were important.

Now she lifted the dessert tray, trying to keep it steady as she carried it into the dining room, where the four of them had been sitting, where they'd been having a sober New Year's Eve. Phoebe was aware that her husband followed her into the dining room.

Everything about this night was different from the way she'd imagined two days before when she'd been at work, writing New Year's copy at the TV station. Then the station's sales manager, Red-Jack Ordall, had dropped the list of "specials of the week" on her desk for the Kansas-Choice Supermarkets account. Rushing, she'd typed, "The month of January is named for Janus, the two-faced Roman god, who has one face looking forward, the other looking back. And in celebration of the turn over of the year, Kansas-Choice Supermarkets are featuring a special on frozen apple turnovers ..." She dated the script for broadcast the next day, Wednesday, December 31, 1958, and dashed out to shop.

Taking her own suggestion, twenty-two-year-old Phoebe bought apple turnovers, thinking that when she served them on New Year's Eve, she could mention the two-faced god and the turn over of the year, since this was Red-Jack's biggest account. And he and his wife, Marcia, would be at the house for supper—which made it seem to Phoebe very unlike New Year's.

But does it really matter? Phoebe had asked herself while trying to accept that this year, for the first time in their three years of marriage, they would be home, rather than out celebrating at a big party at the country club or at a nightclub? Usually when they were going out on New Year's Eve, Niles would look down at Phoebe from his great height and give her a dazzling smile and a hug and say, "Come on, Baby, we'll have a party that won't quit."

Tonight while Niles had been dressing after his shower, Phoebe ran into the bedroom and kissed him on the back of his neck as he sat on the bed, leaning forward to tie his shoes. When the doorbell rang, she removed her apron from her sheer apricot-colored dress. Her dark eyes caught a glimpse of herself as she passed the hall mirror and touched her abundant auburn hair, which swept back from her forehead and fell around her shoulders.

Chilled air swooped in as she opened the door and smiled to welcome Marcia and Red-Jack Ordall, pausing on the porch, stamping snow from their boots. Snowflakes whirled under the streetlights and a car skidded as it turned the corner.

Red-Jack called out to Phoebe, "I feel like I just drove twelve miles through this stuff, instead of twelve blocks." Marcia preceded her husband through the door, bringing in the scent of Balmain perfume along with the cold air.

"The highway patrol is dishing out their usual broadcast bulletins," Red-Jack said. "Due to hazardous driving conditions, motorists are advised—you know . . ."

"Are advised," said Marcia, "to exercise extreme caution."

"Well, anyway, we made it, Pheeb," Red-Jack said.

"Just barely," said Marcia, as if she blamed him for the weather. As if they had been having one of their arguments. Marcia shrugged off her damp mink coat and Niles hung it in the closet. Marcia's young sensuous mouth revealed bunched teeth that protruded ever so slightly as she looked up at him and smiled.

Phoebe smiled too, relieved to see her best friend from childhood look happy, like her old fun self again. Phoebe had worried about her lately. As children, she and Marcia used to laugh so hard they would fall on the floor and Marcia's dad had dubbed them "the Holy Rollers."

Tonight Marcia's smile lasted for only a minute. Niles shuffled the cards to begin their game. They were seated in the living room, at the bridge table set up next to the fireplace, where Christmas cards decorated the mantel. As Red-Jack waited for his wife to bid, Marcia pulled at a strand of her dark hair, and throughout the game kept her blue eyes downcast. Studying her cards, Marcia covered her mouth with her free hand, a habit to hide her teeth. At the age of twelve Marcia had insisted that the dentist remove her braces because a boy at school had objected to "those wires" on her teeth. Marcia's mother, who annoyed Marcia by harping on "the importance of appearances," had chastised her daughter and through the years, had called her "stubborn," and repeated, "You've ruined your chance for beauty."

It was almost ten o'clock when Phoebe excused herself from the bridge table. She tried to understand the downhearted mood of the group tonight, since Niles himself and Marcia had started this plan for New Year's Eve. Niles had pointed out it was his and Phoebe's turn to entertain if they were making it a bridge night. Budget had been brought up. Niles had talked about Christmas expenses.

Now in the dining room, Phoebe leaned over the round table to place the chicken casserole, to move a sprig of holly in the centerpiece, and light the red candles. When she invited the group to come eat, Phoebe saw that Marcia, slumped in the velvet cushions of the sofa, was staring at the men, who stood smoking at the end of the room by the Christmas tree. Niles, usually eager for football talk, seemed unable to keep his mind on Red-Jack's predictions for tomorrow's New Year's games.

At the dining table Phoebe smiled. "What got into everybody? Even if we are budgeting—not even beer?"

"Beer's okay," Niles said and jumped up.

Phoebe stood up too. Maybe she should not have mentioned budgeting again in front of Red-Jack so close to Christmas. Red-Jack called the gifts from Marcia's parents "welfare handouts," as they arrived regularly all year round, Her parents had never accepted him. Last New Year's Eve Red-Jack, who'd had too much to drink, had spotted Marcia's folks at the country club, and charging toward them, he had bellowed that he was fed up with being ignored by them. Her parents, community leaders who owned the grain elevator, were so embarrassed that they proclaimed his actions unforgivable. "Sometimes I hate them all," Marcia had told Phoebe.

Now to brighten the mood to a celebration, Phoebe turned on the radio and came back dancing to the broadcast music: "Whatever will be, will be . . ."

The room smelled of beer as Red-Jack poured. He grinned as he pulled an extra dining room chair closer to the table, propped his boots on its flowered upholstery, and took a swig. "Hey now, this is more like it."

Angrily Marcia told him to put his feet down; he glowered as he straightened in his chair. His face in the candlelight glowed with fire as he ate in a noisy way as if to spite Marcia, who silently stabbed at her salad. He appeared as defiant now as in the company of his dad, a used-car salesman at Keen's Kars, who had belittled him, nicknaming him Red-Jack because of his red hair. Red-Jack hated his real name, John William Ordall, Jr., even more—was he supposed to be a replica of *the old man*? Marcia's rebellion against her own family had been to marry Red-Jack. Now he alternated between defying Marcia and anxiously trying to please her.

When Niles brought in more beer, Marcia's small body was perched on the edge of the chair. Her blue eyes were bright in the candlelight and flushes of red appeared on her delicate face. "Listen!"

Red-Jack, nodding his head over and over, sneered, "Listen! We're listening!"

"We have something to tell you," Marcia said.

"We have something to tell you," Red-Jack mimicked. "Who's we?"

Marcia was twisting her wedding ring and pushing it off and on over her knuckle. "Niles and I."

Red-Jack reared his head back. "Niles and you? What is this?" He turned to Phoebe, who was clearing off the table. "Hey, Pheeb, listen to this."

Niles said, "You better sit down, Phoebe."

Phoebe placed the stack of dishes on the table and sat down with her dark eyes on Niles, who leaned forward as if someone had hit him in the stomach. Phoebe stretched out her hand, reaching toward him, the small diamonds in her wedding ring sparkling in the candlelight.

He did not acknowledge her; he was looking at Marcia, who appeared determined as she picked up her beer glass. Then without taking a sip, she set it down. "Niles, help me out."

Niles sat up straight as though he had suddenly taken over. "Marcia and I have been seeing each other."

"Seeing each other?" Red-Jack said. "What the hell does that mean?"

"It means what you think it means," Marcia said. "That's what it means."

"How could you be seeing each other?" Red-Jack said.

"We have," Marcia said.

Dazed, trying to take this in, Phoebe took the dishes to the kitchen. As if she were in a glassed-in room, she could not quite hear what was being said. Niles came into the kitchen and touched her arm. "Aren't you listening, Phoebe?" He guided her back to the dining room table.

Red-Jack, stomping back and forth in front of the windows, hit his fist in his hand. "Goddamn it, how long's this been going on?" He planted his feet apart. "How come you've decided to come clean all of a sudden?"

Phoebe heard them talking about Labor Day weekend when the four of them had been at the lake. Familiar facts now and then floated across her mind to remind her that she had not been well then because of her miscarriage the week before. The words "miscarriage of justice" kept repeating themselves in her mind; she held her head and tried to concentrate on what was being said.

"I just don't get it!" Red-Jack yelled, smashing his fist on the table, upsetting one of the candles. Niles reached for it, toppling his glass of beer. Phoebe watched the beer drip onto the pale rug, the stain spreading larger. Marcia leaned over the table to blow out the other candle, leaving them in darkness, except for the flickering of the Christmas tree lights from the living room and the faint lights from the snowy street. Niles turned on the ceiling light. The glare made Phoebe blink as she tried even harder to concentrate.

"For God's sake," Marcia said, "we didn't plan it. We just found it happening to us."

Red-Jack slammed his fist on the wall by the windows. "What the hell does that mean?"

"It means," Marcia said, "that Niles and I want divorces."

Red-Jack stared at Marcia, who sat forward in her chair. "Divorces?" Red-Jack said in a suddenly subdued voice. "Are you out of your minds?"

"We want to marry each other," Niles said.

"Goddamn it," Red-Jack said softly. He walked suddenly into the living room.

"Well, not right away," Marcia called after him. "Not this very minute."

"We'll work it out together," Niles said. "All of us."

"The hell we will!" Red-Jack yelled, surging back into the room.

"Let's be civilized," Marcia said. "Can't we?"

"You're damned right," Red-Jack said, lunging toward his wife. "You're coming home with me."

"Hey, now, watch it," Niles said as he stood up to face Red-Jack. "Take it easy."

"Both of you!" Marcia said. "Take it easy!"

"Does anyone want dessert?" Phoebe heard herself say. She sensed the ridiculousness of her question, but, as in a dream, it seemed inevitable that she should say it. "It may not taste very good after beer. I didn't know we were going to have beer." Niles followed her into the kitchen. When they returned to the dining room, it was Phoebe who carried the dessert tray. Now that she had lifted it, it seemed important that she should carry it, a way to prove to herself that she could be in command of something, could hold onto something, even if it was suspended in air as this tray now was. Trembling, she lowered it onto the table.

As if in a kind of strange, social ritual dictated by lack of knowing what to do next, the four of them took their places and picked up their forks from the disheveled table to eat the apple turnovers. Phoebe stared down at her dish. Now that it was before her, it seemed odious and sickened her. She could not bring herself to take any of it into her mouth. She felt the four of them were frozen in time and space at the table, imprisoned against their wills by the dessert she had thrust upon them. Finally, she said, "Well, why don't you go?"

No one replied. They seemed stunned by her words. They looked at her as if she were the only one who had done anything startling tonight. The attention focused on her made her feel that action on her part was necessary. She glanced at each of them, moving her eyes from one to the other so swiftly, it was as if her glance were weighted and connected to a string that she swung above the table and, with it, grazed their faces. "We can't go on forever like this," she whispered. Tears pushed at the back of her eyes, but she was determined not to cry. She had emerged from the dream in which she had been momentarily encased and was now living in the nightmare of reality. "Get the hell out of here," she said.

"We should talk about this, Pheeb," Red-Jack said.

She pushed back her chair and turned so that she faced away from them toward the windows. "Now!" she said. "Go on. I'm not going to turn around till you're out of here." She closed her eyes and the nightmare went on. Opening her eyes, she stared in front of her at the dining room curtains and realized they needed washing. The thought seemed unreal and crazed and out of place to her, as did the whole night.

There were raised voices and she put her hands over her ears. She could still hear them speaking in low, huddled tones, moving about, opening and closing the coat-closet door by the entryway. It seemed a long time before she heard the front door open, the wind blowing hard, felt the cold air sweep through to the dining room. Then the door slammed.

She felt Red-Jack rest his hand on her shoulder. Sympathetically, she reached up to place her hand atop his. Then, gradually, she realized it was not Red-Jack she touched, but Niles. Niles was looking down at her with his deep-set gray eyes and she was so startled, she glanced away. Nothing would stay in place. Everything was changing shape. She grasped the table to see if it remained steady. "I thought you'd gone."

"Did you expect me to leave tonight?"

"If you're going . . . If you're going," she said, "go on. Go on," she persisted. "Get on with it!"

"Where would I go on New Year's Eve?"

"My God, didn't you figure that out? Where would I go for the rest of my life?" She rushed into the living room, past the piano to the stairs, which she climbed, wondering what she was doing, where she was going. At the top she went into the bedroom and closed the door. What should she do now? Floating up from the radio downstairs came the strains of "Auld Lang Syne."

From below: the slam of the front door, the car wheels spinning in the driveway. She ran to the window. Snow was blowing across the street light and across the moving and dipping car lights as he backed out. "Niles," she called. Oh, my God, was there still a way? "Don't leave me, Niles," she pleaded as if in a prayer. She ran down the stairs, pulled back the door and was struck by a force of icy wind, blowing snow. Whiteness swirled about her as she stepped onto the slippery porch. The dark street was empty. "Niles," she called, searching the blackness, broken only by the street light revealing relentless snow.

Shivering, she retreated inside, forcing the door closed against the wind. Whistles and cheers of celebration came from the radio—she rushed to switch it off. In the silence she moved slowly around in the house. Swallowing tears, she stumbled into one chair, then another. She found herself at the kitchen sink, staring at the dirty dishes piled there. Did it matter if she ever did them?

At long last she wandered into the dining room, where the lace cloth was askew on the table, the chairs out of place, abandoned. In the living room the Christmas cards were still there, aging on the mantel.

Niles, she repeated in her thoughts. Niles. Niles. The mantel clock chimed again. Three o'clock.

She lay on the sofa a very long time, not stirring, until it came to her that Marcia had been the last to touch these cushions. She sat up and pounded the back of the sofa; it's mine, it's mine . . . it used to be ours.

She sobbed, leaning forward, holding her face. She needed to talk with someone. Usually, she would have turned to Niles or phoned Marcia. How had all this happened? She had to *know,* she had to ask him. What time is it now? She had to make things right between them . . .

The doorbell was shrill. She rose, startled. Insistent rings pierced the air. "Niles," she whispered. "Niles." Rushing, she unlocked the door and pulled back. Cold wind blew toward her and snow whirled about the policeman who stood on the mat, holding on to the railing of the porch. With his free hand he removed his hat, and the porch light shone down on his young blond features. "Mrs. Stanhope?" his official-sounding voice said.

Phoebe backed away from the door, nodding for him to enter. He stamped his feet on the mat, and she became aware that he had a partner, standing behind him. The two policemen shouldered their way in, unbuttoning their heavy coats.

Words flew through the air, colliding, splitting apart: accident, hospital, your husband, collision, ambulance, highway . . .

Phoebe motioned the men to the sofa and sank down opposite them in a fireplace chair. She whispered, "Where did you say?"

The blond cop sat forward. "He was turning into the Jayhawker Motel."

Phoebe stood and clutched the edge of the mantel. "But the ambulance . . ."

"The ambulance took him to Memorial Hospital."

She leaned on the chair-back, then slid into the chair. "How . . . badly is he hurt?"

The policemen looked at each other. The blond one said, "Ma'am, you'd better come with us."

Two

PHOEBE THREW ON A COAT. It was still snowing. She perched on the front seat beside the blond policeman as he drove down the dark, silent street. His partner sat in back. The windshield wiper scraped back and forth; the police radio sputtered. At Memorial Hospital they drove around to the parking lot. "Wait!" Phoebe said as the car stopped. "Please wait. How is my husband?"

She felt the driver touch her arm.

She leaned toward the windshield. "What am I going to see? How is he?"

"Ma'am, I hate to say this: I'm afraid your husband didn't make it."

The policeman who had been in the backseat helped Phoebe out of the car. "No, no, no! No!" she cried, as he escorted her into a small building behind the hospital. She stumbled in the corridor and he held her arm again. They followed an attendant in dark workman's clothes to a room with a few scattered chairs and a tan window shade pulled down over one wall. The attendant pulled up the shade, revealing a window and behind it an enclosed space. He pushed a button as if ringing for an elevator and within the enclosure a platform rose. Phoebe felt as if she were falling through space as she saw Niles stretched out on the platform, his body covered by a white sheet, his lifeless battered face visible. She turned away, grabbed onto a chair to steady herself.

The attendant said, "Are you ready?" Phoebe nodded, forcing herself to stand up. She tried to hold her hand steady as she signed the forms blurring in front of her on the counter. When she handed them to him, he said, "Which funeral home do you want us to notify?"

"Robinson," Phoebe said, whispering the first name that came to her.

When she returned home with the policemen, the blond one said, "Is there anyone you want us to notify?"

The other one said, "Somebody who can come to be with you?"

"No, no, that's . . . thank you." She nodded to the policemen as they were going out the door. She began to turn on all the lamps, then rushed to call Marcia. Suddenly she stopped, gasped, and leaned on a table while turning away from the phone.

Climbing the stairs, she held the railing and tried to concentrate on what had happened. She paused in the doorway of the bedroom, staring at the wide bed. She heard again her words to him: "If you're going, go on . . . go on . . . get on with it." *Oh, my God, why did I say that?* With her hands clamped over her face, she walked around in a circle.

She felt her stomach heave and ran to the bathroom. After she vomited, she sank onto the edge of the bathtub. Her legs felt weak but she made herself to go downstairs to the desk for her address book. She held her hand on the telephone, hesitating before she called long distance, then hung up before it rang. She placed the call again and let it go through. To Glennerville, Kansas, to Mrs. Bertha Stanhope, Niles's mother. As she listened to the ringing, Phoebe dreaded the sound of her mother-in-law's startled, sleepy voice.

"I'm sorry, Mother Bertha," Phoebe began . . .

In the light of day, the first person to come to the house was gray-haired Lillian Fredericks, Phoebe's next-door neighbor. She insisted on washing the dishes, though Phoebe, bewildered, tried to take over at the sink. The doorbell shocked Phoebe into the memory of the policemen on the porch. She opened the door cautiously to Andy Borton, Niles's red-faced boss at Farm States Implements, Inc., and Mrs. Borton, then to a succession of solemn, sympathetic neighbors, who carried in bowls and platters of food. Phoebe, dazed, thanked one, then another.

Lillian stayed until Niles's mother arrived from Glennerville later in the afternoon. At the door, Phoebe hugged her heavyset mother-in-law tighter than she ever had before. "You're all right?" Mother Bertha said, while crying. "You weren't hurt?"

"No," said Phoebe, guilt rising inside herself.

Phoebe's mother-in-law usually arrived alone, but this time a boy carried her luggage. She introduced him, a Glennerville neighbor who had chauffeured the sixty-year-old woman in her car. She said that after Phoebe's phone call, she had been so distraught she'd been afraid to get behind the wheel herself. She'd driven for years, even had run the tractor when Niles's father had still been alive and they'd lived on a farm, but today, suddenly, she'd been unable to make herself sit in the driver's seat.

Now the boy had taken the bus back to Glennerville and Phoebe and Mother Bertha were alone. Seated on the sofa, Niles's mother held her head between her hands and, through tears, squinted at Phoebe. "Tell me again, I didn't get it all. I've been trying to understand how it happened. Had you been to a party? Where had you been?"

"Marcia and Red-Jack were here."

"Here?" Mother Bertha said. "Oh, you mean he drove them home. Didn't they have their own car?"

Phoebe touched her mother-in-law's arm, wanting to protect her from a new shock. When she handed her a glass of warm milk, Mother Bertha said, "All I thought about in the car was my son lying dead. I think and think and I still can't believe it. He had his whole life ahead." Her deep-set eyes—so like Niles's—were on Phoebe as she took a nearby chair. "I want to get this straight in my mind," Mother Bertha said. "You don't want my son to have a church funeral?"

"I just meant I hadn't been to the church yet."

"Most people find comfort in church."

Phoebe closed her eyes. "I wish I did."

"I'm not arguing. My son wouldn't want us to argue. He never could stand it when his father and I had words."

Phoebe said, "You ought to rest."

"I know I need to." Ahead of Phoebe, Mother Bertha toiled up the stairs, trudged down the hall to the "spare room," called "your room" when she came to visit. Now she cried out, "Oh, dear God, I can't believe—"

Phoebe rushed to hug her. "I can't believe it either."

Alone, Phoebe edged into the bedroom she had shared with Niles. She touched a post of the bed, then opened the top drawer of his dresser and looked at his clean socks she had laundered, tucking each pair into a roll. She picked up a stray sock, a navy-blue one, a sock without a mate. She wiped her eyes with it and kept it clutched in her moist hand, even as she changed into her nightgown and pulled back the heavy blue tweed bedspread. She saw the pillow where his head had lain—quickly she covered it up. She stuffed the sock under her own pillow, sank down on her side of the bed. She clutched her head, heard the words: "If you're going, go on, go on, get on with it . . ." Guilt squeezed her waist, pressed on her chest.

Niles's mother walked heavily in the next room. Phoebe guessed she was praying even as she stepped to the closet to hang up her clothes. She'd said she was tired, but so nervous she wanted to unpack herself, to keep occupied. Phoebe was tortured by guilt for Niles's death, his mother's grief at the loss of her only son. Phoebe thought of the pain she herself had suffered when she'd lost her baby girl by miscarriage.

Phoebe drew on the pale blue robe that Niles had given her for Christmas, then ran her fingers across his dark robe draped over the chair. She stood at the window where last night she had looked down to see Niles back out of the driveway. Tonight the street light revealed the icy whiteness covering the street, trees, shrubbery.

To hide the sight, she grabbed the pull of the window shade and was reminded of the shade at the morgue. She tugged at it and it flew to the top with a ferocious snap. She rushed out of the bedroom and slipped down the stairs.

In the living room she stared at the decorated tree. Among the Christmas cards on the mantel was a red and silver greeting signed in red ink in Red-Jack's handwriting: "Love, Marcia and Red-Jack." Phoebe had a sudden urge to strike Marcia on the face so that her blue eyes, in shock, would look up to see what had hit her.

Phoebe swept the cards from the mantel. She was holding them in her hand when her mother-in-law appeared in her olive green robe, her dyed brown hair in rollers around her large face. Phoebe held her anguish privately inside herself. "You want something else to eat?" she said, leading the way to the kitchen.

Niles's mother re-tied the sash of her robe around her thick waist and opened the refrigerator. She brought out fried chicken and a bowl of shredded carrots and raisins. "You've got to get something inside you, too, Phoebe. You don't want to get any skinnier than you already are."

Phoebe stood at the stove to heat bouillon. "Please don't worry—I'm not really skinny."

"Well, you're not fat, that's for sure."

At the table Phoebe took Bufferin and had a salted cracker with broth, while her mother-in-law chewed on a drumstick. "You don't want to let yourself go now," Mother Bertha said. "I remember how proud my son was when he told me about you: 'She's a knock-out,' that's what he said. Oh, Phoebe, don't let him down."

Phoebe swallowed and nodded.

"If you can't sleep, you've got to make it up for it by eating. I always told that to my son. I tried so hard to keep him healthy. I know that's the robe Niles gave you for Christmas. He saw I wanted a new one too. He said he'd get me one for my birthday."

Quickly, Phoebe said, "I'll get you one."

"You probably don't remember it's the second of March. I may not live that long."

"Oh, please don't say that!" Phoebe said. "Of course you will."

Mother Bertha laid her head in her arms on the table. "I have to pick out the burial clothes. I know that has to be done."

Phoebe leaned toward her. "I'll take care of that."

"No, I want to do it—my son would want me to be brave." Mother Bertha sat up, blotting her wet face with her napkin. "He wore that nice dark blue suit on Christmas. He looked so handsome."

Phoebe had difficulty speaking. "I don't believe he can wear that."

"Why not? Oh, dear God."

Phoebe embraced Mother Bertha, then led the way upstairs. In the bedroom Phoebe brought out from the closet his brown tweed suit and ran her fingers over the roughness. Phoebe forced her voice: "He always liked this."

When Phoebe opened a dresser drawer, Mother Bertha chose a shirt, then moved to the tie rack, pulling out a striped tie. "He and I loved this."

Phoebe lingered at the dresser with the gift box containing the maroon tie she had given him for Christmas. "I bought this tie specially to go with his brown tweed."

"No, you chose the suit. I want him to wear this tie."

"That's fair." Phoebe stared at the blue striped tie draped over her mother-in-law's hand. "You know, Mother Bertha, it just doesn't go with the suit."

"My son wouldn't want us to argue."

Surely we're not really arguing about color schemes, Phoebe thought, agreed to the striped tie, stepped to the closet for a suitcase. As she folded Niles's tweed suit jacket, the odor of cigarettes was strong from the open pack of Camels he'd left in a pocket. Marcia and Red-Jack had given him a carton on Christmas Eve—so that was the last time he'd worn this suit.

Phoebe saw that her mother-in-law had seated herself in a chair and had Niles's robe over her knees. "Mother Bertha." Phoebe tried to make her voice steady. "Tonight you said that you and Niles were always close."

Mother Bertha stared at Phoebe. "You know that. Why are you bringing that up now?"

"I was just wondering whether he mentioned anything about his plans."

"We always talked about his plans."

Phoebe sat down at her dressing table. "I mean at Christmas time."

In the mirror she could see her mother-in-law coming toward her, carrying Niles's robe. "Phoebe, what are you getting at?"

"I wouldn't even know how to say it. He wanted to leave me, I think."

"That's impossible!"

"I guess it came down to . . . he didn't love me anymore."

Mother Bertha slammed a hand on her chest, then sat down heavily in the chair. "Of course he loved you. He loved you and he loved me. He was a good boy, a good man."

Phoebe rushed to embrace her. "I never should have—"

"We have to think of him. We have to do him justice. He didn't like arguments. I remember when he was a little boy—"

"But this was different. He talked about divorce."

"Oh, not seriously. I'm sure not seriously, there's never been a divorce in our family. You mustn't ever say that! Underneath, Niles was proud, he wouldn't want it. His father—oh, if his father could hear this!"

The next morning, a cold Friday, the sky was overcast. Icy whiteness, covering the landscape and rooftops, caused a glare, making Phoebe squint as she drove Mother Bertha's Chevrolet through streets the snowplow had cleared. Snow was piled in the yards and ice hung heavy on tree limbs, some broken off and lying in snow heaps where children tumbled and shouted.

Mother Bertha, seated beside Phoebe, said she hadn't been able to sleep last night. "I wish you hadn't talked about those upsetting things."

"I'm sorry," Phoebe said.

"I'm just so nervous. I hope my heart can stand the strain."

Quickly Phoebe moved her eyes from the road to glance at her mother-in-law. "I can take you to a doctor."

"No, I only like my own doctor."

Phoebe parked near the First Methodist Church, following Mother Bertha's earlier plea that she needed to pray "in a holy place." Phoebe held her mother-in-law's arm as they made their way on the shoveled walk. Their breath showed in the frosty air. As they climbed the church steps, Phoebe recognized the solemn organ music: Mozart's *Ave Verum Corpus*.

She grasped the handle of the carved door, realizing she had seldom entered the church this way—through the front door. Nowadays she didn't attend church, but as a small child she had loved to go in the side door with her father, who had been the church organist. Even as a five-year-old, she'd sat beside him on the organ bench when he'd been practicing and she'd leaned to peek at his worn black organ shoes moving on the pedals.

Now the current organist, with his back to Phoebe and Mother Bertha, appeared to be the only other person in the church. Still bundled up in her cloth coat with the fox collar, Mother Bertha bowed her head, which was covered by a hat that came down over her ears. Seated in the wooden church pew beside her and seeing her lips move in prayer, Phoebe wished that she had her religious faith.

The somber organ music fell over Phoebe like damp, black gauze. She felt she was existing in a ritual: she heard somber chords she did not want to hear, she sat in a place where she did not want to be. Finally, the chords swelled to a close; the pudgy organist, Robert Rowley, stood up.

Phoebe side-stepped her way out of the pew. She'd last seen Robert at the TV station where they both worked. Now, when introduced to Niles's mother, he shook her hand and held it in a consoling way. "If you want me to," Robert said, "I'll come over to the house and play for you. Did Phoebe tell you that her mother was my first piano teacher?"

Phoebe nodded, remembering Jimmy Connordon, age seven, who always had come early to his lessons. Phoebe had told Jimmy that she was five-and-a-half and would be six on her next birthday. Phoebe watched Jimmy take off his cap and together they placed it in the dark coat closet by the entry hall. Jimmy told Phoebe to wait: he would show her his "thing," and pulled it out of his pants, which were already unzipped. Phoebe stared in wonder.

He pointed to her and told her to pull down her panties. She bent to push them down her legs and left them at her ankles. When she stood up, he was looking at her. She stared below his round belly at his small thing he held in his fingers. With her index finger she almost touched the tip of it. They both giggled and said, "Shhh!" to quiet themselves. He chanted in a whisper, "Fuck, fuck, fuck, fuck . . ."

When the piano lesson stopped, neither of them noticed. Phoebe's mother opened wide the closet door. "Phoebe, what on earth?"

Jimmy scrambled from the closet first and ran out of the house. Ducking her head, Phoebe moved to the back of the closet. Her mother picked up Phoebe's panties from the floor, grabbed her by the wrist, jerking her upstairs to her bedroom.

Phoebe stared at the door while her mother shouted to her to stay in her room. As Phoebe tried to hurry to put on her panties, she could hear her mother's footsteps on the stairs, her angry words from downstairs.

Crying, Phoebe ran to the window. In the harsh light, the street below was empty except for Jimmy, running with his cap in one hand, his music book in the other. He stopped, clumsily put on his cap, then ran again. Phoebe thought he must be crying too.

The next morning instead of going to church, her mother stayed in bed with the door to her bedroom closed. Phoebe waited by the door. When her mother finally came out, she informed Phoebe she wanted to talk to her. Phoebe followed her back into the bedroom, where, as told, she sat on a chair. Her mother held her forehead as if she had a headache, paced the rug, then sat down on the unmade bed and said that she had worried all night. She had married too late in life to bring up a child. "It makes me too nervous."

Phoebe ran to her mother, who pushed her away sobbing: "You don't know what you've done. I didn't watch you enough." Phoebe was not to talk to Jimmy or tell her father or anyone else anything about this as long as she lived. "You're to die with this secret," her mother said, "just as I will. You'll be sorry when I'm gone."

In her own room Phoebe ran past the bed to the window. Rather than a view from the second story as always before, the yard and street below suddenly seemed miles down through space. She edged away from the window, covering her eyes with her hands. As if she were blind, she put her hands out before her as she stepped, until she touched the softness of the bed. She wondered if her mother would die that day. She loved her mother.

That night Phoebe kept her panties on under her pajamas and clasped her hands as she knelt by her bed: "If I should die before I wake, I pray the Lord my soul to take." When she climbed into bed and lay on her back, the ceiling light was in her eyes. She was afraid to switch it off. She turned on her side, drawing her legs up. She rubbed her feet against her pajama legs, trying to warm their icy coldness, then pulled the covers about her head. She was afraid to go to sleep for fear she would die before she waked.

No piano pupils came the next Saturday. Her mother was not well enough, she said, to continue teaching . . .

"Phoebe, are you all right?" she heard a man's voice say, bringing her abruptly to the present. She realized that she was standing in the church aisle with the organist, Robert Rowley, and Mother Bertha.

Phoebe ushered Mother Bertha to the car and drove to the Robinson Funeral Home. When the two women stepped into the entrance parlor, Phoebe at once wanted to turn and leave but she felt the pressure of Mother Bertha's hand on her arm. Seeing the heavy dark draperies and deep wine carpet, Phoebe was back to the first time—at age nine—that she had been in this oppressive room. She had held tightly to her father's hand that day after her mother's death.

Phoebe remembered that her mother had long complained of being sick at her stomach. Her mother had told her, "The doctor says it's a bleeding ulcer. I'm so thin, he says I have to gain weight." Often the doctor came and gave her mother a "hypo." She got pneumonia and went back into the hospital. When Phoebe was allowed to speak briefly with her on the phone, Mama had talked to her about her impending death and said she was "preparing" Phoebe.

Phoebe could not keep her mind on her schoolwork or feel enthusiasm for fun with her friends. When Daddy came home from the hospital, he took Phoebe into his arms. "Mama's gone," he said and Phoebe held on to him, knowing he was crying too. He kissed her on the forehead. "You go on to bed and we'll talk in the morning." It seemed to Phoebe that she had stayed awake all night . . .

Now in the entrance parlor of the funeral home, a young attendant took from Phoebe the suitcase containing Niles's clothes. Even before a bald-headed man in a black suit came forward and in a somber voice identified himself as Mr. Robinson, Phoebe recognized him from her mother's funeral and knew that he was Kathy Robinson's father.

Kathy, long ago, had been one of her mother's music pupils and had come up to Phoebe at recess after her mother had stopped teaching. "How come your mom quit giving music lessons?"

"She just did."

Kathy pushed her. "You always say that. My mom and the other mothers think there's something very peculiar about it—the way she stopped—so pfft—sudden."

Phoebe ran from her, across the noisy schoolyard. "Mind your own beeswax!"

Now as Phoebe and Mother Bertha walked along a wide carpeted passageway with Mr. Robinson, a young woman caught up with them: grown-up Kathy Robinson, dressed in black in an echo of her father's suit, her dark hair pulled severely back from her big face. Kathy offered prepared condolences, which Phoebe could hardly stand to listen to. Mother Bertha, as if about to faint, interrupted by grabbing Phoebe's arm.

Phoebe herself felt unsteady as they entered a room where new caskets were displayed, at various levels, on white satin-draped platforms.

"I want the best," Mother Bertha said. "I had the best for his father. I want the best for my son."

That evening when Robert Rowley phoned to say he was on his way to the house, Mother Bertha, who had been resting, was now dressed, as if waiting to be summoned. She smoothed her black dress over her corseted stomach and hips. "I have to be composed," she said to Phoebe. "I mustn't shame my boy."

While Robert and Mother Bertha sat together chatting on the sofa, Phoebe slipped into a chair nearby. Mother Bertha was saying to Robert, "We named Niles for my maiden name. I was Bertha May Niles before I became Bertha May Stanhope thirty-four years ago. I can't believe they're both gone—my husband and now my son." Mother Bertha lowered her head. "It doesn't pay, I'll tell you, to have too many plans."

Robert patted her hand, stepped to the grand piano, and settled his chubby body onto the bench. He stretched his hands, then looked over at Mother Bertha. "Did Phoebe tell you I compose some of . . ." He struck a chord, flourished a down-the-scale movement to low, deep tones.

The doorbell rang. Holding her breath, Phoebe opened the door.

On the porch stood Red-Jack. He staggered. His bloodshot eyes were not in focus as he plunged through the doorway and into the living room. "Hi-ya, Pheeb." With both hands he patted his uncombed hair. He smelled of whiskey as he struggled out of his wrinkled overcoat. When Phoebe started to take it, he yanked it away and dropped it over a chair. "Did you know she's gone?"

Phoebe did not take time to ask what he meant. "Red-Jack, Niles's mother and Robert are here—Robert Rowley."

Robert remained on the piano bench but had stopped playing. Mother Bertha now stood behind Robert. Her eyes followed Red-Jack, who wandered about the room, leaning precariously one way and then another.

Phoebe urged him to sit down. He caught Phoebe by the arm. "I don't want to sit—"

"Red-Jack, Niles's mother's here," Phoebe emphasized, fearful of what he would say. "Listen to me!"

Red-Jack brought his forehead down to Phoebe's and she ducked away. He swung around, rushing toward Robert, and with his fist, jabbed his shoulder. "Hi-ya, Robbie."

Robert stood up. "Hello, Red."

Phoebe turned to Mother Bertha. "Wouldn't you be more comfortable upstairs?"

Red-Jack wailed, "No . . . o . . . o," and threw his arm around Mother Bertha. "You stay here with me."

Robert grasped Red-Jack's arm. "Come on, Red, I'll take you home." Red-Jack lunged toward the dining room. "Let's go, Red," Robert said. "Let's have a drink at my house."

Phoebe and Robert coaxed Red-Jack into his overcoat and escorted him to Robert's car. When the men drove off, Phoebe, who had gone out without a wrap, hurried back to the house.

Mother Bertha opened the door. "What did Red-Jack mean—'she's gone'?"

"I guess he meant Marcia. She probably went somewhere. That wouldn't be too unusual."

"Won't she be at the funeral?"

"I . . . I suppose she will," Phoebe said.

"It still seems peculiar she hasn't shown up."

"We haven't been here every minute."

"Well, it seems mighty odd to me," Mother Bertha said.

The next afternoon when Phoebe's neighbor Lillian Fredericks came to the house, she told Phoebe and Mother Bertha, "Fred has the car waiting, so when you're ready—"

"I'll never be ready for this," Mother Bertha said. "But I must face it. My son would want me to be brave."

She and Phoebe followed Lillian to the green Oldsmobile and Lillian slid into the front seat beside Fred, her husband, the history teacher at the high school. After her mother-in-law had placed herself in the back seat, Phoebe squeezed into the space left over. "I'm glad we're not going in the funeral car to the church," Mother Bertha said. "It's bad enough to ride in the funeral car to the cemetery."

"We'll drive you to the cemetery," Fred said.

"Oh, dear God, I can't believe my boy is going to a cemetery." Mother Bertha's gloved hand reached for Phoebe's sleeve. "Phoebe, you won't leave me?"

"I'm right here beside you."

In the church Robert Rowley was playing Mother Bertha's organ request: "Nearer My God To Thee." Phoebe held her mother-in-law's arm as they walked down the center aisle, breathing in the scent of white roses and carnations. Nearing the front, drawing closer to the casket, Phoebe shut her eyes in dread of seeing Niles as she'd viewed him in death at the morgue. She helped Niles's mother into the front pew, then sank down beside her.

The white satin lining of the raised coffin lid glowed in the light of the large white candles. Phoebe kept her eyes on the flickering light, which blurred through her tears. The elderly minister's voice rose and fell: "The Lord is my shepherd, I shall not want . . ."

In the snow-covered cemetery, Phoebe edged around the gravestones bearing the names of her grandmother and her mother and father, then stood with Mother Bertha and the other mourners. The grave seemed to draw Phoebe into its depth as the coffin was lowered deeper and deeper into the hole, taking Niles away. Mother Bertha cried out and Phoebe, feeling faint herself, put an arm around her.

The mourners began to turn away. It was then that Phoebe saw Marcia and Marcia's mother, both bundled in mink, standing together. With their eyes on her, Phoebe started to stumble, then caught herself and stood erect.

Three

AT THE BREAKFAST TABLE PHOEBE SAID, "I've got to get back to my job."

Mother Bertha looked up from her oatmeal and raisins. "Today?"

"Didn't I mention it last night?"

"But I didn't think you meant today."

Phoebe tried to keep her attention away from the white cover of the family photo album that Mother Bertha had placed beside her dish. In the seven days since New Year's Eve, Phoebe had become intensely aware of anything white. Her eyes seemed to seek it out; at the same time she wanted not to notice. She saw again the white satin lining of the casket, white candles, roses, snow on roads, gravestones . . .

Mother Bertha spread orange marmalade on her toast. "My poor Niles, he'll never go back to his job. Others can go on with their careers." She stirred sugar into her coffee. "You take my car. I won't be driving."

Before leaving, Phoebe said, "Please rest a lot."

In the business district, Phoebe parked in the lot behind the TV station. Then, as she grasped the handle of the heavy glass door leading into the lobby, she guessed that her co-workers would look for a sign from her on how she wanted to be treated this morning. She wished she could avoid this encounter. She felt vulnerable, exposed by tragedy—it would be easier this morning if no one knew her and she came in here as a stranger among strangers.

The monitor in the TV lobby showed Carol Kay holding up a recipe book on *Carol Kay's Calendar,* one of the shows Phoebe usually scripted. During her absence it had been handled by the other staff writer. Phoebe said, "Hi," to Mary Ann, the receptionist but Mary Ann was so occupied with the switchboard, she hardly seemed aware of Phoebe's arrival. Phoebe paused at the doorway to the general manager's office, but he was not at his desk. In the next room, she found it strange to be back at her own familiar tan metal desk, but in unfamiliar circumstances.

She glanced over to the next desk at her fellow-writer, buxom Barbara Hadley, who wore a high-necked white blouse and was busy on the phone. When Barbara acknowledged Phoebe, she said, "Thank the Lord you're back," and deposited an armful of fat file folders onto Phoebe's desk. "This place is a madhouse." Barbara stood up straight, placing her pencil behind her ear. "I'm not good at this but you know how sorry I am."

Phoebe nodded. "Barb, thanks for all your hard work—"

Barbara held up her hand. "You've done plenty for me."

Phoebe's desk calendar for the year 1958 was opened to the last day she had been at the station: December 31. Her hand pounced on the calendar to hide the date. Her incoming box was piled as high as it had been early last summer when she'd returned from vacation with Niles and again in late summer after her miscarriage.

Now she heard: "Phoebe . . ." It was the deep voice of the newscaster, William Eagle—called "Willie" by the staff. He was looking for the general manager. "Jim's not at his desk," Willie said. "Where is he?"

"I haven't seen him," Phoebe said.

"Haven't seen him? You mean not at all?"

"I mean I just came in."

Willie, starting to rush away, stopped. "Oh, I'm sorry, Phoebe. I wasn't thinking."

She shook her head. "Don't worry, I understand." After all, she thought, it was her own personal tragedy. Others could be concerned only up to a certain point.

Coworkers asked her to join them for lunch but she was not ready for small talk. She drove to the Kansas-Choice Supermarket on North Main Street, where she usually shopped because of the commercials she wrote. The last time she'd been here, she had bought frozen apple turnovers. Approaching the store, she forced herself forward but her body rebelled.

She turned away and drove to Dawson's Grocery, near the house where she had grown up. As she entered the small store, the mobile chimes tinkled, a sound familiar from her early childhood when she'd first had the adventure of running alone to the grocery store for her mother. The scent of cleaning powder used on the wooden floor met her now, along with her favorite smells of childhood: fresh bread, celery, and coffee being run through the grinding machine. Mrs. Dawson, as usual wearing a cotton dress and apron with a gray sweater draped about her shoulders, huddled over her desk with the cash register on it. "We're getting along all right," Mrs. Dawson assured Phoebe, "considering we're no longer youngsters."

She gave a little laugh, and after a moment, Phoebe said, "I guess you heard about Niles."

Mrs. Dawson sobered. "We were sorry to hear."

Leaving the store, Phoebe feared she had sounded as if she were asking for sympathy. It was awkward that Mrs. Dawson had not asked her first. Death puts us on uncertain terms, Phoebe thought, when she was again back at her desk. Battling to keep her mind on her work, she would not allow herself to quit for the day until she heard the deep voice of Willie Eagle wrapping up the local evening news.

Outside the wind was cold and the street lights were on against the deepening darkness of winter. Behind the building in the lighted parking lot, Phoebe saw Red-Jack get out of his Buick, stride toward her. "Hey, Pheeb," he said as he opened his briefcase. "I called on our favorite bread-and-butter account. Want me to put your specials-of-the-week on your desk?"

"Thanks," she said, stepping away from him. "It's freezing cold."

"You need a drink."

She opened the car door. "Thanks, not now."

"You want some good hot coffee? We could go over to the Melody." He nodded toward the coffee shop across the street. "We could have a bite."

"No, thanks. I can't right now."

"Pheeb—"

"Please, Red-Jack," Phoebe said, climbing into the car. "Excuse me."

He leaned toward her. "We need each other."

"I'm sorry, Red-Jack." Driving out of the parking lot, she headed for Main Street, then suddenly turned to avoid the Robinson Funeral Home. Out of habit she tried to stop her tears. As a small child, she'd been punished when she had cried, her mother grabbing her by the shoulders, shaking her, "Hush! Now you hush!" Her mother shook her so hard, she forced her to stop her tears before she was ready, so that her crying ended in jerky, hiccupy sounds. "Your face will freeze like that!" Phoebe had kept back tears by blinking and swallowing; then later her mother said, "Cat got your tongue?"

At home, Phoebe found Mother Bertha still in her robe and asleep in Niles's big lounge chair in the living room. She stretched her heavy arms as she sat up. "It's lonely here. I keep thinking about my boy."

Phoebe tried to think of how to help her. "Have you thought about your own job?"

Mother Bertha struggled out of her chair. "What are you getting at?"

"I just wondered if you'd feel better back at work."

"What? And leave everything undone? You're trying to rush me."

"No, Mother Bertha, I just—"

"What about the lawyer and insurance forms? You seem to think burying is the end."

"No, I don't think that." Phoebe turned toward her mother-in-law, who stood in her wide black oxfords and squinted at Phoebe. "Please, Mother Bertha, you don't always know what I think."

Mother Bertha followed Phoebe to the stairs. "Maybe if you'd speak up, I'd know what you think. Didn't you ever talk to my son? It must have been mighty lonely for him."

"Of course we talked. But why should I have to justify how much we talked?" Phoebe climbed a few steps, then came down. "Please, Mother Bertha, I don't want to upset you and I don't want you to upset me. It's a difficult time . . ."

"I'm just so nervous." Mother Bertha looked up with pleading eyes. "Oh, Phoebe, it's just that it's so hard for me."

"I know." Phoebe, running up the stairs, heard herself call out, "As if it's not for me." Oh, God, why did I say that? she asked herself. It only makes it harder to deal with her and she is suffering . . .

The next morning while Phoebe was taking a bath, there was a knock on the bathroom door. Phoebe sat up erect in the tub. "I'm almost finished."

"I just want you to know," Mother Bertha said through the door, "I can take a hint."

Phoebe scurried out of the tub, yanked on a robe. In the hallway, she was surprised to see that her mother-in-law was already dressed, wearing her black shirtwaist. "I did a lot of thinking in the night," Mother Bertha said, "I can tell you want me to leave."

"I didn't say that."

"You don't say a lot of things," Mother Bertha said, following Phoebe into the bedroom.

Phoebe took fresh underwear from her dresser. "I just don't want to say the wrong thing."

Mother Bertha insisted: "I didn't hear what you said."

"I don't want to regret saying the wrong thing, Mother Bertha. Please, I'm sorry, I'm very sorry but I don't have time to talk now."

"Well, excuse me!" Mother Bertha walked heavily from the room.

Phoebe slipped into her underwear and pulled on her navy blue dress. When she stepped into the hall, Mother Bertha came out of her bedroom and thumped down the stairs after her. "Aren't you even going to eat your breakfast?"

Phoebe hurried to the kitchen. "I'll take an orange."

"That's not proper nutrition."

"It'll have to do this morning."

"You need a balanced diet," Mother Bertha called after her. "Breakfast is the most important meal." Phoebe grabbed her coat from the closet. "I suppose you're taking my car," Mother Bertha said, following her to the door. "We'd better see the lawyer at noon since you have so little time for me anymore."

"We don't have an appointment. I plan to make one. But not for today. This noon," Phoebe said, deciding as she spoke, "I'm going to eat with some people from the station. Look, I'll get things done."

"There's a lot to do."

Phoebe held tightly to the doorknob, not allowing herself to scream.

Four

RED-JACK APPROACHED PHOEBE'S DESK at the end of the day. "We have to talk, Pheeb."

"Where?" Phoebe said. "There's too many people we know at the Melody. The Prairie Schooner?"

They left Mother Bertha's car parked and Red-Jack, driving his Buick, headed into the north section of Harkenstown where expansive grounds surrounded large houses. As he swung the car into Cottonwood Street, Phoebe sat forward in the seat. "Where are you going?"

"By Marcia's folks' house."

"What do you think you're going to see there?"

"Marcia, I hope."

"Not with me in the car! Please! Can't you see her when I'm not with you?"

He was driving more slowly now in a neighborhood Phoebe knew as well as her own. She and Marcia used to ride their bicycles after school through these streets. When they had wheeled closer to Marcia's house, they rode single file to make ready for the turn into the long curved driveway. They veered off to park their bikes by the kitchen door. Inside the delicious-smelling kitchen Marcia would edge up to the fat, white-aproned cook, Virginia, and con her into giving them just-out-of-the-oven walnut muffins or a taste of the icing she was about to smear on chocolate cake. Grabbing cookies, Marcia promised

Virginia they wouldn't "strew crumbs," so Phoebe felt she should be careful. But Marcia shrugged, saying her mother was never at home in the afternoons unless she was entertaining her bridge group. Marcia seemed unimpressed with the house that Phoebe and their classmates described in awed tones as a "mansion like a movie star's" with "real silver faucets and phones even in the bathrooms."

Now Red-Jack kept the engine running when he stopped the car in front of the great gabled house. On the grounds, which took up a full city block, spotlights highlighted the shrubbery and winter-barren trees. Phoebe felt uncomfortable sitting here staring at the house, even though it had always been a source of local curiosity, a kind of tourist sight and pride for townspeople to drive around and show their visiting relatives.

Tonight, here and there, throughout the house, lights were turned on. Phoebe saw that the light near the center of the second floor was on in Marcia's bedroom, where Marcia, as a child, used to deliberately leave crayons strewn on the white carpet and to sit on the pink bedspread, against her mother's orders. When Marcia's parents had been away on trips, the two little girls had invaded Mrs. Harkens's dressing room and standing on chairs, they had leafed through dresses hanging there, still smelling faintly of Chanel No. 5. Playing "movie star," they dressed up in her evening gowns and furs—sable, mink, white ermine. Then clumping around in high heels, they tried to hold up the long skirts as they stumbled and paraded in front of mirrors and make-believe admirers.

Now Phoebe turned to Red-Jack in the car. "I don't understand what we're doing, sitting out here, trying to see Marcia. Can't you just call her up?"

"Hell, she won't come to the phone. The goddamned maids say she's not there. All that fancy crap." He drove on slowly, then suddenly speeded up, racing through the residential section.

Phoebe asked, "Do you want her back?"

"She's my wife." He struck the steering wheel with the palm of his hand. "Hell!" He turned onto the highway. "I can't very well put out a search warrant."

"I guess you could talk to a lawyer, to see what your rights—"

"I don't want to talk to any old damned lawyer. They'd love that, to get things going. Her family would get a whole tribe of goddamned lawyers."

He cut off the road into the Prairie Schooner's parking lot, where the fierce, cold wind hit them as they ran inside. The place was almost deserted. Jake Hildebrande, the balding owner, wearing cowboy boots and a sleeveless leather jacket over his plaid shirt, said, "Howdy! Go ahead and take your choice," of tables or booths. There was a mingled odor of beer and something being cooked with onions.

Seated in the back booth, Phoebe looked at the place mats showing pictures of cowboys on bucking broncos. The table lamp with the ceramic base was in the shape of a covered wagon. Or a prairie schooner? "Every time I come here," said Phoebe, in an effort not to rush the real conversation they had come for, "I swear I'm going to look up the difference between a covered wagon and a prairie schooner. Or are they the same?"

"Pheeb, you got me." Someone had put coins in the juke box and the place vibrated with the beat and twang of country music. When a friendly blond waitress arrived with her tray and placed set-ups of club soda on the table, Phoebe noticed that her low-cut blue and white calico-print dress attracted Red-Jack's attention. As the waitress turned to leave, he said, "Thank you, ma'am. Thank you, ma'am honey."

He slid his big body out of the booth. From his coat pocket he pulled a bottle of Scotch, and in the style of those circumventing the Kansas liquor law of the day, he placed it only briefly on the table. After spiking his soda, he took a swig and ran his tongue over his lips. He leaned sideways to place the bottle on the floor under the table. Now his eyes were on Phoebe. "How you been doing? Not so hot, maybe?"

Phoebe took a sip of her drink, and finally said, "It's different from day to day. If I'm able to sleep, I wake up startled and think: *Something terrible's happened*. I'm in a panic, I feel terrified, desperate, and

I ask myself, 'What is it?' And then suddenly it comes to me. I know I won't wake up from this nightmare because it's *real*. And yet at the same time I can't believe it, I just can't make myself totally believe it. It hasn't sunk in yet. Sometimes it almost does and I realize life's never, ever, going to be the same way again."

"I can't believe it either, I know what you mean, Pheeb. You know Marcia always said she'd never go back to live with her folks. Not in a million years." Phoebe's long fingers tightened on her drinking glass as Red-Jack spoke: "Remember how Marcia and I were when we left your house on New Year's Eve? It didn't get any better. We argued all night. Pheeb, I'm sorry, I know this is a rough time."

As he leaned again for the Scotch bottle hidden under the table, Phoebe thought how Marcia would berate him if she were here. Phoebe remembered one of the mornings when Marcia had phoned her at work to complain about Red-Jack. It was during that call that Phoebe had felt the untimely contractions and had ended the conversation abruptly. Barbara Hadley had driven her, speeding, to the hospital, where it was verified that Phoebe was in the throes of a miscarriage.

Now Red-Jack played with the ashtray, moving it in slow circles. "When you feel like talking, Pheeb, I have something to tell you. But I'm not sure you want to hear."

"I don't want to hear," Phoebe said looking up at him, "but I want to know, if you know what I mean."

Red-Jack touched the back of her hand. "I don't want to upset you, Pheeb."

Phoebe closed her eyes. "I keep saying that to Mother Bertha."

Red-Jack told Phoebe that in the early morning of New Year's Day, he and Marcia had been arguing again when the phone rang. Red-Jack, who'd been hung over, rushed to answer to make the ringing stop. "It was Marcia's mom calling to tell us what she'd heard on the local news." Red-Jack paused. "Pheeb, I'm sorry."

"No, I might as well know, I wondered how you'd heard."

Red-Jack said that while he was talking with Marcia's mom about Niles, Marcia grabbed the phone and insisted on hearing for herself. She screamed and ran out the back door. Red-Jack yelled at her that she'd gone crazy, running around in the snow, wearing just a robe. She ran out to the street and stopped a car, a black Ford, and climbed in. He had no idea who it belonged to. He rushed to look for her in his own car, and when he went to her folks' house, two maids kept repeating that everyone was out. Finally, Red-Jack had phoned Willie Eagle, the newscaster, who talked to his police buddies. "They did some undercover work—she's at her folks. Pheeb, do you mind if I ask you something?"

"What?"

"Hell, Pheeb, I feel a little funny asking under the circumstances." As he was filling Phoebe's soda glass, he started to spill it and she took over. "Did you know," he asked, "that Marcia went to see a doctor in Wichita?"

"I don't think she mentioned it. No, I know she didn't."

He hit his fist on the table. "Not to us she didn't."

"What's that got to do with anything?"

"She said Niles knew. Pheeb, I'm gonna tell you—Marcia's pregnant."

"Pregnant! Marcia?"

"That's what she says."

Phoebe sat back, trying to take this in. "When did she tell you that?"

"After we left your house on New Year's Eve."

Phoebe tried to focus her mind as she stared at Red-Jack, gulping the last of his drink. He said, "She never wanted children."

"She told me that too," Phoebe said.

"She's always been very careful."

Phoebe looked away. "Has she?"

Red-Jack pounded the table. "Not with him she wasn't!" He leapt up. Jolted by his news, Phoebe followed him to the car. She jumped in and slammed the door before he skidded out of the parking lot, swerved past a truck, and sped toward town. He whizzed through streets, not pausing at intersections.

Phoebe, sitting forward, said, "Red-Jack." Approaching Marcia's parents' house, he pressed the horn, forcing the loud sound as he drove around the block. He continued to honk the horn as he tore around the estate again.

Phoebe saw more lights come on in the house. "They probably know who's out here."

"Yeah?" said Red-Jack, starting a rhythm with the horn.

"They might call the police."

"Good. Let 'em." He blasted the horn and drove off, heading toward the Prairie Schooner, but this time he passed by it, gaining speed on the back road.

"Red-Jack, slow down!" Phoebe demanded, trying to control herself as well as him. Skidding past a truck, he almost went off the road. "Red-Jack!" she screamed. "You're going to kill us!" He swerved onto another road. "You'll never see Marcia!" she cried. He sounded the horn, then began to slow. "Stop," she said, barely able to speak.

He drew up, parking on the side of the dark road. "Hell, Pheeb."

Phoebe closed her eyes. "Let me drive."

"No. Hell, no, Pheeb." She opened the door to get out. But he grabbed her arm, pulling her back inside and made a U turn, then drove slowly, creeping in the darkness of the isolated road. She wished that he would go faster but she didn't speak for fear he'd speed again.

"Pheeb, I wish Marcia was more like you." Surprised, Phoebe did not answer. Finally, in town and in the TV station's parking lot, he drew up beside Mother Bertha's Chevrolet. The lights in the lot shone down as Phoebe started to get out of the car. Red-Jack caught her arm. "You saw I drove slow. I did that for you, Pheeb."

Phoebe waved to Red-Jack as he roared out of the parking lot. She started Mother Bertha's car but after driving a block, she stopped. She leaned over the steering wheel, weeping, determined to calm herself.

When she arrived home, Mother Bertha stood in the living room, her moccasined feet planted apart. "You had me worried."

"I'm sorry." Phoebe hung up her coat. "But I'm not sure why you were worried. I called you."

Watching Phoebe, Mother Bertha said, "I mean before that. I called up Marcia. I thought maybe you'd gone there. There wasn't any answer."

"You mean you called her at home?"

"Of course, I called her at home. Where else would I call her?"

Phoebe headed for the stairs.

Mother Bertha came after her. "Why shouldn't I call her at home?"

"I didn't mean you shouldn't. I just thought she might be with her folks."

"I get the feeling there's more than what you're saying. Are she and Red-Jack having some kind of trouble?" Mother Bertha said, puffing, reaching the upstairs hall. "Where were you tonight?"

Entering her bedroom, Phoebe said, "At the Prairie Schooner."

"How come? Who were you with?"

Phoebe hesitated, kicked off her shoes. "I was there with Red-Jack."

"What were you doing with him? Is this a common occurrence? Is that their trouble?"

Phoebe answered slowly, "No, it is not their trouble."

"I'm beginning to see why Marcia hasn't been over. Is this the way you treated my poor boy?"

"What do you mean?"

"Going off with other men?"

"I resent that. Damn it, I resent that a whole lot."

Phoebe barely slept that night. The next morning the aroma of coffee was strong when she entered the kitchen. Mother Bertha, wearing her robe and hair curlers, brought out milk from the refrigerator.

"Good morning," Phoebe said, attempting cheerfulness.

Mother Bertha set the milk carton on the table and Phoebe opened a cupboard door for the milk pitcher. "The coffee smells good," Phoebe said. "Thanks for making it."

"I knew you didn't want to bother."

"I've been making . . ." Phoebe, standing at the stove, set down the coffeepot. "I have to go."

"Now you just wait a minute, Phoebe!"

"Mother Bertha, will you please not speak to me in that tone of voice."

"What tone?"

"*That* tone! Obviously, we both need time alone."

"I've been by myself. You're the one who's gallivanting."

"Gallivanting? I'm on my way to work."

"I'm talking about after work—last night."

"Mother Bertha, I think we'd better watch what we say." Phoebe took a deep breath. "Maybe you'd feel better if you were back at your job. I can drive you back to Glennerville. Or will the boy come for you?"

"The boy?"

"The one who drove you here."

"Oh, so you're planning that."

"Damn it!" Phoebe whispered, pulling on her coat, rushing out into cold air.

The next evening after work Phoebe escorted Mother Bertha to the Harkenstown Tower Building and into the attorney's office. She had known Mr. Phillips—Hank Phillips—as a friend of her father and the family lawyer for as long as she could remember. As children, she and Marcia giggled and secretly call him Mr. Hank-kerchief Phillips. Now he leaned over his cluttered desk, and his large hand held a document which he read. He still seemed a very tall man, even though now Phoebe was tall herself. She'd always thought that he looked like Abraham Lincoln and wondered if that was one reason he had become a lawyer. "This is quite a simple and straightforward will," he said. "It's a small estate. I see this will was prepared by a lawyer in Glennerville."

"My husband's hometown," Phoebe said.

"I live there," Mother Bertha told him.

Mr. Phillips said, "As indicated in the policy and in the will, the life insurance in the amount of ten thousand dollars is divided equally between you."

"Equally?" Mother Bertha said.

"Equally. The furniture and personal property are left to the widow. The car was in both your name and Niles's, Phoebe, but I believe you said on the phone you haven't received the insurance company's settlement yet? The only other consideration is about the ring—'wedding ring' is the way it's described here. The will reads: *It is my desire that if my mother, Bertha May Stanhope, should survive me, my wife Phoebe's wedding ring should be returned to my mother, as it had been her wedding ring.*"

"I insisted on that," Mother Bertha said. "I felt it was only right."

Mr. Phillips looked at Phoebe. "You could contest this. Whether it's practical or desirable to do this is another thing—but the ring, as I understand it, was a gift to you and therefore your property."

"It was my property first," Mother Bertha said.

Phoebe held tight to the arms of her chair. "Since Niles said that, I don't want to contest it. I just want to wear it a few more days."

"When I leave this world," Mother Bertha said, "you can have it back. I don't think I'll live much longer."

"Please don't say that," Phoebe said.

"Are there debts?" said Mr. Phillips.

"I can't be responsible," Mother Bertha announced.

"I'll cover them," said Phoebe. "I plan to keep working—in one place or another."

Five

WHEN PHOEBE CAME HOME from the TV station on Friday night, she expected to find Mother Bertha packed and ready to leave for Glennerville early the next morning. But her mother-in-law was still in her robe and seated in Niles's lounge chair, her stocky legs sticking out in front of her with her feet in moccasins. "Are you all right?" Phoebe asked. "Do you need some help with your packing?"

"You're trying to rush me."

"I thought we'd made our plans."

"Your plans," Mother Bertha corrected her. "You're trying to railroad me into doing what you say."

"I guess you remember that Robert Rowley and Lillian and Fred are coming over tonight to say good-bye to you."

"I know that's what you said."

"Do you want help?"

"What? To help me dress? If I was in the hospital, I'd be in this robe."

When Robert arrived, Lillian and Fred came over from next door. Mother Bertha labored down the steps, wearing her black dress and the black beads Niles had given her. Phoebe had secretly shopped for the necklace, as she'd done for all his gifts to her, but Mother Bertha never caught on.

Mother Bertha sat on the sofa between the middle-aged Fred and Lillian while the younger Robert played the piano and Phoebe, the youngest of all, served chocolate cake and coffee. "I'd planned on grandchildren," Mother Bertha said. "You get your hopes up, like I'd hoped for twins when Phoebe was carrying." Mother Bertha laid one hand palm-side-up across her other palm and stared down, as if studying the emptiness. "But it didn't work out—she lost the baby, a little girl. Something was wrong with her little heart. Maybe the poor little thing got that from me." She clasped her hands and cried, "Now I'll never have even one grandchild."

Phoebe stepped around the table toward her, wondering what she would cry out if she knew that Marcia was carrying Niles's child.

Mother Bertha bent over. "Oh, dear God, I can't believe my son is gone."

Phoebe said, "We'd better get you up to bed."

She and Lillian helped her up to her room. Phoebe told her, "I'll be back to sit with you."

"No, I just want to be with pictures of my boy."

Phoebe said good-night to her worried guests and felt worried herself as she locked the door. She sat down by the telephone and re-alized she'd half-expected it to ring with a call from Niles. She went upstairs and kept the light on in the bedroom.

Early the next morning, she heard her mother-in-law moving about in her room. Phoebe went to her door. "Are you all right?" she asked.

"I want to go home now. Don't try to stop me now that I want to go."

As Phoebe drove them through the cold Kansas farm country, winds swept across the open land and hit the car. Phoebe tightened her grip on the steering wheel. All around them, in every direction, the flat land stretched on and on to the horizon, the vastness making Phoebe feel on this overcast morning that they were a tiny speck under a huge gray over-turned cup. Only a hint of green showed in the large fields, a tease of what was to come. Spring would finally arrive, but never again would she drive on this familiar straight road with Niles telling her stories, leaning to grab her knee. There had been times when his hand—or her own—had wandered and he had pulled the car onto a side road. . . .

On a blazing summer day just before wheat harvest, she and Niles had scrambled out of the car to scale a low bluff, the only ground not completely flat. They had looked off into the distance. The miles of wheat, swaying in the wind, looked like waves in a pale golden ocean.

Niles had told her that he dreamed of owning "hundreds of acres—no, thousands" of good Kansas wheat land, someday. Hearing a droning sound and squinting up at it, Phoebe had spotted a Cessna. Niles guessed the pilot was one of his best farm customers, one of the privileged flying farmers who soared over their vast holdings in private Cessnas or Beechcrafts.

But Niles had made it clear that, after having served his country, he personally never wanted to go anywhere outside of the state of Kansas "on vacation or any other time." Phoebe said that just for a change she'd like to visit New York. He'd insisted on only one brand of getting around: he wanted to "pick up and head out," just drive. . . .

"Phoebe," Mother Bertha said. Phoebe glanced at her mother-in-law slumped next to her in the car seat, looking old, her face sagging. "Phoebe!"

"What?"

"I feel funny." Phoebe slowed the car. "Something's wrong with my heart," Mother Bertha cried. "It's pounding fast—it feels like it's jumping out of my body."

Phoebe could see that a farm house ahead on the left was the closest place. She pressed her foot hard on the accelerator.

Mother Bertha struggled to sit up. "What are you doing?"

"I want to get you some help."

"My heart's jumping worse! Don't drive this way—so fast!"

"I'm sorry." Leaning forward, slowing down, Phoebe could feel her own heart thumping against the steering wheel. "You want to be in the back? You can lie down."

"No! I don't want to be back there by myself, Phoebe, I'm scared of doctors, I only like my own!"

Phoebe grasped Mother Bertha's arm in its heavy black coat sleeve. "Everything's going to be all right."

They bumped onto a rutted road leading to the farmhouse, which Phoebe now realized was an unpainted shack with a sagging porch. Rubber tires were strewn about the yard, and leaping over them, a group of yelping dogs charged toward the car.

Mother Bertha crouched in the seat. "Phoebe, don't leave me. Don't get out of the car! They're liable to get in."

Phoebe honked the horn as the dogs barked and wildly circled the car. A huge, sleek, black animal snarled and jumped ferociously at the front window on Phoebe's side and then on Mother Bertha's side of the car, his belly visible as his front paws hit the glass. Phoebe spotted the outhouse so she guessed it was useless to look for telephone lines leading to the shack. If they had no running water, it was unlikely they had a phone. She swerved the car past rubble and tires.

When they were again on the main road, she noticed that Mother Bertha was completely still; seated at an angle with her hat askew on her forehead, her eyes were closed, her skin was strangely gray, and she appeared lifeless. Phoebe began to drive very fast, speeding past a trailer truck, then a car. "Mother Bertha," she coaxed, trying to rouse her while she kept her eyes on the road. She reached for her. "Mother Bertha, can you talk to me?"

In Floyd Center, Phoebe left the engine running, fled the car to dash into a drugstore, interrupting a conversation between two middle-aged women, one a customer and the other attending the cash register. "Where can I find the hospital—a doctor?" The women exchanged startled glances and Phoebe felt desperate to make them understand her terror. "My mother-in-law's very sick. Please. She's out in the car. She may be dead."

"Dead?" said the customer, looking flustered. Phoebe rushed to the back of the store and she talked to the druggist behind the counter, who picked up the phone, calling for an ambulance.

Phoebe hurried outside, paced the sidewalk, looking for the ambulance among the cars and trucks on Main Street. On this shopping day for farmers, a Saturday, vehicles were parked parallel in front of the low buildings of stores.

The woman customer, who had lingered at the front of the drugstore, followed Phoebe outside and said, "You musta drove right past the hospital." She peered into the car at Mother Bertha's slumped body. Phoebe felt she should protect her mother-in-law from prying eyes. She wondered if this is why a cloth is thrown over the dead. She shuddered and was trembling when the ambulance arrived and the attendants moved Niles's mother into the hearselike vehicle. Phoebe expected to accompany her in the ambulance, but the driver, in a hurry, waved her away. Phoebe called out, "Is she alive?"

The siren wailed and Phoebe followed in the car. At the hospital she rushed to watch Mother Bertha being wheeled through the emergency entrance and into an examining room with white canvas curtains, which a nurse pulled around the patient and herself and the doctor, excluding Phoebe. "Is she all right?" Phoebe persisted.

"We'll let you know," said the nurse, pulling the curtain closed again.

"Get her vitals," she could hear the doctor instructing the nurse.

Needing Mother Bertha's medical insurance, Phoebe hurried out to the car. Her mother-in-law's handbag was on the floor and inside it her brown wallet, which had been a gift from Niles and Phoebe. Going through the personal items, Phoebe felt uncomfortable, as though she were snooping, as though she would come across something more than the Blue Cross card she pulled from the wallet. She located an identification card giving Mother Bertha's Glennerville address; her doctor's name, Everett Chaney; and instructions: "In case of emergency notify Niles Stanhope."

"Did you notify him?" the woman in the admissions office asked Phoebe.

Phoebe stared into the woman's squinting eyes behind her glasses. "That no longer applies," Phoebe said. "He's . . . he's no longer alive. My husband . . . her son."

"Deceased? This was recent?"

When Phoebe nodded, the woman added. "You've had your share. You're next of kin?"

"Yes." Phoebe signed the forms, then carrying Mother Bertha's handbag as well as her own, she stepped through the waiting room past men in overalls, women holding fussing babies. Phoebe was near the white canvas curtains when the white-haired doctor came out. She rushed to ask, "Is she alive?"

The doctor nodded, but frowned. "Tell me what led to this episode." As Phoebe explained, he asked questions about her reaction to the dogs at the farm. "Maybe she fainted," he said.

"I thought she was dead," Phoebe said.

"A person in a faint looks dead." The doctor said he wanted to keep Mrs. Stanhope in the hospital. He would confer by phone with her Glennerville doctor.

Phoebe stayed overnight at a roominghouse and the next morning Sunday church bells were ringing in the distance when, with words of caution from the doctor, Mother Bertha was allowed to leave the hospital. The released patient looked uneasy in the car the next morning and sat uncomfortably close to Phoebe as they drove on to Glennerville—population 1,850—and drew up in front of Mother Bertha's small, tidy yellow house.

As Phoebe stepped onto the porch, she found it hard to grasp that she was entering this house without Niles. It seemed impossible that she'd not overhear him on the phone with his hometown buddies, be with him at the kitchen table, see him shake more salt onto his scrambled eggs, hear him tease even his mother.

The house smelled musty from being closed up. Mother Bertha, still wearing her hat, pulled down blinds, blotting out the daylight. "I can't see the neighbors yet. I can't face them without my boy." Phoebe, remembering she was just out of the hospital, put an arm around her "You don't sound like yourself, Mother Bertha. I always think of you wanting people around you."

Mother Bertha lowered her head. "I'm not me anymore."

Phoebe brought in her mother-in-law's leather suitcase, then took her own bag into Niles's bedroom, where he'd been lonely as a child after his dad's death, when he and his mother had moved from the familiar farm to this house. He'd even shown her that he'd still kept his collection of marbles in a shoebox on a shelf in the closet.

Nights she and Niles had spent in this long narrow room, which stretched across the back of the house, making love on the least squeaky twin bed, hoping that Mother Bertha couldn't hear them. Now Phoebe looked around the room—here the same pine furniture, the squat green lamp on the dresser. The twin beds were still placed end to end against the wall. Suddenly she could not resist pulling off the white chenille bedspreads and hiding them in the closet. She was reminded of Niles in the morgue, his body covered by a white sheet, his battered head visible, the blood-matted hair plastered against the dark gash at the top of his forehead, his lower lip slashed, sagging against the chin which in life had been so hard and handsome. She held her own face now, asking herself who else could have seen past the hideous injuries to recognize Niles.

How could she accept that Marcia had known him as long as she had? Yet they had met him together—not in Harkenstown, but a distance away, at the Kansas State Fair. It was bittersweet now to think of herself and Marcia as teenagers as they had been then, in the midst of meandering crowds. She and Marcia had laughed and squinted in the September sunshine on that afternoon ripe with warm early autumn winds and dust, the lively sounds of carnival barkers and merry-go-round music, the smells of hot dogs and pink cotton candy. The two girls had just ridden on the High

Demon Roller Coaster, holding on for dear life, screaming as their car on rails rushed them straight up a high incline, rose over the top, dropped them in a rapid, stomach-sinking nosedive, then shot up and plummeted, only to tear around curves and spirals, the car dipping and slanting on steep embankments, following the harrowing path of ups and downs, until the car looped, leveled, and stopped. They staggered out, giggling. Marcia collided with someone—they soon learned he was Niles Stanhope. He admitted in the party atmosphere of the fair that he'd been watching them, looking for an excuse to introduce himself.

By the time Niles met them, he had served in the Marines, gone to Kansas State on the G.I. bill. He was working at his new job for Farm State Implements, Inc., and this week of the fair he'd been minding the company's exhibit. This afternoon was the first time he'd had the chance to see the rest of the fair and to take in the sights. He told the girls they were the best sights he'd seen so far. Just off work, he wore a blue checked shirt and a knit tie, which he had loosened.

He had offered an arm to each young woman and they walked with him past the Dodge 'Em ride and the freak show. As he maneuvered them through the crowds on the Pike, Phoebe was very aware he was an older man, at least twenty-four. His short blondish hair, thick as a brush, hardly ruffled in the Kansas wind, while Phoebe's own tumble of auburn hair whipped around her smiling face so that she had to push hair from her eyes. She held his arm, feeling delirious so close to him. When he looked down at her again, she thought her fingers might be pressing too tightly on his shirt-sleeved arm. Quickly she loosened her grip, while glancing up again at his tanned face, his high forehead gleaming in the sunshine, the long straight nose, solid sturdy chin, powerful neck and shoulders. By now she had grown tall herself and she found it a rare occurrence to look up, so far, at someone, especially someone so handsome.

He expressed surprise that the girls were so young, still students in high school. Because Phoebe and Marcia strived to look glamorous and sophisticated, they were thrilled by his reaction. Phoebe lifted her head to look more worldly wise, the way she had practiced in front of the mirror. Yet at the moment, he was concentrating on Marcia and her last name, Harkens. He was impressed that, yes, she was the daughter of Charlie Harkens. Phoebe could see that even to a newcomer to Harkenstown, as Niles was, it was not necessary to point out that Marcia was from the big land-owning family whose name was on the grain elevator and whose forebears had founded the town.

But Marcia, always put off by talk of her family she found irritating, looked at her watch and said it was time for her date. Red-Jack was waiting by the ticket booth of the Ferris wheel. While being introduced to Niles, Red-Jack surveyed him, then informed him that he was Marcia's fiancé. Phoebe studied Red-Jack, thinking this was the first time she'd heard him say "fiancé"—he and Marcia were still sneaking around behind her parents' back. "But we're not telling people yet," Marcia had added as she went off with Red-Jack, leaving Phoebe alone with Niles.

Phoebe's first ride with Niles was not in a car but on the Ferris wheel. When she sat beside him in their rocking seat-for-two, she was so excited, she told Marcia later, she could have floated right up to join the blimp that was hovering over the fairgrounds.

Remembering her exhilaration then, Phoebe felt the bleak contrast to today, when she was alone in this house with Niles's mother. All the plans she had made with Niles were gone with him.

Yet even Mother Bertha had said that Phoebe had her life ahead of her.

On Monday Phoebe sat in the office of Mother Bertha's young doctor, Everett Chaney, who spoke reassuring words to his patient about the examination he had just completed, then turned to Phoebe to ask if she could stay on with her mother-in-law. He said it with a smile to Phoebe as if he liked her. But Phoebe, uneasy about taking off additional time from work, suggested a nurse. Immediately Mother

Bertha began to sob and Dr. Chaney said to Phoebe that Mrs. Stanhope, having suffered a series of shocks and recently hospitalized, needed family support. "Just a couple of days," he said.

Hardly had Phoebe nodded than the doctor was smiling again. He patted Mother Bertha's shoulder as he escorted them to the door.

During the midday meal in Mother Bertha's kitchen, Phoebe was surprised to see her take one of the just-prescribed sleeping capsules. "I think he meant for you to take that at night."

Mother Bertha snatched the pill bottle and left the kitchen, heading for her bedroom. Phoebe peeked down the hall to see that her bedroom door was still open. As soon as she was snoring with her mouth gaping, Phoebe grabbed the bottle from the bedside table and counted the capsules—she'd taken only one. Phoebe pocketed the bottle for safekeeping, then considered that Mother Bertha, upon waking and finding her medicine missing, would be agitated rather than calm. Phoebe left the bottle on the table for the moment while she pondered what to do.

After all, she told herself, the doctor had prescribed the capsules. She wandered into the living room and sat down on the brown sofa, where she tried not to be disturbed again by the enormous wood-framed photographic portraits of Niles and his father, which seemed to watch her from the walls.

Niles's farmer father appeared uncomfortable in a suit he had probably worn only to church. Niles in his Marine uniform, sitting straight, shoulders back, stared at her.

The fatal words—"If you're going, go on, go on . . ."—which she had hurled at him in confusion and hurt on New Year's Eve, sounded in her head, echoed around her. She held her face as she peered through a blur into his eyes.

She forced herself away from his gaze and picked up the phone to call again the TV station in Harkenstown. Maybe because of the anxiety in her voice, Mary Ann put her right through to the busy manager. Phoebe explained to him that it was necessary for her to stay on a few days in Glennerville.

"Yeah? Okay, all right." His impatient response signaled that this was the last time he would tolerate a request. Phoebe was torn, feeling she should rush back to Harkenstown, yet held in place by her promise to the doctor and Mother Bertha's need.

During the night when Phoebe was trying to sleep, Mother Bertha suddenly appeared by her bed, wearing her robe and moccasins and saying she felt lonely and strange. "You could live here," she told Phoebe.

Phoebe sat up. "Here?"

"You don't need to sound so surprised."

"I guess I wasn't expecting you to say that, but thank you. It's certainly nice of you." Phoebe adjusted the pillow. "But what about my job in Harkenstown? I need my job."

"I can see you don't want it to work out." Mother Bertha headed for the door. "You're dead set against Glennerville."

Phoebe swung her legs out of the bed. "There just isn't any TV station here where I could work." She shoved her feet into her pink house slippers. "I haven't even thought about it until this very minute. If I've ever thought of moving, I guess I've had my eye on a big place—I've always wanted to see New York."

"So that's what you're planning."

"I'm not planning anything," Phoebe said, following her into her bedroom.

"You said in the lawyer's office you planned to work one place or another." Mother Bertha pushed aside the covers and sat down heavily on her bed. "But maybe you just *said* that, the way you said you'd give me back my ring."

Phoebe closed her eyes against tears she wanted desperately to hide. "Mother Bertha, I don't just say things." She touched the gold wedding band with its row of tiny diamonds. "I planned to give it to you before I left." Phoebe held on to her ring, finally slipped it off, and handed it to her mother-in-law, who tried to force it onto her own ring finger.

"I'll have to have it made bigger." Mother Bertha sighed, laying it on the night table. "It's too bad my son had to have it cut down for you."

Phoebe rushed into Niles's room. She pounded the bed, hearing again Mother Bertha's resentful voice. She had spoken as if Phoebe had persuaded Niles to give her the ring. Except to furnish her ring size, she'd had nothing to do with it until Niles had let her glimpse it before their marriage ceremony held in Marcia's parents' garden.

I can't stay here, Phoebe thought. I can't even stay a few days, but I have to. Then no more. She would say the wrong thing sooner or later. She knew too many things that would upset Mother Bertha even more.

There were some people who should not be together. Did Mother Bertha even realize when she was being insulting? Phoebe felt sorry for her, but that meant more than ever she had to get away. She pulled the covers over her head, hearing Dr. Chaney say that Mrs. Stanhope must be calm.

Phoebe got out of bed, walked around in the room, her feet following the border of the oval braided rug. How could she tell Mother Bertha that her son had impregnated another man's wife? She would be wild with fury, disbelief, become the attacker and the victim all at once, crying out that Phoebe was dishonoring his memory, lying.

It was two days later on the bus heading for Harkenstown that Phoebe leaned back on the seat. Suddenly she sat up. She had to help herself too. Now, before it was too late!

Six

AT HOME, EARLY THE NEXT MORNING, Phoebe zipped up her boots and buttoned her coat over the same navy blue dress she had worn almost like a uniform since New Year's Eve. Once, she thought, she had planned in advance what she was going to wear, choosing bright colors, coordinating her outfits. She had to get back to that.

She set out walking in the cold wind. Striding past a ranch house, she remembered the baby shower she'd attended there. The baby showers that had been planned for Phoebe herself had been quietly canceled. One day such celebration parties would be given for Marcia—she'd have to come out of hiding from her parents' house soon.

Phoebe had hated it when anyone had asked where Marcia was these days, she'd had to scrounge around for a way to change the subject.

Yet, as she made her way along the sidewalk this morning , she pondered why she felt strangely protective of the unborn baby—Niles's child. She felt this was odd of herself—weird—almost as if it were her own baby she was guarding. Since it was Niles's baby, it seemed somehow hers too. She tried to think how she would feel seeing the baby— somewhere. It was inevitable—in a store with Marcia, maybe at a friend's house—especially once the child was walking. How would she be able to stop herself from still looking for a resemblance to Niles?

Now Phoebe turned onto Walnut Street and passed by large, older houses that faced the thoroughfare. Set back behind bare winter trees, many of the houses were homes of families she knew. Or did she know them? It came to her that she'd never really known anyone, not even her so-called best friend from childhood or the husband she loved. How could she still love him after what he had done? Sometimes she didn't.

When Phoebe arrived in the business section of town, she discovered she had hurried so much that the stores were just opening and few people were on Main Street. She walked past stores and office buildings and on to the dealers lot of Farm State Implements, Inc., where farm machinery was on display. She visualized Niles here on the job, climbing onto the seat of a tractor as he pointed out features to a farm customer. Peering into the plateglass windows of the company's showroom, she could see Niles's desk. He had phoned her from here every day, closing with "Take care, hon." Had he then called Marcia? Had she come here to see him?

Phoebe felt doubly betrayed that no one had told her. How many people knew?

How often were Niles and Marcia together? Phoebe asked silently as she entered the TV station. All day she was plagued by painful questions that destroyed her concentration.

After work Red-Jack insisted on driving her home. Parking in front of her house, he said. "You know what I've been thinking, Pheeb? Marcia and Niles admitted everything started with them on Labor Day weekend. And you weren't feeling so hot."

"I'd just had a miscarriage."

"That's what I mean: Niles was probably afraid to touch you then. But goddamn, Pheeb, that's no excuse to be on the prowl."

"The prowl?" Phoebe fumbled for the car handle. "The prowl?" She pushed hard, almost falling out of the car, stumbling her way toward the house. Red-Jack followed her, "Hey, Pheeb, I didn't mean it the way it sounded."

"I can see what crossed your mind," she said as she reached the porch. "If I could have carried the baby through, if I hadn't been pregnant in the first place, he wouldn't—"

"Pheeb, I'm sorry." On the porch Red-Jack pulled her to him. "What I meant was: it was a complicated situation, but that was no goddamned excuse." Phoebe unlocked the door. "Hell, Pheeb, I'm sorry." He followed her in as she switched on lights in the living room, where everything looked blurry to her. "I could use a drink." Red-Jack said, turning around in the middle of the room. "We could pick up a bottle. Hey, let's go to the Prairie Schooner. We're both alone. There's no reason why we shouldn't."

"I can't live here anymore," Phoebe said.

"What? In this house?"

"In this house. In this town. I don't want to be here anymore."

"Pheeb, you can't say that."

"Mother Bertha thought I was planning to go to New York. Maybe I was. Maybe I am."

"New York!"

"New York's not a whole new thought to me."

Red-Jack admitted that Marcia had told him that she and Phoebe used to plan to live in New York. "But that was when you were kids."

"This has nothing to do with Marcia. Well, it does, but I'm doing this myself. This is my plan. I'm doing this on my own. I'm going to New York because that's what I've decided. I just decided."

Phoebe gave her notice to the TV manager two weeks later. Her coworkers pleaded with her not to leave but she held onto her plan. She thumbtacked an announcement to the station's bulletin board: FOR SALE: FURNITURE AND HOUSEHOLD BELONGINGS. Returning to her desk, she heard Robert Rowley call out, "Phoebe," as he waddled up to her. "You don't have the piano listed. Can I have first chance at it? I'll keep it for you."

"I was hoping you'd say that."

Just recently while looking through Christmas music still on the piano, Phoebe had opened the book of carols to find her father's handwriting: "To Phoebe on her seventh birthday, so she can be ready for Christmas, with love from Mama and Daddy." When she had been given this book, her mother no longer taught piano lessons, so her father, who ran the Main Street Music Store, taught Phoebe. Occasionally, in those early days, her mother still joined him in duo piano, her mother on the grand, and her father at the upright. And her mother encouraged Phoebe to go on with her music studies, but once when Phoebe was practicing, her mother cried, "Stop that or I'll lose my mind." Her father had said, "You can't tell her to practice, then raise Cain when she does it."

Her mother covered her face with her apron. "I thought a daughter of mine would have a better ear—"

"Now don't start that again, Pearl."

Phoebe, the child had sat still on the piano bench, ashamed she did not have "perfect pitch," as her mother said she herself had.

Big Barbara Hadley, Phoebe's coworker, drove her home from the TV station the next evening so that she could look at the dining room furniture. She ran her hand over the walnut tabletop once more. She opened her checkbook. "Phoebe, you look like somebody just hit you. You having second thoughts?"

"I felt this way when I sold the marble-top chest that belonged to my grandmother. Niles and I bought this dining room furniture when we were first married."

"Maybe you don't want to do this."

"I want to do it." Phoebe took the check. "My mind just kinda plays tricks on me lately."

"Don't expect so damn much of yourself," said Barbara with a look of distress on her smooth honest face. "You can't help but miss Niles. Just try to remember you were lucky you had such a good marriage." Phoebe turned her head away. Barbara touched Phoebe's arm. "At least," Barbara said, "you and Niles had a wonderful marriage,"

Phoebe's voice came out a whisper: "I'm glad you were at the station, Barb."

"It can't be the same without you, Phoebe."

On the last day of February, Phoebe watched as the few pieces of re-
maining furniture and rugs were carried out the front door by two
workmen and placed in a battered truck owned by a second-hand
dealer. Phoebe had already sent Niles's lounge chair to Mother Bertha.
Now she phoned to tell her a birthday robe was on the way.

"Will you call me before you leave?" Mother Bertha said.

"I'll call you. You know I'll call you."

Phoebe's neighbors Lillian and Fred had been concerned that she
was "going too fast, taking too many big steps at once." But Phoebe
had not confided in Lillian or anyone else about the happenings of
New Year's Eve. Lillian had said, "You got to admit, Phoebe, you don't
know what's in store for you. Stay in our guestroom. We *insist* you
stay with us so we can talk you out of going."

"At least," Fred said, "don't spend money on a room while you're still
in Harkenstown, Phoebe. From all I hear about New York, you'll need
all the money you can get your hands on."

Phoebe's footsteps echoed as she walked through the empty rooms
of the house where she had accumulated too many belongings and not
all the right memories. Finally, she locked the door of the rental house
for the last time. She dropped the key, clanging into the empty mailbox,
then ran next door to the Fredericks's brown stucco house.

That evening in their pink-and-beige guest bedroom, Phoebe,
feeling clean after a lavender-scented bath, slipped on her nightgown.
There was a knock on the bedroom door and Lillian's raised voice:
"Phoebe, Red-Jack Ordall's on the phone." Phoebe, grabbing her
robe, followed Lillian into the hallway. Taking the phone, Phoebe noticed Lillian look away, as if to hide her curiosity.

"Does this mean you're really moving?" Red-Jack said into Phoebe's
ear. "Come out with me, Pheeb, we can talk about it."

"No, thanks, it's late," said Phoebe, keeping her voice low.

"You keep saying no, but I'm gonna keep calling."

Phoning the night before Phoebe's departure, Red-Jack asked to take her to the train station. "Thanks, but Lillian and Fred are taking me."

"I'll miss you, Pheeb. Don't go . . . "

Phoebe returned to the bedroom, where she plopped down on the floor in the midst of luggage and boxes. Lillian offered to help with this final packing. "I'd hate to think," Lillian said, "if Fred and I ever moved. I never can believe those movies where some gal leaves home with just one suitcase."

"Niles always said I took too much stuff on vacations."

"Fred says the same thing about me," Lillian said. "But he's the first to yell: 'Where's my fishing hat, honey? I can't find the camera.'" Lillian placed a hand on Phoebe's shoulder. "I thought you'd like to know something Fred said about Niles."

Phoebe stopped folding a sweater. "What?"

"Sometimes when he and Niles were in the car on the way to the golf course, Niles would pop up with something really nice about you."

"Like what?"

"Usually something funny—about your sense of humor—Fred says Niles really appreciated that. Phoebe, I hope you find somebody, back east there, in New York."

Phoebe pushed down hard on clothes in a suitcase. "That's not going to happen."

Lillian insisted, "You never can tell. You're a beautiful young gal and you know what they say: If you've had one good marriage you can have another. And you and Niles were so happy together. Oh, my soul!" Lillian knelt down beside Phoebe. "I didn't mean to make you feel bad." She cupped Phoebe's chin in her hand. "Don't cry. I'm sorry, Phoebe. Fred tells me I rush things. He says I'm worse than you are about rushing. I'll miss you so much, Phoebe." Lillian hugged her. "I can't believe you won't be next door."

"Oh, Lillian," said Phoebe, holding her close, "I'll miss you so much."

Seven

A T THE DEPOT THE NEXT NIGHT, Red-Jack joined Phoebe and the Fredericks at the ticket window. "Marcia isn't with you," Lillian commented. "I haven't seen her lately."

"She's fine," Red-Jack said, exchanging glances with Phoebe.

Phoebe's group followed her outside where they huddled against the cold wind on the red-brick waiting area. Phoebe, tense with anticipation, sighted the approaching light, heard the train whistle. When the train arrived, its bell clanging, Fred spoke to the redcap: "We want to see her settled."

"Yes, sir." The redcap grinned, hoisting Phoebe's large bag aboard. The group climbed the high steps, and as they entered the train, a small man with a pointed gray beard stepped into the aisle from his compartment and showed Red-Jack a compartment two doors away. "This way," Red-Jack called out.

The bearded man lingered near Phoebe, who watched the redcap stash her bag onto a shelf in the compartment. The redcap asked, "Is there anything else, miss?"

"Thanks, that's it," Phoebe said cheerfully, tipping him. "I checked the rest of my things through." Excited, she thanked Lillian and kissed her on the cheek, then Fred. When she turned to Red-Jack, he kissed her on the mouth, surprising her. "I'll miss you, Pheeb." Phoebe followed them to the doorway to watch them descend; she waved good-bye.

"Have a drink for me in the club car," Red-Jack called as the train moved.

She turned back toward her compartment and suddenly felt the cost of her decision: leaving all that she had known.

The smiling, bearded man made way for her to pass him in the aisle. "That was quite a send-off," he said in his husky, eager voice. "Maybe now you need a welcoming committee."

Phoebe smiled as the train gained speed.

He said, "I heard you say you checked the rest of your luggage through. You must be planning quite a visit." Through the train's mournful cry, he told her his name: "Benjamin Ambhurst," it sounded to Phoebe.

She hesitated before saying, "Phoebe Stanhope." She closed the compartment door. The train jolted her into the shabby green upholstered seat. It smelled of old cigar smoke, reminding her of her mother's complaints about her father's cigars. She looked out the darkened window and saw lights of occasional farmhouses, making her think of farm visits with Niles.

Listening to the rhythmic click of the train wheels on the tracks, she remembered her childhood trip to Kansas City with her grandmother to visit Gramma's sister. In fun, the child Phoebe had bounced on the train seat until Gramma told her to "settle down. Be a young lady." But Gramma had been smiling, having fun too. Later when Gramma had come to live with Phoebe and her father, following Phoebe's mother's death, Gramma had started Phoebe on an allowance. She had counted out the change the first week. She had been sitting in the upholstered chair in Phoebe's room, where she said she had come to visit, making it feel cozy. Gramma pulled Phoebe to her and held her close for a long time. Phoebe hugged her back; Gramma's body felt soft like a big pillow. Releasing Phoebe, she brushed back her hair, kissed her on the forehead. "You're so pretty, Phoebe." Gramma took the box of fresh-smelling lemon drops from her apron pocket and Phoebe opened it for her. Each popped a lemon drop in her mouth.

When her grandmother died, Phoebe was seventeen and after her death, in dreams Phoebe had said to her: "I don't think you know how much I love you." Finally, in one dream, Gramma said, "Well, do you want to tell me?" And Phoebe had said, "I love you very much, I've always loved you very, very much." But that had not seemed enough and Phoebe had felt desperate to reach her to let her know . . .

Now the wailing train whistle echoed across the plains. Alone, enclosed in the train compartment, Phoebe experienced a cold gloominess. She grabbed a magazine and her handbag, stepped into the aisle, and opened the door into the lounge car. She edged past people engrossed in games of chess or cards and was reminded of the bridge game on New Year's Eve.

She sat down on a banquette at the empty end of the lounge car. The window directly opposite herself was like a black mirror reflecting her image, showing her perched on the edge of the seat. Her large eyes looked at herself while her hands touched her auburn hair. She glanced down at the skirt of her cranberry suit and felt encouraged that she had stopped wearing the navy blue dress and had left it for Lillian to give to a rummage sale.

As the waiter approached her, she recalled her promise to Red-Jack to have a drink for him on the train. At the depot he had said, "Why don't you change your mind?" I did the right thing in leaving, she told herself, trying to feel total conviction. She ordered a Tom Collins, and while sipping it, imagined Niles's amused and teasing voice, "Honey, that's a summer drink."

"But it's what I want," she felt like shouting now, when she really did not want a drink at all. She felt tense from exhaustion, the good-bye call to Mother Bertha.

She must become a part of the life right here on the train; it would be practice for the future. She had to get her life in order.

She opened *Broadcasting* magazine and turned to the employment section. Her attention was interrupted by a large man carrying a briefcase, who sat down on her side of the car, at the other end of her long banquette. He placed his briefcase on the seat and she was aware that he continued to look at her. He was probably in his early thirties and his curly hair was clipped short around his head, which was large to go with his massive body. Out of the corner of her eye she now saw him place his briefcase flat on the cocktail table in front of him.

She returned to her magazine but she heard him snap open the briefcase. Taking out a pad, he flipped back pages, then slid his hand under his dark blazer and withdrew a pencil from his shirt pocket. As he busied himself with his pencil and pad, Phoebe was conscious that he was staring at her.

She shifted her position away from him. She heard him order Scotch and soda. "Scotch was what Niles drank most of the time," she wanted to tell someone. Or beer. She remembered the odor of beer on New Year's Eve.

The man with the pad and pencil moved along the banquette seat closer to her. "You seem concerned that I'm looking at you."

"Well, not exactly concerned."

He explained that he'd like to do sketches of her. "Do you mind?"

She half-smiled, questioning, "I guess it's all right."

As he worked with his pencil, he continued to study her. He looked back down at his pad, up at her again, then down. "I'm strengthening the lines that describe the fullness of your hair," he said. "Right now I'm concentrating on the area where your hair is combed back from your forehead."

Phoebe started to lean toward him. "May I see?"

"Not yet." Drawing, he commented that the contrast of her fair skin against her auburn hair would make a dramatic painting. He'd been struck by the size of her eyes.

"Oh." Now his attention seemed more familiar to Phoebe, for all her life she'd heard about her "big beautiful brown eyes."

Back in the eighth grade a boy had tickled her when he'd said,

"You got a face full of beautiful. No matter how old you get, you'll always have guys in love with you." When she had quoted this to Gramma, Phoebe had been embarrassed that Daddy had overheard. "Where'd he pick that up?" Daddy had asked "Reading his mama's movie magazines?"

Gramma, hugging Phoebe, had whispered, "He doesn't mean to deflate you, honey. He just wants to be sure you don't get conceited."

Now a group, shouting and laughing, entered the train's lounge car and joked with the card players. Two of the couples loudly announced that they were honeymooners from Lamar, Colorado. The brides were twins, wearing frilly blouses and orchids and swinging plastic handbags by their chain handles. One of the grooms bellowed to the waiter, "Drinks on the house! I've always wanted to say that."

"It's not a house." His bride laughed, hitting him on the arm with her handbag.

"Hell, he knows what I mean."

Making their way to Phoebe's section of the car, the honeymooning couples noisily greeted Phoebe and the artist. Then, as the train rounded a bend, they sprawled, laughing, onto the opposite banquette. "I'm Vilma," one twin giggled. "She's Valma."

"Hell, I'm Mike Lewis," said one groom, thrusting his hand toward the artist.

"Gilbert Bradley," the artist answered, as if surprised to be included in their celebration, to be served one of the "drinks on the house." He raised his glass, "To the happy couples." He turned to Phoebe, who held up her drink while remembering she'd once believed she was part of a happy couple. After the next round, when standing, she found herself staggering from the motion of the train and the drinks she was not used to having. "Where you going?" one of the grooms called after her. She collided with passengers crowding the aisle watching the chess game. Someone grabbed her arm, pulling her toward the bar. "Remember me?" the small man said. "Benjamin Ambhurst, Chief of your Welcoming Committee." Benjamin the Gray Beard, she thought as she stared at his chin with its pointed gray beard. "Let's have a drink," Benjamin said.

"I'd better not," said Phoebe as the train swayed. They fell into seats side by side.

As the train neared the station in Chicago the next morning, Phoebe awoke in her compartment with a crush of pain in her head. She moved under the covers from a cramped position and extended her long legs until her feet hit the wall. After hurrying to dress, she stepped into the aisle and met Benjamin, who instructed the porter to take her bags as well as his. "I'm catching another train," she told him, "from another station."

"That's why I said last night I'd take you in a taxi."

Departing the train, she said, "Thank you, but I can go in a taxi myself."

But inside the train station, Benjamin insisted, "It's my pleasure to take you." He bombarded her with eager words as they followed the redcap hauling their luggage. People seemed to come toward Phoebe from all directions, as if her headache were a magnet pulling the crowds.

Squinting her eyes through the pain, Phoebe looked around to see if she could spot the artist or even the honeymoon couples as an excuse to get away from Benjamin. "Thanks for your help," she said, "but I really can go by myself now."

"You're not going to deprive my wife and me—"

"Your wife?" As conversation from last night grew more distinct in her mind, Phoebe recognized that he was now repeating a dinner invitation. She remembered he had talked earnestly about her plans to get a job in New York. Now he told her that he was stopping off here in Chicago for business appointments but that he was flying home to New York the next day. He would phone her at the Barbizon Hotel for Women, the place which, as she now realized she had told him, had been recommended to her by her former college English teacher.

She sensed Benjamin's eagerness to help her in her "job-search," as he called it. Shaking her hand and saying good-bye, he seemed reluctant to let her go. "I look forward to seeing you again," he said, gazing into her eyes. When he handed her his business card, showing he was president of his company, she said, "Oh—thank you"

When she took a taxi alone to the LaSalle Street Station, snow was falling, making it seem as if New Year's Eve had followed her here. Seated in the large waiting room of the train station, she remembered the TV script she had written that day. *January is named for Janus, the two-faced Roman god. One face looks to the past, the other to the future.*

She took more aspirin, then studied Benjamin's business card. She wished she felt less squeamish about accepting help from someone who made her feel a bit uneasy. Yet, she reminded herself, since New Year's Eve she was less sure of *everyone*—not only this recent acquaintance. She'd have to think about this, but now she tried to deal with nausea and a headache. She took Alka Seltzer and fell asleep in the waiting room before she boarded the New York Central's 20th Century Limited.

That evening she stood, balancing herself with the motion of the train, at the end of the dining car waiting to be seated. She heard a deep voice behind her say, "Excuse me." She thought he could not be speaking to her. "Excuse me," he said again. "We met yesterday in the club car on the Santa Fe."

She glanced back, then turned more fully to see the large smiling man in a dark blazer, standing behind her in the narrow aisle. Smiling, he reminded her he was Gilbert Bradley and commented that at the moment he didn't have the sketches of her with him.

"Oh," she said, "I'd like to see them." Embarrassed, she said she usually didn't drink as much as she had yesterday. "I hope they'll serve me that small an order. All I want is tea and dry toast."

He smiled. "Well, if you're worried, I'll make it up for you." He buttoned a gold button on his dark blazer, then as if finding the jacket too tight, he unbuttoned it. When they were seated at the table, Gilbert's steady hazel eyes stayed on her as he told her he'd been in Kansas City and was now headed home to New York. Seated across the white tablecloth, he cut into his steak. "I had a hunch I'd said the wrong thing to you."

"When?"

"Last night in the club car. We were talking—suddenly you left in a big hurry."

"Oh." She set down the teacup. "I'm sorry. I can see why you thought that. I plan to change. I plan a lot of changes."

"I wouldn't think you'd need that many changes."

"Let's just say I want to change my life because my whole life has changed." Phoebe glanced at the darkened windows, imagining the land covered by snow. She sat up straighter. "I've promised myself to look forward, not back." She smiled at him. "Do you think spring will ever come?"

"Well, if it'd come before, I wouldn't be on this train." He usually flew, but this winter he'd run into snow storms, planes were diverted, and he'd missed appointments.

He stopped speaking, his attention drawn to a tall, slender blond man, standing by the table, smiling down at them, saying, "Hello, Gilbert." Relieved by this interruption, Phoebe had a chance to close her eyes for a moment and warm her hands on the teapot. Gilbert had half-risen to shake hands. "Edward, you made it. How was Chicago?"

"Splendid," the man said with enthusiasm.

Gilbert introduced Edward Hibbard. "Edward represents The Royal Rose, that great hotel in London—real luxury."

Phoebe noticed that the Englishman seemed to be a kind of advertisement for the hotel. He wore a red rosebud in his lapel and his necktie had a row, down its center, of one red rose after another.

Edward smiled at Phoebe and, accepting Gilbert's suggestion of another coffee, he sat down at the table beside her. She noted his finely tailored clothes and his ramrod posture. He spoke warmly to her: "I've had a marvelous journey. I'd never realized how vast your country is." He had stopped in a number of cities to promote the hotel, to be interviewed by the press and on "the telly."

Phoebe said, "I worked in television."

"Well done, you!"

"In Kansas—in Harkenstown, Kansas. I don't suppose you've ever heard of it."

"Oh, I've been there. I passed through on the train." Edward told her he had been in America before but this was the first time he'd traveled so far into the heart of the country. "I realize now an oversight. I should have stopped to be interviewed in Harkenstown."

Phoebe smiled. "If you had, we'd have met before. I met all kinds of people who came to the station."

"So you see how inevitable . . ." said Edward, still smiling at Phoebe.

There was a hint of annoyance on Gilbert's face, as if he regretted that Edward had joined them to dominate the conversation. Edward was saying now that when he'd been interviewed in Kansas City, Gilbert had been watching the program in his hotel room. He'd been surprised to see Edward on the screen and had called up the station.

"No," Gilbert overrode Edward. "I wasn't surprised to see you. You'd talked a great deal about your plans at Selmabelle's party."

"Oh, I see." Edward raised his blond eyebrows as if not used to being corrected.

"At Selmabelle's party?" Phoebe repeated. "You mean Selmabelle Flaunton?" She noticed that Gilbert frowned. She glanced at Edward, worried she'd spoken out of turn.

"You know Selmabelle?" Gilbert asked.

"Oh, not personally." Phoebe hurried to explain that the station where she'd worked had carried the *Selmabelle Flaunton Hour* until it had gone off the air.

Edward smiled at Phoebe. "We could perhaps take you to one of her parties."

"Really?" she said.

Edward turned to Gilbert. "I'd be glad to see about it, Gilbert. For you—with your wife and family connections—perhaps you'd find it difficult."

Family connections, Phoebe repeated silently, trying to guess what that meant. From now on, it would be even harder to figure out someone's life than it had been in Harkenstown. As she listened to the men talk about the rise and multiple holdings of Selmabelle Flaunton's new business, Phoebe realized she had followed her famous career and knew something about her life. "Maybe I could get a job with her," she said.

Gilbert looked concerned. "I'm not sure that's a good idea."

"But that's why I'm going to New York," Phoebe said. "To get a job."

"Good for you," Edward said, then looked at Gilbert. "Let's not discourage her."

"Oh, I don't want to do that," Gilbert said. "I just don't want to give her false encouragement. Do you take shorthand?"

"Why does everybody ask me that? Does Selmabelle Flaunton take shorthand? Do you take shorthand?" Phoebe suddenly realized the tone of voice she had used.

"There I go," Gilbert said. "I've said the wrong thing."

"No, it's all right," Phoebe said. "I take shorthand." Then she added, "But I didn't plan to use it, I've never had to use it in a job. I just want a start."

"I say," said Edward, "you'll do splendidly."

Eight

PHOEBE REPEATED TO HERSELF, "You'll do splendidly," as she squeezed past the bed and luggage in her tiny room in the Barbizon Hotel for Women. These cramped quarters on noisy Lexington Avenue were not what she had envisioned when she and Marcia, at age fourteen, used to dream of their move to New York. Then she had imagined herself a peroxide blonde, in a satin evening gown, living in a luxurious apartment, perfumed and admired as she strolled in her sunken living room among her guests—mostly strong, handsome men who would besiege her with invitations and who could dance like Fred Astaire. That image made her laugh now.

At the end of her first full day in the city, she was still contemplating her toned-down, adjusted-to-reality version of New York and planning what she would write on the March pages of her 1959 diary. Already she had marked "Help Wanted Female" ads in *The New York Times*. And checking her tourist's map, she had walked noisy streets in Manhattan, with increasingly sore feet; and she had eaten cheesecake while eavesdropping on tourists, instead of the celebrities she had expected, in Lindy's famous Broadway restaurant.

Tomorrow, she decided, she would take the tour through NBC to move forward with her ambition to work in bigtime broadcasting or "something interesting," as she and Marcia used to say to each other.

When the phone rang in her hotel room, she stepped around and over boxes and luggage, then sprawled on the bed to grab it on the third ring. A man's husky voice asked, "Do you still have my card?"

"Benjamin!" cried Phoebe, catching herself in time, before she'd said the full "Benjamin the Gray Beard."

"I just flew in from Chicago," she heard him say on the phone.

"You were very nice with all your offers of help," she said.

"You think so? Look, how about tomorrow night?" he said. "My apartment?"

"Apartment?" said Phoebe, suddenly cautious. "I think I'm going to be moving tomorrow. From this hotel—it's too expensive."

"Friday then. That's even better. My wife says she'd love to meet you." He gave a penthouse address. "Dress casually. We're just going to relax."

"I'm glad you told me." She laughed. "I wondered if I should wear my sequins."

As Phoebe rolled her hair in curlers, she thought of stories she'd heard of New Yorkers who were so cold and unfriendly they just left people lying on the sidewalk. "What would you do all by yourself in New York?" Lillian had asked. "You might get sick or something." Fred had warned her: "It's a big city." Phoebe began to ask herself *why* Benjamin and his wife had given her this invitation. Maybe they were considering her for a job and wanted to size her up in a social situation. As Phoebe tried to sleep, she felt keyed up. She slipped out of bed, opened her handbag, and found Benjamin's engraved business card still there, tucked into her billfold. She counted her dwindling money again; she was going to have to watch it.

The next morning she darted into the booth in the hotel lobby, for she had learned it was cheaper to use a pay phone than the phone in her room. When she dialed the number on his card, the company operator confirmed that, yes, S. Benjamin Ambhurst was president of Ambhurst, Kinsley & Hays International, Inc. "Who's calling please?"

Phoebe hung up. The next day she told Jill Flaxmore about Benjamin's invitation. She had met Jill while waiting in the reception area of the Opportunity Employment Agency on Madison Avenue. Jill, who had blond hair and straight bangs down to her eager blue eyes, had confided that she'd come to New York two years before from Omaha, Nebraska, and now was thinking of changing jobs because she'd not advanced in the ad agency where she worked. Since her boss was out of town, she admitted to Phoebe, she was exploring job possibilities this morning.

The employment agency had no jobs that interested Phoebe or Jill so they walked together to a nearby Chock Full O' Nuts coffee shop. Seated at a counter, Jill held the card of S. Benjamin Ambhurst, President, in her manicured fingers.

"Wow!" Jill said. "You might get a really great job through him." She smiled. "Hey, then you can help me find one."

"I don't want to get my hopes up too high," said Phoebe, studying the card again. "Things don't usually work out—"

"They do sometimes," Jill said. "Otherwise you wouldn't keep hearing about being in the right place at the—Look! You can always leave if his wife's not there. And what if she's not? What's he like?"

Phoebe grimaced. Jill laughed.

The next day Phoebe searched for a room on the Upper West Side of Manhattan where rates were cheaper than where she'd been staying. The room clerk at a hotel in the West Seventies agreed to let her take the keys to look at several rooms. She chose one on the sixteenth floor even though the closet was tiny and the easy chair lumpy. She liked the blue flowered bedspread, which was only slightly faded, and the French windows that faced south and opened onto a tiny balcony. From here she had an expansive view of Central Park down to her left and, in the distance, a skyline of hotels and apartment buildings. Would she soon live in one of them? Until then, this hotel room would do for a few days. She shoved her trunk by the bed, placed a hotel towel over it, and pretended it was a coffee table. Then she called Jill to ask what it meant to "dress casually" to a person who lived in a penthouse on Sutton Place.

Jill didn't know too many people who lived casually in penthouses—"unless you count a sixth-floor walk up. Make the most of it, kiddo!"

That night when Phoebe approached the entrance to the large, white brick building, she straightened her shoulders and tried to look as if she were used to visiting fashionable New York apartments. After checking on his switchboard, the Sutton Place doorman admitted her into the large lobby. On the way to the elevator, she passed a shallow, kidney-shaped pool, edged by greenery, and in the mirrored walls she caught reflections of her black coat, flashes of her blue skirt and sweater.

On the penthouse floor the apartment door was flung open with alarming speed. Benjamin the Gray Beard bowed to her in a playfully exaggerated way, as in a ballet. His red flowered shirt, open at the neck, exposed gray hairs and his yellow Bermuda shorts revealed bony knees. With a grand gesture of his hand, he swept her into a small room like a den, where she took off her coat. She left it on the sofa, along with her handbag.

When they entered the large living room, Phoebe saw walls that glowed an orange-red as if on fire. Recorded symphonic music played in the background. "Darling, she's beautiful!" Benjamin called out to his wife in his husky voice. Immediately he added, "This is my wife, Ninon," as she came into the room, holding out her chubby manicured hand to welcome Phoebe. In spite of her high heels she was short, and dressed much less casually than Phoebe had expected. As if warmed by the walls of fire, she wore a summerlike dress with an oval skirt of white silk flowers and a halter top overloaded with large breasts. Phoebe imagined her whiling away afternoons on a chaise, eating chocolate cream puffs. She appeared to be middle-aged but her skin was taut and her rosy cheeks so puffed out that when she smiled, her tiny eyes almost disappeared.

Benjamin said to his wife, "Isn't Phoebe beautiful, darling?"

Phoebe felt uncomfortable with such a comment to his wife and took this moment to excuse herself. In the den she telephoned Jill, according to plan, and gave the prearranged verifying code: "I received the package so you won't have to wait," meaning: "His wife is here so all is well."

Phoebe smiled as she returned to the living room, although when she and her hosts sat down on low-slung chairs around a large glass cocktail table, an enormous plant centering the table seemed to stab at her with daggerlike leaves. Glancing about at the orange-red walls, she was aware of the bright abstract paintings, but when Benjamin asked her what she wanted to drink she felt her mind go blank. She could not bear another Tom Collins after her queasiness on the train and she hated the taste of Scotch. As Benjamin waited for a reply, she felt a slight panic to name something quickly. "A little bourbon, please."

Benjamin stood up. "An Old Fashioned?"

Phoebe had heard the name but had no idea what was in the drink. "That'd be fine."

"Wow!" his wife said. "A strong drinker."

Phoebe glanced from Ninon to Benjamin, both smiling. "Make it light," she said.

"Not more than three ounces of bourbon," Benjamin called from the kitchen. When he returned with the drinks, he proposed a toast. "Here's to fun."

"And delights!" Ninon's voice rang out.

"People always think the next generation is going to hell," Benjamin said, "but it's restraint—not freedom—that's the problem."

Ninon smiled. "You're so right, darling."

Their conversation sounded rehearsed as if they'd said these same words before. Phoebe had the feeling of watching a play, but she felt awkward, as if she'd been seated on the stage with the actors.

Ninon tottered off in her high heels. "I'm doing the cooking tonight."

Benjamin moved his chair closer to Phoebe's and placed his feet on the cocktail table. "We don't like to have any of the help around when we're relaxing. We give the cook the night off when we plan these evenings." He leaned toward Phoebe, sliding his arm around her shoulders.

Phoebe crouched away from him. He caught her, holding her in a grip. Pushing his bearded chin toward her, he moved to press his wet lips to hers.

She pulled away, turning her head. "Please!" She spurted out of the chair, remembered her grandmother's words: "You can be a lady under any circumstances." She told herself to "act natural." She spotted the double glass doors at the end of the room. "Is that the terrace Ninon mentioned?"

Benjamin ceremoniously offered her his arm, which Phoebe pretended not to notice. "You want to see it?" he asked, then left the doors open as they went out on the narrow balcony that ran along the back of the building. "It's kinda chilly tonight," he said.

They looked down at small rear gardens. "It's nice here, Benjamin," she said in a tone so pleasant her grandmother would have approved.

"Call me Ben. We've been formal long enough." As they leaned over the railing he put his arm around her and strongly pulled her to him. She tried to twist away but he held her tighter.

"Are you crazy?" she said quietly. "Your wife might see us."

"I told you we were just going to relax." He eased his hold. "You think she's jealous?" Ben followed Phoebe inside the apartment. "Darling," he called to his wife, "she thinks you're jealous. Do you want me to do the steaks?"

As Ben left for the kitchen, Ninon came out, stretching her plump, rosy arms, then sat down on the carpet near Phoebe's chair by the cocktail table.

"Ninon," Phoebe said, pronouncing it "Nee-non," as Ben had. "That's a pretty name."

"My name used to be Ann. But when I was nine, I heard that Ninon was the French version of Ann, so I changed it. I believe in doing what I like." Ninon leaned back on her hands. "Who'd you call a while ago?"

"A girl friend."

"Single?"

Phoebe nodded, remembering that Jill was divorced.

"You single girls must have quite a life. Tell me about the life of a single girl." Ninon moved into the chair where Ben had sat next to Phoebe. "I'm just an old married woman myself. Tell me what you single girls do."

"Work. I'm looking for a job."

"I don't mean work. I mean for fun." Ninon reached for a glass on the table and her hand brushed Phoebe's knee. Phoebe shifted position and Ninon picked up the glasses, calling to Ben: "How're you doing, darling?" She went toward the kitchen.

Ben came out, slipped into the chair beside Phoebe and leaned toward her. "Didn't you realize on the train that I was interested? I was very interested." He moved closer to her. "I'm very interested now."

She bent away from him. "Don't be crazy. Your wife really *will* see us here."

"You think she'll be jealous? Darling," he called to Ninon, "she thinks you'll object, isn't that funny?" Ben looked at Phoebe. "You really are amazing," he said slowly. "Don't you realize she would enjoy you just as much as I would?"

"No." Phoebe tried not to show the extent of her surprise. "No, I didn't realize."

"Darling," he called, "we have Miss Innocence with us." When no reply came from the kitchen, he said to Phoebe, "Are you afraid of adventure?"

"No."

"You act like it."

"Do I?" Phoebe stood up. "I like to choose." When he stood too, she sat down. "I like to choose my adventure."

He settled into the chair beside hers. "Why do you think we invited you here?"

"I don't know. You asked me to come to dinner."

"Didn't you think it was strange?" He grabbed her.

She wrenched away and tried to make her voice calm: "You forget I have a choice in this." She glanced toward the den, where she had left her coat and handbag: the door now was closed. She asked Ben where the bathroom was and when she entered the small mirrored room, she discovered that there was no telephone as in the bathrooms at Marcia's parents' house. Nervously, Phoebe thought, as long as she was in the bathroom, she might as well use it.

She was sitting on the toilet when the door flew open: Ninon asked, "What are you doing?"

"Well, I'm going to the bathroom." Phoebe got up, pushing Ninon out, slamming the door, then she leaned on it. Would they let her leave? If she didn't antagonize them, could she go to the den, collect her coat and handbag, and walk out? But what if the door to the den, now closed, was also locked? She must think carefully: This was known as having your wits about you, she told herself, as if labeling would help her know what to do next.

When she opened the bathroom door, she found Ben and Ninon in the hall confronting her with eager smiles of good intentions. "I wanted to tell you dinner is ready," Ninon said.

Phoebe walked with them to the dining table, hearing in her mind the wild silent question: *Will I be able to tell in time if the food has been tampered with?* Phoebe forced a smile in return to theirs, asking herself what else she could do at the moment. She was sure Gramma had never experienced a situation like this.

Ben escorted Phoebe to the side of the table near the terrace doors. After seating her, he ceremoniously held the chair for Ninon at one end of the table, set with gold-rimmed salad plates. He dashed to the kitchen and brought the steaks, one at a time, on sizzling platters.

Ninon draped her hair back over her ears before she began to eat. "We can tell you're a Midwesterner," she said to Phoebe. "You like your steak medium well."

"You like yours rare." Phoebe sensed they thought she was gauche for liking her steak as she did. *Why am I even thinking about this now?* "Delicious," she blurted out, after sampling a green been.

"You said you were looking for a job," Ninon said.

Ben leaned over the table toward Phoebe. "Any leads?"

"Well, I met some people on the train . . ."

Ben said, "Were you leading other people on?"

"I wasn't lead—"

"People that lead other people on get into trouble. And foolish people who try blackmail—"

"Or spread rumors," Ninon said. "We've known some foolish people."

"And we've ruined them," Ben said.

"Anyone," Ninon said, "who has been foolish enough to talk about us to anyone else has been very sorry."

Phoebe kept her eyes on her plate and cut more steak. Chewing and chewing small pieces, she was determined not to gag when she swallowed. She pretended to sip more wine while her hosts continued to reminisce about unwise former guests. She felt disoriented as she stared at the silver salt and pepper shakers in the shape of birds with long tails. She heard herself murmur, unusual.

Finally, Ben smiled and said, "Are we ready for coffee?"

This is madness, Phoebe thought. Why am I still here? Because I don't know how to leave without making them angry, she answered herself. After coffee, Ben cleared the table while Phoebe sat down at the cocktail table with Ninon. Phoebe declined her offer of brandy. "Well," Phoebe said, trying to sound off-hand. She stood up. "It's getting late."

Ninon said, "Don't you want to say good-bye to Ben?"

Phoebe headed for the den. "I'll get my purse and coat first." She was about to try the door when Ninon, tottering on her high heels, slipped around her and, with a sudden gesture of peculiar deference, opened the door for Phoebe with her chubby perfumed hand. Phoebe rushed into the den and grabbed her coat and handbag.

Were they allowing her to leave or would they surprise her again? Ben joined them and all three went into the corridor where they waited for the elevator. Ninon suddenly said, "I'll bet you're disgusted with us."

"No." The elevator door opened. Phoebe said, "No. To each his own."

As the elevator descended, nearing the ground floor, Phoebe had the sensation that her stomach was sinking even deeper within the enclosure. When the elevator stopped and the door opened, she stayed still for a moment. Then she stepped gingerly into the mirrored lobby, where she felt her trembling legs might give way. She could hardly make herself move past the decorative pool.

Outside on the sidewalk she assured herself she would regain strength here in the open air. Touching the building to balance herself, she began to walk. Past great apartment buildings with doormen wearing white gloves and watching her from behind heavy glass doors. Her legs still trembling, she asked herself why it hadn't occurred to her to lie her way out of the predicament. She could have invented a policeman-boyfriend waiting downstairs for her. No, they would have checked with the doorman. In childhood when she had tried to lie, she'd been shamed by Mama and Gramma, who had quoted from Grandpa's church sermons. Mama had asked if she was sure she was telling the truth. "Cross my heart / Hope to die / Stick a needle in my eye." Phoebe had felt that needle coming closer to her eye.

Tonight, by having arranged the code for the phone call to Jill, she had presented a lie, a deception supported by Jill. Yet she should not look for support. In New York she must show herself she can make it on her own. She would never again bank on anyone as she had relied on Niles and Marcia.

She felt tired and torn between the therapy of walking farther or taking the bus. Waiting for the cross-town bus at Sixtieth and Park Avenue, she noticed small trees centering the famous avenue—traffic speeded on both sides of the narrow strip of park—and she realized for the first time that Park Avenue was literally a park-avenue. Knowing that it was not just concrete, lined by large buildings, made the street seem friendlier, a link to the Midwest. Though at home she would never have noticed such a narrow strip of land! Why was she looking for the familiar when she longed for change?

Concerned that no bus had arrived, she hurried to Sixty-seventh Street and waited so long for the cross-town bus that she began to wonder if buses ran this late, now past eleven o'clock. But surely they must in this big city, which she'd once imagined was utopia.

Finally she trudged west, cut across Fifth Avenue, and into Central Park, heading to the West Side of Manhattan. The road and sidewalk were at a lower level than the park, so that to her right was a shoulder-high stone wall. As cars whizzed by on her left, she moved closer to the wall. This route across the park had seemed a short distance on the bus, but not now on foot at night. She trudged on. Although she was budgeting, she looked to see if any taxi rushing by might be empty, then realized that a cab could not stop here without piling up traffic. Her high heels no longer clicked on the sidewalk, which here were encrusted with dirt. Catching a whiff of urine, she began to feel more apprehensive. Suddenly she knew that more than anything she wanted to be back on Fifth Avenue.

She turned around, and as she started to run, she tried to stiffen her ankles, which felt unsteady in her high heels. She forced herself to increase her speed. She was aware—or was it just a feeling?—that now someone was behind her. Propelled by terror, she moved her legs faster, faster.

When she stumbled, the ground seemed to come up to meet her with gigantic force. Stunned and frightened, her face against the sidewalk, she put her arms over her head to protect herself. Gradually she realized she was alone.

In the dim light she saw glimmers of broken glass surrounding her. Her most severe pain was in her left ankle. Trembling, she forced herself to sit up and found her left shoe in the gutter; the high heel had snapped off. She spotted her handbag at an angle against the wall; the handle was broken. She had to find a way to walk. She put her hands on the sidewalk and pushed. Shaking, she leaned against the wall and slid slowly up against the pain. She stood with her weight on her right foot. Leaning to look for the heel of her shoe, she almost fell over into the path of a car.

Cold and dirty, she longed for a warm bath in her own bathtub at home. The tub she wanted was the big one in the green bathroom of her childhood. Anxiously, she gave up looking for the heel of the shoe and limped as fast as she could toward Fifth Avenue.

When a taxi finally stopped for her, she could hardly climb in because of pain. "I fell and hurt my ankle," she told the driver. "I'm sorry I'm slow."

"Want me to take you to New York Hospital? To the emergency?"

"Oh, no, thanks."

"My wife broke her ankle, but she didn't—"

"Oh, please don't tell me that. Thanks." When the cab stopped in front of the hotel, she gingerly got out and hobbled into the lobby. The room clerk at the desk handed her the key to her room. "Well, what happened to you?"

"I had a fall."

Feeling unsteady, she unlocked the door to her room. When she turned on the ceiling light, she was comforted by the sight of her familiar cosmetics on the dresser and the trunk covered by the hotel towel. She pulled off the towel and wiped her face. The towel was dirty from her skin. She sat on the bed to examine her swollen ankle. Throwing off the dirty coat, she tried to phone Jill, but there was no answer.

Should she call Niles? Would he care?

She took off her clothes, painfully padded her way naked into the bathroom. She eased into the bathtub, and lying on her back, hoisted her leg onto the edge. At least it was warm, the water was warm. The hotel's small cake of Ivory soap smelled clean.

She lay soaking for a long time before it came to her that she couldn't call Niles.

Nine

PHOEBE'S ANKLE STILL PAINED HER a week later as she elevated her leg onto the daybed in Jill's apartment. She forced herself to phone Mother Bertha and to tell her about meeting Jill Flaxmore. "Right now I'm sharing her apartment—"

"I don't see why scrounging around, back east there in New York is better than being here with me," Mother Bertha said through the phone. "Well, did you find a job?"

"Temporary. A company called Gotham Temps is sending me out to work at different companies."

"I'd think you'd want something more settled. Everything you're doing sounds pretty fly-by-night. You could be here with me—not staying with a stranger. Who is this person? Is it a decent place?"

"Of course."

"You say 'of course' but in New—"

"Don't worry, Mother Bertha." Phoebe added that she was grateful to Jill for her kindness in letting her share her apartment. "It's small; I'm only staying here for a little while. I'll write you," Phoebe said in a rush to say good-bye.

She dialed, this time reaching the Englishman she had met on the train. "Phoebe, how lovely to hear your voice," Edward Hibbard said.

Quickly she reminded him of his offer to introduce her to Selma-belle Flaunton.

The next evening, though still suffering from pain in her ankle, Phoebe tried to hurry as she climbed the subway steps. She imagined the tall, blond Edward, his very English self, peering at his watch as he waited impatiently for her. Reaching the square called Gramercy Park, she rushed, limping, along the sidewalk beside the high wrought iron fence at the park's west side. Nearing the end of the block, she could see Edward standing in front of a house and, as she'd guessed, he did look at his watch. He glanced up, but did not look at her.

Instead, he watched a young blond woman in a striking red evening gown and cape, carrying a small white poodle. In front of the house, the young woman placed the puppy on the sidewalk and held its leash. She rang the bell at the house and was admitted.

Phoebe kept her eyes on Edward as he adjusted the red rose in his lapel. When he looked up again, she waved to him. She felt happy to greet him and he kissed her on the cheek and said, "Not to worry," as Phoebe, her brown eyes large, apologized for being late.

It was growing dark and the streetlights were already on. While Phoebe stood with Edward in front of Selmabelle's house, a taxi drew up and a couple got out. As they came toward the house, the woman said, "I've read—"

"Look," the man said, "it's hard to describe Selmabelle in person. You have to *experience* Selmabelle."

Phoebe's eyes met Edward's as they stood with the couple at the entrance. A maid opened the door, revealing the lighted marble hall and a wide staircase beyond. Inside the entryway, a mirror invited Phoebe to inspect her hair. Brushing it back with her hand, she caught a glimpse in the glass of Edward, tall and slender in his dark, well-tailored suit. When the maid took Phoebe's coat, she told Edward that "Miss Selmabelle" had something to discuss with him right away.

Phoebe and Edward climbed the broad, soft carpeted stairs, where the banisters were festooned with wide golden ribbons. Reaching the top, Edward apologized for leaving her and Phoebe made her way alone into the high-ceilinged rooms. Guests stood drinking and chatting in clusters near Victorian settees or bay windows that gave view to the darkening Gramercy Park beyond. Lights from the chandelier caught the jewels of the women, a few in long gowns. A fair-haired woman in a wine-colored gown tilted back her head as she laughed with admirers surrounding her. Was she Lauren Bacall? Betty Bacall, Phoebe had heard she was called.

In the midst of all these chattering strangers, Phoebe touched the dark beads she wore with her pale green wool dress and wished that she had added dangling earrings—yet she was here to apply for a job. She busied herself inspecting a wall of landscapes and portraits, then became aware of a man standing nearby. When they exchanged glances, he said, "Does your husband always run off so quickly?"

"What?" Phoebe said, "Oh, he's not my husband."

"I thought he looked a little old for you."

She turned to face him, a small man in a checked suit and bow tie. Grinning, he told her, "You look as though you'd like to write a memo to God. 'Dear God,'" he said, pretending to quote from the memo, "'I don't understand.'" He stared at Phoebe. "You look lost. How long have you been lost?"

"I don't believe," Phoebe said, "I want to answer that." She felt shy but was determined not to appear that way. "I'm not lost," she said.

They went into the bar in the next room. As they sipped their drinks, he said, "Then who was the guy you came in with? Your boss?"

Shaking her head, she smiled at him. "May I ask you a question?"

"Shoot."

"I wondered if you always interview people."

He laughed. "It's an occupational hazard."

"Oh?"

"Now you can guess what I do," he said.

"Well . . . you're with the Census Bureau?"

"No. Hey, you don't want to play *What's My Line?* with me—I used to be with that show. Now I'm with the *Richy Rand Show*—I produce the New York segment."

"Really?"

"You sound impressed."

"I am. I'm looking for a job."

"Don't look to me—we just cut our staff. What do you do?"

"Write, research, search—"

"Search? For what?"

Phoebe hesitated, then tossed off, "My life." He grinned and Phoebe attempted to sound like everybody else: "Job, everything." Her face hot, Phoebe said, "I don't think we've actually met, I'm Phoebe Stanhope."

He looked out at other guests. Then he answered, "Toby Weaver. By the way," he grinned, "how long have you known her?"

Phoebe studied his teasing face, trying to understand. "Oh, you mean Selmabelle Flaunton?" she said. "I'm meeting her tonight."

"Don't admit *that!* There's a parlor game they play here: I've Known Selmabelle Longer and Better Than You."

"Oh."

"Where are you from? Not New York."

"Kansas."

"Kansas!" He tilted his head, as he looked at her.

Was he going to say again, don't admit that?

"Excuse me," Phoebe said.

She found the powder room where two women in evening dresses were at the mirror. One finished applying her lipstick and said, "I was surprised at how she did it."

"Umm," the other said, smoothing the back of her pale orange hair, coiled atop her head. She leaned toward her friend and spoke softly. Phoebe overheard: ". . . amazed she used Lysol. Knowing her . . ."

"What would you have thought?"

"Is there such a thing as a platinum gun?"

The two women laughed together as they left the room. Phoebe followed them into a large room where waiters were moving chairs away from a long dining table.

"Oh, *there* you are," a slightly built man drawled in a Southern accent. He came toward Phoebe, lifting his head, gazing at her through his eyeglasses. "I was looking for *you*." He stared at her as he adjusted his glasses. "Oh, no, I wasn't, I beg your pardon. I thought you were someone else—she wanted to get a job."

"So do I," said Phoebe.

He leaned toward her as if confiding a secret. "I'm better with *figures* than faces I always say—as a *joke*. I don't want you to get the wrong impression." He introduced himself as Selmabelle's accountant, Wilbur Z. Monroe. He emphasized the "Z" so strongly that Phoebe said, as if on cue, "What does the 'Z' stand for?"

"Zachariah," he said proudly. "That's . . ." Phoebe tried to keep track of what he was saying but she had caught sight of the artist Gilbert Bradley from the train. He was in the next room with a group of eager men clustered around the young woman in red, holding the small white dog in her arms. Phoebe felt someone touch her elbow and Edward Hibbard appeared at her side. He shook hands with Wilbur Z. Monroe, then said to Phoebe, "I had a chance to mention you to Selmabelle."

Guided by Edward, Phoebe headed down a corridor, decorated with dark patterned wallpaper. While walking, she turned to Edward to ask, "Do I mention that I want a job? Or should I make an appointment, I mean during office hours?"

"All hours are office hours with Selmabelle—you should think about that. She expects an awful lot. She has a big turnover of assistants."

Phoebe took her folded résumé from her handbag. "I'll work hard— I just want a chance." She and Edward walked down a passageway leading from the main house, which fronted on Gramercy Park, to the house in the rear on Nineteenth Street, which comprised the offices.

Edward told Phoebe that Selmabelle was now being interviewed by a writer for the weekly magazine, *Persona*, for a series on famous hostesses. Elsa Maxwell had let Selmabelle know that she, Elsa, had been the inspiration for the articles. Not to be outdone, Selmabelle planned a *triple* angle on her own story: (1) Selmabelle, Hostess "At Home" (2) Selmabelle, Outspoken Hostess on the Air—even though her show was off the air now, she assumed the magazine would name her the *best* broadcast interviewer—and (3) President of Selmabelle Flaunton Enterprises, Inc. Her international public relations firm represented clients noted for hospitality, with such spokesmen as Edward Hibbard of the luxury hotel The Royal Rose in London, and owners of some of Britain's choicest stately homes and castles open to the public.

Phoebe felt a sense of expectancy as she and Edward entered the office section. Hearing Selmabelle's famous deep voice, Phoebe thought how often, while working at the Harkenstown TV station, she'd heard this voice on the network program *The Selmabelle Flaunton Hour*, which the station carried. Phoebe remembered how hard it had been for her at first to write copy and to listen to the station's programs at the same time.

Now Phoebe peeked into Selmabelle's book-lined office, where in the center was a gilt-encrusted desk. Its high-backed chair resembled a gold throne with posts on the corners. At the moment Selmabelle was not at the desk, but seated on a sofa, speaking to the female journalist, who was writing in a notebook while perched on the edge of a chair. Selmabelle's voice proclaimed: "I have no near relatives surviving, thank God! Jane is Max's niece—my deceased husband's niece. She has more sense than her sister and most of the other Flauntons. Jane can be amusing—thank God!—since she's visiting me."

Selmabelle Flaunton held onto the arm of the sofa to brace herself as she stood up. Phoebe had known she was tall, but now she guessed she must be at least six feet. Her yellow-blond hair, parted in the middle, did not look quite real. It gave her the appearance of a giant walking doll as she moved about stiffly. Except for her throne, the furnishings seemed too small and out of proportion to her. She gestured toward a bookcase containing leather-bound volumes. "I like good things." She put her hands on her generous hips. "Good food."

"You've done so many things," said the reporter trailing Selmabelle about the room, "and had such success."

Selmabelle stared at the reporter. "*What* is success?"

"Well, I mean how do you get what you want?"

"I *insist* on it."

"I understand some people brought you birthday gifts. May I ask which birthday?"

"Certainly not. Discussing age is a waste of time. What's important is what people *do*. And what I want people to *do* is tour the choicest castles and stately homes in Britain." Picking up a page from the top of a stack, she held it toward the reporter.

Taking it, the reporter glanced down at it. "Yes, I know this is your client. But may I ask how you respond to the statement: 'People who entertain as much as you do are basically lonely.'"

Selmabelle straightened her shoulders, stood tall. "I was brought up entertaining."

"Yes, and about that family tradition—which I believe goes back a long way—didn't your grandfather often host Mark Twain? I understand they played billiards together."

"I told you before I'm not going to talk more about my family— too much has been written already." Selmabelle adjusted her rose-colored scarf, which began at the scoop neck of her long black lace dress and wove its way in and out of the lace past her heavy hips to the hem. "Everyone tells me I should do a book of my own someday." She looked at Edward. "Come rescue me. Is this the girl you were telling me about?"

Phoebe offered her résumé but instead of taking it, Selmabelle placed a cigarette in her holder and Edward provided a light. "Why do you want to work for me?" Selmabelle asked Phoebe. "I emphasize the word 'work.' Most of the girls are interested only in expanding their contacts. You know, Edward, employees forget why they're hired. Lord Ravensleigh tells me he employs someone as an estate agent at Ravensleigh Castle and pretty soon the fellow takes on airs, upsets the staff, strolls the gardens, and forgets why he was engaged. As Lord Ravensleigh says, 'The fellow becomes too lordly for words and one simply has to fire him.'"

Blowing smoke, she turned her head on her statuesque shoulders, and stared at Phoebe with her deep-set golden brown eyes. "I suppose you have—what's that quaint phrase—good skills? Edward tells me you've worked in television."

Phoebe held out her résumé, which this time Selmabelle took and read. "You're quite sure you don't want to be *on* the air? From my experience, Edward, they begin to think they know so much they can take over, or they're so helpless it takes all your time telling them what to do." Selmabelle looked again at the résumé. "Edward says you have good references. They'd better be, I'll check them, you know. You can have a two-week trial."

Selmabelle named a salary lower than Phoebe had hoped for. As Phoebe started to speak, Selmabelle turned to the journalist, who was ready with her notebook and pencil.

The reporter said, "You were well known before your latest venture, but you're unusual as a public relations person."

"I hope I'm unusual for any person."

"What I wanted to ask you—how do you get away with it?"

"With *what*?"

"I've heard it said that you're so outspoken."

"Some people find her frankness refreshing," Edward said.

Selmabelle laughed. "Don't be devoted, Edward," she said. "It doesn't become you." But as soon as she had said it, she took his arm and smiled at him.

The reporter asked if she had many regrets. "Regrets?" Selmabelle repeated, as if this totally mystified her. "Why should I have regrets?

Have you met my new assistant?" She turned to Phoebe. "What's your name again?"

"Phoebe Stanhope."

"Phoebe, take care of her." Selmabelle nodded toward the reporter. "Get her a drink. Notice I didn't say 'another drink.' You don't have to rub it in that they've been drinking all evening. Of course, I'm not talking about this young lady," she added, indicating the reporter. She instructed Phoebe: "Be here at nine in the morning. We have a lot to do."

Phoebe smiled, "Oh, thank you, Mrs. Flaunton."

"Selmabelle. Please! You must remember *everyone* calls me Selmabelle."

Phoebe and the reporter, Josephine McPherson, walked down the hallway, heading toward the lively chatter of the party. Josephine asked Phoebe, "Where did you work before?"

"I just got to New York three weeks ago—I worked in TV in Kansas."

"That figures. I did a story on getting so-called glamour jobs in New York and you followed what the experts advise: get out-of-town experience first."

"That's interesting! Employment agencies kept telling me I needed New York experience to work here. Well, anyway, let's get you a drink—I never would have guessed that'd be my first job assignment."

Toby Weaver, in his checked suit and bow tie, grinned as he took an arm from each of them. "Be on your guard for this one," he advised Phoebe, referring to Josephine. "You never know what she'll write," he said in a teasing voice, as if they were longtime friends.

"Don't feel you have to stay with me," Josephine said to Phoebe.

In the next room, Phoebe skirted around tables and chairs toward tall, heavyset Gilbert Bradley, standing at the bar. "Well, hello," he said, his hazel eyes revealing appreciation. He leaned an arm on the bar and inquired what had happened to her since their meeting on the train. "I still have my sketches of you."

"You'll never guess what happened tonight," Phoebe said. "I got a job!"

"Well, congratulations!"

"With Selmabelle. I'm her new assistant."

He stopped smiling and, turning his massive shoulders, faced the bar. "Very good."

"You don't look all that happy about it."

"Phoebe, I just want everything to go well for you." He said it as if that closed the subject.

Phoebe looked for something else to say. "I saw you earlier," she said, "talking to a girl in red."

"I'm about to do her portrait."

Oh, then you're a real artist, Phoebe thought, realizing that all artists aren't super-sensitive otherworldly beings. That some were able to be encouraging to others. At least Edward would be glad for her—although he'd probably give her a warning or two. She felt more grateful than ever to Edward and she told Gilbert that she had a lot to thank Edward for.

Gilbert nodded without comment, then followed her into the next room, where people stood drinking and singing. A group watched a man play the electric organ and other guests danced. Gilbert asked Phoebe, "Do you play?"

"The piano. But not very well." She admitted that she was from a musical family and had probably disappointed her parents. "In fact I know I disappointed my mother."

"My mother," Gilbert said, "says I'm about as grand as a plumber. She'd like it better if I were more like my brother. She still uses a linen handkerchief and when she comes to my studio, she keeps it over her nose against what she calls 'unpleasant odors'—she can't stand the smell of turpentine. And worst of all, in her opinion, she says my fingernails prove I'm an artist—she claims she can tell what I'm painting by looking at my fingernails."

"Gilbert, darling," came a whispering voice. It belonged to the young woman in red carrying the small white poodle. His little paws overlapped her arm. "Fetchy wants to know if he can be in the portrait with me," she said in a coy little girl's voice.

Phoebe put out a finger toward the puppy's black nose. His beady eyes looked up at her. "Does he bite?" Phoebe asked.

"If I tell him to. I haven't seen you here before."

Gilbert introduced them. She was Jane Flaunton, Selmabelle's niece. Phoebe noticed her curly blond hair and tiny features. She was little and, like her dog, cute. Jane put the puppy down on the carpet and held him by the leash. When Gilbert explained that Phoebe was Selmabelle's new assistant, Jane seemed to dismiss her as if she were a servant. Jane took Gilbert's arm and looked up at him. "I want you to paint me with Fetchy. I'll be like Chekhov's *Lady with the Little Pet Dog.* Only she ended up losing and I plan always to win."

"I hope you do win," Gilbert said as they turned away, "but in what?"

"In everything," Jane said. "I'm very greedy and I love it. Does that sound awful?"

"Not from you, it doesn't," he said.

Not from you, it doesn't, Phoebe repeated silently. She thought: he'll have red paint under his fingernails before long. The thought of Jane's presence made her question working for Selmabelle. But why should Jane stand in the way of a job she needed?

Phoebe felt the pressure again of so many things happening in recent months. It seemed as if her own internal clock could not keep up with the events that were the legacy of New Year's Eve. And the legacy was just beginning.

It was at that moment Phoebe became aware of guests wandering about with plates of food, looking for places to sit. She found her way back to the dining room where earlier she'd seen waiters extending the table to its fullest length, and covering it with white linen. Entering the room now, she saw that the large table was filled with heaping colorful dishes surrounding a silver centerpiece in the shape of a swan. Greenery circled the swan's neck and rode on its back. In flickering candlelight an assortment of salads crowded an oblong bowl of trout in aspic that trembled at the jostling of a neighboring dish. Glistening baked ham and a golden brown turkey had been partially cut and slices lay on platters garnished with parsley and radish roses. As Phoebe picked up one of the gold-rimmed plates stacked on the end of the sideboard, she watched groups of guests, apparently long acquainted, laughing at inside jokes, commenting on delicious aromas, pointing at fattening pastries on a side table. They paid no attention to Phoebe, who helped herself to shrimp from a bowl decorated by a ring of shrimp, hooked like claws around the rim.

Even the waiters—one wearing a tall white chef's hat—who offered hot food from steaming pans seemed more interested in helping those whose faces they recognized. They beamed and competed when a woman, who looked like Zsa Zsa Gabor in a white gown and diamonds, nodded to a chafing dish and said to the man with her, "Darling, vot iss zat?" A man whose face Phoebe felt she had seen on TV had his mouth open for a copper-haired girl poised to drop a shrimp into it.

Standing near the pastry table was the couple who had arrived by taxi as Phoebe and Edward had entered the party. Holding a plate, the woman was deep in conversation. Phoebe felt envious, for she was talking with—was it?—Mary Martin, the musical star, who looked interested in what the woman was saying. Phoebe wondered how the conversation had started. It made Phoebe feel shy again. She thought of articles she'd read of celebrities being pestered by people following them about, interrupting their dinner in restaurants. Yet this was a private gathering; she would have to learn to fit in, especially now that she was to be Selmabelle's assistant. Even these people probably loved admiration—they would be lost without their fans. She imagined herself saying, "Hello, I watch your newscasts . . . I loved your book . . . You were wonderful in the show."

Except she could see how occupied they were, commenting eagerly to one another in an exclusive way. Holding her plate of food,

Phoebe walked through the crowded rooms and caught sight of tall, elegant Edward with his red rose and eager business expression; he was busy entering the bar with two men and Selmabelle. Busy and business were the same.

At a front bay window, Phoebe pulled aside the curtains and looked out at the quiet street. She gazed beyond, past the darkened space of Gramercy Park, to the distant lights of other streets, other buildings. She was alone here in this noisy room, not really knowing anyone, and not knowing any of the people under the lights beyond. Where did she belong? Life at this moment seemed a struggle and a longing to belong.

She carried her plate deep into other reception rooms. So many paintings of gloomy landscapes in heavy frames. She settled into an armchair in what seemed to be the library. No other guests were here but the room was crowded with chairs and bric-a-brac on tasseled, brown velvet cloths on end tables. She was eating when the clock on the mantel began to chime and strike the hour of nine. She found herself counting the slow dong . . . dong . . .

She spotted, next to the clock, a glass statue of a naked male figure standing on one foot with the other foot out, as if gleefully about to lose his balance. When Phoebe set down her plate and stood up to inspect the figure, she was tempted to touch parts of the fat body and the tiny face with the impish grin.

"Hello." It was a deep male voice. "Excuse me, hello." The resonance of the voice was like the ringing of a heavy bell which lingers in the air. She slowly turned. A man in a dark suit, she discovered. She felt his presence and caught the clean smell of his shirt, then looked up. Holding a drink in his hand, he had anticipation in his blue eyes as he concentrated on her. "Do you want to talk," he said, "or do you prefer to be alone?"

"Oh, I'd like to talk."

"Are you a collector?" He nodded toward the statue. "Is this Mr. Eros here?" His voice was melodious. She so enjoyed the music, she almost missed some of the words he spoke.

"Eros?" she questioned.

"You sound pleased with that idea."

Phoebe shook her head, while smiling. "I hope not."

"Why? You're not a cynic?" he said in a teasing voice.

Phoebe did not answer.

"I admit I'm a cynic," he said. "Look at this god of love—he's laughing. Don't you think there should be signs up here with him: *Fragile! Made of Glass. Handle With Care!*" He smiled at her. "Maybe you're not a cynic. I wish you could see that look on your face! I'll bet you've even read Edna St. Vincent Millay."

Phoebe smiled back at him.

He quoted: "'We were very tired, we were very merry—'"

"'We went back and forth all night on the ferry,'" she quoted in answer.

He grinned. "See! But the cynic in me says that sooner or later you'll get tired of going back forth on the ferry."

"I hope it doesn't have to be quite that way."

"Want to bet? We could test it."

"Test it? You mean ride the ferry? Tonight? I've never even ridden on a ferry."

"Now you're going to tell me it's a cold night."

"No," said Phoebe. "No, it's not that cold."

He held out his hand.

She hesitated. She looked into his eyes. "I'd go if I could."

"Maybe you're more of a cynic than I thought," he said.

They rushed through the ritual of getting their coats, decided against good-byes and thank yous, and in a conspiracy hurried out. But as he pressed her arm against his side she realized: I don't know this man. On the sidewalk in front of the house, she stopped. "I can't do this. I came with someone. I'm sorry."

"You're thinking now. Sometimes you have to play things by ear—let things happen."

"I'm really obligated to this person. I want to—it's just—"

"All right, it's just as well," he said. "I have work to do."

"Tonight?"

"Tonight." He guided her back to the door, excused himself, and turned away. She watched him leave her, his shoulders filling out his coat, the back of his hair visible under the street light. His determined stride resounded on the sidewalk. He turned the corner at Irving Place. *I don't even know your name.* She wanted to run after him. She started to walk fast, despite her painful ankle, then stopped. The moment for that had gone too.

She found herself rushing to the corner. Near the end of the block on Irving Place the lights of a car moved out from the curb, then, motor racing, the big car took off.

She was filled with disappointment. How do you know, she thought, when to follow your impulses? When she followed hers, she was sometimes sorry. When she didn't follow hers, she was sometimes sorrier.

Ten

$\mathcal{P}$HOEBE ARRIVED AT HER NEW JOB early the next morning but the maid informed her that Selmabelle Flaunton was not yet in her office. Phoebe waited in the parlor overlooking Gramercy Park. Determined to be here promptly, she was instead ahead of time, in the way of the maid running a noisy vacuum over the flowered carpet. Phoebe skirted around the machine, lingered in front of a bookcase, admiring a Chinese vase filled with pink carnations that smelled of cinnamon. She noticed on the grand piano a framed photograph of Selmabelle holding a microphone toward a distinguished-looking, white-haired man. The stone building shown in the background of the picture looked like a castle—Phoebe guessed it was one Selmabelle had mentioned to the reporter from *Persona* magazine.

It's amazing, Phoebe thought, that she might deal with clients who owned castles. If she wrote Lillian and Fred about her new job, they would read and reread the letter, question if Phoebe was having delusions. She would have to stress to them that her job had to do with travel. People traveled. People visited castles. Still . . . a far cry from Kansas.

Gramma's highest compliment had been that a person was down-to-earth. It was hardly run-of-the-mill down-to-earth here. Phoebe had to admit to herself that it had seemed strange to hear Selmabelle talk about such people as her friend Lord Ravensleigh in England, who had hired an estate agent, a "fellow who had strolled the gardens, taken on airs, upset the staff, and become too lordly for words, and one simply had to fire him."

If he had become too lordly, Phoebe reviewed in her mind, he had forgotten he was an employee. Well, that would not be her problem; she needed this job. She thought of warnings she'd received about the big turnover in this job.

But she would not get fired, she promised herself when a buzzer sounded. As the maid led her down the long corridor. Phoebe thought of Dorothy in *The Wizard of Oz*, saying to her little dog, "Toto, I have a feeling we're not in Kansas anymore." But here Phoebe did not have a dog. Selmabelle's snippy niece, Jane, had that dog.

Now the maid left Phoebe alone in front of Selmabelle's office door, which was ajar. Selmabelle was on the phone as Phoebe cautiously stepped just inside. Wearing a flowing green silk coat, Selmabelle stretched her free arm toward the ceiling as if to exercise while she finished the conversation with "You're an angel," then slammed down the phone. Seated in her throne chair, Selmabelle leaned toward a yellow leather tulip in a flowerpot on her desk and pulled from the petals her black-rimmed spectacles. Shuffling papers, she glanced up at Phoebe, who prepared for dictation. It soon began in Selmabelle's deep voice. Suddenly Selmabelle interrupted herself: "Now this is urgent. We're dealing here with urgency."

Phoebe promised to rush with the letters, then walked into the next office, a square room with two desks. Following instructions, she hurried to the rear one where the desk chair had wooden arms and was fairly comfortable. Remembering her two-week trial period, Phoebe opened desk drawers to find pencils, paper clips, rubber bands in disarray and press releases headlined AMERICAN TOURISTS INVITED TO VISIT CASTLES AND STATELY HOMES IN BRITAIN. And printed at the top, left, of the page: Selmabelle Flaunton, Public Relations Representative in the U.S.A., The Association for Castles and Stately Homes in Britain.

Phoebe was typing the second letter to England when she heard a buzzer and tried to decide if this signal was for her or the maid. The buzzer sounded again and Phoebe rushed to the door of Selmabelle's office.

Selmabelle had removed her green silk coat to reveal yellow lounging pajamas, which matched her yellow hair. "That's what I said," Selmabelle said into the phone, then hung up. "Why can't people pay attention? I've had too many phone calls this morning." She sounded as if she were accusing Phoebe. "You'll have to handle them."

Selmabelle swung her body in her throne so that her feet were planted beside the desk. She pulled up the flowing pants legs of her yellow hostess pajamas to show her black orthopedic oxfords. "See these shoes," she said in her famous deep voice. "I have trouble with my feet."

Phoebe nodded as she looked at her wide shoes and thick ankles.

"One of your duties will be to do my walking for me."

Phoebe tried to think what that meant.

"My clients and everyone else I've ever known sooner or later comes to New York and expects to be taken around. Lord and Lady Petwell are in town now, staying at the Pierre." She looked at Phoebe. "Have you written that down? Good. Now this morning Lady Petwell needs to be taken sightseeing, which means walking. She'll be expecting you at eleven-thirty."

"Oh." Phoebe looked at her watch. "The only thing—I was just thinking . . ."

"About what?" Selmabelle demanded.

"You said the letters were urgent."

"Do I hear doubts that you can handle this job?"

"No," said Phoebe, standing up. "I can handle it, definitely."

It was on the eighteenth floor of the Pierre Hotel that a maid opened the door and asked Phoebe to wait in the living room of the suite. As Phoebe sat on the edge of a wing chair by the windows overlooking Central Park, a group of men came out of an adjoining room, led by a large, white-haired man in a pin-striped suit. Phoebe recognized him from the photograph she had seen: Selmabelle interviewing him in front of the castle! Phoebe guessed that he was Lord Petwell. Smiling warmly, he crossed the carpet to Phoebe and, shaking hands, he said, "You're waiting for my wife." Then, with his entourage of men, he left for a business meeting which Selmabelle had said he would attend. Phoebe wondered if the man with the musical voice might possibly be at that meeting, then told herself to stop thinking of him.

This is my job, she again reminded herself, unusual as it seemed.

Now Lady Petwell emerged from the back of the suite, wearing a beige tweed suit and a brocade hat set back on her head to show yellow curls across her forehead. Her face, like her husband's, was rosy red, and she let out little giggles and seemed excited, leaning to look out the window. "We'll cross the road and walk there by the park," she said, referring to Fifth Avenue and Central Park.

As she spoke in her upper class English accent, her nasal passages seemed closed and the clear words formed precisely in the front of her mouth, aided by large teeth. "Then we'll take a taxi, shall we?" She clapped her hands as though they were embarking upon a great adventure. "Let's go over to the Empire State Building. We'll have luncheon," she said with the excitement of a child, "on top of the building."

"I think they may only have snacks up there," Phoebe said, even though she'd not yet visited the landmark. Recently Phoebe had suggested lunch there to Jill, who had said the only restaurant was on the street level.

"We'll see. We'll take a *taxi,* shall we?" said Lady Petwell with intense excitement. It seemed that Lady Petwell had never before ridden in a taxi. In all sixty-five years of her life she had apparently ridden only in a baby carriage, in chauffeur-driven cars, special trains, and rickshaws in Hong Kong, where she and her husband had once lived before returning by ship to live in his family's castle in England.

The taxi ride was without incident except for Lady Petwell's enthusiasm. When they stood on the sidewalk and looked up, Lady Petwell confided to Phoebe that she was frightened. She knew a woman, she emphasized, who had become *so* frightened by the heights in the Empire State Building that she had fainted on the fifty-seventh floor. Lady Petwell did not want to faint: "We'll go up in sections. We'll start with the second floor."

"But Lady Petwell, you're staying on the eighteenth floor of the Pierre. Couldn't we start on the eighteenth floor?"

In the crowded elevator Lady Petwell announced to the operator, "We're going up in sections. We want to see if we faint." Phoebe was aware that other passengers looked at them curiously as they got off on the eighteenth floor.

Lady Petwell was inspired as she stood in front of the elevator door. "We haven't fainted, have we? We could go to the twentieth."

Phoebe pointed out there were 102 stories to the Empire State Building. "Couldn't we go to the thirtieth?" When the next elevator stopped and passengers got off, Phoebe urged Lady Petwell to step in first.

"But that's going down," Lady Petwell said.

Phoebe tried to hide her impatience. "No, it's not."

"Yes, it tis," Lady Petwell cried out as she got on.

The elevator went down, returning them to the ground floor. Chagrined, Phoebe apologized and Lady Petwell announced on the next elevator that they were going up in sections. When they finally got off on the thirtieth floor, a man followed them, and listened, as Lady Petwell told Phoebe: "We'll look out the windows to see if we faint." As they walked along the corridor, no windows were visible, only doors to offices. Lady Petwell lamented.

The man, catching up with them, asked, "Are you sure you don't want to commit suicide?" Ignoring his question, Lady Petwell told him with delight of their conspiracy and he trailed them in their progression. On the fifty-seventh floor he asked again, "Are you sure you don't want to commit suicide?"

"I don't want to commit suicide," said Phoebe, beginning not to be sure.

Lady Petwell insisted that at the next door, Phoebe must knock and ask if they could look out the window. Phoebe reminded herself that this was her new job and she depended on it. When the door was opened by a secretary, Lady Petwell's voice rose high as she emphasized that the fifty-seventh floor was where her friend had fainted. A stern-looking man faced them from behind the counter. "No," he said. "No one is permitted behind this counter."

With the door closed on them, Lady Petwell said to Phoebe, "We haven't fainted, have we?"

On the eighty-sixth floor the elevator operator said they had to transfer to another elevator to reach the Observatory at the top. Not only that: they needed tickets, which were on sale only on the first floor. "Why don't we have tickets?" Lady Petwell accused Phoebe.

"Is there a restaurant on top?" Phoebe asked the attendant.

"First floor," he said.

As she got off the elevator on the first floor, Lady Petwell seemed fresh out of bravery. Looking at a line of people waiting to buy tickets, she said, "Oh, I never wait in a queue!" The man interested in their suicidal intentions departed; Phoebe assumed he was with the building's security office.

As the two women sat across a small table from one another in the crowded first-floor restaurant, Phoebe realized that she had grown fond of Lady Petwell, and because of their experience together, they seemed to share a buddy-buddy feeling.

Leaning toward Phoebe, Lady Petwell said, "Phoebe, dear, are those separates you're wearing?"

Phoebe looked down at her olive green woolen blouse and matching skirt.

"Off-the-peg?" asked Lady Petwell with hopeful delight.

Phoebe stared at her, trying to grasp her meaning. Lady Petwell lifted her hands, and, smiling broadly as with delicious understanding, she cried, "Oh!" Now Lady Petwell spoke as if confiding, "I believe in *America,* you say"—she paused, then spoke bashfully—"'off-the-rack.'" Lady Petwell turned her head, eyeing Phoebe from the side. Shyly but with excitement, she divulged, "I want to see separates hanging in a store."

Phoebe had bought her separates in Kansas, but she thought that a nearby department store, Lord & Taylor, would have them. This suggestion filled Lady Petwell with joy and amazement. Soon they were in Lord & Taylor and she was ecstatic when looking at blouses and skirts, the separates she had longed to see. "Off-the-peg!" she continued to exclaim.

Phoebe had never before heard anyone use the expression "off-the-peg." She felt an urge to admit this to Lady Petwell, but decided to keep her mouth closed while Lady Petwell opened hers. Lady Petwell beamed as she told clerks and other customers that she was in this store to see separates hanging in a store and behold, "Here they are!" Apparently it was one of the miracles of the world she was looking at. Other people seemed to find it difficult to share her wonderment. Instead they seemed to wonder about her. Phoebe was aware of many people turning to stare at Lady Petwell and then at Phoebe herself.

It occurred to Phoebe that, in addition to this being the first day Lady Petwell had ridden in a taxi, she had seldom, if ever, been in a store. Shop employees brought merchandise to her London flat or to the castle, or her servants shopped. Clearly dressmakers had come to her for fittings—nothing "off-the-peg," nothing ready-made.

Outside, as they walked on Fifth Avenue, Lady Petwell seemed thrilled by a sign on a corner store: F. W. Woolworth Co. "Oh, that's where our neighbor in London bought a stopper for his champagne bottles." Phoebe had the feeling she somehow had the wrong store. Inside, Lady Petwell asked one clerk after another where she could find a stopper for champagne bottles. They were directed to the basement where they were told Woolworth's did not carry stoppers for champagne bottles but they did have them for Pepsi bottles. Lady Petwell decided that would perhaps do. Not knowing American money, she held out a handful of coins for Phoebe to identify the amount to pay the clerk.

Lady Petwell took the small paper bag containing the stopper. She held it against her suit jacket, above a pocket, as if she were about to deposit it there. "Do you think," she asked Phoebe, "that it would be all right if I put it in here?"

Puzzled, Phoebe said, "Well, I believe so."

Only then did Lady Petwell slip it into her pocket. Realizing it was almost four o'clock, she said she must go back to the Pierre Hotel. But first, she insisted, she would take Phoebe to Selmabelle's. "I'll take you in a taxi," Lady Petwell said with such joy, Phoebe expected her to clap her hands. The taxi headed down Fifth Avenue and at Thirtieth Street stopped for a traffic light. Phoebe was surprised to see a man about to cross the street whom she thought she recognized. "Oh, look, there's Lord Petwell!" said Phoebe, assuming this would delight his wife.

Lady Petwell leaned forward in the seat to look at the man. Turning back to Phoebe, she narrowed her eyes and glared at her through half-closed eyelids. Her face was menacing, her eyes weapons. She spoke in a slow, ominous voice: "How dare you!" She had changed from Lady Petwell to Lady Macbeth. She took an audible breath, and her voice rose. "*That* man is carrying a *parcel*! Lord Petwell never carried a parcel in his *life*!"

"Oh," said Phoebe. She turned to see that the man was not only carrying a parcel, he was carrying three. The taxi stalled in traffic. Phoebe was aware that the bald-headed cab driver had turned around and now stared incredulously at Lady Petwell, who continued to glare at Phoebe. The driver looked in disbelief at Phoebe, as she apologized to Lady Petwell: "Oh, I'm so sorry. How could I not have noticed?"

Phoebe looked prayerfully into the driver's eyes. Please do not say a word, she said silently. If you say anything, it will be the end of my job, the end of my money which I need, the end of my chance in New York. Please, do not speak.

As if she had willed him to do so, the driver turned to face the front. Phoebe closed her eyes in relief. "Can you ever forgive me?" she heard herself say to Lady Petwell.

The driver steered his way through traffic, heading for Selmabelle's address on Gramercy Park. The eyes of the driver and Phoebe's met in silent language again as she got out of the cab. Phoebe thanked Lady Petwell for the ride and the "lovely day," and Lady Petwell began to look pleased while Phoebe, standing in the street, waved to her.

As the taxi drove off, Lady Petwell suddenly leaned her brocaded and curled head out the window and threw kisses to Phoebe, then turned, throwing more kisses through the back window. Phoebe threw back kisses in amazement as she watched the taxi head up town.

Phoebe was eager to report to Selmabelle that Lady Petwell had been pleased with the day before she changed her mind again. Phoebe knew she very much wanted to keep this job, unusual as it was. She hurried into Selmabelle's house only to learn that she was not in.

Phoebe realized that she had better finish the letters before Selmabelle's return and rushed into her own office. Passing the tidy front desk, she noticed that above it, the bulletin board displayed a large photo of Selmabelle's niece in an evening dress: blond Jane, bare-shouldered, beautiful, and smug. As Phoebe sat down at her own desk, she hoped that she would not see much of Jane in person, though she was curious about the portrait Gilbert planned to paint of her.

Phoebe glanced up from her typing and recognized Selmabelle's skinny accountant, Wilbur Z. Monroe, who had been at the party. Coming into the room, he placed a large black ledger on the front desk, making Phoebe realize he was her office-mate. Taking a chair next to her desk, he lifted his head and peered at her through his glasses, which had slipped down his long nose. Dragging the words in his Southern accent, he said, "I looked it up."

Phoebe was wide-eyed. "What?"

"Your name. It means *shining*. Phoebe means *shining*."

"Really? Nobody ever told me that before. I was named after my grandmother."

"Names are a hobby of mine." He stood up. "I hope this job works out for you. You know, a lot of people have had it. But they don't last long."

Phoebe nodded while thanking him. And during the day she noticed that when Wilbur began a sentence with "You know"—he thought she did not know and was giving her the benefit of his wisdom and especially his gossip, which he seemed to relish—"Selmabelle's a widow."

Phoebe wondered if he was about to spring another question about her own personal life. She had stated on her employment form that she was a widow and he had already asked her how her husband had died. "Car accident," she'd answered but had not given details. Now she was relieved when Wilbur went on to talk about Selmabelle, saying her late husband had been Maxwell Flaunton, the scientist; that her maiden name had been Surrey of the textile fortune; and her parents' family estate near Hartford, Connecticut, had been called Surreyview, but the huge house had burned to the ground due to faulty electrical wiring. Wilbur was sure that was why Selmabelle was so interested in stately homes and castles in Britain. "That and the fact she knows all these owners of those big places. Selmabelle knows everybody, just like her daddy and her granddaddy did."

Wilbur lifted his head to peer at Phoebe. "What goes on with you and Edward Hibbard? I wouldn't think a girl like you would go out with a married man."

Phoebe, opening drawers to inspect her office supplies, felt herself pause. She remembered that on the train Edward had mentioned Gilbert's marriage, but not his own. "I really didn't know he was married."

"I'm not married," Wilbur said.

"You're not?" said Phoebe, though preferring to stay away from the subject of marriage. At the apartment she had told Jill that her husband had died in a car accident on New Year's Eve but had said nothing more. The complications of Marcia and Niles and his death were still too painful to manage in conversation even with Jill. She experienced life now as a tug-of-war between memory—which forced her back into the past—and will—her determination to move forward.

She thought of her TV script for New Year's Day: January is named for Janus, the two-faced Roman god of gates, the god of beginnings, with one face looking forward, the other looking back. She thought also of the theatrical masks of tragedy and comedy and imagined herself choosing to wear the smiling one. Even in childhood with her obsession to guard her secret, having promised her mother never to tell, a part of herself was able to keep sadness in the background of her mind, hidden behind her eyes where her tears about her mother remained, so that she was able to giggle and laugh and have fun like the other kids—she tried not to remember that her partner-in-fun had been Marcia. Lately she lived behind the mask of newness, not really knowing anyone here. Her masks were placed on her face by her feelings. No, she thought now, her masks were her feelings, feelings covering deeper feelings.

Selmabelle's insistent buzzer suddenly sounded and Phoebe rushed into her office where Selmabelle gave her new instructions in an impatient tone of voice while her ringed fingers thrust more papers at her. Back at her own desk, Phoebe was determined to decipher Selmabelle's big, hurried handwriting in margins, or on yellow note paper bearing the printed name SELMABELLE across the top. Invisibly written on each paper was the message, "You're still on trial."

By seven o'clock, Wilbur—having gossiped away much of the day by way of the phone or by interrupting Phoebe—was hard at work at his desk. During business hours, he seemed curious about Phoebe, watching her, asking questions which she answered vaguely, disliking his surveillance. He also advised her often, as if she constantly needed guidance. He pointed out that almost every evening Selmabelle was in the front parlors, hosting twenty or thirty "personages," as he called them. Or he

was quick to tell Phoebe that Selmabelle had just left for a function else-
where, such as the farewell dinner for Lord and Lady Petwell which she
was attending tonight.

Phoebe still found it hard to get it settled into her brain that she—
Phoebe Fields Stanhope from Kansas—had anything to do with Lord
or Lady Anybody, even if they were in America to promote tourism.

Phoebe, striding home to relieve tension, recalled party evenings
she had spent with young friends at Marcia's parents' house—once
her "second home," though she tried not to think of it that way now.
She compared her memories to the childhood evenings of Selmabelle, who from an early age had stood with her eminent parents in
the receiving line at Surreyview.

On Lexington Avenue, in the Murray Hill section of Manhattan,
Phoebe walked into Jill's small apartment building. Taking the tiny elevator to the third floor, she reminded herself that she lived here too, but
unlocking the door, she still felt like a visitor in the one-room apartment, where she slept on a rollaway bed.

Yet she liked the down-to-earth feeling here. Since Jill was from
the Midwest too, it gave Phoebe a feeling of the "real world." She felt
a strong need for this grounding and comfort of the familiar to coun-
teract her new job. This realization made her know that she didn't
want to give up altogether on her past life.

"Hi," Jill called out as Phoebe entered the apartment. Jill, wearing her
yellow terry cloth robe, was propped up against colorful pillows on the
sofa, which became her bed at night. Jill's blond hair was in rollers, except
for bangs falling even with her eyebrows. Jill's blue eyes always seemed to
sparkle, no matter if she was thoughtful or mischievous, or even as she
complained about her job. Now she smiled and held up one of the
brochures which surrounded her on the sofa. "I got these from the Italian
Government Tourist Office." Jill emphasized that since she and Phoebe
were splitting the rent, she could be serious about her travel plans.

This apartment-sharing arrangement was great for both their budgets, Jill told Phoebe while Phoebe was fixing lamb chops and a salad for their dinner. Jill had cooked the night before. Phoebe thought: We're trying to make each other a substitute family.

"I have to absolutely *dwell* on budgets," said Jill at the coffee table they used even for meals. "I spent a fortune on clothes to wear with that guy and it still didn't work out." She spoke of her former lover, Bill, a married account executive in the ad agency where she still worked as an assistant to a department head, rather than as the copy-writer she wanted to be. Jill admitted that she had been crazy to have spent money on clothes for Bill because he just wanted to get her out of them—once he'd complimented her. It was a kind of routine: "Darling, you look beautiful in that dress." And then he'd start un-zipping it, helping her to take it off.

Jill had stayed in that affair too long, just as she had stayed in her marriage too long. As she spoke of her ex-husband Vic, who still lived in Omaha, Jill looked at Phoebe, who sensed they were dangerously close to discussing Niles. Jill sprang up to carry dishes to the sink as if knowing Phoebe's reluctance to confide. Phoebe closed her eyes, touched by Jill's thoughtfulness.

Phoebe went to shower and enjoying the force of warm water on her shoulders, she experienced a loosening of her tense muscles. Scrubbing her hair, she imagined the musical sensation Mary Martin singing her famous "I'm Gonna Wash That Man Right Outta My Hair." Phoebe recalled seeing her, or at least someone who looked like her, at Selmabelle's party.

When Phoebe turned under the shower, she tried to guess how she'd feel now if she'd gone on the ferry with the man who had the musical voice. As she stepped out of the shower, she heard the phone was ring-ing. Jill came to the bathroom door. "It's for you, it's a man."

At once Phoebe could feel herself smiling; she had the notion that the mystery man might have learned who she was and had tracked her down. But when she took the call, she heard Edward's English voice: "Did you get my message? Wilbur said you had gone out to do something for Selmabelle."

Phoebe's shoulders slumped. "I guess he forgot to tell me."

"He seemed surprised I was ringing you," Edward said.

"He made a point of telling me you were married."

"Oh, did he really! Well, you didn't want to marry me anyway, did you?"

Taken aback, Phoebe started to laugh, then recalled Edward's usually serious face.

"Come and tell me about the new job, Phoebe," Edward said, almost as if he could see Phoebe and Jill exchanging looks. "We'll have dinner."

"Oh, I'm sorry, I just washed my hair."

Edward reminded her that he was returning to England the next day. "You'll have to come to London with Selmabelle. By the by, I don't think you realize what an impression a certain American girl named Phoebe has made on me. God bless."

When Phoebe queried Wilbur about Edward's call the next morning, he answered vaguely, "Didn't you get the message?" He stood up from his desk; Selmabelle and her niece Jane had just passed in the hallway and he hurried to look out at them. He likes to check up, Phoebe thought. Even his job was accounting.

Wilbur turned back to Phoebe. "Red-Jack Ordall sends regards."

Phoebe must have asked aloud the question in her mind because Wilbur was answering, "Harkenstown. I called him after you left last night." Selmabelle had told Wilbur to check Phoebe's references and he had phoned the TV station to speak to the manager, who wasn't in, so he had talked instead to the sales manager. "How well do you know him?" Wilbur asked. "Pretty well, I take it. The switchboard operator gave his name as John Ordall, but he said you called him Red-Jack."

"Everybody calls him Red-Jack."

Wilbur grinned. "He gave me the impression y'all were great friends." Wilbur moved to sit by Phoebe's desk. "He said he'd call you up when he gets to New York." Wilbur pounced on her sudden intake of breath. "You didn't know he was coming?"

Phoebe hesitated, needing the two parts of her life—Harkenstown and New York—kept separate. "Of course I knew there was a possibility."

"I'd think you'd at least thank me."

"Oh, I do thank you, Wilbur. What did Selmabelle say about the reference?"

"What makes you think she said anything?"

"You mean you didn't give it to her?"

"Now don't get on your high horse," Wilbur said.

"I think it'll be a good reference."

"You sound worried."

"No." Phoebe went back to a memo she was writing, anxious not to appear anxious. She assured herself she had earned a good reference. She was determined not to return to temporary work—sneaking out to the pay phone, marking want ads, making lists as she looked for another job. She heard again Mother Bertha's voice: "Everything you're doing sounds pretty fly-by-night."

Periodically, during the day Phoebe silently repeated: *I have to get my life in order.*

On leaving the office that evening, while buttoning her coat, she paused at Wilbur's desk. "Did you get a chance to pass on my reference to Selmabelle?" When Wilbur did not answer, Phoebe added, "I just thought I'd ask since we both know Selmabelle likes everything done in a hurry."

Wilbur gave her a hostile look. "You don't need to tell me how Selmabelle works. I've been with her a good deal longer than you have."

Phoebe nodded, trying to appease him. "You've been saying you want to take me home on your motorcycle."

He shrugged. "I didn't bring it today. Selmabelle thinks it's too noisy to bring here much."

"Oh." She smiled at him. "Then maybe tonight's the night you might want to walk home with me?"

He shrugged again and gradually seemed so pleased with the arrangement, she hoped she had not made a mistake in going out of the office with him. They crossed the street where he unlocked the south gate of Gramercy Park, using Selmabelle's key. Phoebe had never before been in the park, but on sunny days she had looked between the iron bars of the fence and seen mothers and nursemaids running after toddlers running after pigeons and squirrels. Now on this chilly, dark night Wilbur slammed the south gate after them, heavy metal clanging against metal. "You can't get *out* without a key either," he said.

She could not see anyone else in the park. Just enough light from surrounding streets allowed Phoebe to watch her step on the gravel walk. In the center of the square Wilbur waved his cigarette in its holder toward a lifesize statue. Wearing a toga, the bronze man stood on a pedestal with his head bent and his hand over his heart. "This," said Wilbur, as if introducing him, "is Edwin Booth, who played Hamlet and lived over there at the Players' Club—you know, his brother shot Lincoln." Looking up at the lifesize statue, Phoebe thought of Selmabelle's small statue of Eros and the words: "We were very tired, we were very merry—We went back and forth all night on the ferry." "Wilbur," said Phoebe, suddenly describing the glass statue. "Do many people know about that little statue?"

"I don't know what you're talking about, but I usually know what I'm talking about, and when Selmabelle gives me an assignment, I don't dawdle. I admit you peeved me."

"I'm sorry." Phoebe tried to placate him as they walked up Lexington Avenue, where the street changed markedly from charming, old-world structures to the dreariness of small, shabby hotels and rickety buildings—one had boards over the windows. After they crossed busy Thirty-fourth Street, Phoebe told Wilbur she was amazed that in Manhattan you would see a good neighborhood and next to it run-down streets, then another good section would appear, the way a needle goes in and out of cloth.

At Jill's apartment, Phoebe unlocked the door to discover Jill seated at the coffee table with a shoe box in front of her. "I'm doing my box," she said to Wilbur after being introduced. Opened to reveal three-by-five index cards at one end, the box was stuffed with tissue paper in the rest of the space. "I figure," Jill said, "that if you can't live *within* your means, you have to find a way to live *beyond* it. I owe money to nine stores and each card here represents a debt. I just wrote a check to pay part of my Bloomingdale's bill. So now, this Bloomingdale card goes to the back of the other cards. Gradually as I pay other bills, this card will reach the front again—that means I have to pay more on it."

"Jill," Phoebe said, "did I mention that Wilbur's the accountant in our office?"

Jill's blue eyes smiled up at Wilbur. "I'll bet you don't think much of my system."

"It's not standard," Wilbur said. Taking the easy chair, he put a cigarette into a holder as if copying Selmabelle and looked about, appearing to inspect Phoebe's life.

Phoebe stepped to the so-called kitchen, an inset in the wall of the main room. The kitchen's blind could be lowered to hide the half-refrigerator, the small sink and the stove, topped by cabinets. But, as usual, the blind was up. While spreading cream cheese on crackers, she heard Jill tell Wilbur, "Phoebe and I now call the Midwest 'the Land of the Big Kitchens.'"

"Phoebe doesn't like to talk about Harkenstown," Wilbur said. "I told her I'd called the TV station for a reference and she about jumped out of her skin."

Phoebe laughed, pretending to take this as a joke. "I'm concentrating on New York."

"Let's drink to that," Jill said. "Or my Nebraska toast: 'Here's to you and here's to me / May we never disagree / But if we ever disagree / To hell with you and here's to me.'"

Jill, laughing, clinked her glass to Wilbur's. He talked about his home state, Louisiana, calling it *"Lewsiana."* When he finally left, Phoebe locked the door and said to Jill, "Lord, I thought he'd never leave."

Jill grinned. "Remember, single men are scarce." Lounging in the chair with her legs over the arm, she leaned toward the coffee table to grab a cracker. "How'd you like all that talk about his daddy? Picture it—his old man making pews for churches. Wilbur reminds me of something out of a Victorian novel." Jill gave a laugh in appreciation. "A *heroine* out of a Victorian novel."

"Bingo!" Phoebe said, then admitted, "I haven't quite figured him out. I just wish he weren't so nosy."

Eleven

LONE IN THE APARTMENT a few nights later, Phoebe repeatedly returned to the windows to look down at Lexington Avenue. Lights were on in the streets and on taxis noisily speeding by, and when at last one pulled over to the curb, she saw Red-Jack Ordall get out, then lean into the cab's front window. Only out-of-towners wait until they get out of the cab to pay the fare, Phoebe thought. She imagined Red-Jack telling the driver that in Harkenstown you don't tip unless the driver carries a trunk or something up to the attic. She guessed that Red-Jack had let the driver know that he didn't frequent taxis since his old man sold used cars and he and most Kansans had their own cars. This lack of taxi experience was about the only thing Phoebe could think of in common between Red-Jack and Lady Petwell.

Phoebe imagined Red-Jack stepping into the small entryway downstairs, looking at the mailboxes, one for apartment 3B with a card-insert identifying the occupant as FLAXMORE, as well as an additional card, taped on, naming STANHOPE. Phoebe listened to the arrival of the elevator, then the doorbell. She opened the door, partway at first. With his weight on one foot, Red-Jack swung around toward her. "Hey, Pheeb."

He greeted her with awkwardness, his hands jammed into his pockets as if ill at ease in his double-breasted pinstripes. He would have looked more at home in his checked shirt and baggy pants, which Marcia used to complain about, along with his lack of social graces.

Phoebe stepped aside as he came in, jarring himself against the frame of the door. He still had his hands in his pockets, his elbows close to his body. "How the hell are you, Pheeb?" He sounded as though he were trying to think of things to say, to cover what he was feeling, just as she was. She smelled his whiskey breath. He circled the coffee table as if wondering where the rest of the space was. "Hey, Pheeb, we'll have a party that won't quit." He turned away. "Oh, hell, Pheeb. Niles used to say that. I'm sorry, I forgot."

Red-Jack told her he'd heard a lot about the Rainbow Room. When they were on their way there in a taxi, Phoebe mentioned that she and her apartment-mate Jill had been to the Rainbow Room, but only once, just for a drink because of their budgets.

"Hell, Pheeb," he said, "what are you living here for, if you don't go to these places?" Phoebe began to feel more relaxed when he leaned to look out the taxi window. "Hey, this is our night on the town," he said. "That's what they say in the movies."

In the Rockefeller Plaza elevator, Phoebe and Red-Jack laughed at the pressure in their ears when they neared the top of the building. "Now, this," he said as he followed her through the revolving door leading to the Rainbow Room's cocktail lounge, "*this* feels like New York." They ordered drinks, then abandoned their seats for a moment to stand close to the windows and look down at the glittering city far below. Phoebe said that this was an exciting view for her too as she lived on the third floor at Jill's and worked on the second floor at Selmabelle's. "Hell," he said, "I always think everybody's up real high in New York."

While he was finishing his second drink, Phoebe suggested, "If you don't want to eat here. I know a little Italian place."

Slipping Phoebe's arm through his, Red-Jack sang as they charged to the nearby restaurant. Entering, they were in the midst of a noisy crowd at the bar. "I like a place like this," he said. "Dimly lit." He downed another Scotch before they were finally seated across from one another at a small table, wedged between parties of older couples.

Opening the large menu, Red-Jack discovered a saying in Italian at the top of the first page. "I gotta remember that," he bellowed. He ordered a bottle of Chianti and repeated the translation the waiter had just given him: *A meal without wine is like a day without sunshine.* "That's pretty good," he said as if congratulating the waiter, the restaurant at large, and all the patrons. Phoebe noticed couples on either side of them glancing their way, shifting in their seats. Cutting into his veal parmesan, he thundered out the beginning of his questions about her job. He seemed impressed, as if Selmabelle's celebrity status had rubbed off on her.

She wanted to subdue him as Marcia used to try to do, then saw her mood influencing his. He confessed he had appointments with bigwigs at ad agencies and the network, and his troubled eyes signaled that he was feeling inadequate.

"Oh, Red-Jack, you can do it," she said. She asked herself why she should care what these couples seated at too close, neighboring tables thought about anything? Why should she give a damn that they looked at Red-Jack with subtle disdain or laughter? In Harkenstown she had grown up with too much emphasis placed on other people's opinions. "This is New York," she said aloud as they left the restaurant.

Red-Jack darted into a liquor store for a bottle of Scotch. He seemed happy now with her earlier-in-the-evening protest that she had to go right home after dinner. In the small enclosure of her apartment elevator, he leaned unsteadily toward her. "Hey, Pheeb, I thought this was the big-time. What's this contraption?"

"It'll hold us," she said, "but we might get stuck."

He nudged her. "Would you like that? Huh? Just the two of us?"

He followed her into the apartment. "That guy in your office who called about your reference. He said we should have lunch when I got to New York."

"What, the two of you?"

"Nah," said Red-Jack, hugging her. "You come too."

"Wilbur's very nosy, Red-Jack."

"Ah, come on. He sounds like good people." Red-Jack wandered around the apartment, as if getting acquainted with her new life. Staring at the blue candle in its holder atop the chest of drawers, he took an unsuccessful aim at the wick with his cigarette; then with the cigarette dangling from his mouth, he brought out a lighter from his pocket and the flame caught. He turned off a lamp that Phoebe had just switched on. When she objected, he said, "I thought you New Yorkers were night owls."

He plopped down unsteadily into the lounge chair. He dropped the gold lighter and it clattered onto the coffee table in front of him. Phoebe recognized it as his Christmas gift from Marcia. They still had not mentioned her, which seemed bizarre, but Phoebe was relieved.

Suddenly she imagined Marcia, her tiny body swelled by pregnancy with Niles's child. Marcia tilted her head to the side, viewing herself in the three-way mirrors in Wilsons' maternity department, parading in one expensive dress after another. Marcia's hands were on her bulging belly, her lips clamped over her teeth, her blue eyes looking at herself in triple reflection. She was shopping with her mother, who would charge all items to her own account, mentioning "little gifts."

Phoebe tried to extinguish thoughts of Marcia as she moved the candle in its heavy silver candlestick to the coffee table. She took a chair near Red-Jack. His pink eyelids drooping, he said, "How you getting along? I don't suppose you ever get lonely."

Phoebe hesitated. "I'm glad I know Jill. Do you get lonely?"

"Hell, you know it—all the time."

She stared at the candle in its silver candlestick, a remnant of Jill's marriage which had ended in divorce. This apartment is furnished with leftovers of marriages, she thought and looked at Red-Jack. We're leftovers, too.

"When you coming back to H.T.?" he said, using the abbreviation for Harkenstown. "You're not gonna stay here forever, are you?"

"Probably. How can I know?"

"You like it then?"

"Some things. This probably sounds funny, but sometimes when the sun slants down through the side-streets here—I don't know, it seems like freedom. Hope maybe."

"Is that the main thing?"

"Being where people don't know . . ."

"Do you miss things? I mean—"

"One of the things I miss most," she said, "is something I never really thought about in Kansas. Something you never hear in Manhattan: the sound of a back screen door slamming, echoing across back yards. I told Jill and she said, 'Oh, I miss that too, and I didn't even know it.'"

"I miss *you*, Pheeb." He was suddenly down on his knees by her side. "You know I do, goddamn, we need each other." Phoebe tried to stand but he grabbed her around the knees. "Pheeb, please." She attempted to move her legs and he suddenly released her, rolled away, then sat on the floor. He put his hands over his face; his voice was muffled: "You both wanted Niles. Neither one of you wanted me."

"Don't say that," she said, "ah, Red-Jack, don't say that."

Sitting on the rug, he kept his head bowed.

"Do you want a cigarette?" she said. She took one from the pack on the coffee table and looked at the gold lighter. She was tempted to drop it the minute she felt the cold metal that had come from Marcia. But with the cigarette in her mouth, she forced herself to flick the lighter. When it responded with a flame, she was startled even though she had been expecting it. The whole evening seemed like that.

She handed the cigarette to him, then rose to make instant coffee. When she gave him a mug, he said, "I wish Marcia was more like you."

"Niles wished it were the other way around," she said and suddenly sat down on the rug beside him.

"I guess Marcia wouldn't agree with you," he answered. "She thinks Niles wanted you."

"*Me?*" Phoebe said.

"Both of you. He wanted both of you."

"How do you know Marcia thinks that?"

"She said so."

"*She* said so?"

"It's one of the few things she's said. We're back together," he said in a deadened voice, "if you can call it that." He bowed his head to his knees. "Marcia could be right. Remember on New Year's Eve after Niles and Marcia said they wanted to marry each other and you told us all to get the hell out of the house?"

Her eyes downcast, Phoebe said, "I wish I didn't remember."

"When we were leaving, the three of us were all standing by the front door and Niles said, 'I don't think I can go through with this.'"

Phoebe sat up straight. "Wait! What do you mean? Niles said, 'I don't think I can go through with this.' He actually said that?"

"Yeah, Pheeb."

"Exactly that? You mean he was *not* going to leave me?"

"I guess he was trying to decide what to do and Marcia grabbed ahold of his arm. She said, 'Phoebe already kicked you out, Niles. Come on!'"

Phoebe put her hands on her cheeks and closed her eyes. "What did Niles say?"

"Pheeb, I don't know. I don't remember—"

"Try!"

"I may not even have heard."

"Please *TRY!*"

"I can't remember. I was so goddamned mad by then, I yanked Marcia out the door. I said, 'Goddamn it, you're coming home with me!'"

Phoebe held her face. *If I hadn't forced Niles out of the house, he wouldn't have left me. He would have stayed with me. We'd be together now.*

Phoebe stared at the coffee table. "Pheeb, how did everything happen? The whole thing, everything these last few months. Marcia thinks that Niles may have been so upset in his mind, he wasn't careful enough when he was driving."

Phoebe struggled to speak. "What do you mean—'not careful?'"

"I mean he agonized back and forth, trying to make up his mind between the two of you."

"What?" Phoebe whispered.

"Marcia said he'd told her that he'd get up at night and watch you sleep, then at breakfast he'd want to talk to you or else talk to his mom when she was there visiting. He'd start to say something but then he'd wait. During the day he'd talk to Marcia and feel guiltier and guiltier—she thinks it wasn't entirely an accident . . ."

"Not entirely an accident—what? You mean he deliberately—"

"Maybe," Red-Jack said, "he didn't know exactly what he was doing."

"Oh God, help me! Help me! Red-Jack, why didn't you tell me this before?"

"Hell, Pheeb, I didn't know all of it before you left H.T. I thought of calling you, Pheeb. Goddamn, I wanted to call, but before you left you didn't want to talk. It seemed like you didn't even want to hear. Anyway, I was thinking you probably already knew since Niles stayed with you New Year's Eve. He stayed after Marcia and I left. He didn't leave—"

"Not right away," she whispered.

"What happened after Marcia and I left?"

Phoebe turned away. "Please don't ask me that! Oh, Red-Jack, don't ask me that!"

Red-Jack slammed his fist on the table. "Goddamn, you're doing it again! It gets me down. You say you want to talk and then before I know it you say, 'Don't ask me that—don't say anything.' I know it's tough for you, but goddamn, Pheeb, this is hard on me too."

"I know it is, Red-Jack."

He went down on his knees before her. "Please understand, Pheeb. Don't you know you're the only one I can talk to? Don't you feel this too? Marcia won't talk to me now." Red-Jack stood up. "That's what I need to tell you. Since she came back, she won't talk. The doctor says she's depressed. Goddamn, as if the rest of us aren't." He walked about as if not seeing what he looked at. "Marcia's mom hounds her. Now especially since Niles's mother phoned—"

"*Mother Bertha* called up?" Phoebe said, wide-eyed.

"Yeah, about the accident."

"You mean she called up Mrs. Harkens? She doesn't even know her. It's a big deal for her even to call long distance."

"Yeah, she said you acted strange when she'd ask you questions. She tried to call Marcia at home, and when she couldn't reach her, she called up Marcia's mom, one mother to another."

"To say what?"

"That she'd instructed her lawyer to get hold of the official accident report, and that spelled out that Niles had been alone in the car. She got real upset when she saw that report because you'd told her that Marcia and I were in the car with Niles."

"I didn't tell her that." Trying to think, Phoebe ran her fingers through her hair. "Heaven help me, she must have just got that idea. What else did—"

"She wanted Marcia's mom to explain the discrepancy and her mom said she'd call her back, but then she didn't. But her mom hounded the hell out of Marcia, kept asking her questions over and over. Finally Marcia broke down and told her about New Year's Eve."

Phoebe closed her eyes.

"Marcia's mom laid down the law that Marcia couldn't tell a soul about her and Niles. 'He's dead,' she kept saying, 'so keep your mouth shut about it. It's not necessary for other people to know. As far as the world is concerned, Red-Jack's the father of your child.' That's the first time her mom ever accepted me, Pheeb."

"How do you know this? You said Marcia won't talk now."

"Her old man told me. Can you imagine her *dad* having a man-to-man with *me*?"

"I can if Mrs. Harkens was behind it."

"Her folks find me convenient now."

"Knowing the way they think, I can just imagine." Phoebe leaned forward over the coffee table. She was silent for a time, then said, "I hate thinking about this. But I see now they want you as the husband, the father for the baby. Lord, especially if they've had hints of rumors about Marcia and Niles. It makes my face burn just thinking about this. 'Respect in the community,' that's what Mrs. Harkens lives for—they need you now on their side."

"Yeah, and they need me to look after their daughter. Pheeb, I'm so confused, but, goddamn, I don't like a lonely life. But it's lonely now with her. I've *never* been so lonely. The only thing Marcia says is she won't go back to her folks' house." Red-Jack began to pace in front of the coffee table, then knelt in front of her. "Pheeb, I keep thinking *maybe* the baby is mine . . ."

"You could find out. Blood tests."

"I'm not sure I want to know, it's rough sometimes."

"I know it is, Red-Jack."

"Pheeb, let me put my arms around you. That won't hurt." She extricated herself as gently as she could, and thought: Poor Red-Jack.

He said, "What do you want, Pheeb?"

"I want things to be the way they were."

"Hell, Pheeb, they're never gonna be."

Red-Jack smiled at Phoebe the next night as she sat beside him in a large booth at Pete's Tavern, a couple of blocks from Selmabelle's. Red-Jack wiped beer from his mouth with the back of his hand. Glancing about at the groups of lively people at nearby tables, he seemed to approve of the noisy, what-the-hell atmosphere. "Now this is my kind of place, Pheeb."

Wilbur, facing them across the red-checkered tablecloth, dabbed at the corners of his mouth with his napkin. "I want to find out what's so fascinating about Harkenstown, Kansas," he said to Red-Jack. "You know the way they talk about the Mysteries of the East—well, Harkenstown must hold the Mysteries of the Midwest. Phoebe almost had a heart attack when I told her I wanted to meet someone from her hometown."

Red-Jack reared back his head. "Hey, Pheeb, what is this?"

"Now, listen, you guys!" Phoebe forced a smile, determined not to be put off by their teasing. Wilbur seemed so curious about her that she wished she had not agreed to introduce him to Red-Jack. She'd been out at a library for Selmabelle this morning at the time Red-Jack had phoned her at the office, and Wilbur had taken the call. When finally Red-Jack had reached her, he'd said, "Hey Pheeb, that guy in your office, he still wants to meet me. Come on, Pheeb . . ."

Now as the trio sat together over drinks, Wilbur said, "You know as a general rule you learn to read people whether they want you to or not. Don't you find that?"

Red-Jack signaled the waiter. "Let's get us another round of drinks going here."

Wilbur smiled. "People tell you about themselves one way or another. You just wait and listen. And watch." Grinning, he stared at Phoebe, who glanced away. "This is quite a treat," Wilbur added, "visiting y'all. I find it hard to get Phoebe here to talk—"

"We're very busy at work," Phoebe said.

"I'm glad we're not at work now," Wilbur said.

"Hell, yes," Red-Jack agreed. "This beats work. Though it must be downright engrossing, working for a celebrity like Selmabelle Flaunton." Red-Jack brought out from his pocket the lighter that Marcia had given him and lit a cigarette. When he laid the lighter on the table, Wilbur looked at it with raised eyebrows and seemed to calculate the heavy weight of the gold and to read the engraved initials.

Red-Jack said to Wilbur, "You must meet a lot of interesting people."

Wilbur looked pleased by the suggestion. "Well," he shrugged as if being modest, "a few now and then." Propping his elbows on the table, he gazed at Red-Jack. "I'd be enthralled to hear y'all talk about Harkenstown."

"Wilbur's been to lots of Selmabelle's parties," Phoebe said. "Haven't you, Wilbur? You've been with her so long."

"We're talking about your hometown now, aren't we?" Wilbur said to Phoebe, then smiled at Red-Jack. "See how she tries to change the subject? That tells us something." Wilbur lifted his arms to put his hands on the back of his neck. "Generally speaking, I've noticed that when people change the subject or are secretive, they're shouting: 'I have something to hide.'"

"You're quite a philosopher," Red-Jack said.

Wilbur inserted a cigarette into the holder and reached for Red-Jack's lighter. Quickly Red-Jack leaned toward him. "Here," said Red-Jack, taking the lighter, "allow me. I feel like one of those sophisticated bastards in the movies saying this—*Allow me.*"

Sucking on the cigarette, Wilbur nodded in thanks.

Phoebe quickly looked away from the lighter. "I told you I could stay only a little while."

"I'm fascinated," Wilbur said to Red-Jack, "that she should mention she has to leave, just when I want to hear about her hometown."

"Excuse me," said Phoebe. "I'd be interested to know what you've discovered about a person who's very curious."

Wilbur peered at her through his glasses. "I believe in saying what I have to say, Phoebe. I'm sorry to hear you use innuendo."

"Ah, now, I think Pheeb was just speaking in general terms," Red-Jack suggested, as he deposited the lighter in his suit coat pocket. "Weren't you, hon? I think it's time for another round."

"Thanks, I'd better pass," said Phoebe, pulling her coat around her shoulders.

"Here," said Red-Jack removing her coat. "Let's just hold our horses. Waiter! More drinks!"

"Please! Not for me," said Phoebe, feeling trapped, knowing she could not leave unless Red-Jack moved out of the booth to let her out.

"Hey, now, Pheeb, hold on—let me at least pay the check." Red-Jack leaned to one side so he could extract his billfold from a hip pocket. As he opened the wallet and turned the plastic pages of business and credit cards, Phoebe caught a glimpse of a photo of Marcia. Red-Jack said to Wilbur, "You're interested in Harkenstown, maybe you'd like to see a picture of my wife."

Phoebe looked away but was aware of Wilbur leaning over the table. "Oh, you're married, I was wondering. Isn't she pretty?"

"This picture was taken a while back."

"What's her name?"

"Marcia."

"I'll have to look it up," Wilbur said.

"Look it up?" asked Red-Jack.

"The meaning. Like Phoebe means 'shining.' Do you have children?"

"No, no children. Not yet. One on the way."

"Oh, well! Congratulations!"

"Thanks. Pheeb and Marcia were best friends all their lives. Pheeb, I hope you don't mind . . ."

"Why would I mind?" Phoebe whispered. "Maybe you could let me out of this booth," she said to Red-Jack as the waiter arrived and caught Wilbur's attention.

"Hey, now, Pheeb," Red-Jack said, "you two have to work together. I'm just trying—"

"Red-Jack, that's the point," she said under her breath. "We work together." When she said she had to leave, Red-Jack said he'd go with her.

Phoebe was quiet on the way home in a taxi. She said good-night quickly. Red-Jack handed money to the driver, and not waiting for change, hurried after Phoebe. Talking loudly, he followed her into the apartment. She did not want to sit down—he'd see this as an invita-

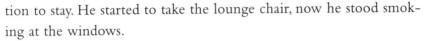

tion to stay. He started to take the lounge chair, now he stood smoking at the windows.

"I'm very tired," she said.

"Do you want me to leave? Is that it? Hell, Pheeb, you don't have to kick me out." He walked heavily toward the hall. He closed the door, a final sound. She felt anxious, reliving her words: "If you're going, go on . . ."

In a sudden irrational panic, she thought: I'll hear about an accident! She hurried to the door, then stopped, rushed to the windows, looked down on Lexington Avenue and saw Red-Jack climbing into a cab.

She turned away and began to prepare for bed, removing her earrings, placing them on the coffee table. Spotting the gold lighter on the table, she found herself concerned and annoyed that Red-Jack had forgotten it. Again she noticed the engraved initials, J.W.O.,Jr., for Red-Jack's real name John William Ordall, Jr.

Marcia would have had to special-order this well in advance of the holidays. This might have been a present to try to ease her conscience. Had she seen this as an expensive farewell gift, as well as Christmas present? Had she already been planning that she and Niles would make their announcement on New Year's Eve?

As Phoebe unfolded the rollaway bed, she attempted again to guess how long Marcia had been scheming. It was unlikely she would have just forgotten to be careful with Niles when she'd been cautious every time with Red-Jack. Now Phoebe readied Jill's couch for sleeping too, knowing Jill would probably come in late.

Lying in bed, Phoebe told herself she should have listened to her inner voice warning her to keep the two parts of her life separated. "Never the twain shall meet . . ." She did not want to discuss New Year's Eve with Wilbur, not even with Jill yet.

She remembered she had suffered secretly when her mother had been unhappy. Her mother had forbidden her to express her feelings, while she herself had indulged in tears. She would *not* become like her mother. Or Mother Bertha. She would not pass on her own distress.

Phoebe moved the pillow, changed positions, then finally sat up. From across the hall came the clack, clack, clack of a typewriter; a shoe dropped in the apartment above; there was the constant rumble of traffic. In the jungle of sounds, people were quarreling; there was the rush of water filling a bathtub; car horns; now and then sirens; the wheeze of buses on Lexington Avenue. Jill came home and crept into bed.

Phoebe replaced a towel over her eyes as light from the street and apartments across the street disturbed her. She had left the blinds up and had opened the windows for Jill, who liked "fresh air," even though the air was filled with traffic fumes and smoke that drifted over from the Con Edison stacks. Phoebe felt the decision on light and air was Jill's privilege, not her own. That was part of her problem now, she was living on the fringes of other people's lives, not in the center of her own. She was a misplaced person no matter how she coped or how kind Jill was, with her talk of budgets. Phoebe did not want to have to receive that kind of kindness. She and Jill were making too many concessions to each other. People, she thought, when they are least able to compromise are forced into all kinds of compromises.

She drifted into sleep, and when awake again, she felt tense, having struggled in a dream. The subterranean sadness she felt flowed through the back of her eyes; that was where her tears lived, pressing against the back of her eyes, but they did not come out. She tried to find the dream again but it was gone. In her troubled sleep she was a wife. That much she knew of her dreams: she was Niles's wife.

She wondered if, after all, there was something to the old-fashioned idea of a long formal mourning. If she had to wear widow's weeds, would it be easier? Feelings don't follow fashion, or do they? Now people expected you to get on with your life. *She* expected it. Phoebe sat up in bed. She'd have to find a way to wake up happier every day.

Jill was asleep when Phoebe dressed and left early for work.

In the office Wilbur grinned and made remarks to Phoebe about her "special friend from Kansas" being married. She nodded but kept her eyes on a chart she was making.

At noon Phoebe stood in line at the post office, telling herself that by mailing back the lighter she was saying good-bye to Harkenstown. She had addressed the package to Red-Jack in care of the TV station, but suddenly now she imagined Mary Ann, who handled the station's mail, telling one person after another that Red-Jack had received a package from Phoebe. Like Mother Bertha, Mary Ann might assume that Phoebe had come between Marcia and Red-Jack. While still in Harkenstown, she had hated it when people wanted to know why she and Marcia were no longer seen together. Phoebe guessed that when they finally had learned that Marcia was pregnant, they had believed she envied her for her pregnancy because Phoebe had suffered a miscarriage and now her husband was gone. That part of the rumor was true, but they knew so little of the truth. At least, Phoebe thought, Red-Jack claimed he hasn't told anyone about New Year's Eve.

And now more than ever she wanted to protect the baby. Now that Red-Jack was taking on the father's role, Phoebe could not take away from the child's future; the child would have a hard enough time with Marcia for a mother. She wanted the rumors to die out now that she had left Harkenstown.

Phoebe crossed out the station's address on the package, substituted Red-Jack's home address. Suddenly she imagined Marcia's blue eyes scrutinizing Phoebe's return address. *So what if Marcia has a possessive nature,* Phoebe asked herself, so what if she finds out that Red-Jack saw me in New York? Surely Marcia would have expected that. But as soon as the postal clerk had tossed the package into the outgoing bin, Phoebe felt less settled than she had hoped for.

When Phoebe heard Red-Jack's voice on her office phone the next week, she held the phone tightly. "This is confidential, Pheeb— Marcia's folks are keeping it a secret but she's in the hospital with a nervous breakdown. She tore down the drapes in our bedroom and set them on fire—"

"Oh no!"

"I stomped out the flames and she went into such a rage, I had to restrain her. Somehow I made a mistake, I handled it all wrong, I feel like— I don't know. God, Pheeb, we didn't talk enough while I was in New York."

"I'm sorry. Oh Lord, Red-Jack, can you talk to someone there— your folks?"

"No! *My* folks don't know about Niles and Marcia. My mom says there's nothing wrong with Marcia, she's just spoiled rotten. I told this to the doctor and he said, 'I think it's interesting your mother can reassure you like that, when her doctors can't.' He said when a depressed person makes threats you have to listen."

Selmabelle's buzzer sounded. Phoebe said, "Talk more to the doctor."

"He's Marcia's doctor."

"Could you get your own doctor?"

Selmabelle's buzzer became insistent. Phoebe tried to comfort Red-Jack before she said good-bye. As she rushed past Wilbur's desk, she realized he'd been listening.

Twelve

"DIDN'T YOU HEAR ME BUZZ?" Selmabelle glared as Phoebe slipped into the chair next to her desk. "We have to be ready for Sir Chatham Wigans."

"Excuse me, please," Phoebe said. "Who is Mr. Wigans?"

Selmabelle was indignant. "*Not* Mr. Wigans! He's been knighted. He's Sir Chatham Wigans."

"Oh, I'm sorry, Sir Wigans."

"No! Not Sir Wigans! It's Sir Chatham, Sir Chatham, Sir Chatham. Call him Sir *Chatham*." Selmabelle clamped her big hands over her ears. "A knight is addressed—oh, I can see I have to start with the kindergarten of protocol with you. Learn your forms of address! I thought you were qualified for this job."

"I am. We just don't have many sirs in Kansas."

Selmabelle held her head. "No! You don't talk about 'sirs.' You talk about 'knights.' Oh, God, when I was trying so hard to be patient." Watching her, Phoebe could see that despite events in her personal life, she had to be ready for Sir Chatham Wigans.

Two weeks later, inside the airport's international arrivals building, Phoebe unzipped her portfolio and withdrew a photograph from a file folder she had labeled SIR CHATHAM WIGANS. Anxious that she might miss him, she watched the stream of newly arrived international passengers.

It was some time before the elderly man appeared, his cape moving gracefully as he swaggered through the double doors. Holding his cane, he stopped in front of the doors so that other travelers coming out from customs, some carrying luggage, had to move around him. His white hair rose from his high forehead in a pompadour, then swooped down and out to form wing-tips at the sides of his thin cheeks. He looked about, then lifted his head as if used to being photographed in this pose.

Phoebe compared his long, narrow face to the glossy photo she held in her hand, then slipped the picture into her portfolio. Stepping closer to him, she could see that the skin under his eyes was crinkled like old tissue paper but his cheeks had a pink glow.

"Sir Chatham Wigans?" she asked.

His white eyebrows lifted and his pale blue eyes searched her face. "And you? Are you from *The New York Times?*"

"No, I'm Phoebe Stanhope, Selmabelle Flaunton's assistant." He smiled as if delightedly. They shook hands and his grasp, like hers, was firm. "Welcome to America," she said. "Selmabelle's sorry she can't be here herself. She asked me to tell you."

"How very kind of you, my dear." He busied himself with his three-pronged walking stick and the round seat attached to the cane dropped, to make it a three-legged stool. "This, my dear, is a shooting stick," he said, sitting down on it, "They're dandy for outdoor sporting events, but I make more use of mine. They're jolly useful for someone eighty-four years old." Still seated, he grasped her arm and turned her to face him. "Here, let me look at you." His old eyes studied her face. "Splendid! You mean I'm to have your company? I was afraid I might be met by reporters."

Seated bolt upright in the taxi, Sir Chatham was again smiling and eager. "We made jolly good time," he said of his flight, then removed his cape and suitcoat to reveal a timepiece collection, watches strapped over his white shirtsleeves. The watches started at his wrists and were lined up his arms, one next to the other so there was hardly room for a rubber band between them. "I have the watches on my left arm on London time, and the ones on my right arm on New York time. So that way, the right time's on my right arm and the time I left behind on my left." Checking one and then the next to assure they were properly wound, he worked his way up both arms.

From a vest pocket he took a watch with a gold chain. "But this is my favorite," he beamed. It had no gold cover but was set in a glass case so its tiny nervous workings were visible. "See, you can see the movements. I like to watch it tick. I bought it in Switzerland and paid for it on my numbered bank account. An equivalent of about three thousand of your American dollars."

Phoebe said, "Amazing."

"I like to be on time."

Phoebe remembered his words the next morning when she sat up in bed and turned off the alarm clock before it rang, so not to disturb Jill. She crept to the bathroom, where she had left her clothes in readiness.

Outside on Lexington Avenue, the sky was surprisingly light. At ten minutes past five, the streets were relatively empty and her high heels echoed on the sidewalk as she searched for a cab. She wanted to feel as awake now as she had during the restless night when her mind had dwelt on questions of Marcia in the hospital.

Hailing a taxi, Phoebe instructed the driver to stop at the Waldorf, where she sighted Sir Chatham in front of the hotel, chatting with the doorman. He beamed getting into the cab.

The young production assistant greeted them at the studio entrance on the seventh floor of the network building and advised Sir Chatham that his interview would follow the news and sports segments. She led them to the green room, where the friendly TV crew wandered in for coffee and sweet rolls, prior to airtime.

Then standing on the sidelines in the studio, Phoebe found the atmosphere stimulating as she compared preparations for this elaborate network production to the small local TV shows on which she had worked in Harkenstown. Once only in New York had she gone with Selmabelle to a competitive morning show as part of her training; Lord Petwell had been the guest.

Sir Chatham was incredulous that millions of Americans watched television at seven o'clock in the morning. In England, he was quite certain, the telly did not start at such an uncivilized hour. He protested when Phoebe took him to Make-up, where he had to sit in what looked like a barber's chair. The perceptive make-up man went "easy on him," brushing his white eyebrows and silky hair and saying how much he enjoyed meeting such a distinguished Englishman.

Sir Chatham Wigans was in a top-of-the-world mood by the time he was in front of the cameras and on the air. He sat at a table beside the program host Don Hayes and was introduced as "the Chairman of the Association of Castles and Stately Homes in Britain." Sir Chatham hardly waited for his introduction before he invited the people of America "to come to visit our great houses in Britain." As he spoke, filmed scenes of huge, magnificent houses and castles were shown on the TV screen. Commenting on the richly furnished rooms, he said the owners might take you round and tell you what it was like to grow up in a castle.

When Don Hayes asked why the owners wanted to open their homes to the public, charging admission, Sir Chatham said, "By Jove, what would you do if you had to pay heavy death duties—what you in America call inheritance taxes? It might be millions of pounds. Then the owner has to keep his house in repair, which means buying acres of roof or carpets. Can you imagine if you had to keep up a hundred rooms?"

"I wouldn't get very far with my little vacuum cleaner," Don Hayes admitted, then told Sir Chatham that he could hardly believe he was eighty-four years old.

"Oh, I won a swimming contest in Hawaii last year." Sir Chatham showed more delight as he said that his diet included fish and brandy daily. "And I don't allow myself to fall into the syndrome of elderly people concerned about aging in their friends. They look at a wrinkled face and think, 'Never send to know for whom the bell tolls, it tolls for thee.'" He suddenly removed his suitcoat to display his collection of watches.

"Speaking of time," the show host said, and the interview was over, to Sir Chatham's displeasure. He had expected more time for his timepieces.

After the show he made it plain to Phoebe that he did not want to be left on his own in the city, even though he'd made "thirty-seven crossings of the dear old Atlantic." Phoebe was not to abandon him and he wanted a "proper breakfast." In the Waldorf coffee shop, when he ordered porridge, the waitress looked puzzled. "Porridge?" Then the dawn of recognition came over her sweet face. "Oh, that's what bears eat."

Sir Chatham roared with laughter. "How delightful!"

Phoebe admitted that as a child the only times she herself had heard the word *porridge* was through Goldilocks and the Three Bears. "I always thought it was potato soup."

His old eyes looked at Phoebe with new pleasure. "Extraordinary!"

Following Sir Chatham's press and radio interviews, Phoebe arrived alone back at Selmabelle's, just as Gilbert Bradley was coming out of the house. Gilbert had dropped by Selmabelle's after lunching at the nearby National Arts Club. He invited Phoebe to his studio to see the sketches he had done of her on the train. His hazel eyes studied her. "Selmabelle's out," he said as if to persuade her.

Phoebe said, "It'll have to be fast."

Phoebe set the pace as they rushed around the block to his Eighteenth Street building. In the elevator Phoebe was aware of the scent of Gilbert's leather jacket as he stood beside her. When he ushered her into his fifth-floor artist's studio, the light from the long north windows illuminated the room, which seemed as large as a warehouse and filled with as many paintings as a gallery. Empty frames were stacked against the white walls and there was a long table holding tubes of paint and two jars filled with bouquets of clean paint brushes, the brushes sticking up like drab flowers. On a platform was an armchair, where, Phoebe guessed, Jane and her poodle must pose for their joint portrait.

Glancing about at the landscapes and still life oils on the walls, she told him she was fascinated as she'd never been in an artist's studio before. "But somehow I thought you were mostly a portrait painter—I expected to see mostly portraits."

"I've done plenty of them," he said, handing her a glossy, colorful brochure, depicting portraits he showed to prospective clients. He opened a portfolio containing more photographs of his portraits which hung in government buildings, private houses, clubs, and corporate headquarters.

"You've done so many," Phoebe said. "I'm amazed you wanted to do sketches of me on the train."

"An artist is always drawing."

Phoebe smiled at him.

"It's wonderful," he said "to see you look happy like that. On the train you seemed—well, I remember the line of your mouth when I was sketching you."

Phoebe glanced down, avoiding his eyes.

"There it is again! That expression—all of a sudden." Gilbert grasped her arm. "I've said the wrong thing again?"

She pulled away from him. "It's all right."

"When can we have more time together?"

Phoebe said, "I have to run."

"What's the matter? I'm married, you mean? There's more to the story . . ."

There always is, she thought as she headed for the door. But knowing he was a friend of Selmabelle's, she guessed it might be dangerous to her job to part from him under strained circumstances. And he did seem nice.

He said,. "Phoebe, you haven't seen the sketches—"

"Another time. I'm sorry, I really do have to rush back now. I'll see you tonight at the reception."

Preparing for that reception in Selmabelle's front parlors, Phoebe helped Bessie the maid shove the velvet Victorian loveseats and chairs back closer to the walls. Phoebe felt it was exciting to make room for the many guests who would mingle under the glittering chandeliers. Then quickly Phoebe arranged table displays of travel guidebooks featuring British castles and stately homes.

Bessie, blond and like a Kewpie-doll with her chubby feet planted together and her stomach protruding under her maid's uniform, had stopped again to view Phoebe. Bessie's eyes studied Phoebe's blue satin cocktail dress and inspected her slender legs in sheer stockings and her blue satin pumps. "That's a nice blue, Miss Phoebe. Is it—"

"Sapphire blue, I think."

"You look just like you belong here."

"Why, thank you, Bessie. That's a real compliment."

"Oh, Miss Phoebe, I hope you'll stay here. They don't last long." At once Bessie looked distressed, as though she had spoken out of turn. Before Phoebe could reassure her, she rushed off.

Phoebe herself hurried out to the hall at the top of the grand staircase and, sitting at a table, reviewed the guest list.

Bessie was soon in the entryway below, opening the door for the first guests. After the visitors climbed the stairs, they gave their names to Phoebe to check off the list. Phoebe liked to hear the representatives of British organizations speak with their British accents. It made her feel she was living in a play; even the New York accents sounded like stage speech to her.

Glancing up from her check-in table into the faces of arriving guests, Phoebe thought she recognized some people but she was not always sure whether it was because they were famous or whether she had just seen them at a party here at Selmabelle's. She hesitated about asking their names in case she should have known them, so she began not to look up, but tried to wait for them to volunteer their names.

With people arriving in greater numbers, she was relieved when Wilbur came to help her. He bobbed up from his chair to greet some of the guests, though Phoebe noticed they did not always know just who he was. He kept up a commentary to Phoebe under his breath, letting her know that he was a human *Who's Who*.

"Here come the Bradleys," Wilbur said to Phoebe, who checked the guest list and found "Bradleys (5)"—presumably five members of the family were expected. But now there was just an older couple coming up the stairs with something rather grand and arrogant about their attitude. "Gilbert Bradley's parents," Wilbur confirmed and seemed impressed that they were a branch of a distinguished American family that had come to America in colonial days—he felt sure the Bradley ancestors had known Selmabelle's forebears. Phoebe, having just visited Gilbert's studio, found his parents of interest too.

But even if they were Americans, Phoebe thought, they looked unfriendly, not like Gilbert. His mother was plump and her black cocktail hat had a feather haughtily sweeping back from it; she held her husband's arm as if he would protect her from unpleasant encounters. Gilbert's father's piercing blue eyes were trained on Phoebe. His white hair was parted on the side, as though he had taken great care with the part, just as Phoebe supposed he had taken great care with all parts of his life. He looked at Phoebe as if everything he had done had been precisely planned and executed and he thought Phoebe had been carelessly imprecise but she didn't know about what. They swept past the table as if they need not identify themselves. Proceeding to the receiving line in the first parlor, they shook hands with the guest of honor, Sir Chatham.

Watching them, Wilbur said to Phoebe, "Americans love titles." He said it proudly as if he were personally responsible for Sir Chatham's knighthood and his visit here.

Sir Chatham, shaking one hand after another, managed to evoke laughter from guests that mingled with his own exaggerated guffaw. His new laugh sounded suspiciously forced to Phoebe. Did he think this was what was expected in America? Perhaps it was, since he was making such a hit.

By now a great number of people had arrived. The receiving line broke up and Sir Chatham, released from handshaking, caught sight of Phoebe at the table. "I was quite afraid you'd deserted me," he said coming toward her. "You must never do that!" He held out his hand to Phoebe. Under his scrutiny, Wilbur agreed to Sir Chatham's suggestion that for a time he tend the table alone.

But, glancing back, Phoebe saw Wilbur giving her a resentful stare.

Sir Chatham drew Phoebe's hand into the crook of his arm. He smiled now, as if pleased to be the focus of attention. Nevertheless, he said to Phoebe: "You must protect me from all these people."

As she held his arm, they strolled together past groups of guests who smiled and greeted them. Then Phoebe and Sir Chatham huddled together at a small table in the bar. She hoped that Selmabelle would see them—that might improve her opinion of Phoebe, to see his approval of her. Savoring a brandy, he said, "Now, my dear Phoebe, we must plan for the future, you and I. I always plan for the future; it keeps me vigorous. And in any case, we can't plan for the past, can we?" He laughed as if he had just thought of that. "If I could plan for the past, I'd jolly well see to it that I'd met you sooner." He took both her hands in his, saying he wanted her to know how he planned for the future: "I work with my gardener and plant flowers in my dear garden and greenhouse in Devon. My favorites? Five-year orchids. I have to be around to see them bloom, don't I?" He grinned mischievously as if he'd gotten away with something. "Look at a gardener," he said, "and you look at an optimist." He laughed as if enjoying himself immensely.

Phoebe felt this was a special message for her. It seemed like an omen that Sir Chatham was talking about what she had come to feel was her own private question: how to focus on the future, how to face it—though looking forward had its hazards too. She had planned for her baby, then she'd had a miscarriage. And in the aftermath of that loss, Niles and Marcia had "discovered" each other.

Sir Chatham said, "Right now, my dear Phoebe, we must plan a trip for you. You must come over and see what you're publicizing." But his invitation was interrupted by Selmabelle and Gilbert's parents. Selmabelle walked between the smiling couple, holding an arm of each of them as they came up to the table. How differently the Bradleys looked at Phoebe now that she was in the company of Sir Chatham Wigans.

Phoebe tried to smile as broadly as everyone else but finally excused herself. She much preferred to talk with Sir Chatham alone.

As she took over from the disgruntled Wilbur at the check-in table, she noticed that Selmabelle's niece Jane hovered nearby. Holding the little white dog by the leash, Jane looked down the staircase toward the door as if waiting for someone. She knelt to straighten the puppy's ribbon, which matched the red cape she wore, then stood and held her head high, as if to show off her curly blond hair and her small-nosed profile. Wilbur had gossiped to Phoebe that Jane, as a child, had wanted even more than her rich parents had given her and she had become increasingly insistent that she would have everything she chose. She demanded privileges everywhere she went.

But how had she done this, Phoebe tried to figure, because if Jane spoke at all, she whispered in a little girl's voice. Wilbur also had revealed that Jane someday would come into her own personal money as an heiress from North Carolina. She'd hated the women's college she'd attended. That's why she was in New York going to fashion-design classes and "staying with family—with her auntie Sel." Wilbur claimed she wouldn't be so happy with "family" if her aunt weren't known for her parties and her broadcasts. "And you can bet Jane expects to inherit from Selmabelle when the time comes, as the saying goes. Even if Jane is already rich on her own by then—you know the rich can never be rich enough," Wilbur had told Phoebe as if he spoke from intimate knowledge.

Phoebe watched Jane and her puppy go back into the parlors, where Jane in her peppermint-striped gown dropped her cape over the back of a chair. Then she pulled away from a group of guests and returned to the head of the staircase. Her Joy perfume scenting the air, she stood in front of Phoebe, ignoring her.

Suddenly from below, in the entryway, came a deep male voice greeting Bessie. Phoebe stood up from the table. The first time she had heard this musical voice had been on her first visit to this house, the night she had been hired for her job. Even tonight, while dressing for the reception, she had wondered if he would be among the guests. She stepped to the end of the table so that she could see around Jane and look down the stairs. There at the entryway, handing his coat to Bessie, was the dark-haired man she remembered, his erect shoulders encased in a dark suit. She wanted to call out to him, "I'm ready to go back and forth on the ferry," and to rush down the steps to meet him.

Jane put her puppy down, dropping the leash on the carpet at the top of the stairs. "Go after him, Fetchy. Fetch him." The puppy pressed his nose onto the carpet. As the man came up the steps, he playfully clapped and clapped his hands at the waiting puppy, which finally backed away. The animal turned and darted in one direction, then another, running under the table and chair where Phoebe had been sitting.

Phoebe, the closest person in pursuit of the dog, tried to grab him by the leash, then caught him by the red bow. She picked him up in her arms, where he barked and squirmed, until she set down the wiggling bundle, holding onto the leash. Phoebe looked into the blue eyes of the man. They held their gaze until Jane snatched the dog's leash from Phoebe.

Selmabelle charged into the hall. "Haven't you got that dog out of here yet?" Starting back into the party, Selmabelle added, "And don't leave his damned toys around for someone to fall over!"

"Fetchy needs walking," Jane said to the man who offered to take the leash but she held on to it, asking him to wait while she got her cape.

Phoebe was aware that he was watching her. "I didn't get your name," she said. "I'm supposed to check everyone's name."

"Bradley. Lawrence Bradley." He smiled. "And yours?"

"Phoebe Stanhope. I think I may know your brother—Gilbert Bradley?"

"It's inevitable! That figures. He always knows the pretty girls before I do."

Phoebe looked down at the list. "I still haven't been on the ferry."

After no reply came from him, Phoebe looked up to see that Jane was back with her poodle.

Why didn't I keep my mouth shut? Phoebe asked herself as she watched them descend the staircase together. Going out of the house, Lawrence placed his hand on the small of Jane's back. Phoebe imagined the pressure of his fingers on her own back.

The door closed behind them, reminding Phoebe that Janus was the god of *doors* as well as *beginnings*. The beginning month of the year— the door to the new year. This reflection further depressed her. She picked up one of the glossy travel guidebooks from the table, turned the pages, to look at pictures of castles, then put the book down.

She stepped to the archway leading to the parlors. Enough guests had arrived by now, surely, for her to leave her post for a moment. She took hors d'oeuvres offered by waiters and did her best to smile at other people being served, but they turned back to their conversations. These encounters only deepened her sense that she was an Outsider, an Unknown.

A bald man with a double chin stood alone, looking uncomfortable at being by himself at a cocktail party. Phoebe forced herself to approach him. When they shook hands, he seemed so grateful it became a hearty handshake.

But his wife, who had an elongated face and oily hair, came to make her presence known. When she learned that Phoebe worked for

Selmabelle, she let it slip that she was a world traveler and veteran magazine editor who had been with Selmabelle in radio in the "olden days." "You're from Kansas?" she asked in a condescending voice. "I've been in Kansas. I'll bet you don't meet many people in New York who've been to Kansas. And this is your first job in New York? My, what a wonderful one!"

Phoebe thought: *She thinks I should be selling can openers at Macy's.* Phoebe returned to the check-in table.

She realized that Gilbert Bradley was coming up the steps. She had only vaguely noticed his arrival. But now she had a duty to perform. She located on the list: Bradley—five members of the family were expected—his brother and his parents were already here. "Is your wife with you?" she asked Gilbert, then realized how abrupt she'd sounded.

His hazel eyes under their heavy brows were looking at her intently. "No. Why?"

"I'm supposed to check the names."

"Is that really the reason you asked, just for your list?"

"Not entirely." And Phoebe's mind was not completely on this conversation. Below in the entryway Jane was coming back into the house with her puppy, followed by Lawrence Bradley. The little dog, tumbling now and then in his effort, led the way up the steps.

Gilbert turned to his brother, who had reached the top of the stairs: "You still want to see Jane's portrait? I was about to ask Phoebe if she wants to come see the sketches I did of her." Gilbert smiled at Phoebe. "Finally. You have to stay long enough this time to really see them." He turned back to his brother. "Maybe we could all go over together."

Carrying her dog, Jane swept past Phoebe.

"It's a great idea, Jane," Lawrence called after her. "Let's do it."

Phoebe, feeling she was in an awkward position, said she had to work.

"I meant later," Gilbert said.

Lawrence caught up with Jane where they greeted acquaintances and Jane grabbed Gilbert's arm, bringing him into their circle, excluding Phoebe.

Phoebe caught sight of Wilbur standing with a woman who had her mouth open while grinning at him, as if drinking in his gossip. Phoebe herself was ogled by several men as she moved along the chain of chatter.

She spotted Lawrence Bradley standing near a bookcase in a group whose attention was on a middle-aged woman with dyed pale orange hair coiled atop her head. Phoebe realized she was the woman she'd noticed her first evening at Selmabelle's, laughing with a companion about platinum guns. Tonight as she had arrived, Wilbur had told Phoebe that she was the close friend of Selmabelle's named Henrietta Tibbold, called "Henny" for short. "Once upon a time," Wilbur had said, "she was the wife of a producer—both film and Broadway."

Henny Tibbold, laughing now, talked about the memory course she had taken. She had astonished people because she was able to remember names, faces, dates, even entire magazine articles. Then one day she had run into her memory teacher buying an umbrella at Bloomingdale's and he hadn't remembered her. So immediately she forgot everything she had learned from him. Her audience laughed.

The party was winding down and guests began to leave. Phoebe saw Lawrence back away from his place and edge around the group. His eyes were on her. Walking toward her, he set his glass on the bookcase beside a vase of pink carnations. "I remember you," he said.

"I remember you too," she said.

"What do you remember?" he said.

"You tell me first," she said.

He grinned. "Didn't we mention something about going on the ferry?"

"We might have. Yes. I think we did."

He said, "Do you think we might consider it again?"

"I think we might," Phoebe said.

"I consider this an excellent idea," he said. "What about now?"

Thirteen

HUDDLING TOGETHER IN THE CHILLY WIND, Phoebe and Lawrence leaned over the railing to look at the dark water below. They had just boarded the ferry again on Staten Island, having earlier made the crossing of New York Harbor from Manhattan. Now the engines started and the ferry pulled away from the Staten Island slip on her return to Manhattan. Phoebe had hoped to appear worldly-wise but she found herself telling Lawrence that she was as excited as she would be on an ocean liner. Having lived in the center of the United States, in Kansas, so far from an ocean, she'd never been on a ship. Even this ferry, which Lawrence estimated was about three hundred feet long, seemed really big to her.

Phoebe was aware Lawrence surveyed her. "I like your hair, I like long hair." He stroked her hair back from her forehead. "I like to see it ruffling in the wind. I like your dress," he added, even though now that he talked about it, the blue satin cocktail dress was covered by her coat. She'd worn it last to the Harkenstown Country Club; since her wardrobe was limited, she was relieved that he liked it.

As he put his hand over hers on the railing, she felt it was her turn to speak. She told him she'd gotten her job with Selmabelle the night they'd met. "I remember you said that it was just as well we weren't going on the ferry as you had work to do."

He smiled at her. "I always have work to do."

"I've been trying to guess what kind of work."

"I'm flattered you gave it a thought."

"I noticed your voice and thought maybe you're a singer. Or maybe you're an artist since your brother's an artist."

He grinned at her. "Do you want me to be like my brother?"

"Oh, I didn't mean that."

"I'm going to have to watch you, I can see that." He looked out at the water, commenting that it was just as well he wasn't an artist. His family gave Gilbert a hard time about his profession. All except their grandmother, the Grand One. "She's always encouraged us in our passions."

"The Grand One?" Phoebe said. "Grand as in grandmother, or grand as in wonderful?"

"Both. We've always called her that, as long as I can remember—I think Gilbert started it when she agreed with him over Dad's opinion. The Grand One doesn't always agree with Dad. Dad thinks if you're successful, you're *not* the artist. You're the person who's posing for the artist." Lawrence laughed, saying, "Of course, you could mention Van Dyke or Reynolds or some other great portrait painter and I'll bet hardly anyone could come up with the names of people *in* their paintings. But anyway, my father thinks the successful person sits for a portrait to be hung in board rooms or—"

"Is that what you want? To be in the paintings?"

"No! I sat for Gilbert enough times when we were kids to last me a lifetime. The other kids loved it. They'd say, 'Draw me—Gilbert, draw me next.' But not me, I hated it. I couldn't stand to stay put. I'd only sit still for him when I lost a bet to him."

Phoebe smiled. "How were they—the drawings—paintings?"

"Usually drawings then. They weren't always flattering."

"On purpose?"

Lawrence laughed. "Well, he *claimed* he drew me the way I looked but I hope he'd admit now that he sometimes exaggerated my shortcomings." Phoebe tried to imagine the pictures and shortcomings of Lawrence the little boy. She wondered when the creases in his forehead had started. They gave his face a rugged masculine strength. She liked the way his straight, dark hair had a tendency to fall in a slant onto his forehead but not enough that it hid the creases when he raised his eyebrows or frowned or grinned.

As Lawrence talked about his brother, Phoebe remembered Gilbert's curly brown hair, much lighter and clipped shorter than Lawrence's. Gilbert's eyes were hazel with heavy brows, Lawrence's eyes, dark blue. Gilbert was unusually tall with bulk. Lawrence was svelte and, while standing beside him on the boat, she decided he was, at most, only an inch taller than she was in these high heels.

Lawrence was saying, "All my life I've heard about my brother's talent. He was two years ahead of me in school." Leaning over the railing of the boat, he turned to look at Phoebe. "You're beginning to sound awfully interested in my brother."

"Well, he was kind of my introduction to New York. We met on the train."

Lawrence smiled at her. "And then what?"

Phoebe paused, looking into his eyes. "Nothing has developed between us, if that's what you mean."

"Does he know that?"

"He should—to begin with, he's married."

"There's that," Lawrence said.

While they talked, in the back of her mind Phoebe wondered how involved Lawrence was with Jane. She found herself mentioning that Gilbert was painting a portrait of Jane.

"His sister-in-law," Lawrence said.

"Jane is Gilbert's sister-in-law?"

Lawrence nodded. "Gilbert's married to Gloria, Jane's sister."

"Oh," said Phoebe, trying to adjust to this new information. Lawrence took her hand as they walked along the chilly deck. The Statue of Liberty was visible from where they stood. The boat glided close by and at this distance the famous figure was impressive as she stood on her pedestal with one arm raised, holding a torch high above her head.

"It's kind of interesting that the Statue of Liberty wears a crown," Phoebe said. "And she's so huge. I knew she was big but I didn't think this gigantic. I remember thinking the same thing when I met Selmabelle."

He laughed.

"Maybe I shouldn't say that." Phoebe shivered and he put his arm around her, saying they should go inside where it was warm. At the snack bar he ordered coffee for them. She breathed deeply, enjoying the aroma. With steam coming into her face, she added cream as they stood side by side at the counter.

"Hot dog?" he said.

When she held the warm split roll containing the frankfurter, he squeezed mustard onto it for her. His eyes were concentrating on what he was doing and he was smiling, "Phoebe, you'll always remember our first dinner together."

She laughed, loving it.

They sat together on a bench, then as if guided by the same force, they held hands and rushed again to the staircase. On the top deck, they found their spot at the railing. Lawrence identified the lights of Ellis Island and Jersey City to their left, then peering ahead, he pointed out the lights of Manhattan on the horizon, the Woolworth Building, the Empire State Building.

Phoebe told him of her day at the Empire State Building with Lady Petwell and of their shopping for a champagne stopper at Woolworth's midtown store. They laughed as the boat was turning, moving into the slip at the lower end of Manhattan, easing closer and closer. The ferry jerked to a stop, jarring them. They raced down the stairs and joined the people departing. Together they ran through the passage out of the terminal and on to the car. "Where do you live?" he asked, driving out of the parking space.

"On Lexington—I'm sharing an apartment." As they headed through Chinatown, the car radio played, "I Could Have Danced All Night." "Where do you live?" she asked Lawrence.

"On Park—"

"Park Avenue?"

"Want to come for a drink?"

"Oh, no, I wasn't hinting. I didn't mean that."

He told her he hoped they wouldn't tear down his apartment building to erect an office tower. "After you've lived in New York a while, you'll find they're always tearing buildings down and putting new ones up. You suggest a restaurant, and when you get there the building isn't there anymore."

It sounds like people, Phoebe thought.

While driving, Lawrence slipped his arm around her, drew her nearer. As she settled into place, she was aware of her own outstretched legs in sheer stockings, next to his legs in their dark trousers. She used to sit this way with Niles—she had the strange feeling that it was really Niles she sat beside.

In the past few months, she'd had the feeling that she could never depend on things to stay in place. She longed for life to go on in an orderly way, her own internal clock in sync with the calendar and the clock.

The music on the car radio closed in on her. Niles always had the radio set to go on whenever he started the car—what last music had he heard New Year's Eve?

"Sure you don't want to come for a drink?" Lawrence said. She moved away from him and sat sideways. She could see his profile against the window. "Or coffee?" he suggested as their car shot ahead of the others.

"Thanks, not tonight," Phoebe said. "I have to be up very early in the morning."

Lawrence double-parked near her apartment, leaned to open the car door. His lips brushed her cheek. "I'll call you," he said.

As Phoebe entered the apartment, Jill turned in bed, groaned in her sleep. When Phoebe herself was lying on the roll-away bed, she had an inner debate as to why she cared so much that Lawrence hadn't asked for her home phone number. When he'd said "I'll call you," had he just tossed that off as a way of saying good-night? Or was he saying good-bye? She sat up, shook her shoulders in an effort to relax.

When she finally slept, she was submerged in deep water. She battled something heavy, something tugging. She was naked and struggling in terror; someone was caught under a huge rock. She awoke in a panic, sat up. Who was drowning? Niles? She remembered the dark water under the ferry. Lawrence? Herself?

She questioned if she was making a mistake in trying to start a new life. No, she answered. Yet the nightmare remained with her,

She was determined to keep her thoughts on Sir Chatham when she greeted him at the Waldorf. She knew she had to concentrate totally on him as he checked his watches and frowned. Prior to his New York visit, he had written Selmabelle that expenses for his American trip should be kept down, but now he believed they should not rely on taxicabs. He feared that he and Phoebe might not be on time for their morning appointment even though they rode in a chauffeured limousine. When they arrived a couple of minutes late at the old west side building housing the production office of *The Richy Rand Show,* Phoebe tried to reassure him.

Inside the lobby of the building they had to wait for the elevator, which annoyed Sir Chatham further. He had a regular walking stick this morning rather than his handy gadget on which he could sit. Finally, the huge door opened; a bald-headed man stood at the helm.

"Good morning," Sir Chatham said as they entered the elevator, which was as large as one used for freight. The door clanged closed and they made a slow ascent. The elevator man did not reply. "I said, 'good morning,'" Sir Chatham said. Without answering, the man opened the big door on the second floor. Sir Chatham stomped off the elevator. "Scoundrel. Scandalous."

They were now in a dingy space that looked very much like a warehouse but with temporary walls about halfway up to the ceiling. Sir Chatham set his walking stick heavily as they headed for the reception desk. "Please don't let him get you upset," Phoebe said to Sir Chatham. "Don't let him put you in a bad mood."

"Mood?" he snapped. "I haven't had a mood since I was two years old."

"No, of course not," Phoebe said weakly. "I've told them how charming you are."

"Why are you telling me that? You want me on my good behavior, is that it?"

Phoebe gave their names to the receptionist at the desk. Then she and Sir Chatham waited in chairs placed against the wall.

The elevator door opened and a man followed by three chimpanzees in short pink ballet dresses came into the reception area. Holding hands to form a chain, they went to stand in a row before the receptionist's desk.

"What kind of program is this?" Sir Chatham asked.

"A variety show," Phoebe said. "Interviews and variety. It has a big audience."

"I must be on a dignified program."

"Don't be put off by the offices. I know in the movies, TV offices are glamorous, but this is the way most of them are in real life—even the best ones."

"But who are those gorillas?" he said, referring to the chimpanzees.

"You'll be seen by millions of viewers," she reminded him. "If it works out."

A producer came into the reception area and shook hands with the trainer. The chimpanzees followed them to the offices. "They came in after we did," Sir Chatham said to Phoebe. "What will they make me do?" His faded blue eyes looked at her. "I have to be on a dignified show. They won't make me act like a clown?" he said in a questioning voice. "I won't be a clown."

"It's all up to you and the producers. They may not be able to work you into the schedule."

Selmabelle had written Toby suggesting Sir Chatham as a guest for the show. When Phoebe phoned Toby, he admitted he could not find Selmabelle's letter; it was buried on his desk. "Look, we're rushing," Toby had said. "Tell me fast—who is Sir Chatham Wigans?"

"He has the longest Who's Who in Britain," Phoebe said into the phone.

"I beg your pardon."

"Well," said Phoebe, "certainly one of the longest."

"This I gotta see." Toby, laughing, repeated her words to someone in the room with him.

"What I mean is," said Phoebe, trying to cover her double entendre, "his biography is so long in the British *Who's Who* because he's lived so long and done so many—"

"You'd better quit while you're ahead," Toby had said, still laughing.

Now a secretary ushered Phoebe and Sir Chatham into Toby Weaver's office. Toby invited them to be seated. Then leaning across his cluttered desk toward Sir Chatham, he asked, "What about the suits of armor?"

"Suits of armor?" Sir Chatham said, baffled.

"That you and Richy are going to wear?"

"What's that?" said Sir Chatham, alarmed.

"Look, this is a busy show, let's get on with it." Toby turned to Phoebe. "You mentioned suits of armor."

Phoebe cleared her throat. "When you asked me on the phone, I was trying to explain about Sir Chatham being a knight and I said, 'You know, like a knight in shining armor.' I didn't mean he would *wear* a suit of armor."

"It would be a funny bit," Toby said.

Sir Chatham scowled. "We don't wear armor these days."

Two men in overalls came to the office, and each lifting an end of a table, carried it into the hall. When they returned for Toby's desk, he followed them, trying to catch the papers falling off. They took Toby's chair, then Phoebe's, and when they stationed themselves like bookends on either side of Sir Chatham's chair, he frowned, stood up, and turned to watch his chair's departure.

"I like the idea of the suits of armor," Toby told Sir Chatham. "You can wear one, show Richy how to walk in one. We could have you and Richy peek at each other through the visors. Is that what you call them? Visors?"

"Peek at each other?" Sir Chatham said in a disbelieving voice.

"Toby," Phoebe said quickly, "could he talk about his contributions to Anglo-American relations?"

"Maybe have a duel," Toby said, warming up to his idea.

"Toby," Phoebe raised her voice. "Sir Chatham's had a distinguished career and is chairman—"

"Look," said Toby, suddenly annoyed, "we have an entertainment show. We have millions of viewers, we're not in the business of education." He named shows on which Sir Chatham already had appeared. Toby didn't want to use the same material, the same visuals, he wanted something new. "We can name him 'The Foremost Knight of the Twentieth Century on the Foremost Night Show.'"

"He doesn't want to wear a suit of armor," Phoebe said. "Couldn't we have toy knights to illustrate—"

"Toys?" Sir Chatham glared at Phoebe. "You want me to play with toys?" He charged out, saying, "Selmabelle, I need to talk with Selmabelle."

Phoebe tried to appease Toby, who said he was busy and moving his office. Sir Chatham was passing the reception desk when Phoebe caught up with him. Walking just behind him, Phoebe told herself to be composed, but she was leaving Toby, one of Selmabelle's favorite "contacts," in a decidedly annoyed unreceptive mood.

And now Phoebe sat in the back of the limousine with an enraged Sir Chatham, Selmabelle's chief client. When the car came to a stop in

Gramercy Park, Phoebe leapt out and raced ahead of Sir Chatham to explain the situation to Selmabelle.

Selmabelle glared at Phoebe.

When Sir Chatham burst into her office, Selmabelle said, "Look, Chatty, this is a big important show with millions of viewers. Toby knows his stuff and a lot of people in the TV audience would visit the castles if you took this opportunity to talk about them." She sat forward in her throne. "But it's up to you, as I said, it's up to you."

Sir Chatham paced in front of the desk. "I've been privileged to count the crowned heads of Europe my friends. I was a Cabinet Minister and a member of Parliament. I've known all your American presidents since dear Teddy Roosevelt. I entertained your grandfather, and father—not to mention you—and you want me to play with toys on the telly on a program with gorillas"—he raised his cane, barely missing the edge of the desk—"in ballet costumes?"

"Chatty, I'm sure," Selmabelle said, "they wouldn't dream of having you on at the same time as the gorillas," but she agreed he should not do this show. "Let's just concentrate on the rest of your tour. Why don't you go rest? Have a nap this afternoon."

"Nap? Nap? I haven't had a nap since I was two years old."

"Lunch?" Phoebe suggested.

"That's it," Selmabelle said. "A whopping big lunch, Chatty. You'd like that."

He sat down in a chair. "I won't like it."

"We could go back to the Waldorf Coffee Shop," Phoebe said. "You might see that waitress." As Phoebe told Selmabelle about the porridge, Sir Chatham grew calmer, then followed Phoebe to the limousine. Phoebe suddenly suggested that they could tour the birthplace of "dear Teddy Roosevelt," his old departed friend. "It's just down the street a couple of blocks."

And leaving the Roosevelt house, Sir Chatham pronounced, "Splendid! Splendid!"

The next morning Sir Chatham, wearing his cape and carrying his walking stick, was talkative as he stood with Phoebe at the airline departure gate, eager to board his flight to Toronto. He looked forward to his visit with his Canadian relatives, he told her, but he looked forward even more to his return to New York and what he called his "journey" with Phoebe.

Now he gave her two more eminent names to phone. Phoebe was to advise them that he would visit their cities on his goodwill tour of America and that she would officially accompany him. "Just tell them you're a darling," he instructed her, before saying good-bye. Phoebe laughed to herself; she could just imagine phoning someone: "Hello, I'm a darling." What would Lawrence answer to that? In any case, she felt uplifted by Sir Chatham.

But on her return to the city, Phoebe hovered in the doorway of Selmabelle's office. Selmabelle stormed back and forth behind her desk, shaking a rolled magazine over her head. Wilbur, with his glasses in place atop his long nose, stood with his back to the fireplace, looking as though he wished it had a fire in it.

Selmabelle noticed Phoebe in the doorway. "There you are. I told you to look after her."

Phoebe stepped into the room, stood on the edge of the thick gold rug. "Who?"

"That reporter," said Selmabelle, her famous voice rising. "That *creature* who says she's a journalist."

"Josephine McPherson," Wilbur said to Phoebe.

"Oh, you mean the first night I was here?" Phoebe said. "I got her a drink." Then she remembered she had not, that Toby Weaver of *The Richy Rand Show* had interrupted, taking Josephine to the bar himself.

Selmabelle had the pages of the magazine folded back and rolled in her hand so Phoebe could not see the print. Phoebe gathered from the conversation that Selmabelle was outraged by a woman who had played the organ briefly during the At Home party. "That reporter saw her."

Selmabelle slapped the magazine with the backs of her fingers. "It says here: 'Bouncing breasts!'"

Wilbur looked at Phoebe. "At the organ," he said primly. "She performed in the nude."

"Played the organ nude?" said Phoebe. "You mean stark naked?"

"*NEVER* SAY 'STARK NAKED'!" Selmabelle demanded. "'Naked' is enough. You can tell a lot about people by the adverbs they use."

"She kept her shoes on at the organ," Wilbur said.

"Oh, yes. Sparkling *rhinestone* shoes," Selmabelle said in such an enraged tone Phoebe guessed that she was quoting from the article.

"Barefoot is difficult at the organ," Wilbur said. "She jumps around on the pedals."

Selmabelle spread the open magazine on the desk. "She shouldn't have been allowed near the organ when that so-called journalist was here doing a story." She looked at Phoebe. "That was your fault."

"I didn't even see her playing," Phoebe said.

"Oh, are you always that observant?"

"I heard the music but it didn't occur to me to make sure the organist was wearing clothes."

"I did the best I could," Wilbur said, as if he were being accused.

"To be *my* assistant," Selmabelle said to Phoebe, "you must anticipate *my* needs. Keep your eyes open, and assume a reporter's at work."

"I put my coat around her," Wilbur said. "And hustled her off before many people saw her."

"Quit saying that!" Selmabelle ordered. "That *creature* Josephine saw her!" She slapped her big hand on the magazine that lay open on the desk. "There was no need for her to include this. Unnecessary!" She glared at Phoebe. "We can't even ask for a retraction. There were witnesses!"

"I saw a man playing," Phoebe said, "but he was wearing clothes." She glanced away from Selmabelle, determined not to be thrown by her attitude. It was hard to believe that she was expected to mourn this—especially since she secretly found it funny—though, she had to admit it was not exactly good P. R. Yet, Phoebe told herself, she certainly took her work seriously; she would do whatever was necessary to hang onto this job. But if you make everything a tragedy, she thought, how can you go forward?

Too bad the organist isn't a client if she got this much space. Who was it that said, "I don't care what they say about me as long as they spell my name right."

She found it interesting that Selmabelle was so upset, as outspoken as she was. As long as Selmabelle did the talking, it was all right. It was fine for her to say what she pleased, but just let anyone else try it.

From time to time, their conference was interrupted by a ringing telephone on Selmabelle's desk. When Phoebe answered, she followed Selmabelle's crisis instructions to say she was not in. While on the phone, Phoebe read the headlines upside down: SELMABELLE— CELEBRATED HOSTESS TO THE CELEBRATED. She still could not make out the smaller print.

Selmabelle spoke of the organist with such contempt Phoebe had the impression she was not a privileged Somebody about whom you're careful or forgiving. She had to be a Nobody, eligible for scorn. Yet Phoebe had picked up Gloria as the name of the organist.

"What's Gloria's last name?" Phoebe said.

"Bradley," Wilbur said. "It used to be Flaunton before she married Gilbert."

Phoebe kept her surprised reaction to herself. When the phone rang again, she answered to hear a deep, musical male voice on the line: "Do you want a real dinner?"

"What?" said Phoebe, excited.

"You don't want a steady diet of hot dogs, do you?" Phoebe hesitated, caught by Selmabelle's penetrating eyes. Lawrence suggested seven o'clock.

As Phoebe hung up, Selmabelle said, "Was that someone from the reception? I understand you went sneaking off that night."

"Sneaking off?"

"You seem to forget you *work* here. You're not here to be entertained, you weren't hired to expand your contacts, social or otherwise. Is that clear? And don't view your job as an entree to a social life! You're here to save me time, not waste it. I don't want to have to listen to more complaints about you."

Phoebe started to leave Selmabelle's office, now she returned to stand in front of her desk. "May I ask who complained?"

"You may not!"

At her own desk, Phoebe silently repeated: Never say stark naked.

Stark terror, she thought. That's what I'd like a few people to feel.

As she pasted press clippings about Sir Chatham into his publicity scrapbook, she recalled how he had chuckled over the favorable comments written about him. He had glowed when TV producers had congratulated him on his performances and wit. These were his emotional pick-me-ups. She thought how people, even heads of organizations, try to convince others how good they are. Including Selmabelle. Even Sir Chatham, on his return to England, could show this scrapbook of photographs and press clippings to the owners of castles and stately homes and they in turn could tell him, their chairman, what a good job he had done in America. Like a chain letter, the message of you-are-good must not be broken.

Maybe she could weave these thoughts into her conversation at dinner tonight with Lawrence. Should she mention that Selmabelle had accused her of "sneaking off" last night? Or would that put him off? She had to hold on to the job—her work had to be her top priority—but she wanted to be with Lawrence again too. She had to be really careful.

She noticed Wilbur morosely unwrapping a sandwich as he sat at his desk. When she invited him to eat with her, he spread his handkerchief on a corner of her desk and on it set his American cheese sandwich and 7-Up. He seemed so pleased by her friendliness that he started to chat, and when Phoebe mentioned Gloria's name, he told her that Gloria had wanted the job she had. He warmed to his own gossip: "Selmabelle gave Gloria a trial but she wanted to get herself on TV, instead of other people."

Phoebe unwrapped her own sandwich of chicken salad. "Then how come Jane treats me the way she does, if my job was good enough for her sister? Jane treats me like a servant."

"You mean she treats you like a sister."

"A sister!"

Wilbur smiled slyly, his look of knowledge. "You know they hate each other."

"No," said Phoebe, "I didn't know."

"Jane threw a flowerpot at Gloria once and it almost killed her." Wilbur nodded. "She'll do anything, *anything* to get her way."

Fourteen

THAT EVENING PHOEBE AND LAWRENCE hurried out of the wind into a hotel in the east Sixties. "It's not so big," he said, "and it's not as well known as the Plaza or the Waldorf." He placed his hand on the small of her back, as he had with Jane, guiding her from the hotel lobby into the mirrored entryway of the restaurant, where a line of people waited. Lawrence said, "Excuse me a minute." Going to the head of the line, he shook hands with the maître d', who then seated them side by side in a green velvet booth, where pink carnations set off the white tablecloth and crystal sparkled before them.

Phoebe smiled at Lawrence. "I thought we didn't have a reservation."

"I never make reservations, I like to keep my options open."

"You got this table with all those people waiting."

He grinned at her. "I just told him I knew you."

Phoebe laughed. "I'll bet."

"You happy here?"

"Oh, yes." She looked around the dining room where smoky mirrored walls reflected lights from the tiny table lamps. Like Lawrence, most of the men wore dark suits, but they appeared older than he and years older than Phoebe. The perfectly coifed women seemed subtly attentive to each other's dresses and jewelry. Phoebe touched her own sparkling green earrings, and sitting up straighter, she smoothed the small waist of her emerald-green silk dress. It seemed magical that she'd chosen to wear green, now that she and Lawrence were seated in this green velvet booth.

Nearby, the gray-haired piano player, fingering "Everything's Coming Up Roses," wore evening clothes with sleeves too short and leaned intently over the keyboard. Phoebe hoped she looked accustomed to this kind of evening. She wanted to fit into his world—Selmabelle's world. She wished that the pianist would be inspired to play "Sophisticated Lady," but guessed that making a request would not be sophisticated.

She wondered if sophistication had allowed Gloria to play the organ in her special way, though Wilbur had insisted she had done it for attention and spite. Wilbur was sure Gloria wanted publicity for a career in entertainment. She'd known very well the reporter saw her.

Phoebe was aware that Lawrence had turned in his seat to look directly at her. "It occurs to me," he said, "a beautiful woman goes through life differently from other women."

Phoebe suddenly realized he was waiting for her to speak. "You mean me?"

"Don't you know you're beautiful?"

"I'd be crazy to answer that," she said, laughing.

He took her hand and held it between them on the seat. "Did I put you on the spot by asking that?"

"Not really," she evaded the truth.

Phoebe tried not to show that she was watching as he looked over his menu. She studied her own menu, noticing the expensive dishes, and glanced at him as he made suggestions from the less costly items. Then he ordered with confidence.

She smiled. "I admit you did a little—put me on the spot—when you called this morning. I probably sounded funny. I was in Selmabelle's office."

"We'll have to have a code," he said.

She felt a glow inside herself. "Yes!"

He took her hand again. "Tell me how I put you on the spot."

"Oh, I wasn't accusing you, I didn't mean that. Maybe I put me on the spot."

"*You* did?"

"I should have stayed with the reporter." Looking into his eyes, she told him of Selmabelle's outrage at the magazine article. As she spoke, she began to remember that Gloria was not only Jane's sister and Selmabelle's niece, but also *Lawrence's* sister-in-law. Phoebe hurried to end her story.

Lawrence was laughing. "So you should never say 'stark naked.' Naked is enough. Hmm." He squeezed her hand. "And here I thought it was just the beginning. Darling." He paused, then said, "After we finish, I'd like to suggest we have our coffee at my apartment."

She said, "This probably sounds funny . . ."

"Try me."

"In Kansas we have coffee *with* the meal. I'd really like some now."

As they left the restaurant, he tucked her arm into his. "My car's parked on the west side," he said. "You mind a walk?"

"I like to walk."

"Another thing we share."

This was *not*, she thought, the time to talk about Selmabelle's prohibition on seeing him.

He squeezed her hand as he said, "You want to stop by my apartment for that second cup of coffee, darling?"

Phoebe wondered how to answer, then tossed off, "Don't tempt me."

"I have Sanka."

She hesitated. "I have a big day tomorrow."

"I always have a big day."

When Lawrence drove out of the parking garage, he told her, "It's highway robbery what these garages charge." Phoebe was fascinated to hear him go on about "jacked-up parking fees" as they luxuriated in his Lincoln. He double-parked in front of her apartment building, then took her hand. While other cars honked and whizzed by his double parked Lincoln, he said that he sometimes left his car "out on Long Island. At the Grand One's," he added, referring to his grandmother's house. "Now I know how my grandfather felt," Lawrence said. "He used to rant about the damn Long Island Rail Road having the gall to raise ticket prices at the very time they lowered their services."

Phoebe wondered just how much he realized he was presenting a humorous picture of a complainer who was obviously well-off. Now with his arm around her, he pulled her to him. "Didn't I tell you the ferry's the only bargain around?"

Phoebe was smiling. "I loved it."

"We have a lot of exploring to do, sweetheart." He leaned to open the door on her side. "I'll call you tomorrow."

But he did not call on Thursday and on Friday Phoebe tried to forget that it was the beginning of the weekend. Friday night, in the apartment, she told Jill, "I want to be ready when he does call." Phoebe stood on a straight chair, turning slowly as she looked in the mirror at the skirt of the gold satin dress which Jill had offered to lend her. She tried to keep disappointment out of her voice. "This dress is just too short for me. But thanks very much anyway, Jill."

Jill, doing her exercises on the floor, stopped to study Phoebe's image in the glass. "Men like to see skirts short," Jill said.

Phoebe stepped down from the chair. "But this is really short."

"Would Lawrence know it's too short?"

Phoebe unzipped the dress. "He might even know it's too late in the season to wear satin."

Jill warned Phoebe not to fall into the same trap she had: going into debt to buy clothes. "I m not saying it won't work out with Lawrence. I just don't want you to count your chickens."

Phoebe pulled off the dress and stood in her slip. "But there's this other saying: 'Be prepared.' I'm going by that."

"Okay." Suddenly Jill said, "Phoebe, you know, it just occurred to me—do you realize there might be a saying to fit *any* way you look at something? Like: 'A stitch in time saves nine'—as opposed to 'Haste makes waste.'"

Phoebe said, "Wow, that's kind of a liberating thought."

"You're the one who started me thinking of it," Jill said. "Do you want to borrow one of my dressy blouses?"

"You mean pick up a skirt to go with it? Great! Lawrence talked about going to a lot of places."

"Phoebe, he may be tied up with plans he'd made before he met you."

"Oh, no, he doesn't like to plan in advance—which seems ironic when I'm trying to look ahead in everything."

"Keep looking ahead," Jill said.

"I gave him our phone number. I hope I didn't sound too eager."

"You just got through saying he hadn't called because you were too aloof, now you're too eager."

Jill joined Phoebe to look in the closet. Jill pulled out a sheer apricot dress. "What about this? I've never seen this on you."

"Oh, no!" Phoebe took it from her.

"Why not? It's gorgeous."

"I just don't want to wear it." She made herself meet Jill's eyes. "I wore it New Year's Eve." Phoebe threw the dress over a chair and rushed into the one place of privacy, the bathroom.

Finally after splashing cold water on her face, Phoebe saw in the mirror that her eyes were red from crying. She used eyedrops and told herself she had to go back to face Jill. She returned to the main room and hung up the dress in the closet. 'I can't make myself wear that dress and I can't make myself give it away."

From her chair, Jill glanced up at Phoebe with a look of concern.

Phoebe hesitated. "I'll tell you more about that night some time." She slipped into a chair at the coffee table, where Jill was going through Sunday's *New York Times,* which, as usual, they had saved for further browsing. Phoebe picked up a section, relieved that their news reading rescued her from premature confidences. After a time, she glanced up from the page. "They have these articles on gardening when the whole town is concrete—"

"Except for the parks, where you can't garden," Jill said. "I know what you mean. When I moved to New York, I kept going to Central Park. I missed trees so much, a gal in my office said I had a Druid complex."

"I miss all kinds of flowers outdoors," Phoebe said. "When I was growing up, we had hollyhocks—"

"We had a lot of roses—"

"So did we." Phoebe leapt up. "But I wasn't going to think about the past."

Jill lowered her paper. "So now you think about Lawrence."

"I'm not going to think about him either."

"You're kind of limiting yourself, aren't you?" Jill said.

"Maybe. Maybe I am."

"You know what I wish?" Phoebe said to Jill later that night as they talked across the room, one bed to another. "I wish there could be some kind of insurance policy for a relationship before you got into it."

"Maybe we should call up Mutual of Omaha."

"Quit teasing me," Phoebe said. "I've been thinking about this. What I want is a guarantee so that each one cares exactly the same amount as the other."

"I'd say the odds are against you on that."

"They are. That's the point. It's lopsided too much of the time. One person cares more than the other one."

Jill's response came from across the darkened room: "I guess you're talking *generally* about couples—spouses, lovers . . ."

"Not only couples—*all* kinds of relationships."

"How personal is this—what you're saying?"

Phoebe paused, anxious not to reveal more than she wanted to. "Think of all the uneven feelings between people. You hear about it, read about it, see it around you all the time. No, it's not just couples. It happens in other situations too—whenever someone needs you more than you need that person." Phoebe's mind was on Mother Bertha. "A person like that holds you back when you're desperate to get away."

Phoebe waited for Jill to speak but she was quiet now. In the silence, Phoebe could not stop the thought of Marcia saying many times that she wanted to get away from her folks and from Red-Jack. "It haunts me," Phoebe said, "what lopsided emotional situations can lead to. They can lead to tragedies."

"Umm," came Jill's reply.

Suddenly Phoebe said, "And if it's the other way around, if you're the one who cares more than the other person—*that* is hell, and can lead to tragedy too. Even after it's too late to try to make things right, you're obsessed, you lecture yourself: stop thinking about it. And you feel deprived, no matter how hard you try not to." Phoebe sat up. "From now on in my life, I want equal feelings, I don't want to care more than he does."

"But how do you get it equal?" Jill said.

"That's what I'm trying to figure out. It's more than what they call 'a delicate balance.' It's more like a teeter-totter that gets stuck and you can't even it out . . . when you were little, did you say teeter-totter or seesaw—"

"It keeps the lawyers busy," Jill interrupted. "And I'm not joking."

"Sometimes it seems almost inevitable for relationships to be off balance," Phoebe said, "but some people make it work somehow."

In the semi-darkness Phoebe saw Jill sit up. "Some people are lucky," Jill said.

"I guess what I'm afraid of," Phoebe said, "is that I might really fall for him."

"Him? I believe the name is Lawrence. Phoebe, I hate to tell you this."

"What?"

"I think the law of gravity has already taken over."

"I hope not—God, I hope not."

Phoebe slid out of bed and walked barefoot to the windows. "Jill." Phoebe turned toward her and said, "I just thought of something. Teeter-totters reminds me of something I'd forgotten all about until just now. When I was little, I fell off the teeter-totter in the schoolyard at recess. There was broken glass underneath it and it cut my head in a lot of places so I was bleeding and blood got on my dress, my white dress. I remember the teacher sent me home from school. My mother washed the blood off and sent me back to school in a clean dress but I was too shy to go back into the classroom. Maybe it was because the teacher had sent me home and I knew she expected my mother to keep me there or to take me to the doctor. But my mother was sick herself. Anyway, when the kids were let out of school and saw me in the schoolyard, they said, 'Ah, you weren't really hurt.' I don't know why they thought that since they'd seen the blood."

Where was Marcia then? Phoebe suddenly wondered without speaking the thought aloud. Strange, she had no memory of Marcia that day.

Selmabelle's buzzer sounded long and urgently as Phoebe arrived at her desk Monday morning. She rushed into the next office. Selmabelle, at her desk and wearing her yellow lounging pajamas, thrust a sheet of paper toward her. "You can get started on this."

"What's that?" asked Phoebe, grasping the paper and hurrying to take the chair next to Selmabelle's desk.

"The party for Jane."

"Jane!"

"I've decided," Selmabelle said, "it's the way for Gloria to learn she can't get away with her idiocy. When Gloria finds out that Jane is being honored—of course, Phoebe, you should think of your *own* actions! You should have been careful with that reporter. Call up Cognac!"

"Excuse me?"

"You don't know who Cognac is? You're with Selmabelle Flaunton Enterprises and you don't know who the caterer is?"

"I just didn't know his name."

"Names are important. What's in a name? I'll tell you a *lot* is in a name. In *this* business." Selmabelle withdrew papers from a drawer of her desk and pointed out Cognac's catering service as an acquisition of Selmabelle Flaunton Enterprises, Inc.

Selmabelle swept on with her orders, instructing Phoebe to tell this to the caterer and that to the servants. "And you're responsible, remember that! You look a little out of it. Do you take multiple vitamins? Try them. We'll unveil Gilbert Bradley's portrait of Jane. You'll see there in my notes—well, look at the *notes*! Not at me! You'll see in the notes that Gilbert's brother is Jane's special friend, so always bear that in mind: Lawrence Bradley."

Phoebe looked down at the paper.

"You really must do something about that look you get on your face," Selmabelle said. "You'll never get any place in this world with a look like that." Leaning back in her chair, Selmabelle raised her heavy arms and clasped her hands atop her head. "'Make dreams come true'—that's what my parties are all about," said Selmabelle, quoting herself. She had said the same thing to Josephine McPherson, who had used it in *Persona.* "

"I believe in lavish displays of food," Selmabelle told Phoebe. "Guests at my parties say, 'I'm starting a diet tomorrow.' Remember: never that night. Lots of chocolate—this party may be to teach Gloria a lesson, but it's also a celebration."

"A Rite of Spring party?" Phoebe suggested.

"*Le Sacré du Printemps*?" Selmabelle said. "You mean inspired by the ballet? What, and watch a girl dance herself to death?"

"Death? Oh, I forgot that part of it."

"Well, remember!"

Phoebe could hardly believe that she had to plan a party for Jane. "Could we call it a Celebration of Spring?" she heard herself say. "Though it'll be kind of late in the season—"

"*Jane's* Celebration of Spring," said Selmabelle, enlarging on Phoebe's idea. "Good! We'll make it a costume party. My guests like to use their imaginations."

Phoebe visualized Jane and Lawrence together and tried to stop her own imagination. That afternoon in preparation for the party, as she entered Selmabelle's vast kitchen, she found huge copper pots and skillets overhanging the gigantic stove. In this kitchen used for servicing the entertainment rooms were row after row of freestanding cupboards, which reminded Phoebe of the rows of bookstacks in a public library.

That night, describing the kitchen to Jill, Phoebe said she now had a new concept of New York kitchens.

"Unfortunately," said Jill, as she leaned to open the small, crowded half-size refrigerator under the kitchen counter, "it doesn't change the size of our refrigerator."

"You've never seen so many cupboards full of dishes—great big platters. Beautiful. I have to find out from Jane what her favorite pattern is."

"What a thrill!" Jill said.

"Jill, Lawrence still hasn't called."

"And you still talk about him all the time. You want me to tell you what crossed my mind? That he's married."

Phoebe frowned.

"That was my first impression, Phoebe—the way he took you on the ferry where I'll bet his crowd doesn't go. Can you visualize Selmabelle on the ferry—or any of her fancy guests?"

"No."

"Except Lawrence with his stingy streak?" Jill said. "And he took you to that hotel restaurant, where there'd be mostly people from out of town. Believe me, Phoebe, I know about dating a married man.

And this gal in my office is always telling me about her married boyfriend who takes her on the ferry. That's the only place he takes her and she's afraid to complain for fear he won't even take her there. Phoebe, the only place married men really want to take you is to bed. I can tell you that makes you feel used when you know all the places he takes his wife—or at least you think he takes his wife. I was haunted by places Bill took his wife. And the gifts he—"

"We went on the ferry," Phoebe said, "because we were quoting that poem by Edna St. Vincent Millay."

"But isn't Lawrence the one who brought up the poetry?"

"It's Jane," Phoebe said. "I know it's Jane! He tries to hide me because of her. He's supposed to be her special friend. You know I don't talk about him at work. Selmabelle thinks I'm trying to take advantage of my contacts."

"Good for you. I hope you do. I shouldn't have said anything. Phoebe, I'm sorry."

"No, no. It's better if I think about everything. Maybe it's just as well he hides me *for the moment,* the way Selmabelle talks. But I'm going to work this out, Jill."

Jill smiled. "Without getting emotionally involved?"

Fifteen

WHEN PHOEBE ARRIVED AT HER OFFICE on Monday morning, she stopped—startled—in the doorway. Jane Flaunton was sitting atop Phoebe's desk, swinging her legs as she spoke to Wilbur in French. Dressed in a short white tennis dress, Jane held her puppy in her arms and stroked his head. Phoebe had never noticed before how stocky Jane's legs were for her petite size. Neither Jane nor Wilbur formally acknowledged Phoebe's presence but Jane slipped from the desk, cooed *"Au revoir"* to Wilbur, and almost knocked Phoebe out of the way as she passed, carrying her puppy, en route to her aunt's office next door.

"Maybe I should have said *Bonjour*," remarked Phoebe. "That's about all the French I can remember."

Wilbur smiled from his desk. "I went with Jane again to walk her dog."

"Oh?" said Phoebe, having not been aware that their friendship was so cozy.

"Jane says we're taking our 'language walk' cause when we walk her French poodle, we speak French." Wilbur seemed to think this clever of her. But Phoebe guessed he thought the cleverest thing about her was that she was the boss's niece. "You know I'll bet they don't have many people speaking foreign languages in Winston-Salem, North Carolina," he said of Jane's hometown, as if to illustrate her alleged brilliance. "Winston-Salem's not like New Orleans, where I grew up bilingual. Of course," he added, "I'm like Jane, in that I have a smattering of other languages."

Until the verbal display this morning, Phoebe had assumed that Jane could speak *no* language. Jane did not speak to her, even now that Phoebe was planning her party.

Appearing pleased, Wilbur walked out of the room, carrying his coffee cup, heading for the tiny auxiliary kitchen.

Phoebe could not stop her mind from asking if Lawrence had been with Jane over the weekend. When she found herself dialing Lawrence's office number, the switchboard operator at the law firm connected her. "Mr. Bradley's office," said the female voice, sounding stern, rushed, and middle-aged. Phoebe gave her name and Lawrence came onto the line: "I'll call you back."

Phoebe stayed by the phone; she did not want gossip-addicted Wilbur to know that Lawrence was in touch with her. It would be expecting too much for Wilbur not to pass on this information to Selmabelle. Or to Jane, in one language or another.

But by noon when Lawrence hadn't called, Phoebe dashed to the cleaners to pick up Jill's black lace dress, which Jill generously had insisted Phoebe should borrow and lengthen. In Selmabelle's powder room, Phoebe quickly dotted the black taffeta lining with perfume to cover traces of cleaning fluid that still clung to it. She could change into it tonight after work if Lawrence asked her out. The spring weather had turned surprisingly warm. She hoped black lace would not look too wintry.

Lawrence phoned just before five. "You like Italian food?"

"Love it."

"How'd I guess that?"

Phoebe was smiling when she put down the phone. Rushing through her work and to change, she hurried again from the subway and arrived at the address on Lexington Avenue earlier than planned.

She made herself walk to the end of the block and back before entering the noisy, narrow restaurant. She found that Lawrence was not here and had not made a reservation. In hopes that he'd rush through the door, she waited near the entrance and watched people coming in.

Lawrence hurried in forty minutes late and kissed her on the cheek. "Darling, it's been one of those days," he said in an apology for keeping her waiting. "Forgive me?"

"I'm not sure."

"You must want to shoot me. I'll help you pull the trigger."

She examined his regretful, but still confident, expression. She laughed. "All right," she said.

He took her hand as he looked into her eyes. When they were seated across from each other, Phoebe tried to concentrate on the Italian menu but was distracted. It was so much more stimulating to be dining here with Lawrence than in that Italian place with Red-Jack, the one Jill had originally suggested.

Yet here, she noticed hanging baskets of plastic flowers, which confirmed her first impression. This place was not as nice as Jill's favorite restaurant.

"I like an informal place like this sometimes," Lawrence said. "Just to relax. You in the mood too?"

Smiling, Phoebe nodded, swirled spaghetti on a spoon, copying his skill.

"How about some more wine?" he said, then talked about a day in the life of a trusts and estate lawyer. "Now tell me," he said, "how are you? How's our Selmabelle?"

"She's fine too."

There was a pause in the conversation as Lawrence's flattering, appraising eyes were on Phoebe. He said, "We could go to my apartment for an after-dinner drink."

As they left the restaurant, she commented, "I was thinking it'd be fun to see your office."

"I was thinking of my apartment," he said.

"Isn't your office near here?"

He grinned. "I can see you want to see the office." They walked to a nearby building on Madison Avenue, and because it was after hours, the night-maintenance man had to run the elevator to the eighth floor. In the corridor, Lawrence knelt to insert a key in the lock at the bottom of the glass door, which had gilt lettering: Bradley, Rimington, Beechorde & Thorpe, Attorneys at Law. "My grandfather was the first Bradley," he said, pointing to the name, "to represent Selmabelle's family in New York."

Phoebe wondered if she should warn Lawrence not to let Selmabelle know she'd been here. But why would he tell Selmabelle? Phoebe laughed silently at herself—after all, *she'd* been the one who'd suggested this! Maybe she shouldn't have. Lawrence's father was Selmabelle's long-time friend and lawyer. Why hadn't she thought of this earlier? Because I was trying to think of a way *not* to go to his apartment, she answered herself. I wasn't thinking it through, I was just thinking fast.

Using a panel by the door, Lawrence switched on lights. The waiting room smelled of the leather sofas and of furniture polish used on the tables, which displayed *Fortune, Time,* and *Newsweek.* Lawrence ushered her into a large interior room resembling a library, where Phoebe stopped.

"What?" Lawrence said.

Laughing, she said, "You'll never forgive me if I tell you."

"Try me."

Phoebe stared at the rows of bookstacks. "It reminds me of Selmabelle's kitchen."

"You're right. I won't forgive you."

With both of them laughing, Phoebe explained that the rows of cupboards in Selmabelle's kitchen reminded her of freestanding bookcases in a library. "When I'm in a library, I'll think of Selmabelle's kitchen, and when I'm in Selmabelle's kitchen, I'll think of a library—you see, it works both ways."

He grabbed her and held her close.

Caught in the embrace, she felt herself stiffen in spite of herself. He pressed himself against her, which confirmed his intention and readiness.

The evening was leaping ahead of her emotions. She tried to hold on to their mood of lightness.

"Does this work both ways?" he said.

"I can't speak for both sides."

"You could," he said, "if you paid attention to the vital signs."

"Aren't you liable to get sued or something, doing this here in front of all these law books?" She pulled away and they strolled past the books, his arm around her shoulders. They turned right down a corridor, passing a line of offices, first his father's, and after a few more doors, they entered his own. His sofa was dark red and the large desk stood at the end of the room. Phoebe smiled, "Let me see you look official."

He moved into the swivel chair behind the desk. "Mr. Lawrence W. Bradley," she said. "I just realized—Well, to tell you the truth, I thought of it this morning . . ."

"What?"

"Your first name begins with 'law.'"

"Is that the kind of thing you think of when you're supposed to be working?"

Smiling, she said, "Now, listen, don't tease me. You know I work hard. What does the 'W' stand for?"

He leaned, looking into a cupboard. "Winters."

"I would never have guessed that."

"My mother's maiden name. I didn't make it up—I mean about us having an after-dinner drink. If Mrs. Cartright hasn't drunk it all up."

"Is she the one who answered your phone today?" Phoebe said.

"She's the one." He brought out two glasses and a bottle of brandy.

"Mrs. Cartright?" Phoebe said. "That sounds very formal. You call her Mrs. Cartright?"

"You're damned right. She doesn't even smile."

"Maybe she thinks smiling is against the law. After all, this is a law office."

"No," Lawrence said, "I think she's afraid of losing her virginity."

"If she's *Mrs.* Cartright, I assume she's already lost it."

"Don't be too sure. Some men are perfect gentlemen."

They laughed as they touched glasses. Seated beside her on the sofa, he held his globelike brandy glass, looking down into it thoughtfully, as if he were a fortuneteller. Then he placed his glass on the end table, and when he reached for hers, she kept it to gulp a larger swallow than intended. She coughed.

"Easy, darling." She felt his arms slide around her, tighten in an embrace. His lips traveled down her throat. She let out another cough. "This is our time together, sweetheart," he said as he leaned over her, inviting her to lie back.

She tried to sit up. She was tempted to admit that after betrayal by the two people she had trusted most, she needed assurance of how he really felt about her. Should she tell him she'd met Niles when she was very young so she'd had no other man in her life? "Things are moving too fast for me," she said.

"Let's just relax, darling," he said.

Sitting up, she was not as relaxed as she wanted to appear.

Lawrence lifted a footstool that had fronted a chair and brought it over to the sofa. "Now, there," he said as they both put their feet on it. With their legs outstretched before them, Lawrence moved so that his hip and leg touched hers. When he kissed her, he unbuttoned the top button of the black lace dress.

"Lawrence," said Phoebe, standing up, "if your father comes back to the office, will he come here?"

"Don't worry, we chose a good night, sweetheart. He's out of town." Lawrence took her hand inviting her back to the sofa. "Are you always this sensible?"

She smiled at him. "I would never have believed Winters was your middle name—a cold name like Winters."

"What would you have believed it was?" he whispered, as he unbuttoned the second button of her dress.

"Umm . . . wonderful, wicked."

"Now we're getting some place."

"Wilbur says—"

"How'd he get into this conversation? You mustn't try to make me jealous."

"I'm sure he makes you very, very jealous. Wilbur says Phoebe means 'shining.'"

"I can think of better . . ." His exploring fingers started to enter her bra and she quickly pulled away, saying, "Lawrence . . ."

"Sweetheart."

Phoebe stood up. "This probably sounds funny, but I feel that inside of me is this internal clock and it's telling me I'm not ready for this yet."

He took her hand, pulled her onto the sofa, and leaned down to her. "Sweetheart, tell me what you want."

"I'm sorry." She struggled, against his protest, to sit up again, "I want to leave."

With a push of the foot, he shoved the footstool away, toward the middle of the room. "We both have to want it."

In front of the building they searched the almost empty street for a taxi. His car was parked on Long Island at his grandmother's. "I guess I'd better drop you off at your apartment," he said.

"Thank you."

"I have work to do tonight," he said.

"I thought your father was the workaholic."

"It's a family trait, sweetheart." Even speaking an endearment, he sounded evasive, preoccupied. They said goodnight in the taxi and Phoebe, feeling anxious, walked alone into the apartment building.

Phoebe awoke early, startled, in a panic. In a dream-struggle she had tried to rescue Niles from a pit, even though she could no longer hear him call.

Disoriented, she sat on the edge of the rollaway. It came to her that the night before she had not been with Niles, as in the nightmare, but with Lawrence in the office.

The phone rang. Sleepily Jill handed the phone to Phoebe.

"Pheeb?" It was Red-Jack, telling her that Marcia was out of the hospital and under the home care of a nurse. "This new doctor's a psychiatrist—they called him in. I think Marcia worries about you now. She's mentioned you several times."

Phoebe hesitated. "I'm surprised."

"You two go back a long way, Pheeb."

Phoebe said, "I hope she'll be all right." She hung up, held her face in her hands. She experienced the old close feeling of longtime friendship with Marcia, but it collided with all that had happened. Phoebe walked slowly to the office. She had to move into the world of the morning—Selmabelle's world.

At her desk she read her note on her calendar: *Work on Jane's party.* She knew she had written these words but they seemed alien to her now.

Snap out of it, she said silently. You've got a job to do. Your job is all you have.

Soon she would travel with Sir Chatham Wigans. Everything *had* to go smoothly on that trip. But first she must get through Jane's party.

As she was writing a memo to Selmabelle about the party decorations, the phone on her desk rang. A resonant male voice asked, "How hungry do you think you'll be tonight?"

Phoebe grasped the phone tighter. "I'd say . . . as hungry as you'll be."

"*WON*-derful," Lawrence said. "We'd better team up."

Phoebe felt chagrin. She had told herself she'd never be excited by him again. Still she felt herself smiling. To stay at her work, she pretended an airplane seatbelt held her to the chair. But she glanced often at her wristwatch.

Finally at ten minutes to twelve, she stood. She was aware of Wilbur's eyes following her as she strolled past his desk. Once in the hallway, she rushed from the building and took the subway to Bloomingdale's. When she emerged from the better skirt department, feeling triumphant, extravagant, and swinging a box, she told herself that it was necessary to go beyond her budget, just this once.

Phoebe hurried through her work during the afternoon, but again had to stay overtime. Running late, she ignored her budget and took a taxi home to change, another to meet Lawrence at the Plaza, which turned out to be just their meeting place. They walked from the hotel to a nearby Japanese restaurant.

"I hope you like it here, darling," he said. Following Japanese custom, they removed their shoes, then while seated on mats, they shared shrimp tempura and beef sukiyaki. Phoebe felt intoxicated by the delicate aromas and mingling of flavors.

She was aware that Lawrence observed her in the low-cut black chiffon blouse, which she wore with the new black skirt, which was fashionably tight—"all the rage" this season of 1959. The superior-acting saleswoman had told this to Phoebe as if she were just in from Timbuktu. Now with Lawrence watching her, Phoebe tried to adjust the skirt while sitting on the mat.

Lawrence said, "Don't worry, darling, you're beautiful. It's too bad you had to take off those high-heeled shoes—I always notice those long slim legs."

Phoebe was aware of the skillful way Lawrence used his chopsticks. "Here, let me show you," he said, placing one chopstick under her thumb. She tried not to be affected by his touch and to keep her mind on his instructions: "Now, this second chopstick goes on top of the first one. The top one you hold like a pencil."

She captured a crunchy bean sprout and brought it to her mouth. With each biteful, they looked at each other as if they were clinking glasses and drinking a toast. She poured more scented tea for them both.

But when he invited her to his apartment again, she declined.

Upon entering her own apartment alone, she found Jill asleep. She was tempted to awaken her to ask if she'd made a mistake in again saying "no." But in the morning, Phoebe knew that she had to decide for herself. Was she paying too much attention to Grandma's old warnings? She already had recognized a feeling in herself that she had to be faithful to Niles. Yet he had been unfaithful to her.

Reading *The New York Times,* Phoebe found herself focusing on the word "unilateral." Lawrence had said that was what she was doing—making unilateral decisions—not giving him a chance. She tried to accept: he would not call.

Then he called! At three in the afternoon. They returned that night to the *same* Japanese place, the *same* table. Starting a "tradition," she happily named it in her mind.

Again seated on the mat, she struggled with the tight black skirt, but she pretended to be unfazed. A bright pink stole hugged her shoulders and during the meal she slipped it off and smiled at Lawrence. She was smiling too as they left the restaurant.

He said, "Do you want to walk? I like a walk—"

"So do I."

He strolled along, his hands in his pockets. "I don't mean *too* far. My apartment's only a couple of blocks away."

She smiled at him. "I remember you said that."

He pulled his hands from his pockets. "I was hoping you'd remember. I hoped I'd be so lucky." Increasing the pace, he took her hand in his. On Park Avenue, Phoebe recalled walking on this famous street, trying to recover from her visit to lecherous Ben and his wife, Ninon. Looking up at the tall apartment buildings, she realized that back then she'd not even known that a person named Lawrence Bradley lived on Park Avenue—or that he existed at all. Now she walked with him, hand in hand. And in public. She could tell Jill: "So he wasn't trying to hide me." She thought of Selmabelle's prohibition against her seeing Lawrence, then remembered the saying, "New York's a big place but it's a small world." But she wasn't going to worry about a thing.

She felt a certain pride at being with a man people seemed to notice wherever they went. At the entrance to his stately apartment building, Lawrence warmly greeted the smiling, white-gloved doorman.

Phoebe already had seen how popular Lawrence was with Selmabelle's guests, including women of all ages, distinguished-looking men—even taxi drivers liked the way he started conversations during a ride.

She had told Jill about his sense of fun that everyone enjoyed. "Everyone? What a man!" Jill had said, and Phoebe, making a face, picked up a pillow as if about to throw it at her. Phoebe explained that he gave each individual so much attention he made people assume an unexpected appreciation of themselves. It was as if he held up a flattering mirror to them, so they suddenly accepted that they *really were* what they secretly had always wanted to be.

Now in his apartment house, the uniformed elevator operator smiled broadly in Lawrence's friendly, flattering presence. No one could accuse Lawrence of being snobby like Jane. On the penthouse floor, as he inserted the key in a door marked P2, Phoebe wondered if Jane had been here.

She noticed again the spicy scent of his after-shave lotion as he brought her into the apartment. In the entry hall, bright with a red abstract painting, she could see beyond to a large living room. Designed, she thought, with the kind of masculine decor that would be featured in *The New York Times Magazine* for the bachelor who liked space and could afford it. Browns, beiges. Strong, straight lines.

Lawrence flicked a switch in the living room so that more lamps went on and tango music began. Phoebe, feeling the rhythm and try-ing to appear at ease, danced a few steps. He moved toward her. Taking her stole, he dropped it over a chair, pulled her to him. To the beat of the music, he swept her, charging and dipping, around the room. She felt she was impressing him by how well she followed. But suddenly missing a step, she apologized. He interrupted by kissing her on the mouth. He removed his coat and tie, then kissed her again. Her heart was drumming faster than the music, now a rapid rumba.

"How about a brandy?" he said, slipping behind the bar. "Or maybe a brandy for me and a Grand Marnier for you." Phoebe sat on a barstool and waited for him to join her. Instead he leaned toward her across the bar: "You look as if you're not quite sure you should be here."

"Oh, no!" she said, hoping she sounded convincing.

"You looked this way when I showed you my office."

She smiled, accepting the drink. She tried not to notice the burning of the sweetness on the way down.

He sipped his brandy. "Happy, darling? Want to see the rest of the apartment?"

Following him, Phoebe clutched her small purse, wondering if she should leave it in the living room. But she was not sure so she kept it with her.

At the open doorway of the bedroom, she paused. The room was large, with a large bed and she caught a glimpse of Lawrence and her-self in the mirrors. Light from the hall came into the bedroom and, with it, the question of how he really felt, and 1959 rules and warn-ings she'd heard before leaving Kansas.

Misgivings on how he really felt about her made her turn to leave. He caught her arm and, pulling her to him, kissed her on the mouth. Phoebe dropped the purse onto an upholstered bench. He unbuttoned, then yanked off his shirt, and began to work with the hook on the back of Jill's sheer blouse, this one with silver threads.

How would she get out of this tight new skirt? Phoebe fled to the bathroom. She had not considered enough how it would be outside of marriage, her own bedroom, bathroom, her own husband. Standing on the brown bathroom rug, she kicked off her shoes and wiggled out of the skirt and draped it over the shower rod. Taking off her underwear, she rolled it together and then, not sure where to set it, carried it with her. After some hesitation, she opened the door.

Without clothes, she felt awkward walking across the bedroom, which now seemed the size of a ballroom and the bed a long way off. She left her rolled underwear on a chair, then tiptoed further, to where Lawrence had removed the brown and gold textured bedspread and now lay under the beige sheet.

"Sweetheart," he said, pulling her into bed, offering his warm-as-a-heating-pad body. At once she remembered that Niles, in Kansas winters, used to say he was her human heating pad. Moving her legs now, she was reminded that Niles had been taller than Lawrence so that her feet had reached different places on Niles's legs than what she was aware of here with Lawrence. She wished she could quit having so damn many thoughts.

The phone on Lawrence's night table was ringing—the phone's bell volume had been turned low. Answering, Lawrence murmured, "Hold on a minute." As if preoccupied, he excused himself with a quick kiss. By the light from the hall, she saw him throw on a robe, and go into the next room, the study, which she'd glimpsed from the hall when Lawrence had led her here to this bedroom.

She sat up, realizing the study had two entrances, one from the hall and one from the bedroom. Now that he had disappeared into the study and had closed the door, she silently volunteered I'm happy, knowing that was part of her feeling, but another part was anxiety. Everything's all right, she told herself.

But what phone call, at this late hour, could be so damn important as to last this long? Who is *this* interesting? Jane? Another woman?

She should dress and get out of here. She stared at the telephone on the night table. She put her hand on it, tempted to listen in—he might hear a click. She forced herself instead to pick up his watch he had left beside the telephone. Slipping the heavy gold band over her hand, she placed it next to her own small watch, the way Sir Chatham lined up watches on his arms. Lawrence's band was much too large, and taking it off, she turned the watch over to peer at the back: 18K. No other engraving. No TO LAWRENCE WITH LOVE FROM JANE. No evidence. *What is happening to me? What am I turning into?* She was like a detective in his apartment tonight. She held his watch to her ear to listen to the ticking, then put it back on the table—she hoped exactly as he had left it.

She slipped out of bed and walked around the room, barefoot on the thick carpet, reminded by two mirrors of her nakedness and her too thin, imperfect body. She stopped before the wall of books. She noticed that some were paperback but most were hardcover. Suddenly she realized they were categorized: reference, history, golf, novels alphabetized by author, drama, art, poetry. For someone who did not like to plan ahead, she thought, these books are well organized. Did he see his *life* was as well organized as his books? Did he figure that once you're really well organized, you can play things by ear?

If she were well organized, would she leave now? If she walked out, she would have second thoughts later and want to call him back. *Admit it—I'm where I want to be.*

Phoebe seized a small, cloth-bound volume, *A Little Treasury of Modern Poetry*, to find their Edna St. Vincent Millay poem. Then, conscious of passing time, she replaced the book on the neat shelf. She didn't want him to know that she'd even noticed the length of his blasted phone call—better if he thought she slept through it all. She went back to bed. But in protest, she turned onto her side, facing away from his side of the bed.

She heard the doorknob turn. The mattress sagged, as pulling back the sheet, he kneed his way into bed. He moved closer to her, bringing his warmth. "Darling," he whispered and kissed her shoulder. "Hey, darling, did you miss me?" He tongued the edges of her ear. "I missed you. Sweetheart, Phoebe, you haven't gone to sleep on me, have you?"

The next morning, when Phoebe was about to leave his apartment, she stood before the front-hall mirror examining the sheer evening blouse, wondering how Wilbur and Selmabelle would react if she strolled into work wearing this. Lawrence already had kissed her a quick good-bye before he had stepped into the shower, and now out, he padded barefoot toward her once more. His hair was wet and no longer tousled as it had been when they had made love again this morning. He was wrapped in a damp towel and smelled of expensive soap. I was happy *most* of last night, she thought. "I was happy last night," she said aloud, canceling the rest of the thought.

"What about now?" he teased.

"Yes." She smiled.

He kissed her on the tip of her nose. "I'd hoped I'd be so lucky."

"Will you call me later?" she heard herself ask.

He leaned to kiss her on the mouth. He tasted of toothpaste. "Sweetheart." He clasped the towel with one hand and opened the door with the other. "When I can snatch a minute." He kissed her forehead. "I'll call you."

Going down in the elevator, she felt more assured. But the rest of that day and the next, she heard in her mind, "I'll call you." In the evening, alone in the apartment and in the shower, she again lathered with Ivory soap and thought of the scents of Lawrence's expensive soap and after-shave lotion. In his apartment she had noticed fancy gift boxes of toilet articles stored on his bathroom shelves. She had found herself looking to see if she would discover Jane's gift card, but all evidence had been removed.

Having not slept much the night in Lawrence's apartment or the next night in her own, Phoebe now went directly from the shower to bed. When Jill returned home from a party given by a coworker, she reported to Phoebe: "Nothing exciting."

Phoebe sat up in bed. "Lawrence still didn't call."

"Hey, gal," Jill said, "don't worry."

"His voice is so beautiful, Jill, sometimes I think I pay too much attention to that. Do you think that's possible?"

"Anything's possible," Jill said.

The next morning, Friday, Phoebe again told herself to forget him. But when he did not phone by eleven o'clock, according to her watch, which she had been watching, she speculated on how he'd feel being interrupted at his office. She recalled his smiling at her from his desk and hoped he now viewed his office differently than before her visit. If she telephoned him, his secretary, Mrs. Cartright, who thought it was against the law to smile, would answer, and she'd know that she should not have called. Wilbur left the room and she dialed the number. When Lawrence himself answered, she almost hung up the phone.

"Hello," he said again.

"This is Phoebe."

"Okay to call you back?"

"Of course," she said, dreading the wait.

At three that afternoon he phoned. "Feel like dancing?"

Phoebe felt herself beam. "All night."

"I'll call you later."

In an attempt to distract her thoughts, Phoebe reminded herself of how particular and demanding Selmabelle was. He phoned just before six and gave her an address on the Upper West Side. She caught the subway, located the place, and hurried through the door into a bar that was dark, noisy, and so crowded she wondered if she would ever find him.

"Hi ya, honey," breathed a short stocky man with a greasy face and squinty eyes. She stepped back. "What's the matter?" the man said.

Phoebe pulled away and squeezed her way out the busy door. Seeing Lawrence striding toward her on the sidewalk, she ran to meet him. "Darling," he said, "that's quite a welcome." Inside the restaurant, he looked around the darkened interior. "This place must have changed hands." He led the way through the crowd to the back where tables surrounded a small dance floor. They danced with their arms around each other.

When they were about to leave, Phoebe visited the ladies room. Returning to the dance area, she saw Lawrence talking with a black-haired woman in a tight, blue-sequined dress.

In the taxi Phoebe did her best to smile at him. "Have you been busy at the office?"

"I'm always busy." he whispered, pushing aside a scarf at her neckline, sliding his hand inside her dress and bra.

"I don't want things to be too casual," she said. "I mean you don't always call, I mean when you say you'll call." She twisted and he removed his hand.

"Hey, what is this, sweetheart?" He mocked astonishment, teased, "Next thing, you'll be carrying a stopwatch! You've been around Sir Chatham Wigans too much."

Phoebe forced herself to smile.

"We're together, aren't we?" he said.

"But I like to plan."

"Maybe you plan too much. Don't spoil things, sweetheart."

"Is that what I'm doing?"

"I'm not good with plans outside the office." He laughed. "Someone once sent me a sign saying *Plan Ahead.* Gift wrapped."

"Someone? Do you still see her?"

He smiled. "Of course."

Phoebe turned away and he caught her in a tight embrace.

"You make everything sound very unimportant," she said.

"What *is* this?" he said, grinning. "I should bring my attorney when I talk to you. Hey, you're not laughing."

"I got the joke."

"You're angry," he said.

"Lawrence, I don't want to be angry but it's hard."

"Haven't you heard?" He was using his charming, teasing tone. "Men don't like possessive women."

"Some men do. You said yourself you get jealous. I have just as much right."

"I don't want to be unfair, darling. Isn't this what you want?"

"Do you have to work tonight?" she said.

"What a question, sweetheart."

"Because I have work to do early in the morning," Phoebe said. "I think the driver should let me off at my apartment."

As the taxi neared her address, Lawrence said, "Are you telling me something?"

"Just that I have work—"

"Am I allowed to say I'll call you?" he said as he let her out of the taxi.

"If you mean it," she said and, with a smile, waved.

Sixteen

JILL WAS AWAY, WEEKENDING IN EAST HAMPTON with friends from her office. Phoebe, alone in the apartment, opened the windows wide just after five on Saturday morning to bring in cool air, which she wished were not so filled with fumes. Face it, she told herself, it's the only air that's available if you're going to live in midtown Manhattan.

Still in her flimsy nightgown, she leaned over the table to eat her corn flakes. Peeling an orange, she reviewed last night, feeling rather proud of herself for the way she had ended her evening with Lawrence. She dwelled on her comment to Lawrence that she had work to do this morning. He hadn't said what he would do and she hadn't known what work she had in mind when she spoke of it.

She began to plan her day. The word *plan* seemed a dirty four-letter word today, but she would cleanse that along with a lot of other things that needed cleaning, she decided, as she looked around the room.

While she cleared the table, she questioned if she should ever admit to Lawrence that she herself was *not* big on planning. She could add that she planned only what she had to and what seemed important to her, and she guessed he did too—so where did that leave her as far as his priorities were concerned? Maybe she should just drop the subject—and yet . . .

She heated the coffee and poured herself another cup. Then she deposited the orange peels and dumped the coffee grounds into a plastic bag and carried it to the incinerator in the hallway. Suddenly she heard the apartment door slam shut.

She rushed to it and just as she feared—knew—it was locked. Oh, my God, she thought, as her heart pounded its anxiety beat. What could she do? She looked around the small hallway as if it would know the answer. The only person besides Jill she knew in the building was Ginger, the skinny, freckled woman who lived across the hall—and she was away on vacation in Portugal. Phoebe rushed to her door and found it locked too.

What made you think Ginger would go off to Europe and leave her door unlocked? Desperation, Phoebe answered herself.

Jill had once told her that the super of their small five-story building lived in a basement apartment in another building about half a block away. Could she run down there, plead for him to let her in? He must have a master key.

Phoebe looked down at her short, sheer revealing nightgown and thought she might as well be naked—it was *stark naked,* no matter what Selmabelle said. If she ventured out on Lexington Avenue in this, she might be arrested for indecent exposure. Did they arrest women for indecent exposure? That was usually a male arrest, wasn't it? One thing in favor of being female. She must hang onto any positive thought.

As she made her way barefoot down the steps—she had decided to avoid the elevator—she guessed that most tenants in the building were away for the weekend and if they weren't, they were asleep on a Saturday morning. She wished she were asleep and this only a nightmare.

Since she didn't know tenants in the building, how could she ring their doorbells especially at this hour on a Saturday morning and expect a cordial greeting? Or if it was *too* cordial, maybe she should be alarmed herself, dressed—or undressed—as she was.

She wished she were wearing her watch, but it couldn't be much more than six-thirty by now. When she reached the first floor, she peeked out the entrance door to see if any pedestrian would walk by.

Maybe someone could alert the super? But she was in a vulnerable position alone in this lobby in this attire. Better be cautious—she was in enough of a fix now. She watched a few taxis speed by but none stopped at the building. The traffic was lighter than she'd seen it, except when she'd been up very early to accompany Sir Chatham to the morning show.

Inspecting the lobby, she found that the only door, besides the elevator door, led to a broom closet, which was empty except for a dirty mop and a bucket. She picked up the bucket wondering what she could do with it—wear it on her head? She looked ridiculous enough already. She set it down, picked up the mop, and holding up the mop end, stared at it. She pulled a blackened string from it. She looked down at the spaghetti straps at the top of her full, gossamer nightgown. Then, with the string, she tied the sheer fabric of her nightgown into a few folds over her left breast. Good thing she was thin so that there was extra material. She tied another string onto the right side. As she stared down at herself, she thought this short garment was really misnamed to be called a gown. She wished she had left on her underwear, but who would have thought?

At least with the mop strings, it was better than it had been. Could she strike out now and run barefoot down Lexington? But which building did the super live in? What if she rang the wrong bell? She didn't even know his name—Jill just called him "the super."

She needed to go to the bathroom. She thought of the bucket but felt that was going too far.

Traffic seemed heavier now and there were a few pedestrians on the sidewalks—Saturday shoppers probably, safe in their chores. She sat down on the floor, wondering when it had last been mopped, and leaned her back against the wall. Having gotten up so early, she was sleepy, except that her bladder needs were keeping her awake.

What the hell? she asked herself. She went into the closet to relieve herself. Returning to the lobby, she wondered what the super

would think the next time he started to mop. Would the odor of
urine permeate the lobby?

Her hope was that the postman would be along soon. Every time
she heard footsteps outside, her expectations arose again. She had
never actually seen the postman but she knew he came around nine
on Saturday because she or Jill went down soon after that for the
mail. Phoebe was standing by the entrance door when the fat, uniformed, middle-aged man arrived, large envelopes and magazines
protruding over the top of his leather shoulder bag.

"Oh, thank God," Phoebe said. "You've got to help me."

He looked at her, then averted his eyes. She could imagine him saying: "This is not a part of my job description."

"I'm locked out of my apartment. Please help me, please, I'm desperate." Phoebe stepped from the lobby into the tiny entranceway,
where the mailboxes lined the wall. She pointed to the card bearing her
name. "I came out in the hall and the door slammed shut. Do you know
the super for this building? Do you know where he lives? He could let
me in. He should have a key."

"Stay right there," the postman said.

"Oh, I promise," Phoebe said. This was not the way she had planned
her day. Maybe Lawrence was right—better not to plan too much.
Would she have a chance to tell him? Had he called while she was
down here in the lobby?

On Monday morning, at her desk, Phoebe checked her work calendar, determined to concentrate on work only. Going through the office mail, she came across a plain white envelope addressed to her in
printed ink, with no return address. She ripped it open, took out a
theater ticket for Tuesday night for the play *J.B.* Examining the
empty envelope, she found nothing to identify the sender.

She tried not to be excited but was seized by expectation and the
next night at the ANTA Theater she followed the usher down the

aisle to the third row center, in the orchestra section. She took her seat next to the empty one on the aisle. People in seats near her appeared dressed up and Phoebe felt pleased with her own lime-green silk top with the halter neck, which only this noon she'd bought on sale at Saks to wear with the black skirt. She hoped Lawrence would admire the way she looked tonight with her hair swept atop her head, rather than falling around her shoulders.

She cautioned herself that Lawrence might not have sent the ticket. Yet she reasoned that with his sense of fun, maybe this was a grand gesture in lieu of a phone call after their argument. The later it became, the more likely it seemed he would slide into the seat beside her. He would arrive just as the play was about to begin, take her hand in his, say something amusing. Probably comment on the stage setting, a circus tent scene, which was in full view of the audience upon entering the theater. Phoebe thought of her college English teacher Miss Thompson, who posed such questions as: "Is the poet-playwright Archibald MacLeish perhaps suggesting that the world is a circus?" She remembered Sir Chatham's words in the office of *The Richy Rand Show*: "I won't be a clown."

Phoebe read in the program notes that the play was about two unemployed actors "reduced to selling balloons and popcorn in an ancient circus." They had "traveled the towns and cities of the earth . . . playing the Old Testament story of the suffering of Job . . ."

The Book of Job. Was Lawrence suggesting that she should have more patience, the patience of Job?

She had to admit she was impatient. Her father used to tell her: "Hold your horses." He'd said the same thing to her mother. She remembered her father had complained that her mother wanted "everything now and everything perfect." When Phoebe had felt unhappy in childhood she had wondered how she could ever do everything the way Mama wanted. Gramma had told Phoebe that religion represented perfection, the Ideal. Phoebe remembered turning away from Sunday School, realizing she could never be perfect and never believe. Still, she experienced guilt and believed in punishment. When her mother died, Phoebe had envied her Catholic friends who were able to go to confession and leave their guilt behind. She heard again her mother's words: "You'll be sorry when I'm gone."

She swallowed now and tried to hold down her anxiety and excitement. The overhead chandeliers shone down on the theater audience. There was a mingling of perfumes and the rustling of late arrivals. Then the usher was standing at the end of the row, handing him his Playbill.

He took it in his big hand and smiled at Phoebe. "You're here." As he sat down beside her, he said, "You look wonderful, Phoebe."

She made a quick mental adjustment as Gilbert settled his large body into the seat next to hers.

She was unprepared for more of the unexpected. The house lights dimmed and the drama of Job began. Phoebe felt hemmed in her seat. She attempted to make her breathing easy. But the play unfolded as a nightmare of fear and remorse, a horrifying succession of tragedies. She tried not to hear tormented voices shriek at the death of Job's children. "The Lord giveth / The Lord taketh away," Job cried out and begged: "Speak to me of the sin I must have sinned."

Phoebe covered her ears and shut her eyes. All the events of her life suddenly seemed to topple over her like boxes. She placed her hands atop her head to protect herself. Her heart was trying to pound its way out of her body. She grasped the arms of the theater seat and, in an attempt to calm herself, she sat up straighter. She watched Job's wife return to him as they planned to start again, to rebuild their lives.

Finally, it was over. Trembling, she got up to leave the theater with Gilbert. She stood erect but then she steadied herself by touching the backs of seats she passed on the way out. It seemed as if the play had given her a message: Life tests you. She must rebuild her life. Destiny had meant for her to live through this terrifying drama. But she would not have guessed that Gilbert would have been the one to bring her here. Had Lawrence sent him? No, Lawrence always objected—though in his charming, teasing way—if she even mentioned Gilbert's name. Why was he jealous if he didn't really care?

Touching her elbow, Gilbert guided Phoebe through throngs of people in the theater district to a lively Greek café, where musicians and dancers were enjoying themselves so much she could hardly believe the contrast from the play. They sat at a small table covered by a white cloth, where Gilbert, ordering for them, asked for a hearty vegetable soup and Greek pastries.

Phoebe, still under the influence of the play and the jolt of being with Gilbert, commented, "I was surprised you sent the ticket. Thank you, but I was surprised."

Gilbert studied her. He had moved his chair back from the table to accommodate his bulky body, but now he leaned forward as he spoke, "You mean surprised by the ticket, or that I was the one who sent it?"

"Both," she said. Conscious of music and laughing, joyous people around them, Phoebe noticed a certain wildness of appearance about Gilbert with his thick curly hair and heavy eyebrows, making her think of a genius scientist as he peered at her.

"Phoebe, I've wanted to be with you since I first saw you on the train. Gloria and I aren't living together—we haven't been for a long time. Does that matter to you?"

Matter? she repeated silently.

"I've said the wrong thing again, Phoebe. I want to say the right thing to you so much—I'd better not talk about it anymore tonight. Except . . ."

"What?"

"I want to be sure you understand. Gloria and I both agreed on a divorce. Our trouble started a long time ago—she married me on the rebound. Phoebe, I'm interested in you."

She looked into his eyes. "What if I already have someone in my life?"

"Do you?"

"You didn't know?" Phoebe could feel Gilbert waiting for her to say more, but if Lawrence had not told his own brother . . . "I think you're right," Phoebe said. "We shouldn't talk about it anymore tonight."

When the apartment phone rang two mornings later, Phoebe struggled to be alert and realized it was Saturday. Jill, answering, handed the phone to Phoebe, who sat up. "No, no, I'm awake," Phoebe said when she heard Lawrence's voice.

Now he said, "What are you going to do later?"

Phoebe tried to think what to answer.

He said, "I might call you."

"Do you know when?"

"My plans are a little uncertain at the moment."

"So are mine," said Phoebe. "But if I knew when . . ."

"I can't say now, but don't stay home."

Hanging up the phone, Phoebe told Jill, "I don't know whether to stay home."

Jill, carrying her breakfast dishes to the sink, said, "Good luck."

"I want to see him, if that's what he meant. But I don't want him to keep me dangling. I'm not going to sit around."

"Good for you," said Jill, leaving for her Saturday shopping.

Phoebe dressed and finally started out to do her own marketing. On Lexington Avenue, she walked briskly, but feeling worried, she slowed. She took a few more steps and turned around.

In the apartment, she busied herself by sitting down to balance her checkbook. When the phone rang, she insisted that she walk calmly and sound unconcerned in her "Hello?"

"Oh, you *are* there," Lawrence said. "I phoned a while ago and there was no answer."

"I was out."

"Want to go to the country? I thought we'd take a drive."

"It's a beautiful day," Phoebe said.

While she changed into her blue sweater and skirt, she thought of Jill's stories of trips with Bill to Connecticut, where they'd stayed at an inn and taken walks if they ever managed to get out of bed. Phoebe wondered what Lawrence had in mind. By now it was almost noon and she felt the beginning of hunger. She guessed they would stop somewhere for lunch in the country; she ate only a few peanuts, then hurried downstairs and stood in the sunshine in front of the building.

Lawrence maneuvered his long black Lincoln out of the traffic to stop for Phoebe, then sped to Long Island. She sighted huge elms and oaks, splashes of red, pink, and yellow tulips. "There's a reason for this drive here," he admitted, as he swung the car into the curved driveway of a large white house, which had a long porch and pillars, southern style. "I have to return a set of golf clubs." He opened the trunk of the car. Phoebe watched him sling the bag of clubs over his shoulder and carry his load up the steps of the porch. When a maid opened the door, he disappeared inside.

Lawrence had not mentioned lunch. Phoebe opened the glove compartment in hopes of finding a candy bar, but at that moment he leaped down the steps. She slammed the compartment shut. As he slid in beside her, he leaned toward her. "Miss me?"

"Madly," said Phoebe, laughing.

"That's more like it." Driving along, Lawrence talked about his longtime pal, who lived in the house; they had gone to Harvard together. He hadn't been home just now so Lawrence had left the clubs with the maid.

Phoebe recalled Niles's way of announcing his plans to play golf at the Harkenstown Country Club. "I'm going to make you a golf widow on Saturday," he used to say. Then, the word *widow* had fit into their joking banter. It chilled her now. She wanted to avoid more talk of golf and thought to say, "Tell me about your grandmother who lives on Long Island—the Grand One. I like that name."

"We could give her a call." He suggested they return to his friend's house and he could phone from there.

"Oh, I didn't mean—"

"It's a good idea, darling," Lawrence said, squeezing her hand.

After he made the phone call, he told Phoebe he liked this drive out here. He'd been borrowing his friend's golf clubs for years, since he didn't play often enough to have his own set. "But I'm more a sportsman than my brother, even if he does have his own golf bag. He doesn't have clubs, just the bag." Lawrence laughed and explained that Gilbert got the idea to travel with a golf bag from another artist, who had told him to carry his rolled-up canvases in it. That way, arriving at an airport or a hotel, looking like a golfer, Gilbert would get great service, since all the skycaps and bellhops would expect to receive big tips.

Phoebe, who had been wondering how to tell Lawrence about being at the theater with Gilbert, asked, "Do you think they do get big tips?"

"Gilbert always overtips."

"Does he?"

"All the time. Hey, you sound very interested in my brother." But Lawrence's attention was now on his driving as he sped along Middle Neck Road, where a sign read the Village of Sands Point. He finally turned, heading down a tree-lined country road, slowed as he approached the next estate, then passed between stone gateposts onto the private drive. The windows of the Lincoln were open and Phoebe caught the scent of lilacs lining the road. "God knows where we'll find her," Lawrence said of the Grand One, his eighty-three-year-old grandmother. Just a few years before, his father had driven out here to see her and she'd been up on the roof, checking the shingles to see if the roofer had done his work properly. His father had called to her that if she didn't quit climbing up there on the roof, he wouldn't come out to see her again. "Suit yourself," she had called back.

Phoebe laughed with Lawrence.

The wheels rattled the gravel as he drove into the Grand One's private parking lot. With all this space for cars, Phoebe thought, at least at one time, there must have been many parties here on the estate. She wondered what Lawrence's late grandfather, who had growled about money, had said about the entertainment expenses.

Phoebe heard a dog barking and a beautiful golden retriever bounded toward them. As Lawrence opened his door, the dog wagged his tail and sniffed Lawrence's outstretched hand. Lawrence patted his head, then leaned down for a face-to-face greeting, calling him Horatio. Phoebe stroked the soft reddish hair, and the dog lifted his head with pleasure, joining Phoebe and Lawrence as they started in the direction of the side lawn of the house. Horatio suddenly trotted ahead of them toward a small, erect, elderly woman in a pink dress and wide straw hat. Walking to meet them, she passed a wheelbarrow and dropped her gardening gloves into it. Removing her hat, she offered her cheek to Lawrence, then smiling, welcomed and shook hands with Phoebe.

The trio strolled the sunlit lawn behind the house where, in the distance, evergreens formed a backdrop for the sweeping green of the grounds. Lawrence, patting the large trunk of a silver maple, said to his grandmother, "You having these trees sprayed?"

"And it cost a fortune," the Grand One said, squinting at Lawrence. "Oh my, did you hear that, darling? I sound like your grandfather."

Lawrence laughed. "So do I."

Horatio darted in and out of the azalea bushes, shaking blossoms of coral, salmon, and pink until the Grand One called to him and the dog accompanied the group into the house, and through the large kitchen. Phoebe, now famished, secretly wanted to stop at the giant refrigerator, but Lawrence ushered her into the dining room, where glancing at the long table, she imagined a feast. In the spacious living room, bright with oriental rugs and windows overlooking the garden, she scanned the coffee table in vain for mints. They took seats around the table and when a maid appeared with a tea tray and set it down before them, Phoebe smiled with relief, then realized there was only tea with lemon.

A portrait above the mantel showed the Grand One, seated erect in a carved chair, and attired in a pink silk gown and pearls. The real, in-the-flesh woman, seated across the table from Phoebe, wore a pink, long-sleeved shirtwaist dress. She had been younger when the picture had been painted, so even though she was still pretty, by comparison, the portrait now made her appear more fragile and aged. The opposite of Dorian Gray, Phoebe thought. In the painting she was quite beautiful and serious. Phoebe said, "I've been admiring your portrait."

"I like it too," the Grand One admitted as she poured more tea. "My grandson painted it—Gilbert. Do you know Gilbert?"

Phoebe glanced at Lawrence. "Yes, I know him."

"People tell me," his grandmother said, "that the portrait looks like me when I'm concentrating. I like that. It sets a good example for me." She smiled at Phoebe. "When you're my age, you'll see it helps to set good examples for yourself, and new goals. It gives an illusion of long life. When you're young, you take life for granted."

Phoebe, thinking of Niles, did not reply.

"It helps to start something new," the Grand One said, "like a new pet economy. Lawrence, your grandfather would be amazed if he could hear me say this!" Her latest economy was to save used envelopes to write notes to her housekeeper or to make grocery lists. Her friends had pet economies too. "I have one friend who says she's still extravagant in some ways"—the Grand One leaned toward Phoebe—"but every Sunday she waters her eye lotion." Phoebe, amused by the questionable logic, noticed his grandmother smiling and Lawrence appearing to enjoy himself. "Do you have a pet economy?" the Grand One asked Phoebe.

"Oh," said Phoebe. "I have to have so many economies."

"Good for you!" His grandmother clapped her hands. "My husband would have approved of you, wouldn't he, Lawrence—someone with so many economies?"

"Amen," said Lawrence.

"I must tell you then," the Grand One confided, "once in the Dallas airport gift shop, I bought three pretty little scarves for myself. Of course, my husband didn't offer to buy them for me. And do you know what he said to me? I'll never forget it. He said, 'It never ceases to amaze me what a woman would rather have than money!'"

"Oh!" Phoebe smiled broadly. "I'm going to remember that!"

"Bravo!" said Lawrence, standing up. He touched Phoebe's shoulder, then excused himself, leaving her with his grandmother. Phoebe wondered if he might be going to see about some lunch.

"My grandson's good about bringing his friends to meet me, my dear," the Grand One said to Phoebe, "but not telling me about them first—then he says I mix up his friends. I'm sure you do whatever you do very well."

"I'm Selmabelle's assistant."

"Oh, lucky you! My family's devoted to her. You know where you stand with Selmabelle. Then I'm sure you know she's planning a party for Jane. I'm really looking forward to it. I've known Jane and Gloria since they were babies."

"I can't find Gilbert's scrapbook," Lawrence said, coming back into the room, "the one you put together of Gilbert's early artwork. I promised to show Phoebe some drawings he did of me when we were kids." Phoebe was encouraged that he had remembered their conversation on the ferry, yet she felt now that this might be an imposition. "Oh, please, don't bother if it's—"

"I think Gloria was looking through it," the Grand One said. "Or was it Jane, when you and she were out here the last time?"

As they left the house, Phoebe went out the door first and Lawrence stayed back to say to his grandmother that he hoped she had not minded their impromptu visit. "Can I help it if everyone wants to meet you? I told you about my Catholic friend at college—"

"You may have, darling."

"He's the one who said that all his non-Catholic girlfriends wanted him to take them to Midnight Mass on Christmas Eve. Well, with me, everyone wants to meet you."

His grandmother laughed. "Heavens, darling, what a comparison! I don't think you should say that again."

"It's true."

"But don't apologize, darling, about stopping by. I love to see you, you know that. But did I get it wrong? I thought Jane was coming with you today."

Phoebe, listening from a distance, fingered the leaf of a bush.

Lawrence lowered his voice so much that Phoebe could hardly hear: "She had to take Fetchy to the vet."

"Oh, dear, is it that pesky virus? I hope Horatio doesn't catch it."

"Don't worry," Lawrence said. "He won't. He's out here and Fetchy's there in the city—"

"I know, Jane tells me. Fetchy loves all those enticing smells on the sidewalks. Give her my love, darling."

During the drive to the city, Phoebe looked out her window so that her expression would not give her away. So Jane had been his first choice for this day in the country. Jane had been the reason he had kept her dangling. Would he have asked Jane if she'd had lunch?

"You want to stop by my apartment for coffee?" Lawrence asked.

"The tea was just fine," Phoebe said.

"You're sure? Maybe a drink?"

"No, thank you."

"Unfortunately," he said, "I have an appointment later on."

"So do I," said Phoebe, trying to sound convincing. When he stopped the car in front of her apartment house, he leaned toward her, kissing her cheek. "I'll call you, sweetheart."

Seventeen

"I'LL CALL YOU, SWEETHEART," Phoebe still repeated in her mind three days later. Well, it won't do you any good! She wished she hadn't met him through her job; it made it harder to shove him out of her mind, especially now while working on Jane's party.

"There's too many guests for one table," Selmabelle told Phoebe. "There will be two long tables, placed side by side. As hostess I'll preside over one." She directed that her throne chair be moved from her office to the head of that table. "People will see at a glance where *I'm* to be seated. Jane can head the other table, as guest of honor. That way, *all* guests will be at an *important* table."

On the night of the dinner Phoebe was dressed in her gown of peacock blue chiffon, which she'd last worn to the Harkenstown Country Club. Holding a chart, she double-checked the forty-eight place cards on the tables set up in Selmabelle's main dining room, which was so large Phoebe thought it could be called "the banquet hall." Tiny lights twinkled on the ceiling and blue iris, pink tulips, and lilacs centered both tables covered by spring green tablecloths. She picked up the place card for Lawrence W. Bradley, then put it back where it had been, on Jane's table.

This was the first time ever that Phoebe had worked on place cards when she herself was not to be seated at the dinner, and against her will and reason, she felt left out. She felt in a strange position because when Selmabelle had instructed her to add the name of her "distinguished physician," Dr. John Broden, to the guest list, it had become clear, by the number of places available, that she was not to be at either table. Lord knows, Phoebe thought, I'm not a personal friend of the guest of honor.

On the "professional staff," Phoebe had been assigned to be "in charge of the party." She had told Jill she guessed that meant if anything went wrong, she'd get the blame. She doubted that she'd receive much credit for the arrangements, certainly not from Jane. "I don't even know why I want credit," Phoebe had said to Jill the night before.

"If you do a good job," answered Jill, "you want credit for it. That's only natural."

"I've been thinking," Phoebe said, "all my life I've been praised for depriving myself. It makes me feel pushy if I want very much. Even Lawrence's grandmother clapped her hands when I said I had *economies*. It's like when I was little, I was praised when I didn't do this or ask for that. I've always been encouraged to deprive myself."

Jill's blue eyes looked concerned. "I probably have too. But I'd never thought about it before."

Now Phoebe was determined not to feel deprived, even if she was not a guest at this Celebration of Spring party in honor of Jane Flaunton.

The red-cheeked trumpeter, already dressed in his troubadour costume and carrying his instrument case, reported to Phoebe, assuring her he had arrived on schedule. He confirmed that he would await the nod of her head as his cue to start the fanfare for the picture ceremony.

Then Phoebe, hurrying into the kitchen, heard chopping, a clatter of pots, and Cognac giving orders to his underlings, cajoling, scolding. She could see she was not needed here.

Starting to push open the door leading to the dining room, she glimpsed Henrietta—"Henny"—Tibbold, the ex-wife of a movie producer. Phoebe remembered her stories of the platinum gun and the faulty memory teacher. Around her shoulders Henny wore a green stole decorated with artificial flowers of many colors, and her pale orange hair was coiled with more flowers atop her head. Her green gown set off Jane's white one.

As Jane leaned over the table to inspect place cards, Henny peered at the white orchids wreathing Jane's curly hair. Examining her white gown, Henny said, "Now *that* is stunning." She placed her hands on her wide hips as if to measure herself against Jane's small figure. "Jane, darling, someone could take you for a bride." Henny laughed. "Well, listen to me, I didn't plan to make a pun but I'll bet someone *will* take you for a bride!"

Jane pretended a little girl's shyness. "I can't imagine what you mean!"

Henny continued to study Jane. "You're still taking your design classes?"

Jane smiled as she nodded.

Hetty said, "And you designed that dress yourself?"

"I didn't have time. Auntie Sel bought it for me at Bergdorf's."

"What are you two up to?" Joining them was a plump woman with a high headdress of blue feathers.

Henny said, "Well, look at you!"

Phoebe, still watching from the crack in the doorway, saw the bird woman reach up to touch her feathers, making them sway, "I'm your feisty Blue Jay," the bird woman announced. "Your fine feathered friend." The women laughed together. The feathers looked like dyed ostrich feathers to Phoebe. When the bird woman brushed back her feathers, Phoebe recognized her as Lawrence's mother, Elizabeth Bradley. Phoebe remembered her hat with the haughty feather when she had entered Sir Chatham's reception on the arm of her white-haired husband. Now she leaned over the table to read place cards. "Where am I seated?"

Henny, smiling, bent toward her. "Across from me."

"Oh, good."

At that moment Lawrence's grandmother, the Grand One, her white hair decorated with daisies, hurried into the room to embrace Jane, saying she wanted to hug her before she was surrounded by all her other admirers.

Henny insisted, "Doesn't Jane look like a bride?"

Jane, tilting her head, smiled coyly.

"Well, I've done my part to encourage it," said Lawrence's mother, the bird woman, hugging Jane, who kissed her on the cheek.

"I don't want to ruffle your feathers," Jane said in a high, little voice, causing laughter as the group walked into the front parlors.

Phoebe told herself that this chatter about Jane was just party talk. If she weren't feeling left out, she wouldn't pay any attention to it. She rushed past the group of hateful women, through the parlors, down the wide staircase, out of the house, ignoring the people coming in the front door. As she walked up and down the block on Gramercy Park, she kept her head down and queried herself: why should she feel left out? They were silly women. Is this what she'd left Kansas for? Phoebe looked up and wondered what she was she doing, walking out here?

"Where have you been?" Selmabelle demanded of Phoebe when she came back up the stairs. "I looked for you—"

"I had to have some air."

"I put you in charge and you want *air*? I have to have people I can depend on."

"You can depend on me. I *promise* you can depend on me." At once Phoebe stepped away as more guests spoke to the hostess, exclaiming over the rooms transformed into a garden. New arrivals cooed over each other's costumes and clustered around Selmabelle, who wore a lei of green orchids on her flowered gown, and more orchids at the back of her yellow hair. Suddenly Phoebe collided with a woman clutching a bouquet of balloons. Phoebe apologized but the jolt brought the party into focus.

As if in competition with the three-piece orchestra in the corner, a heavy woman in a robe shook the bells on her fingers and bells on her toes. One man, draped in a white sheet, waved his hairy arms about, showing off his bracelets of flowers. Phoebe, moving away, faced Toby Weaver, who strutted toward her in a cowboy outfit instead of the checked suit and bow tie he sported in his TV office. Greeting Phoebe, he pulled out two toy guns from their holsters. "Is this the way to the spring roundup, pardner?"

"It sure is," said Phoebe. But her attention did not stay on Toby. She realized by the scent of his after-shave lotion that Lawrence was by her side. She did not look at him directly as he said into her ear, "I'd rather go back and forth all night on the ferry."

Smiling, Phoebe turned to Lawrence just as Toby stuck out his hand to him. "Put it there, pardner."

Jane rushed into the parlor on Gilbert's arm. Pulling him with her, she ran up to Lawrence: "You're here, darling." Standing between the two brothers, Jane summoned the photographer: "Here, Jimmy, right now, before the ceremony—take a picture of The Three Musketeers." After the flashbulbs, Jane insisted for the next shots that Lawrence's mother and grandmother pose with them. When the Grand One brought Selmabelle into the photos, Selmabelle lifted her head in a majestic pose and out-smiled all the others.

As the group disbanded, Lawrence's grandmother caught Phoebe's eye. Phoebe imagined the surprised frowns on some faces—those of Selmabelle, Jane, even Gilbert—if the Grand One came to greet her and mentioned that Phoebe had been a guest in her house. Phoebe remembered Selmabelle's pointed description of Lawrence as Jane's "special friend." She felt it wise now to make a quick exit. With Selmabelle's prohibition of her seeing Lawrence, how could she explain having met the Grand One?

Rushing from the parlor into the dining room and encountering the trumpeter troubadour, Phoebe looked down quickly. The trumpeter sounded his fanfare. Phoebe, startled, remembered she'd told him she would nod to him when time to start.

As he played his way into the parlor, Phoebe stepped forward to tell him to stop, that he was ahead of schedule. But already he had moved toward Selmabelle, who hesitated only a moment, then got into an awkward step behind him. Parading through the parlor, the two inspired the orchestra and guests to follow their lead to form a chain. Phoebe placed herself at the rear of the line behind the woman with the balloons. The long line pranced and snaked through the entertainment rooms, some eager drinkers downing cocktails as they kept the pace. When the trumpeter led the group back into the second parlor where they had started, the crowd broke up. Everyone seemed to be laughing, running into one another.

The trumpeter again sounded a call-to-attention and Selmabelle bowed stiffly. Then, as if the lively parade had been too much for her feet, she took laborious steps to the easel set up against the bookcase wall. There was a hush punctuated by the popping of flashbulbs. "I've always wanted," said Selmabelle in her deep voice, "to be a magician."

She whisked away the cloth to reveal a large, gilt-framed portrait of Jane, in a red gown, haughty in a high-backed upholstered chair and holding her white puppy, which was seated bolt upright on her lap. Both Jane and the dog stared out of the painting; it seemed their eyes met Phoebe's. The crowd responded to the picture with applause and cheers, moving toward the portrait and around Jane.

"Look at little Fetchy," the woman with bells said to a woman dressed as a maypole with colorful streamers falling from the top of her head. In the portrait Fetchy wore a red bow, but now at the party he modeled a bow that was even whiter than his clipped poodle-fur. Weaving his way around the legs of the guests, the dog raised his head when the maypole woman leaned to pet him.

"Wasn't Lawrence sweet to give Jane this darling creature?" the maypole woman oozed.

Phoebe whirled away from her and caught sight of Jane, the guest of honor, being kissed on one cheek, now the other by a young couple who had arrived with Ambassador Kerby and a group that had just flown in from Washington. "See if Cognac can delay another five minutes," Selmabelle said to Phoebe, who hurried to the kitchen.

Cognac, standing at the stove while sampling his delicious-smelling lobster sauce, stamped his foot to protest her message and cried, "Delay! Delay!"

But Cognac's words were interrupted by screams. Phoebe rushed back to the parlor, making her way into the crowd. Selmabelle let out another scream. Her face was creased with pain. She was half-sitting, half-sprawled, at an odd angle on the carpeted floor. Her flowered gown had slipped up, showing thick ankles and orthopedic shoes, which Phoebe knew she would hate having revealed.

Dr. John Broden pushed people away and knelt beside Selmabelle. He looked serious, asking questions as he touched her here and there.

All the guests seemed to be talking at once, recalling what they had been doing when the screaming began. Some said they had predicted problems as soon as the man in the sheet began to tease the dog.

"No," the draped man protested, claiming that Selmabelle had backed up to talk with Ambassador Kerby and had tripped over the dog.

Phoebe leaned down to Selmabelle. Orchids dangled from her yellow hair. Between gasps, Selmabelle instructed Phoebe, "You sit at my place. Cognac can't hold dinner forever." Selmabelle cried out again, then added, "You can't just stop the party."

Because Dr. Broden was to accompany Selmabelle in the ambulance, Phoebe hurried to the dining room ahead of the guests to remove the doctor's place card and place setting. She heard the chatter and caught the perfume of guests entering the room. "It's nice to see you again," the Grand One greeted Phoebe, who noticed Jane lingering nearby, within earshot.

"Thank you, you too," Phoebe murmured quickly, trying not to be rude but knowing she'd better end the conversation. As the crowd surged into the dining room, Jane was arm-in-arm with the Grand One; Phoebe wondered anxiously how the Grand One would answer questions that Jane was sure to be asking.

When people had found their places, Phoebe herself sat down in Selmabelle's throne-chair. She discovered that she had forgotten to remove Selmabelle's place card. She felt awed that she should be replacing "America's premier hostess"—one of Selmabelle's favorite descriptions of herself. From this position, it seemed to Phoebe that the table, decorated with flowers and candles, had stretched and was still lengthening. The man in the white sheet, at the opposite end of the table, was like a ghost in the distance.

Phoebe was aware that guests, including Ambassador Kerby, seated to her right, waited for her, as hostess, to sink her fork into the salmon mousse before anyone else at the table would take a bite. She felt pressured to say something aloud. Comments sounded secretly in her head: "I'm sitting here because Selmabelle ordered me to and I *need* this job."

Mid-table, Lawrence's father with his usual critical look, sat fork-in-hand, nodding, frowning at remarks made to him. What would he say if he knew of her nighttime visit to his law office? She still had not looked at Lawrence, seated at the other table with the younger guests. Wilbur would be gossiping at that table—he'd boasted to Phoebe that he'd been invited "personally" by Jane during a French-speaking walk.

Phoebe glanced at the head of that table where cute, small-nosed Jane, with white orchids like a crown on her curly blond hair, held court. Phoebe could tell that she had Jane's attention when her small, gray eyes—like those in the painting—met hers. Phoebe imagined Jane suddenly forgetting her usual whispers and screaming, "What are you doing in Auntie Sel's chair? What are you doing at my party?"

Phoebe straightened in her chair—Selmabelle's chair—telling herself that she was where she belonged: she had been *assigned* to be here. But now she had to think of what Selmabelle would do now: give a toast to Jane.

How could she personally do that? Jane would be enraged, would report her to Selmabelle. Phoebe must ask someone else to do the honors. Not Ambassador Kerby—he might resent being called upon to give a toast since he'd probably done that almost nightly in his old job. Selmabelle had said he was really a retired ambassador living in Washington, but he liked to be invited to parties.

Phoebe looked down the table where Henny Tibbold, in green stole and flowers, seemed to be telling one of her stories to guests straining to hear it. If Henny were to give the toast, there was the risk she'd mention that Jane's dress was like a bridal gown. But if there was to be a wedding announcement, Phoebe told herself, she'd better hear it now.

Phoebe rose from the premier seat and stepped to Henny's chair. Leaning over Henny's sweetly scented shoulder, she made the request.

Henny seemed modestly taken aback. But as Henny started to answer, Jane appeared. In her little girl's voice, she asked Henny if anything was wrong, as if Phoebe were causing trouble. "Do you need help?"

Henny laughed. "I may, darling." She explained that she was to give the toast. Jane looked suspiciously at Phoebe before she returned to her seat.

"I'll give you the signal after the dessert," Phoebe told Henny.

Phoebe was back in Selmabelle's chair when she realized that a disturbance had started at the other table. Jane's voice had risen to reprimand Anita, Bessie's younger sister, who was working as a waitress tonight. Phoebe heard Jane say, "She wouldn't dare be so slow if Auntie Sel were here."

The eighteen-year-old waitress, turning pale, walked stiffly from the room. Bessie, her face showing distress and wisps of blond hair escaping her maid's cap, stayed on duty. She served more wine to guests who paused in their conversations, then pretended everything was as it had been.

Phoebe wanted to hug Bessie and run after Anita, but she remembered Selmabelle's words: "You can't just stop the party." After dessert of chocolate lilies filled with raspberries, Phoebe tapped a wine glass. The chatter quieted.

Henny stood up, seeming about to lose her balance, and held up her champagne glass, liquid spilling from it. "Some of you may remember my story about forgetting my memory course." Guests at both tables laughed and applauded. "Now that I'm standing here, I feel I've forgotten my course in public speaking too. Oh, Lord, I need Selmabelle. I forgot something else—I was supposed to acknowledge people, like the Ambassador." When he chuckled, Henny said, "You'd better come here and help me say this."

Laughing, white-haired, ruddy-faced Ambassador Kerby rose to stand next to Henny. "Not to worry, Henrietta, you're doing fine." Everyone applauded.

"I don't want to let our poor, dear Selmabelle down," Henny said. "I'm going to do this right, so help me!"

Phoebe felt a shock that the crowd was smiling, nodding, pretending that Jane was as sweet as Henny and the ambassador were saying she was. But what should I expect, Phoebe asked herself, at a party given by Selmabelle? Guests want to be invited back. Wilbur had said: "Selmabelle's parties are her power base, just as they were for her daddy and her granddaddy. Nobody wants to be left out of her next party."

Henny smiled at her audience at both tables, then turned to Jane. "I told Selmabelle when Jane was a little girl that 'Darling Jane' should be her name. Tonight I told Jane she looks as radiant as a bride. But she hasn't admitted a thing!" Ambassador Kerby and the crowd found this funny and endearing. Henny held up her champagne glass. "To Darling Jane!"

Voices echoed, "To Darling Jane!"

Finally guests, many of them taking after-dinner chocolates, began leaving the tables.

Phoebe felt Lawrence's familiar touch on the small of her back. He stood beside her and pulled her to him.

"The dinner was delicious," he said under his breath, "but it should have been hot dogs." Phoebe smiled and pressed against him, she felt encouraged that he'd thought of their ferry ride.

The next minute, his eyes were on Jane, who was followed by other admirers. He edged around the crowd to catch up with her as she headed upstairs to the ballroom.

Setting her jaw, Phoebe pushed hard on the swinging kitchen door. But someone caught her arm.

She turned to Gilbert, who was wearing a tuxedo decorated with a large, spring green bowtie for the party. She had barely glimpsed him earlier when guests had surrounded him, congratulating him on Jane's portrait. Now he said, "I tried to catch your eye all through dinner."

She silently recalled the seating chart, his place at Jane's table. She stared into Gilbert's questioning eyes, wondering how to explain that she'd not glanced in his direction because she had not wanted to see his brother. She might never want to look at his brother again.

"Phoebe," Gilbert said, "I don't want to say the wrong thing but you said that night after the theater you might have someone in your life. You said we could talk—"

"Please, Gilbert, not right now. I'm so busy with this party . . . Forgive me," she said before leaving him to go into the kitchen.

"Oh, Miss Phoebe," Bessie said when Phoebe put her arms around her and held her close.

"Miss Phoebe!" Anita ran to Phoebe to be comforted too. Phoebe tightly hugged Anita, then Bessie again. The warmth of their bodies and the rush of this sudden new good feeling brought back memories of Gramma. As a little girl, Phoebe had run to her grandmother to be taken into her pillow-soft grasp.

Now giving comfort, Phoebe felt suddenly older, needed, comforted herself. Selmabelle may be famous for her At Home parties, Phoebe thought, but this is the first feeling of home for me.

But why should I feel at home? she asked silently. She was at work.

Phoebe burst into the dining room, where Gilbert waited. "I'm on my way to the ballroom," Phoebe said to him. "Selmabelle told me to take her place tonight."

If Selmabelle were still at the party, Phoebe thought, she'd be up there in the ballroom, seated at the opposite end of the dance floor from the orchestra, talking with guests, surveying the room as if it were a kingdom.

Phoebe and Gilbert hurried up one flight, peeked into the room where flower-decked trellises covered the walls and costumed guests danced and clapped their hands above their heads to "Everything's Coming Up Roses." As Phoebe entered, already dancing with the surprisingly agile Gilbert, she saw that Lawrence was not with Jane, but standing on the sidelines with his unsmiling father.

Phoebe glimpsed Lawrence's eyes following her and his brother. She felt a certain triumph that she and Gilbert danced so smoothly together.

"What's the earliest you want to leave?" Gilbert asked Phoebe just as the music changed to a tango. Hearing the beat, Phoebe at once glanced at Lawrence, wondering if he remembered their tango in his apartment. She imagined he'd suddenly swoop her into his arms, announcing to Gilbert that he and Phoebe always danced the tango together.

But at that moment Jane rushed to Lawrence and his father, then coyly pulled Lawrence into the tango. Phoebe guessed Jane had noticed Lawrence's eyes following his brother and Phoebe dancing. And what had the Grand One told Jane about Phoebe's visit to her house?

Phoebe reminded herself that she was here *only* because of her job. She said to Gilbert, "I have to go downstairs to congratulate Cognac on the dinner. I'm still on duty."

"I'll go with you. I'll take you home."

"Gilbert, I want to *walk* home. I need to walk."

"Sounds very good to me," Gilbert said.

Phoebe was aware she was on duty the next day too as she tiptoed down a green corridor at New York Hospital. Carrying office papers, she passed the nurses' station, then hesitated outside Selmabelle's room when she heard her deep voice: "Quit harping on it, Jane! There's something haywire in your sense of timing."

"If I were doing it, I'd fire her," came Jane's voice, rising above a whisper.

"Well, you're not doing it—don't wear me out. I *need* Phoebe now."

Phoebe tightened her hold on the papers. Entering the room, she saw Bessie adjusting pillows behind Selmabelle's back. "Bessie," Selmabelle said, "I need some cigarettes. Oh, God, I need to be pampered." A yellow bed jacket draped around her shoulders, Selmabelle sat awkwardly in the high hospital bed, raised at the head. Phoebe forced herself not to stare at her arm, encased in a hard white cast.

Already the room, like last night's party, displayed flowers everywhere, but here they were not unified into a garden scene, but exhibited in competing elaborate containers with florist cards identifying the senders. A nurse's aide, wheeling a cart containing pitchers of fruit juice, had followed Phoebe into the room. Selmabelle waved the aide away just as Henny Tibbold rushed in and kissed Selmabelle on the cheek.

Henny inspected her cast. "Are you going to have people autograph it?"

"Of course I'm not!"

"Sorry, darling."

"On top of everything else," Selmabelle said, "they're testing to see if I bruised my liver. Oh, Henny, I'll bet you never expected to see me like this." Selmabelle tried to sit up but let out a cry of pain. "God knows I didn't expect it. But I don't know *why* I didn't expect it!" Selmabelle glared at Jane, who pouted by the bedside as if being maligned for bringing Fetchy and his toys into her home.

Phoebe stepped toward the bed. "Selmabelle, I hope you'll—"

"Selmabelle," Henny interrupted, "do you remember when we played circus and I slipped on the bottom step of the children's slide?" Henny laughed. "I remember actually saying, 'Accidents are so accidental.'"

"Don't be so damned jolly," Selmabelle said.

"I thought laughing was supposed to be therapeutic," Henny said.

"Not with three cracked ribs—it kills me to laugh! And my damned elbow hurts—forget painkillers! I need to know what I'm doing. Oh, God, Henny, my broken funny bone probably seems hilarious to my friends."

"Don't say comical things, darling, if you don't want me to laugh."

As Henny and Jane left together, Selmabelle, with a dejected expression, said to Phoebe, "I feel isolated. Pain makes me isolated."

Phoebe said, "I'm sorry." In Kansas, she thought, we call the funny bone the crazy bone, and she remembered how painful it had been when she'd only hit her elbow, not broken it. She was about to say this to Selmabelle but noticing her sudden rigid expression, she decided that Selmabelle didn't want to discuss this further with her employee. Phoebe quickly sat down beside the bed, reviewed the office papers.

When Selmabelle's eyelids drooped, Phoebe stood up, "I'll take care of everything."

Selmabelle said, "Don't think you can take over." She turned her weary eyes toward the door. "Come in, Gilbert."

He leaned to kiss Selmabelle's cheek. "I found you," he said to her, then faced Phoebe with a smile. Greeting him quickly, Phoebe moved from the bedside so not to draw attention away from Selmabelle in her present mood.

Gilbert placed a gift package, which appeared to be a book, on the night table. "I hope this inspires you to get well fast."

"Everybody wants to inspire me." It sounded like a complaint.

"Did I say the wrong thing to her?" Gilbert asked Phoebe later as they walked out of the hospital together.

"Don't worry," Phoebe said. Rain was coming down and at the hospital entrance a crowd was growing around a doorman.

As arriving taxis deposited passengers, the doorman helped them, then held the taxi door open for new passengers. When one yellow taxi stopped at the entrance, the passenger who emerged from it was Lawrence. With his raincoat, he wore a shapeless felt hat and suddenly a smile. He grinned at Gilbert, then Phoebe. As he looked into her eyes, she sensed that he displayed more exuberant delight in running into them than he felt.

"Have you met my brother?" Gilbert said to Phoebe.

Phoebe nodded. Lawrence patted his briefcase. "I'm here to see Selmabelle briefly on business." He stepped toward the hospital door. "Great party," he said over his shoulder.

Phoebe wanted *not* to accept that he'd looked handsome even in that dowdy, goofy hat which he probably kept in his office for rainy days. She turned to look at him once more and found that he had glanced back too. Her face felt suddenly hot, despite the coolness the rain had brought. She rushed into the taxi and bumped her head on the door-frame. "Damn," she whispered, blinking, flinching from pain.

Chagrined, Phoebe smiled at Gilbert beside her in the cab. Yet her thoughts took her back to breakfast this morning, when she'd half-defended Lawrence, saying to Jill that, after all, the party had been in honor of Jane and given by her aunt. "He'd naturally pay attention to the guest of honor." She still tried to believe this argument herself.

Phoebe leaned forward when the cab stopped in front of a Chinese restaurant not far from Selmabelle's. She suddenly realized that Gilbert had suggested take-out food. The plan he had initiated during the taxi ride now registered: they would eat in his studio, where at last he'd show her the sketches he'd done on the train. Boosting himself out of the cab, Gilbert admitted he'd had this plan in mind for a long time.

In his studio Gilbert found plates while Phoebe, seated at the table, opened the food cartons, from which wafted the aroma of shrimp

and ginger. Gilbert settled his large body snugly into a worn upholstered chair, unlike the elegant chairs used in portraits at the front of
the studio. As they ate, Phoebe noticed that near their table, hanging
on the wall, were vividly colored papier-mâché masks.

Propped against a child's highchair was a guitar, making Phoebe
wonder if Gilbert and Gloria were parents and if he was a musician
as well as a painter, but she did not take time to ask for he was saying: "I didn't have lunch. It's probably a good thing after all I ate last
night. I've been thinking: you were awfully quiet when I walked you
home." When Phoebe delayed her answer, he said, "Phoebe, I just
want to understand you."

He left the table to open his metal flat file, which had wide shallow
drawers. From the bottom drawer he pulled out drawings and spread
them on an old paint-stained table. Phoebe recognized that they were
sketches of herself, mostly in profile, drawn on the train to New York.
She remembered how stiff her mouth had felt as she tried to control
her feelings of wanting to break down and sob with no restraints.

Suddenly while studying her own facial expressions in the sketches,
she had to hold herself back from ripping up the drawings. "We didn't
plan it," she heard Marcia say again. "We just found it happening to us."
Phoebe felt an overwhelming anger at Marcia and Niles. She picked up
another sketch to view it closely, but she was so afraid she would de-
stroy Gilbert's work that she set it down again. She became aware that
Gilbert had hold of her arm. "Phoebe, are you all right?"

She leaned on the table a moment longer. "I'm fine," she said and
began to move about the studio, rubbing her arms, pretending to
study the paintings.

"Phoebe," Gilbert said after a while. "I want to tell you something. I
hope it's all right to say this: I like to study you—your facial expressions.
I think I told you I've always been fascinated by faces and you have so
many moods. I'd like to do all kinds of studies of you. And I'm interested in figures in movement—I like to watch you walk."

"Oh?" Phoebe remembered Lawrence, in a flattering appraisal, had said that one of the first things he'd noticed about her was the "wonderful way" she walked. Only later she'd realized that on their first meeting, she'd still been limping from her fall in the aftermath of Ben's and Ninon's attempts at seduction. Now once again Phoebe found herself questioning Lawrence's sincerity. But maybe he meant a little later—even Niles used to compliment her on her walk.

Phoebe realized Gilbert was still speaking: "Most of all, Phoebe, I want to paint your portrait." She began to tour the studio again, considering his idea, which surprised her. When he'd first suggested it on the train, she hadn't expected it to happen. Now she thought that in a new portrait her expression would have to be different than in the drawings. She stopped pacing and looked at Gilbert, who seemed anxious for her answer. She told herself that her own commitment and focus in life now had to be on *right now* and on whatever she would do *from now on*. "All right. Yes, Gilbert, thank you!"

Eighteen

PHOEBE PHONED GILBERT THE NEXT MORNING to describe her wardrobe, as well as Jill's, so they could choose what she should wear for the portrait. Gilbert asked if she had a dress in a color that would echo the auburn highlights in her hair.

At once Phoebe visualized the apricot chiffon dress she had worn on New Year's Eve. Niles's dark suit of that night had become his death suit. She wished this had not come into her thoughts. But New Year's Eve was *always* with her—it stayed below the surface, then sprang up to choke the breath out of her.

Maybe, she thought now, it *would* help if she wore the dress for the portrait. But as soon as the idea emerged, she felt herself cringing away from it.

"I'll do this," Phoebe said into the phone to Gilbert, who was still talking about her auburn hair, her large dark eyes. "I'll bring some dresses with me tonight to the studio."

After she hung up the phone, it rang at once. She stared at it, letting it ring before she finally answered. Lawrence's deep melodious voice said into her ear, "I was thinking of someone named Phoebe."

"Were you? I guess I'm surprised to hear from you."

"We run into each other in the most interesting places," Lawrence said, his voice taking on its teasing tone. He remarked on his surprise in seeing her lately in the company of his brother. When she did not com-

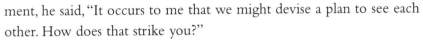

ment, he said, "It occurs to me that we might devise a plan to see each other. How does that strike you?"

"It has possibilities," said Phoebe, attempting to slide into his banter.

"Tonight?" he said.

Phoebe hesitated. "Tomorrow night?"

"Tonight is out?" he asked.

"Yes."

"I'll give you a call," he said brusquely.

That night as she carried her suitcase of dresses to Gilbert's studio, Phoebe still replayed in her mind Lawrence's voice of dismissal. She pulled her load off the elevator and rang the bell. She heard the twist of the doorknob immediately, as if Gilbert had been by the door.

He picked up her suitcase, then ushered her into the huge, now familiar room.

"My brother's here," Gilbert said at the moment Phoebe caught sight of Lawrence. Wearing a white cotton sweater, Lawrence stood with his hands in the pockets of his dark trousers, and he was smiling at her.

Was he as surprised to see her, as she was to see him? His eyes continued to watch her as they exchanged greetings. Had he just come in or was he about to leave? He had to have seen Gilbert take the suitcase from her. She was tempted to explain it but that would be awkward.

Lawrence had his hand on the doorknob when he said to Gilbert, "I don't want to interfere with your work." Had he emphasized the word "work" to be snide? No, Phoebe answered herself: Lawrence likes to flatter people, bring out grateful smiles.

With the brothers standing next to each other, saying good-bye, Phoebe witnessed how large Gilbert was. Gilbert was a giant, fully half a head taller than his brother. She remembered Lawrence's description of what it had been like to have a talented older brother, to have followed him in school where Gilbert carried off the prizes.

Gilbert closed the door after Lawrence, then took Phoebe's suitcase to the center of the studio and placed it flat on the large old table. As Phoebe opened it, she ventured, "I hope I didn't interrupt your appointment with your brother."

"It wasn't an appointment. I'm surprised he just dropped in," Gilbert said, "if that's what he did."

Phoebe pulled out the sapphire blue dress. "What did he say?"

"He said he was driving by the studio and happened to see the lights. But that doesn't hang together."

"No?" said Phoebe, feeling her way. "I didn't think New Yorkers dropped by—"

"I know his habits—he had something on his mind. There's always something with him . . ." While talking, Gilbert looked at one dress, then another, which Phoebe held for his inspection, then draped over a chair.

But she left the apricot chiffon from New Year's Eve at the bottom of the suitcase.

Gilbert said, "Lawrence called on the intercom from downstairs to see if I had a client with me at the moment. At least he did that."

"And then he came up," Phoebe said, attempting a casual tone while sweeping Jill's bright pink stole around herself to show Gilbert the color. She recalled wearing this to Lawrence's apartment, his removing it from her shoulders.

Gilbert frowned as if still puzzled by his brother's visit. "He wasn't here long."

"I'm sorry I interrupted."

"You didn't interrupt, I had this planned with you. If he had something on his mind, he'll tell me. Or *maybe* he will—we don't confide much."

"I'd think you would, being brothers."

"There's plenty of reasons why we don't." While talking, Gilbert held a dress against her face, then her hair. "I'd prefer to paint you in natural light," he said, "but I know you're busy with Selmabelle in her condition. We'll have to work at night."

"You're busy too."

"I'll take time for this." He stepped back to view Phoebe. "This will be a major work, a full-length portrait—I've wanted to do this for a long time. Which is a departure for me. I usually like big volup-tuous curves—Renoir's women. He's not my favorite painter but I like big curves. For me, the ideal model is not just fat, but a woman who can strike great positions."

"Oh," said Phoebe, remembering Mother Bertha's criticism: "You need more meat on your bones." Suddenly Phoebe said, "Gilbert, I'm thinking: you painted Jane. She's not fat, she doesn't have such big curves as all that."

"That was a commission. My brother commissioned it."

"Your brother!"

"Why? You think I shouldn't do business with my brother?"

"No, I didn't mean anything," said Phoebe, keeping her eyes away from Gilbert.

"I gave him a special price, a *very* special price. He's always looking for a deal."

"Is he?" Phoebe said.

"He takes after Granddad and Dad in that. Yeah, he still wants to please Dad. All his life he's tried to win him over. Oddly enough, Dad likes *me*—though he doesn't like me being a painter. It's *Mother* who loves Lawrence. That's how our family's divided. When we were kids, I didn't knock myself out to impress Dad—Lawrence did. And he's still doing it. It's strange, even now I seem to do all right with Dad without trying a whole lot."

"That's interesting," Phoebe said, urging him on.

"I married a woman with money," Gilbert said, "or at least she'll have money of her own someday, unless her sister gets it all."

Phoebe pretended to be only mildly interested. "You mean Jane will get it all?"

"Yeah. Dad's always preached to both of us to marry into a substantial family. But I married Gloria in spite of the money. Yet now that the marriage hasn't worked out, Mother's the one who criticizes me. If it had been Lawrence whose marriage had ended—well, she sees Lawrence in a different way than she sees me. I'm not sure Mother wants any other woman to have Lawrence. She puts on a good show, maybe for the sake of Dad. Maybe she thinks she's supposed to."

"Supposed to?"

"All I know is that Mother dotes on him. All women love Lawrence. All women have *always* loved Lawrence."

"Really?"

"You seem surprised, Phoebe. Why? Do you find Lawrence unattractive?"

"Oh, no." Phoebe groped for something to say: "I was wondering about your grandmother."

"You mean how she feels about Lawrence? I doubt if any woman in the family wants to let him go. It's fascinating." Gilbert said. 'The more the women in the family worry about Lawrence leaving them, the more they push him to marry the girl in question. Maybe because that way Lawrence backs off—he looks around for other females on the horizon. Of course, Mother's always there to spoil him—that's what Dad says. I think that's part of it: Dad gets his nose out of joint. And then Lawrence tries harder to please him. Maybe Lawrence even sees it as a problem having so many women in love with him. I'm sure all guys would love to have his problem."

"I guess they would," Phoebe said.

"But he's always having to squirm out of something. By this time it's practically a way of life. I watch him flatter the hell out of somebody. If people try to get him to do something he doesn't want to do, that's when he'll *really* flatter them. Or maybe if he feels guilty about something—well, I'm not sure about guilt."

Gilbert looked again through the dresses now draped over the chair. "You asked about the commission for Jane's portrait. There's an example: my hunch is that Lawrence wanted to flatter Jane. Me too, for that matter. Flattery is a way to keep things on an even keel. If he rocks the boat too much or gets himself in too deep . . ."

"That's interesting," Phoebe said. Gilbert walked toward her, then stepped back to look at her. "I find *you* interesting, Phoebe. There's something about you that's different from other women I've known. I thought that on the train. I sensed something."

"I wasn't even sure you liked me. You didn't encourage me about a job. *Edward* did."

"Edward's in England most of the time, he may not be as aware. . . . Phoebe, you were coming to New York for a job. I wanted to protect you."

"I don't think I need protecting, but thank you, that's nice of you, Gilbert." She picked up the sapphire blue dress. "I thought this would be the choice," she said, hoping to distract Gilbert, who was now lifting the apricot chiffon dress from the suitcase.

He held it against her hair. "*This* is what I was talking about on the phone. No! I don't want you to look like that! There's *no question.*" With a smile, he handed her the dress. "*This* is the one."

Holding it, looking down at it, Phoebe suddenly wanted to wad it up and throw it. Her impulse was to aim it at Gilbert, who still insisted this was the right choice. She felt to wear the New Year's Eve dress for the portrait—a still, unmoving picture—would trap her forever in that night.

Yet earlier, she had thought it would be a step forward to wear the dress. As she went into the bathroom to change, she told herself: All it takes is courage. What, in reality, could possibly happen because she was wearing the dress?

She readied the dress to slip on. She pulled it down over her head, her breasts, her hips. A feeling of pressure rose within her throat. As she zipped up the apricot chiffon, she had an overwhelming nausea. She took deep breaths. Her wet eyes closed, she asked herself why she had brought this dress tonight. Gilbert would never have known it existed if she'd left it in the apartment.

Shaking, she was sick.

At last, she washed and splashed cold water on her face, then pulled off the dress, dropping it on the floor. Standing in her bra and panties, she placed her hands on the basin, pondered what to do. She had agreed to the portrait. Finally she combed back her long hair. Earlier tonight Gilbert had brushed her hair back with his hand, saying this made her dark eyes even more prominent; he wanted that for the portrait.

Gilbert was different from his brother, Phoebe thought. Gilbert always made clear his *preferences*. He showed an intense sincerity and commitment to whatever inspired him that was close to alarming at times. His dedication verged on stubbornness, and when it concerned her, it forced him to hold on, to insist on being persuasive.

As she leaned against the wall, she noticed, on a hanger on the back of the door, a large robe, as ornate as a Persian dressing gown. She lifted the clear lightweight plastic covering the robe. She touched the heavy silk and its cords of gold and tried to visualize Gilbert wrapped in it. She was surprised to see something so elegant hanging here, just a door's thickness away from paint and turpentine.

Possibly the robe was just back from the cleaners or perhaps Gilbert sometimes bathed here before going down to his apartment, which he had told her was on the floor below. She tried to imagine what his apartment might be like—magnificent, like this robe? She'd never before thought of Gilbert in terms of elegance, except when considering his mother's complaint that he was about as "elegant as a plumber" with his paint-stained fingernails. "Down to earth," Phoebe's grandmother would have said. More a plumber than a potentate wrapped in a silk robe.

Phoebe ran her fingertips over the fabric, rough in places because of the gold embroidery. She found herself removing the heavy robe from its hanger, inserting her arms into the voluminous sleeves. When she pulled the great mass around her slender body, it was huge and weighed her down as she walked out of the bathroom wearing it. It trailed behind her. She struggled to pick up its folds so not to drag its hem through any dust, maybe even paint, from the studio floor.

She continued on, moving toward Gilbert. Suddenly she felt like a child about to please someone with a surprise.

Now wearing a blue painter's smock, Gilbert had his back to her as he adjusted lights at the front of the studio. Phoebe, close to him, held up the skirt of the robe as she stepped onto the platform and settled herself in the high-backed brocaded chair he had placed there.

She realized at once that he had stopped moving and stared at her. Within minutes, Gilbert, while not speaking, moved the couch from the side of the studio onto the platform. "If you want to use that dressing gown," he said finally, "take it off and lie down on top of it— *that* would make a picture."

"Can't you paint me wearing it?"

"No, you're lost in it. What's wrong? You look pale. Why aren't you wearing the dress?" Gilbert asked her to lie down on the sofa. She felt the weight of the robe and she trembled as she stepped across the platform, but instead of stretching out on the couch, she sat down on it. It appeared to be an antique sofa; its back curved gracefully to the rolled arms of beige satin. She spread the skirt of the robe on both sides of her.

He leaned to help her. "You sure you're all right? Want to slip out of the robe?"

Phoebe tried to be subtle as she hunched away from him. "When you say to take off the robe and lie down *on top* of it . . . I didn't plan that."

"I didn't plan it either," Gilbert said, "but I like it."

Stalling, Phoebe said, "Gilbert, I'd like to see examples of your favorite models."

He frowned as if impatient to get on with his work. "Phoebe, are you getting cold feet? If you feel like it, come on, I'll show you."

"If I walk around in this robe, it's liable to get paint on . . ."

"Here." Gilbert pulled off his painter's smock, handed it to her. She stayed seated on the couch while he strode to the back of the studio, then held up a large painting to show her. Even from this distance, she could see that it portrayed a side view of a stout nude, her back straight, her head uplifted triumphantly.

When he turned away, Phoebe removed an arm from the sleeve of the robe. Her arm had never felt so bare. She guessed that he was placing sketches of nudes on the table. She imagined Lawrence's jealous reaction if she posed nude for his brother. She felt confused now by thoughts of Lawrence. She tried to force her attention back to the robe. She followed the rough gold thread on the fabric. She called out to Gilbert, "Is this robe yours? It's beautiful."

"My mother's."

"Your *mother's*? Oh, I'm sorry," Phoebe remembered Mrs. Bradley, Selmabelle's close friend, the plump bird woman who had talked of Jane as if she might be the bride for her son Lawrence.

Now wearing Gilbert's painter's smock, Phoebe joined him at the table. She couldn't resist saying, "Please don't tell your mother I had on her robe."

"I was going to give it to her as a birthday present after I had it shortened. You may know, she's not very tall."

Phoebe said lightly, "Then we *can't* use it for the painting, she'd recognize it."

"I don't plan to give it to her now."

"Why?"

"I want *you* to have it after we're finished."

"Oh, no!"

"Here's something else." Gilbert lifted a large framed picture from a storage rack, held it to show Phoebe: a montage of six studies of nude pregnant women lying on their backs, some with their hands over their rounded stomachs. "Pregnant women are beautiful," he said. "Look at those curves. You'd be beautiful, Phoebe."

She remembered that during her pregnancy, Niles had patted her tummy and said, "Junior's in there." Then she had miscarried and they had learned it was a girl they had lost. She wondered now what Niles would have said to Marcia as she grew larger. Suddenly Phoebe tried to stop the gnawing questions. She hated it the way unwanted thoughts continued to surface in her mind.

She tried to keep her mind on the present as Gilbert pulled from a cabinet some different drawings of nudes and arranged them on the table. These models did not look pregnant to Phoebe, but because they were far from slender, none had an especially flat stomach. Now Gilbert talked in the mode of a professor giving a lecture, saying what he had been trying to achieve in each composition. He spoke of "physical mass," "attitudes," and "expressiveness of the body."

One model, lying on her side facing the viewer, had large eyes, a puffy cloud of curly hair, and thick lips and thighs. Phoebe said, "What about this one?"

Gilbert finally answered: "That's Gloria."

"Oh," Phoebe said and realized her voice had sounded as surprised as she felt. Somehow she'd expected Gloria to look more like Jane. Phoebe tried to find a family resemblance, then found herself concentrating on Gloria's breasts, remembering Selmabelle's outraged: "Bouncing breasts!" She imagined Gloria seated at the organ "stark naked." Nudity as an artist's model is within bounds, but nudity as a musician is considered excessive, Phoebe thought.

"Gloria's not pregnant in any of these. That's because she didn't want children." Gilbert's face was gloomy as he said of the drawings: "I have dozens more of Gloria. And I'm keeping every one of them. Now we're getting close to something close to me."

"I'm sorry," Phoebe said.

"No, I'd like to talk about it."

"No, please don't! Let's wait!"

Gilbert was frowning.

Phoebe said, "Gilbert, I don't want either one of us saying things we might regret later on."

"I *want* to say this, Phoebe. I'm keeping these drawings because they remind me *never* again to fall in love with a woman on the rebound. I married Gloria when she was on the rebound. From Lawrence."

Phoebe nodded, trying to look as if a mention of Lawrence did not affect her personally. Gilbert was still talking, no longer lecturing. He pointed to another drawing of Gloria, appearing belligerent, as she stood facing the viewer, her solid naked legs apart, hands on her hips. Gilbert had learned that at the time she'd posed for this, even though she was married to him, she was still calling Lawrence.

Lawrence, Lawrence, Lawrence! Phoebe found it hard to listen. She mumbled, "Excuse me," rushed back to the bathroom to dress in the clothes she had worn to the studio. She stared at the apricot chiffon on the floor, finally grabbed it, and, taking it with her, returned to the studio and threw it into the suitcase, piling other dresses on top of it.

Gilbert frowned. "Why are you doing this?"

"Gilbert, I told you there might be someone in my life. It's Lawrence."

Gilbert stared at her, then began to stride across the studio. "And you just didn't bother to tell me?" He returned to her. "You let me go on talking. *That* must have been entertaining!"

"Remember I was reluctant—"

"You had plenty of chances." Gilbert paced again. "You could have told me. Both of you could have spoken out. For your information, I don't make a habit of baring my soul. I was brought up not to talk outside the family. But I wanted to know you, I wanted you to know me—"

"I don't want things to be this way," Phoebe said.

"How do you want them to be?"

"Peaceful."

"Peaceful?"

Phoebe looked directly at Gilbert. "There's been a lot of things in my life," she said. "I didn't want to stir up trouble. I'll tell you this much: I came to New York to get my life in order."

"And you hooked up with my brother?"

"Don't make fun of me, Gilbert! You don't know everything."

"I'm not making fun of you," he said, putting an arm around her.

"You don't know how your brother feels."

"I just know his history." Gilbert embraced her, holding her close. "I don't want you to get hurt. I don't think you know how I feel."

She pulled away. He gave her a stricken look. She grabbed up the suitcase, which felt heavier as she headed for the door. "I didn't start trouble between you two." Phoebe did not wait for the elevator but clattered down the four flights of stairs.

Not finding a cab, she heaved her suitcase onto the uptown bus and, with shoulders aching, leaned forward in the seat. She reviewed Gilbert's saying that he'd tried to protect her on the train by *not* recommending a job with Selmabelle. Well, he'd been *wrong* in *that* judgment. I want this job, she thought, I *need* this job. So that showed his views of people and situations weren't always perfect, even if he had said that one reason he'd wanted to become a portrait painter was that he liked to stare at people and study them, and, as an artist, he could get away with it. He'd said, "I've found that when people sit for me, they somehow have a tendency to bare their souls as though I'm a psychologist." He could still be wrong about Lawrence. She didn't doubt he had studied Lawrence, but, she bet, unfairly. Both brothers had told her they'd been rivals all their lives—jealousy and prejudice had to have been involved.

Gilbert hadn't even guessed why Lawrence had been to his studio tonight. She'd been encouraged, experienced a touch of achievement, seeing Lawrence there—or had she herself misinterpreted that? Why was she defending him so much?

Yet, she could have told Gilbert that all her life she too had done her own share of trying to understand people. And in New York, especially with her determination to keep her job, she'd closely watched people in Selmabelle's world. Come to think of it, even though Gilbert had been born *within* Selmabelle's world, he seemed somehow, an *outsider*. Like me, Phoebe thought. No, we're very different, she corrected herself as she carried the suitcase into the apartment.

Jill, reading in bed, greeted Phoebe: "Your mother-in-law phoned."

Phoebe, setting down her suitcase, said, "I can't bear to call her back tonight."

Nineteen

It was early the next morning, before work, when Phoebe forced herself to phone.

Mother Bertha commented, "You must have been out late last night."

Phoebe hesitated. "How are you, Mother Bertha?"

"I can't be alone on my boy's birthday. I suppose you won't come to Glennerville—"

"Oh, I *can't* do that," Phoebe said. "I'm sorry, I'm very sorry."

"I've never been on a plane before but my boy would want me to be brave."

"You mean—do you mean you're thinking of coming to New York?"

"Well," Mother Bertha said, "you don't need to sound so surprised."

Phoebe still felt surprised a few nights later as she searched faces of arriving passengers at LaGuardia Airport. Mother Bertha was the last one from her flight to come through the arrival gate. She came out slowly, looking about shyly, as if she were a child in an old woman's stout body. Dressed in a short-sleeved black dress, she wore a hat that came down over her forehead; her gray eyes peered out.

Phoebe rushed toward her. Embracing her, leaning to accommodate her shorter stature, Phoebe found her fat arms hot and damp— apparently from stress as the early-summer night was cool. Mother

Bertha, looking worried, fumbled in her handbag. "I can't find the stub for my suitcase."

"Maybe it's stapled to the envelope—your airline envelope your ticket came in?"

"Oh, I remember now."

As they waited at the luggage claim, Phoebe sensed that her mother-in-law was so anxious she'd become hysterical if something had happened to her suitcase. When Phoebe saw the familiar gray bag come bouncing out and begin its round on the carousel, she rushed to grab it. Mother Bertha called after her in an alarmed voice: "Phoebe!"

"I'm just getting your suitcase."

On the way to the city in the speeding taxi, Mother Bertha sat on the edge of the seat, glancing about, peering at the traffic. She settled back, then quickly sat forward again. Phoebe attempted to calm her and, nearer the city, pointed out skyscrapers on the lighted skyline.

In the apartment her mother-in-law, seated at the low round table, sipped bedtime milk while Phoebe tried to make her feel welcome. When Jill came in and joined them, Mother Bertha watched her as if she were an intruder. Jill, seated on the edge of her chair as if ready to spring up, smiled and told Mother Bertha that she was from the Midwest too. "From Omaha. Have you been there?"

"No, I don't have any reason to go to Omaha." Mother Bertha kept her eyes on Jill, who smiled encouragingly as they spoke of the older woman's plane flight. Jill assured her that she would be used to flying the next time, on her flight back.

"I'll never get used to it. People keep saying I'll get used to things." Finally Mother Bertha said, "I'm tired."

"Let's fix her bed," Jill said to Phoebe.

"Yes," Mother Bertha said as if she liked to be taken care of in the solicitous way Jill's sweet voice implied.

While Mother Bertha changed into her nightgown in the bathroom, Phoebe and Jill pulled out Jill's sofa bed and arranged it for sleeping. Phoebe had rented an extra rollaway bed for the visit, but Jill had insisted that she herself would sleep on it, leaving the better bed for the older woman.

Now Mother Bertha lumbered out of the bathroom with rollers in her dyed brown hair. She wore moccasins and her flimsy pink robe, which revealed the outlines of her stocky body. She climbed into Jill's sofa bed and sighed when she leaned into the pillows.

The next morning as Phoebe was about to leave for her office, Mother Bertha insisted that she couldn't stay alone.

"I gave you a list," Phoebe said, "of places to visit—"

"I don't want to go by myself. Can't I just walk with you and wait outside?"

"Outside Selmabelle's? You mean wait on the sidewalk? Don't you want to at least see one of the places I put on the list for you?"

Mother Bertha looked away from Phoebe.

"Mother Bertha, you know I want you to have a wonderful visit but remember I told you: Selmabelle's just out of the hospital. I can't take time off. But you can call me every once in while at my office so you won't get lonesome."

Walking down Lexington, Mother Bertha said above the traffic noise, "I notice you didn't offer to introduce me to Selmabelle Flaunton."

"I didn't know you especially wanted to meet her."

"It's not every day I get to meet somebody famous."

"I guess not," said Phoebe, thinking of Glennerville.

Wilbur arrived as Phoebe and her mother-in-law continued their conversation in front of Selmabelle's house. When introduced, Wilbur shook Mother Bertha's hand and held it, peering at her through his glasses. "This is a real pleasure, ma'am." He used his key to open the front door instead of ringing for the maid. "Aren't y'all coming inside?"

"Phoebe says I can't," Mother Bertha said.

"Can't come in?" Wilbur said.

"I explained to her this is Selmabelle's first day back," Phoebe said. "I offered to bring her here for a short visit on Monday instead."

"Aren't you going to show her our office?" Wilbur asked as Mother Bertha stepped into the entranceway; she gazed up at the grand staircase they were about to ascend. She touched the smooth marble wall. "She has the whole house?"

Wilbur, smiling, assured her that Selmabelle had the whole house. He peered at Phoebe through his glasses. "I've already been in the office this morning," he said in his earlier-than-thou tone. "I just dashed out for a second. Oh, Red-Jack Ordall called up."

Mother Bertha's gray eyes widened. "Red-Jack?"

Wilbur watched Mother Bertha's face as if he smelled gossip. "I got to meet Red-Jack," he told her, "that time when he was in New York."

Mother Bertha turned to Phoebe. "You didn't tell me Red-Jack was in New York."

"She keeps things from you too?" Wilbur said as he escorted Niles's mother along the corridor leading to the offices, with Phoebe following. Wilbur turned to look back at Phoebe with a grin. "He left quite a message."

Mother Bertha touched his arm. "What kind of a message?"

"Let's talk about it later," Phoebe said.

"You always want to wait till later," her mother-in-law said.

Wilbur smiled. "You've noticed that too?"

Improvising, Phoebe rattled off information about the paintings in the corridor and decorations in the house. Reaching the office, Phoebe pulled a chair next to her desk so that Mother Bertha could sit down.

Selmabelle, wearing yellow lounging pajamas, her arm in a cast, appeared in the doorway Phoebe realized Mother Bertha had her back to Selmabelle so she was unaware of her presence. Hurrying to join Selmabelle in the hallway, Phoebe asked in a soft voice, "How are you feeling?"

Selmabelle demanded, "Who is that woman?"

"A fan of yours, Selmabelle. She's thrilled to be in your house—"

"Who is she?"

"My mother-in-law."

Phoebe followed Selmabelle back into the office where Mother Bertha, still seated in the chair, was leaning over untying the laces of her black oxfords. She looked up, appearing startled when she saw Selmabelle watching her.

"Oh, excuse me." Mother Bertha sounded flustered. "Sometimes I do this—but I don't take my shoes clear off cause my feet swell up." Selmabelle stepped closer to her and Mother Bertha said, "I'll tie my shoes right up."

"Not on my account," Selmabelle said. "Please."

Phoebe, surprised by Selmabelle's amiability, introduced the two women.

"I don't usually act this way," Mother Bertha said. "Untying my shoes. But I've done a lot of walking this morning—"

"I hope you're enjoying yourself," said Selmabelle, settling into a chair next to Mother Bertha.

"My boss told me I'd do a lot of walking in New York and just to grin and bear it. He came here to New York and about walked his feet off."

Selmabelle looked at Phoebe. "Did you tell her about my feet?"

"No," said Phoebe. "No, I didn't."

"I don't like it broadcast," Selmabelle said to Mother Bertha, "but you're a fellow sufferer: I can tell you."

Mother Bertha frowned. "You have foot trouble, too?"

"High arches!" Selmabelle spoke indignantly as if they were intolerable. She lifted the pantlegs of her lounging pajamas to reveal orthopedic shoes. "People talk about flat feet, but what causes real misery are high arches. I have to have special shoe supports."

"I use moleskin," said Mother Bertha, "on the balls of my feet."

"If I did much walking, I'd *live* in my chiropodist's office," Selmabelle said.

"Foot trouble affects every step you take, your whole life, Mrs. Flaunton."

"Selmabelle. Everyone calls me Selmabelle."

"People call me Bertha. Phoebe says Mother Bertha. I was Bertha May Niles before I married. I named my son for my maiden name."

"I've never had children," Selmabelle said.

"That's too bad," Mother Bertha sympathized.

"No, it's not," said Selmabelle.

"But you have nieces, I heard you mention them once. I watched your TV program and listened to you on the radio. You had my favorite show."

"Mine too."

"Would you mind, could I get your autograph?"

Selmabelle looked up at Phoebe, who moved a sheet of paper on the desk and held it while Selmabelle scrawled her name.

"Thanks a whole lot. I guess you're taking it easy."

"I can hardly do that. Now if you'll excuse me, Mrs. Stanhope," Selmabelle said, "Phoebe and I have work to do."

"I saw your arm was in a sling but I didn't want to say anything."

"That was thoughtful of you."

"If you ever get out to Kansas, I hope you'll come to Glennerville. I don't have a big house like this, but I have a spare room."

"Thank you, I'll keep that in mind."

Mother Bertha turned to Wilbur. "I'm glad to meet you too. You never did say what Red-Jack's message was."

"More an announcement, I guess you'd say." Wilbur faced Phoebe. "You'll want to buy a baby present."

Phoebe, standing by Mother Bertha's chair, placed a hand on her shoulder.

"Buy pink," Wilbur added, "it's a girl."

"Who had a girl?" Mother Bertha said. "Did *Marcia* have a baby?"

Wilbur nodded and Mother Bertha looked up accusingly to Phoebe:

"You didn't tell me she was expecting—you knew I'd want to know that."

Selmabelle took a deep breath. "Phoebe, we have work! Mrs. Stanhope, *I* don't have spare *time*! You *will* excuse us!"

Mother Bertha stood up, looking terrified. "Which way do I go?"

Phoebe stepped toward her mother-in-law but Selmabelle said, "You show her, Wilbur."

As if now realizing she might lose a worshipful fan, Selmabelle called after her, "You caught us at a bad time, Mrs. Stanhope. Wilbur, I need you back here right away."

Selmabelle glared at Phoebe. Using her good arm, she braced herself on Phoebe's desk. "How could you bring her here and on my first day back? Come in to my office!"

Phoebe was torn between following Selmabelle's orders and running after Mother Bertha and Wilbur. At the same time the phone on her desk was ringing. She grabbed the phone, and hearing Gilbert's voice, she said, "I'll call you back."

Phoebe peered down the corridor. Not seeing Mother Bertha, she hurried into Selmabelle's office where she had trouble keeping her mind on Selmabelle's instructions for Sir Chatham's "goodwill tour of America." Even while worrying about her mother-in- law, Phoebe noticed that the circles under Selmabelle's eyes were as dark as her mood.

"I planned to travel with you and Sir Chatham at the start of the tour," Selmabelle said. "But the doctor warned me against it. You'll have to do it yourself, be his sole escort for the whole thing. And remember *every* minute: the contract with the castles' association is up for renewal—do you hear me? It *must* be a triumphant tour!"

Released from Selmabelle's office, Phoebe rushed to the front of the house but could not spot Mother Bertha standing on the sidewalk. Returning to the office, Phoebe asked Wilbur, "What'd she say? Where was she going?"

"She didn't say where she was going—she was just crying a blue streak, rattling away about you losing your baby—her 'only chance for a grandbaby.'" He waited as if expecting Phoebe to explain.

"I guess Mother Bertha talked to you," she said vaguely. "By the way, when you talked to Red-Jack, he didn't happen to mention what they named the baby, did he?"

Wilbur smiled. "Why? Did you think they named her Phoebe?"

"No." She felt as if her face were enlarging with blood. "No, I didn't think that."

"Well, you sound mighty certain. How come you're so sure?"

"I just didn't think it would happen." Phoebe turned away from him, hurried to check the front sidewalk again, then phoned Jill: "I forgot to give Mother Bertha keys for the apartment."

"You mentioned it to me," Jill said, "but we had so many things going on."

"Something might happen to her—"

"She's so scared of everything in New York, that'll probably protect her."

Phoebe tried to rush with her work so that she could go home at lunch time to see if she might be standing in front of that building. As Phoebe worked on Sir Chatham's itinerary, her desk phone rang. A female voice advised: "A woman here says you work for Selmabelle Flaunton. She showed me an autograph . . ."

Phoebe closed her eyes and said into the phone. "Let me talk to her."

Phoebe heard: "They say I can't stay here."

"Where are you, Mother Bertha?"

"At the phone, down the hall from the babies."

"What babies? Where are you, Mother Bertha?"

"Here—the nurse says she'd talk to you."

Told that Mother Bertha was at nearby Cabrini Hospital, Phoebe rushed out of the office and found her mother-in-law slumped in a chair in a hospital corridor. "Mother Bertha!" Phoebe hugged her. "Come on, I'll get us a taxi." Phoebe took her to the apartment, fixed her a sandwich, and made her promise to rest on Jill's couch until she returned home after work.

"You sure you'll come back?" Mother Bertha called to Phoebe, going out the door.

"I'll be back," Phoebe said.

That night at dinner in the apartment, Mother Bertha finished her dessert of custard pie, then stared at Jill, across the table. "I don't suppose you know Marcia."

"Marcia Ordall?" Phoebe said in a puzzled voice. "I'm not quite sure why you think she'd know Marcia."

"You said Red-Jack had been in New York."

"But Marcia wasn't with him."

Mother Bertha placed a fist on the table. "I thought there was something funny about that trip!"

Phoebe, holding her breath, turned from her mother-in-law to Jill, who frowned as if confused by the conversation.

"You know me," Mother Bertha said. "I believe in speaking my mind. You said Marcia had been sick for a long time—I'm thinking now it's no wonder."

Phoebe answered, "I haven't said much about Marcia—"

"I'm not sure if you've mentioned her," said Jill, looking down as if embarrassed.

"Did you mention Red-Jack?" Mother Bertha said to Phoebe. "Or my son?"

Phoebe shot up from the table and, removing the dishes, took them to the sink.

"I guess you're still tired from traveling," Jill said to Mother Bertha.

"I don't want to go anywhere tonight," Mother Bertha said.

Phoebe picked up the rest of the dishes from the table and noticed that Mother Bertha smiled at Jill as if she liked her attention. Mother Bertha went into the bathroom to change into her nightgown.

When Mother Bertha returned to lie down on Jill's couch, which had been made ready for sleeping, Phoebe said, "Jill and I decided we might go out for a little while."

"You go on," Mother Bertha said.

Riding down in the elevator, Jill turned to Phoebe, "I hope I said the right thing, I mean about Marcia."

Phoebe hugged her. "You did. Thank you."

"Well, it's a miracle since I'm not sure who she is."

Walking out of the building, Phoebe said, "I'm sorry Mother Bertha's so difficult. But I can tell she likes you."

"After she got used to me," Jill said.

Under the street lamps, they sauntered up Lexington Avenue, where yellow cabs speeded by. They both admitted they were not in the mood for a movie.

In the cocktail lounge of the Tuscany Hotel, when the waiter poured beer into their glasses, the smell reminded Phoebe of New Year's Eve. She tried to force herself to drink, then finally set down the glass. "Jill," Phoebe said, leaning toward her over the table, "I want to tell you something—I've wanted to tell you for a long time."

"I thought there was something," Jill said.

Phoebe started to describe the snowstorm on New Year's Eve. She stopped speaking. Then she forced her voice: "I was so upset, I must have just ignored the blizzard. I absolutely insisted that he 'go on . . . go on, if you're going.' He drove off . . ." Phoebe gasped. "The next thing I knew he was dead."

Jill came around the table and hugged her.

"I couldn't believe it," Phoebe said. "I couldn't get it into my head that it was too late. And then Mother Bertha came the next day . . ."

"Does she know?" Jill returned to her seat and leaned across the table toward Phoebe. "I mean how much does she know?"

Phoebe whispered, "Nothing beyond that she's lost her son."

Jill's now very serious eyes looked into Phoebe's.

"When I tried to explain about New Year's Eve," Phoebe said, "she got so upset, I was afraid she'd have a heart attack—literally. I used the word *divorce* and she said I was dishonoring her son. She keeps on asking me questions. No matter what I say, she gets frantic and accuses me. I try so damned hard but I really think she hates me sometimes. But she hasn't got anybody else. Sometimes she makes me absolutely *furious* but, even so, I don't have the heart. I resent her but I feel sorry for her, I know she's suffering. I don't dare let her know the whole story. She absolutely idealized Niles, she's very religious, to her even just the *thought* of a *divorce* in the family is too much. Niles used to say: 'She's from the old school.' It seems incredible that she should hang on to that belief at this point, but maybe she feels she has to hang on to something." Phoebe looked up at Jill, then bowed her head again. "I think about her losing her only child."

Jill took Phoebe's hands into her own.

"When I *hint* about something," Phoebe said, "she talks about her heart condition—that scares me. I don't want to be responsible for something else happening. But when I try to change the subject, I can tell she thinks I'm holding back—just as you could tell . . . Jill, the accident may not have been an accident. Marcia told her husband that Niles may have deliberately . . ." Phoebe, leaning, almost touched her forehead to the table. She could feel Jill's hand atop her head. "I didn't tell you: Marcia was pregnant with Niles's baby."

"Oh, Phoebe . . ."

"And I learned today Marcia had the baby—a baby girl. I almost fainted when Wilbur told me that Marcia's husband had called up. But I had to look calm in front of Mother Bertha and Wilbur. And Selmabelle . . ."

"Oh, God, Phoebe."

"Mother Bertha probably would have liked Marcia better as a daughter-in-law. She's always liked her. And I can tell she likes *you* a lot better than she likes me."

"Is Marcia like me?"

"No, you're very different. But I know Mother Bertha likes Marcia—"

"But Marcia didn't marry her son," Jill said. "If she had, Mother Bertha might not like her either."

"Now she thinks there's something between me and Marcia's husband."

"But if there isn't . . ."

"There isn't."

"Maybe you should take a chance and come right out and tell her the full story."

Phoebe picked up a napkin and dabbed her eyes. "It's ironic she has this new granddaughter but doesn't know it. She keeps saying she'll never have a grandbaby. I know that's why she walked into that hospital today, to look at the babies. But, Jill, I keep asking myself what I can do. What would *she* do if I told her that her son had impregnated another man's wife? She'd be out of her mind, she might really have a heart attack—"

"Oh, Phoebe! What about Marcia's husband?"

"He's claiming the baby, he *wants* the baby. Sometimes he half-believes it's his, but he knows it isn't. Marcia's parents know the real story but *his* folks don't. How are his folks going to feel if they suddenly find out they aren't the grandparents? But Jill, what I think most about is the baby, what's best for the baby. I know people want the best for babies, but there's more here with me. I'm sure this sounds strange after what happened, Jill, but since Niles is the father, I feel almost like the baby's mine too."

"I don't think that's so strange," Jill said. The waiter brought the check and Jill grabbed it, over Phoebe's protest.

As they entered the apartment, Mother Bertha was sitting on the edge of the couch. "I got waked up."

"I'm sorry," Phoebe said.

"By a man phoning you, Phoebe."

"Oh, I'm very sorry." Phoebe said. She and Jill exchanged glances.

Phoebe looked back at Mother Bertha. "Did he give his name?"

"Oh, you don't know who it was?" Mother Bertha narrowed her eyes. "Are there that many men calling up?"

Jill went into the bathroom to change into her nightclothes and Phoebe turned to her mother-in-law, who frowned at her from the couch. "Mother Bertha, I'm sorry, I know you're under a strain, but I think I have to say this."

"Are you going to say something mean?" Mother Bertha covered her ears. "You're taking after that Selmabelle-woman." She placed a hand over her chest. "I can't stand the way things are. My heart can't stand it. Sunday's my boy's birthday."

"Mother Bertha, I have a job and I know quite a number of people now. I have business calls."

"At night? In your private apartment?"

"Please don't sound so damned disapproving," Phoebe said. "I wish we could get along—it'd make your visit so much easier."

"I'm sorry I'm a burden. I shouldn't have made this trip. But I couldn't be alone on my boy's birthday."

Phoebe stepped around furniture to stand by the window. She turned back to her mother-in-law, who was staring straight ahead. "Mother Bertha, please don't feel—"

"I'm trying not to feel anything. I find that works better sometimes. I like your friend."

"Jill's wonderful."

The next day as the three women sat over Saturday breakfast, Mother Bertha asked Jill, "Do you know that Selmabelle-woman?" Jill glanced at Phoebe, just as the doorbell sounded.

Opening the door, Phoebe was surprised by the towering figure of Gilbert standing back a few feet in the dim hallway. She hadn't seen him since their words about Lawrence.

Gilbert explained that one of the building's tenants coming in the downstairs door had let him in. "You didn't call me back," Gilbert said, handing her a florist's cone-shaped package.

Phoebe thanked him, but aware of Mother Bertha standing just behind her, she did not remove the floral wrapping from the flowers. She invented, "I guess these are for me to hold in the portrait." She backed away from the door so he could enter. "Mother Bertha, this is Gilbert Bradley. He's a portrait artist."

Mother Bertha inspected him. "Could he make a picture of my boy?"

Quickly Phoebe suggested, "Maybe he'd make a sketch of *you*. He told me once he's always sketching."

Gilbert nodded. "I could do a sketch," he said, as if trying to fit into plans he wished he understood.

Mother Bertha said, "It's my boy's birthday tomorrow."

"Would you like some coffee?" Phoebe asked Gilbert, then introduced Jill, who set a steaming cup before him at the table. Gilbert kept his eyes downcast, unusual for him. Jill offered cream and sugar for his coffee.

"No, thanks, I drink it black."

"My boy drank his black," Mother Bertha said as she stood up from the table. "Where's my handbag?" Phoebe passed her the large, black, leather bag, which she had stashed under the table. "I don't know how you people get along in New York," Mother Bertha said. "Everything here's so crowded." She rummaged in her handbag and brought out photos. "This is my boy."

Gilbert looked through the snapshots, which Phoebe could see included one of her and Niles, their arms around each other, taken in front of Mother Bertha's house. "Very nice," Gilbert said, handing the pictures back to Mother Bertha. As he spoke, his face became red.

At once Phoebe turned to her mother-in-law. "Maybe he could show us his studio. Or is that inconvenient, Gilbert?"

"*Very* convenient." he said, smiling suddenly. He hurried out to hail a cab.

At the end of the crowded ride, Gilbert ushered Mother Bertha, as well as Phoebe and Jill, into his studio.

Mother Bertha asked him, "How old are you?"

"Thirty-four."

"The first thing I thought of when I woke up this morning," Mother Bertha said, "was giving birth to my boy thirty-two years ago tomorrow." She spotted a painting-in-progress on an easel: a portrait of two small boys seated on a rug. "I guess they're not twins," Mother Bertha said.

"They're five and seven," Gilbert said.

"I hoped for twins when Phoebe was carrying. But then she had a miscarriage. It nearly broke my heart. Do you have any brothers or sisters?"

"A brother," Gilbert's answered, appearing uncomfortable again.

Phoebe, dreading the next question, intercepted. "You're a wonderful painter," she said. Then she slipped an arm around her mother-in-law." You always like to know about celebrities, Mother Bertha. Gilbert's painted a lot of famous people."

Mother Bertha suddenly frowned, "I hope not that Selmabelle Flaunton. You know her?" she asked Gilbert, who nodded. "I don't like her," Mother Bertha said. "I used to, till I met her in person."

Phoebe hurried to say, "It's an honor to have Gilbert do a sketch of you."

"I don't know about an honor. But how would you like to take that chair to sit for me?" Gilbert said, nodding toward the platform. He offered her his arm. Mother Bertha gave him a shy, pleased smile. Guided by Gilbert, she plodded forward, then looked up at him the way she used to look up at Niles.

Phoebe thought: He's doing this for me. She stepped toward Jill. "I'm beginning to feel too obligated to Gilbert," Phoebe whispered. "But I guess he wouldn't do this if he didn't want to."

"He'd find an excuse," Jill said, adding, "He's nice."

"Yes," Phoebe agreed.

"He sure is!" said Jill.

Phoebe studied Jill's eager eyes. "You mean you're interested?"

"I might be," Jill said. Phoebe experienced a tinge of jealousy, which surprised her, making her feel selfish. She and Jill pulled up chairs to watch while Gilbert sketched.

When at last he showed Mother Bertha the drawing, she looked at it bashfully and allowed herself to smile.

Phoebe said, "I'll have it framed for you."

"You three sit in back," Phoebe suggested when Gilbert hailed a cab for their return ride to the apartment. "I'll sit in front." Phoebe winked at Jill to let her know that she was arranging for her to be near Gilbert.

But Gilbert insisted that he would sit in front of the taxi, and when they entered the apartment, Gilbert pulled Phoebe back out into the hallway. "Phoebe . . ."

"Isn't Jill lovely?" Phoebe said.

He frowned, "Yes."

The next morning, Sunday, as the three women joined the line of people waiting in front of the Marble Collegiate Church on Fifth Avenue at Twenty-ninth, Phoebe decided not to offer that this was the only time that she'd been to any church since her arrival in New York. She said, "This is a very popular church."

Mother Bertha said, "I *know* it's popular. I listen to the broadcasts. Glennerville's not at the end of the world, you know."

When seated in the red-upholstered pew, Mother Bertha gazed about, as if in awe of the gold fleurs-de-lis trimming the walls, the Tiffany stained-glass windows. After the choir music, when the tall and imposing Dr. Norman Vincent Peale, dressed in a black robe, rose from his highback armchair, which faced the audience, and stepped forward to stand near his congregation, Mother Bertha remained still, her gray eyes staring at him, her lips slightly parted. He delivered his sermon, as if he talking to a friend.

Phoebe, watching her mother-in-law, thought of a gift she would later give her: Dr. Peale's book, *The Power of Positive Thinking.*

"He's a good preacher," Mother Bertha pronounced as they left the church. "I've never understood people who have a negative view—those who insist on the dark side of life. With all the tragedy in my own life, if I hadn't had a good attitude, I wouldn't be here today, that's for sure."

Amazed, Phoebe glanced at Jill, who wide-eyed her in return. As they walked up Fifth Avenue, Phoebe asked her mother-in-law, "How'd you come by your outlook?"

"Maybe I was just born with it, God-given," Mother Bertha said. "I have positive intentions, even if I don't always succeed. I find it hard that my boy's not here."

Phoebe held back the information that Niles had never wanted to visit New York.

When they were inside the vast, echoing, high-ceilinged lobby of the Metropolitan Museum of Art, Mother Bertha headed for a circular bench, where she sat down and untied her oxfords. Phoebe leaned toward her. "Mother Bertha, is walking in the museum going to be all right for you?"

"My boss at the bank told me he'd never walked so much in his life as he had in New York. He said to expect my feet to hurt. I said I'd grin and bear it."

Jill asked, "Then would you like to see the Impressionists, Mrs. Stanhope?"

"I guess that's as good as any," Mother Bertha said. Phoebe led the way.

"You need more meat on your bones," Mother Bertha told

Phoebe, comparing her to the two plump young women seated on the grass in Renoir's *In the Meadow*. She pointed to the figure clad in white. "I had a dress like that when I was a girl. I liked that dress because the boys untied my sash. I got attention in those days."

Phoebe said, "You got attention from Gilbert yesterday."

A smile came onto Mother Bertha's face. But leaving the museum, she stopped on the wide granite staircase leading down to Fifth Avenue. "I wish my boy could be here."

"Mrs. Stanhope," Jill said with an encouraging smile. "See that hotel over there on the corner across the street? That's the Stanhope Hotel, named for Bertha Stanhope."

Mother Bertha appeared baffled, worried. "What?"

"Jill's making a joke," Phoebe said.

"You're making fun of me," Mother Bertha said, "on my son's birthday."

Jill looked distressed. "Oh, no, I didn't mean it that way. I'm really sorry." She turned away, saying she had letters to write at home. Phoebe tried to catch Jill's eye before she rushed down the steps.

Phoebe put an arm around her mother-in-law. "You'll see it's a lovely hotel." Phoebe paid for their elegant lunch there out of her shaky budget.

Back in the apartment when Mother Bertha disappeared into the bathroom, Jill whispered to Phoebe: "You had a call—Lawrence."

"He gave his name?"

"Not at first."

"You mean you talked awhile?"

"Not too long." Jill grabbed her handbag from under the table. "I said I was on my way out—I am."

It was early the morning that Phoebe took Mother Bertha to catch her plane. Feeling a lightness when leaving the airport, she remembered Mother Bertha saying, "I'm sorry I'm a burden." She may not have been sorry, Phoebe reflected, but she sure was a burden. What a mood-booster to know she now was flying back to Kansas.

"Hallelujah," Phoebe suddenly said aloud, as she sat at her desk in the office. She did not explain when Wilbur turned to look at her.

But in the office, her rejoicing ran out when she did not hear from Lawrence. At the end of the day, she walked slowly home.

From the apartment's mailbox, she pulled out a letter from Barbara Hadley, her co-writer at the Harkenstown TV station. Red-Jack had passed around cigars at the station, Barbara wrote, but no one there had yet seen the baby, his "little beauty."

"Marcia's sick apparently," Barbara added, as if hinting for Phoebe to specify what was wrong, since she and Marcia were such close friends. "And don't you love what they named her: Delia Dawn? I guess you know they call her DeeDee."

"Delia Dawn, DeeDee," Phoebe repeated to herself, trying not to question again if the baby looked like Niles. Could his masculine features translate onto a baby girl?

Phoebe wanted to show the letter to Jill, but she was out again tonight.

The next morning Phoebe awoke to find that Jill had rushed off again. She must be trying to recover from the strain of Mother Bertha's visit.

At once Phoebe's mind was on Jill's phone conversation with Lawrence. The memory of the Kansas betrayal still rose up, made her imagination run wild. It was her imagination, wasn't it? Maybe she really should be cautious. No, she trusted Jill.

She had trusted Marcia too. And Niles. If Lawrence were more reliable, she wouldn't have these thoughts, would she?

But when she heard Lawrence's voice on her office phone late that afternoon, she tried to stay calm as he spoke in his just-for-you tone: "As I was saying . . ."

"Yes?" Phoebe felt herself smiling, blotting out her intentions.

"Our place?" Lawrence suggested, and reminded her of the Japanese restaurant near his apartment. At once she recalled their going from that restaurant to his apartment, her first time there, the first time she'd been in his bed.

Now Phoebe entered the restaurant alone on her return visit. She stood inside the door, where she enjoyed Japanese lanterns hanging around the room. She spotted the table where Lawrence had shown her the way to use chopsticks. Tonight that table was taken. Phoebe walked about near the entrance; she felt restless and eager.

The young head waiter standing near the door looked at her with expectation and bowed slightly. "Would you like to sit down?" he asked again, motioning toward a table.

"Thanks, I'll wait here a little longer."

He greeted a noisy group who came into the restaurant, and after seating the newcomers, he returned to stand near the door again. When Lawrence rushed in, the waiter bowed to him. "Ah, sir, Mr. Bradley, you come again tonight. Nice to see you again."

Lawrence kissed Phoebe on the cheek. The waiter looked from one to the other, as if surprised that it was Lawrence for whom she had waited. He led them to the back where Phoebe sat down on the mat, adjusting the skirt of her lime green dress.

She said to Lawrence, "You come here often?"

"You know me: I like a place I can pop into. I know you like it, darling, that's what counts." The waiter brought a bottle of sake, which had the name "Bradley" written on it.

"We haven't been here for quite awhile," Phoebe said.

"High time." He squeezed her hand, then studied the menu. "Tell me what appeals to you, sweetheart."

She scanned the menu, trying to concentrate. She firmly restrained herself. She would not allow herself to burst out with: "You were joking about this being *our place*. If you come here with other people, how can it be *our place?*"

Lawrence suggested they share dishes, "the way we did before." Phoebe was determined to use her chopsticks skillfully, causing Lawrence to comment, "You must have been practicing."

Phoebe smiled.

"My brother's a great one for Oriental food," Lawrence said. "It was interesting seeing you in his studio."

"He planned to paint my portrait."

"Planned? Is it finished?"

"I doubt it. By the way," she said, "the reason I took that suitcase to his studio—it was full of clothes so—"

"Suitcases often are." Lawrence grinned.

Grinning back, Phoebe made a fist, as if about to hit him on the arm. "I mean it was full of clothes so we could pick out what I should wear for the portrait."

"I remember you told me there was nothing between you and Gilbert."

"He just started to paint my portrait. He's painted Jane's portrait."

Lawrence shifted his position on the mat. While Phoebe poured more sake for them both, he said, "Jane used to be Gilbert's sister-in-law."

Setting down the teapot, Phoebe said, "I think you mentioned that when we went on the ferry."

Lawrence reached for Phoebe's hand. "We'll have to do that again, go on the ferry."

Phoebe nodded, saying, "But tonight I have to go home early."

On Lexington Avenue Lawrence found a parking place and walked with Phoebe to her apartment building. In the entryway Lawrence paused at the mailboxes. "That's you," he said, pointing to the name STANHOPE, then FLAXMORE on the same box for apartment 3B. "And Flaxmore is . . ."

"Jill Flaxmore—it's her apartment. I told you before: she just lets me share it."

He turned to Phoebe. "She must be as wonderful as you, darling." He cupped Phoebe's face in his hands. "Is she like you? What's she like?"

"Jill? She's blond, pretty . . ."

"Hmm." Inside the small lobby, he rang for the elevator. "Is she from Kansas too?" he asked, as they stood waiting for the elevator.

"Omaha. We met in an employment office before I got my job with Selmabelle. Jill hasn't changed jobs yet. She wants to wait until after her vacation."

"She sounds smart. What field?"

"Advertising, but she wants to go into public relations."

"Oh, Selmabelle's world."

"And mine now," Phoebe reminded him.

"And yours, darling. I was just going to say that."

When the elevator clanked to the main floor, ready for passengers, Lawrence opened the door. "Should I come up for a few minutes?"

In the elevator Phoebe told Lawrence it had worked out well for her to share the apartment with Jill on a temporary basis. "It helps both our budgets."

"Good for you!" Lawrence said. "Both of you."

"That was Jill you spoke to on Sunday."

"It's a good thing she was home, darling. You're hard to keep track of."

Rushing ahead into the apartment, Phoebe was relieved to see that the small space was not in as much disarray as it sometimes was when she and Jill were both busy running in and out. Yet even now Phoebe quickly gathered up *The New York Times* from where it had been left, sprawled on Jill's daybed. She visualized the rooms in Lawrence's apartment, thinking how orderly and organized everything had looked each time he'd taken her there, as if the place had been turned inside out so that nothing telltale remained, except that which he meant to convey.

"So this is it!" he said now, stepping further into the apartment from the doorway. He wore a lightweight suit, and in the elevator he had loosened his tie. Smiling, he looked about, lifting his arms in a sweeping gesture as if complimenting her on where she lived.

"Jill's out," Phoebe said.

He turned to the tiny kitchen. "You and your roommate entertain much?"

"Mostly we take turns cooking for each other."

"You must be wonderful cooks."

"I wouldn't exactly say that."

"I'll bet you are."

"No."

"And here I was just about to ask how I get invited." He laughed. "I was only teasing, sweetheart." He pulled her to him. "Maybe I'll see that roommate the next time. I was beginning to think she didn't really exist."

"You've talked to her on the phone. Jill's a good friend," Phoebe said, trying to sound casual.

"Good. Wonderful, darling."

The next morning, after a restless night, Phoebe drank coffee while Jill, seated at the table, buckled on her sandals. "Lawrence was here last night," Phoebe said. "Jill, I think he wants to meet you."

"Me?" Jill looked up at Phoebe, as if studying her, and frowned. "Hey, now, Phoebe, deal me out."

"It made me jealous. I've had all kinds of thoughts."

"Forget that."

"Forget it?" Phoebe swallowed.

"I'm not interested. I've got enough problems."

Phoebe turned away, afraid of tears. "I'm glad you said that. Gilbert says all women fall in love with Lawrence."

"Guys like that get pretty spoiled."

"I wish I didn't care. I try not to."

Jill picked up her handbag from the coffee table. "I know what you mean." Jill stopped. "Phoebe, I'm sorry."

"What for?"

"What I said to your mother-in-law at the museum. I wanted to be helpful but it came out wrong." Jill looked into Phoebe's eyes. "I have another confession. Gilbert interests me more than anyone since Bill."

"Oh."

The next morning when Gilbert phoned Phoebe at the office, he said again that he'd been too hasty. "I want to get back to work on your portrait."

"I'm very busy now, but when I have time, can I bring Jill with me?"

"Jill?"

"You know Jill. I share her apartment."

"But why do you want to bring her?"

Phoebe took a deep breath, "I think she's interested in portrait painting."

"You mean she wants a new *hobby*?" Phoebe could hear the annoyance in his voice. "Phoebe, this is *not* a hobby with me. This is what I *do*! This is how I *live*!"

"Oh, I'm sorry," Phoebe said quickly. "It was just a suggestion."

"All right, bring her," he said, still sounding badgered.

"Anyway," Phoebe said, "I'm going out of town soon."

"I'm going to be traveling some myself. Can I have a copy of your itinerary?"

"I guess you can." During the day Phoebe wondered if she should tell Jill about Gilbert's call. Maybe she should wait until she returned from the tour with Sir Chatham Wigans. By then, she might find a new plan to help Jill with Gilbert.

Twenty

HE NEXT WEEK PHOEBE TOLD HERSELF she would focus *all* her attention on her job, beginning now, this Monday morning. As she boarded the plane with Sir Chatham, she was well aware that without her job, she had no means of support, in every sense of the word. No matter what else was happening in her life, what really kept her going—kept her sane—was her job: knowing that she had duties to perform.

It was exhilarating, and daunting, to know that this tour with Sir Chatham was her responsibility. On the way to the airport, he'd told Phoebe that two of his annoying relatives had queried him about his assets and holdings in England, as if hinting about his will, while he himself had no intention of soon leaving this world.

Now as the plane taxied down the runway, Sir Chatham sat up alertly, looking out the window to his left. Phoebe, seated beside him, peeked out too, catching a glimpse of LaGuardia Airport in sunlight and the ground, which seemed to be moving. Gradually she could feel the pull as they began their ascent, her first commercial flight, her first air experience since childhood rides in Marcia's father's plane.

Pleased with his roomy, first-class seat, Sir Chatham told Phoebe that his first experience with an airplane had been with his friend Wilbur. Hearing the name "Wilbur," Phoebe thought of Selmabelle's accountant and then it came to her that Sir Chatham was talking about the aviation pioneer, Wilbur Wright of the Wright Brothers.

Sir Chatham said he had met "the birdman" through mutual friends "in 19-ought-8." That was when Wright had first shown him his "flying machine. Phoebe, I stared at this most peculiar-looking biplane, trying to take in that this heavier-than-air contraption could go up in the air and stay there. And it did. For four minutes! It wasn't on wheels, like this plane; it was on runners like a sleigh. When it catapulted off, with Wright in the single seat, he looked like a man bicycling in the air. He landed fifty yards from me—a thrilling moment, my dear Phoebe."

"I'm sure," said Phoebe, thinking that Sir Chatham not only enjoyed planning ahead, but looking back too. She watched as he checked his seat belt. "Now I'm tucked in next to you," he said as he chuckled and beamed. "On our first flight together. But my first journey by air wasn't in an airplane."

"No?" asked Phoebe, imagining an angel's wings.

"I was up in a balloon, sailing over London with Charlie Rolls. He took me for my first motorcar ride too. And it wasn't long after this that Charlie founded his firm Rolls Royce." Sir Chatham smiled. "I like firsts."

Phoebe was tempted to ask about his first meeting Lawrence when Lawrence was a little boy but decided to wait for a more appropriate moment; Sir Chatham had just opened his book on the history of clocks and wristwatches.

"Another first for you," said Phoebe the next day in Boston, as Sir Chatham, carrying his cane, followed her into the television station. "Your first TV appearance in Boston."

"Heigh-ho," said Sir Chatham, when escorted by the smiling program host, Hughie Hoburn, onto the stage. "I look for the little red light to know which camera to face—you see, I'm becoming accustomed. I'm quite used to the public platform in England. Jolly good, this," Sir Chatham commented as the two men were seated in twin upholstered chairs. "Ah, we have an audience we can see."

On the air Sir Chatham announced, "We have an important birthday in England in this year of 1959. The thirty-first of May will be the hundredth anniversary of Big Ben. When I say Big Ben, I'm talking about the *bell*."

"The bell?" asked Hughie Hoburn.

Sir Chatham laughed. "Ah, now, I stumped you."

"Do *you* know what I mean?" he asked the studio audience, which began to applaud as if this were expected. Sir Chatham, looking pleased, said that a century ago Big Ben had been nicknamed for a member of Parliament, Sir Benjamin Hall. But the name originally referred to the *bell* of the clock, rather than to the clock itself.

Sir Chatham pulled off his coat to show his watches. "You can see my personal fondness for time pieces." As the audience agreed, Sir Chatham clasped his hands together above his head, like a boxer, which caused more laughter and clapping.

Phoebe, surprised by his action, thought of his insistence that he be on a "dignified program." She guessed that his career in public service and politics made him adapt to new possibilities. When in America . . .

By now Sir Chatham had left his chair and was standing up on the TV stage with the program host. Beaming, Sir Chatham told the audience that "the voice of Big Ben" had made its radio debut by chiming on the BBC on New Year's Eve in 1923.

Watching, Phoebe told herself that it was *good* for her to hear Sir Chatham speak the words "New Year's Eve."

"But Big Ben, at age one hundred, is a youngster," Sir Chatham was saying, "compared to our historic houses and castles. Do you want great pleasure for a small visiting fee?" he asked and the audience cheered. "I thought Boston was said to be staid," he commented and the audience erupted into laughter.

But Sir Chatham seemed mystified when Hughie Hoburn approached him with a stiff straw hat. "We'd like to make you an honorary Yankee Doodle Dandy."

"How's that?" said Sir Chatham, backing away. Hughie Hoburn followed him with the microphone. And the hat. Sir Chatham's upraised arm prevented a closer frontal approach, but the TV host rushed behind his back, placing the hat on his head. The studio audience laughed and applauded. Sir Chatham's face showed astonishment.

"This is an honor, sir," Hughie Hoburn told him.

"An honor?"

"We give the hat to our most important guests."

Sir Chatham reached up to touch the hat.

"You're a good sport, Sir Chatham Wigans."

"Sport?" Sir Chatham did not remove the hat. Once planted, it seemed to grow on him. Clamping the hat to his head with one hand, he bowed to Hughie the host, then to the cheering audience.

"I like an audience," Sir Chatham said to Phoebe that night as they dined at the hotel.

"You'll have a studio audience in Chicago."

"But we have all those cities in between."

"Everyone loves your interviews whether you have a studio audience or not."

He brightened, his old eyes alert. "They do seem to like what I say, don't they?"

At once Phoebe recalled that what she herself had said to Gilbert about Jill. It had annoyed him. Had she said too much to Lawrence about tardy phone calls? Was she expecting too much? Maybe she was being foolish. Selfish? She wanted to get her life in order. But suddenly she asked herself if that meant that she expected other people to fit into her agenda. She recoiled from this thought. But didn't she need to think of herself too? Life, she thought, is a balancing act.

Wearing his straw hat and carrying his walking stick, Sir Chatham hurried with Phoebe to planes and appointments in one city after another, appearing as hearty and pink-cheeked as when they had started the tour. Phoebe marveled at his stamina.

While seated next to him on the flight from Milwaukee to Chicago, Phoebe roused from a nap to see Sir Chatham, sixty years older than she, poring over his book on the history of clocks and wristwatches. She remembered he hadn't had a nap since he was "two years old." Phoebe's own hectic-schedule fatigue had been increased by the stress of heavy publicity responsibility and nightmares during the brief times she could sleep.

After Sir Chatham closed his book, he clasped his bony old hands in front of him. Over the roar of the plane, he told Phoebe that his father had been a barrister; his mother, who loved Greek history, had lived to be ninety-four, three years more than her husband. Sir Chatham himself already had outlived his siblings. His earliest memory was being picked up from his cradle and held in the arms of his beloved nanny. "My lady," as Sir Chatham called his wife, Florence— had been a violinist, had loved gardening, and had died fifteen years ago. They'd had no children. Sir Chatham turned to Phoebe with a contemplative, wistful look: "We had fifty-seven years together."

He sighed, then added, "Our happiest times were at our house in Devon. My lady was born in Devon. I really bought the house for her. We both loved it, I still do, especially the garden. And the greenhouse . . ."

"My grandmother told me," Phoebe said, "that when I was four years old, she was trying to explain the government to me and she said, 'The President lives in the White House.' And she said I piped up, 'Well, that's all right, I'm going to live in a greenhouse.'"

Laughing, Sir Chatham raised his hands. "How delightful! You'd be a flower among flowers! Like my lady." He tilted his head as he studied her. "You don't look like her but at times you *do* rather remind me of her." He laughed again. "You make me laugh, Phoebe, you charm me." He touched her chin. "I'm either going to have to ask to marry you, or adopt you."

After the plane landed late at Chicago's O'Hare Airport, Phoebe hurried to look and look for her suitcase on the moving, roundabout luggage rack. When she reported her luggage missing, the unconcerned airline attendant advised her that as soon as the suitcase was found, it would be delivered to her hotel, The Mallard. Then he handed her a small emergency overnight kit for a man. "We ran out of kits for women."

In her hotel room, Phoebe glanced at the message slip saying Gilbert Bradley had phoned. She hadn't a spare moment now to call him back. She hurried with calls to confirm Sir Chatham's Chicago broadcast and press appointments and wanted to phone Lawrence. But she had given him her itinerary. Surely he remembered . . . She ached for the kind of devotion from him that Sir Chatham had shown when talking of his "lady."

Now was her only time to call Jill to check on her mail. "By the way," Jill said at the end of their conversation, "I finally met Lawrence."

"Oh?"

"He was passing by and said he'd always wanted to meet your apartment mate."

"You mean he just dropped by, like that?" Phoebe said.

"That's what he said."

"Did he stay long?"

"Not too long. I've got to rush, Phoebe."

"So do I. I have to rush too." Phoebe hung up the phone, stunned by what Jill had told her. She couldn't call her back, she was going out.

Phoebe had to hurry too. Her suitcase still had not been delivered and she had no time to shop for an evening dress, even if she'd had the money to pay for one. She had made such a point of bringing a long dress for tonight—so carefully she had packed the peacock blue gown in tissue paper.

Quickly she fluffed her hair with her fingers as she looked in the mirror at herself, still wearing the same black knit suit, which now seemed ugly to her. Meeting Sir Chatham in the lobby, she saw he was trim in his tuxedo and concerned that they might be late.

"You're very brave," he said in the taxi on the way to the important black-tie dinner party. "You're different from my lady in that. If she had lost her suitcase, she'd be in floods of tears." He was stern as he pounded his cane on the taxi floor. "I don't know what I'd do if they lost my cases."

Phoebe did not mention how she herself was feeling. She noticed that he seemed to have second thoughts about her knit suit; earlier he'd said she could wear it anywhere. Now he suggested, "Perhaps our hostess will lend you an evening frock."

Phoebe tried to imagine the look, size, and shape of Mrs. George Yorbrook Adams. "I think Selmabelle told me she's English," said Phoebe in hopes he might describe her. She was indeed English, Sir Chatham told Phoebe, but she was married to an American.

Sir Chatham consulted at least one watch on his right arm as he and Phoebe stood on the steps of the private residence, a structure roughly the size of Phoebe's apartment building in New York. A porch light shone down on Sir Chatham's smiling face. "I don't believe in being what is foolishly called 'fashionably late,' especially when the party is in one's honor. Do you agree, my dear?"

"Oh, yes," said Phoebe, though she'd not had much occasion to think of parties in her honor.

Had Lawrence often excused himself by pretending he was just fashionably late? He was far too late for that! He'd had time to drop by the apartment while she was away. She told herself to stop thinking of Jill and Lawrence just as a servant admitted Phoebe and Sir Chatham into the hallway of the residence.

A high voice called out, "Chatty!" The stout, blond woman flung her arms about Sir Chatham, but her stomach was so large, her arms did not reach far around him. When she emerged from the embrace, she was introduced as the hostess, Mrs. Adams. She wore a black velvet dress handpainted with flowers. The dress seemed to match a flower painting on velvet in an oval frame behind her on the hallway wall. Phoebe tried to decide if the picture had been hung especially for this occasion.

"I understand from Selmabelle you're American," Mrs. Adams said cozily to Phoebe. "I know everyone calls her Selmabelle. It would please me if you called me Cynthia." A necklace glittered below Cynthia's several chins. "May I call you Phoebe? We've adopted American ways, or I should say I have—my husband was born in Oklahoma." Phoebe, noting the difference in Cynthia's size and fashion style, decided that she'd better remain in her suit, tailored and inappropriate as it was.

But already Sir Chatham was explaining that the airline had lost Phoebe's suitcase.

"Oh dear, that happens so often it's almost routine," Cynthia said.

"Perhaps," Sir Chatham said, "an evening garment of some kind could be found for her?"

"Oh, please don't bother!" Phoebe said quickly. "It would be difficult—I'm so tall." She guessed that Cynthia had gained weight since Sir Chatham had last seen her. He had abandoned his earlier wording of an "evening frock," which Phoebe had interpreted as a form-fitting dress, and replaced it by a vague description of a "garment of some kind," which made her think of a flowing coat or a long floating painted scarf. Phoebe knew that she would look as awkward in something borrowed as she felt in this situation.

Cynthia squinted at Phoebe, as if there were a code between women under the circumstances. "Perhaps some jewelry to dress up your own costume?" the hostess suggested.

"Splendid!" said Sir Chatham.

Phoebe, glancing at Cynthia's necklace and drop earrings, saw that the dozens of sparkling stones were small and arranged in clusters, but they were diamonds and rubies—Cynthia was not talking about costume jewelry. Phoebe tried to think of an excuse. Something might happen and she'd spend her life working to pay for the loss, as in the de Maupassant story "The Necklace"—only here what she would choose would not be paste. "Please, I really can't—"

"George will show you," Cynthia said of the suntanned man shaking hands with Sir Chatham. "Won't you, George?"

Phoebe visualized a bedroom vault being opened, as in the movies, and her staring at a cache of jewels. "It's very generous of your wife," Phoebe said to George Yorbrook Adams.

"Hogwash," he said.

Phoebe watched him out of the corner of her eye as they approached the wide carpeted steps. She guessed this was the grand staircase, but no matter what it was called they were on their way upstairs and Sir Chatham and Cynthia and the others would remain below. Even the servants would be downstairs scurrying about. As they climbed the steps side by side, she thought it's too awkward to turn back now. "I don't feel comfortable borrowing jewelry," she said.

"Don't worry about it."

"I'm surprised your wife—"

"She's preoccupied with entertaining and paint designs. Come on, honey," he said at the top of the stairs. "Her room's this way."

"Maybe you could just pick out something for me," Phoebe said, "and I could go back downstairs."

"Oh, hell no. I wouldn't ever claim to know a woman's mind. We're here now." George ushered her into the room, where oval velvet pictures lined the walls, and led her past the bed, decorated with pillows painted with flowers and birds. Phoebe sat down at the vanity table to open the surprisingly large quilted box residing among the perfume bottles.

But before she touched it, she heard him say, "Honey, you hold on in here and excuse me. I'm going down to my room and get me some other shoes."

Phoebe turned toward him. "Couldn't you wait—"

"In fact, if you don't mind . . ." Seated on the end of the bed, he took off his shoes and black socks. "Hell, I thought so—I'm getting blisters wearing these damn sissy shoes Cynthia ordered." Carrying his shoes, he started for the door.

"Excuse me," Phoebe said, "I'd rather not open this box by myself."

He laughed. "You expecting a jack-in-the-box?"

"Something might happen to the jewelry and I'd be responsible."

"You got quite an imagination, girl."

"Well, sometimes I haven't been cautious enough."

He set his shoes down at the end of the bed. "I guess we could all say that." Walking barefoot on the carpet, he picked up a satin-covered straight chair, set it down near her at the vanity, turned it around, and straddled it. His forehead was wrinkled, making him look quizzical, as if he were constantly asking himself questions. He was quiet, watching her.

Pulling open the top drawer of the quilted box, Phoebe found jewelry in such a jumble she might have been at a rummage sale. She picked up a strand of dark red beads, caught in a tangle of other beads. She retrieved a shiny black strand but beads trailed at the end of the broken string.

"There's probably nothing much of value," George said. "I think the best stuff's down in the bank vault."

"Oh, that makes me feel a lot better."

"You're funny, I'm gonna remember you. Take your time, honey. This may be the best part of the evening."

She pulled out a silver pin. "I could wear this."

"That dinky thing? That's hardly worth the effort to put it on. I thought you wanted to doll up, I thought that was the whole idea."

When Phoebe and George descended the stairs, he had exchanged his patent-leather pumps for loafers and she was laden with silver-and-turquoise Indian jewelry from drawers in the box.

In the downstairs hall she touched the earrings and necklace, then held out an arm to admire the row of bracelets.

But Phoebe's hands were bare—Cynthia's turquoise rings had proved to be huge on her. Staring at Phoebe's hands, George said, "I bet you haven't milked many cows. You sure got thin fingers." Phoebe's mind shot back to Glennerville, back to Mother Bertha's bedroom where Phoebe had handed over her wedding band. She heard Mother Bertha's voice. "It's too bad my son had to have it cut down for you."

As Phoebe started toward the dining room, where the guests were assembling, George said, "Wait a minute. I thought Cynthia said you were visiting here from New York, honey, but you don't seem—"

"Kansas. I'm originally from Kansas."

"Kansas! Hell, I'm from Oklahoma."

"Yes," said Phoebe. "Cynthia told me."

"Kansas. Oklahoma. We're neighbors! Where abouts in Kansas?"

"Harkenstown."

"Harkenstown! You know Charlie Harkens? His family started the place, maybe his granddaddy. I've known Charlie Harkens for years."

"I thought maybe you had."

"How'd you figure that?" George said.

"'Cause you're both big cattle dealers, and into grain and oil. I thought you'd probably run into each other some place, here in Chicago maybe, Kansas City . . ."

"You thought all that and didn't mention it? How well do you know Charlie?"

Phoebe forced herself to return his gaze. "I knew his daughter."

"And his wife? She's something, isn't she? Quite a looker. Is the daughter like her?"

"In some ways," Phoebe whispered.

"What's her name?"

"Marcia."

He smiled. "Nice name. Phoebe's a nice name."

Phoebe nodded. Niles had said that too. Phoebe swallowed and looked away. "I, Niles, take thee, Phoebe . . ." Niles had placed the ring on her finger in the rose garden at Marcia's parents' house.

"Well, well," George said, "next time I run into Charlie I'll pass along a word to the daughter for you."

"No . . ."

"I might even see him when I'm in Tulsa next week."

"No, please! Don't say anything on my account."

"Hell, honey, it's no trouble, Charlie and I always shoot the breeze. Hey," George frowned. "You all right? You look kinda—"

"It's just that . . . I'll be . . ." Phoebe hurried ahead. At the entrance to the large square dining room with its dark tapestry walls and flickering candles, she paused, blinking at the trembling lights on the table.

Then she plunged forward. The chairs on the nearest side of the table were filled. She turned away, colliding with a waiter, upsetting his large tray, setting off an avalanche of sliding dishes, which crashed at her feet. Grasping her upper arm in pain from the impact, Phoebe gazed down at her oily, shrimp-stained, tomato-spattered skirt. The waiter crouched on the floor at her feet, nervously gathering up remains of odorous food and dishes. Another waiter rubbed the carpet with a napkin.

Phoebe bent to help them, but when the waiters frowned even more, Phoebe said, "I'm sorry."

"Are you all right?" It was Cynthia.

"Fine," Phoebe lied in a whisper.

George appeared. "Wait! I'll find your place, Phoebe." He began to lead his wife back to her seat.

Quickly, with one clean napkin obtained from a waiter, Phoebe dabbed at the devastation on her clothes. Then, with George, she made her way to the other side of the table. She tried to be inconspicuous as she spread another napkin on the chair seat. As George ceremoniously seated her, the elegantly dressed people at the table subtly glanced or openly looked at her.

Phoebe forced a smile as she looked up to thank George. In memory, she heard her mother's voice: "Don't make a spectacle of yourself!"

Her face burned. She wished George weren't seated so far away. She ached to sweep away the last few minutes and to replace her sodden tailored clothes. If only she could reappear in her own familiar evening gown appropriate for this table of guests, who having assessed her, now ignored her. She could tell they knew one another and their own wealth and importance. As the guest of honor, Sir Chatham was seated numerous chairs away from her.

Phoebe sat ramrod straight and held her head high as though she set her own fashion trends and always attended formal parties in a splattered black knit suit.

She thought of the cook, who must be wondering if there was enough food left to serve after the crash. Phoebe could not get up from the table to check with the kitchen nor could she leave the party. She felt strongly her responsibility as an employee of Selmabelle, whose implied threats in her long distance phone calls had invaded Phoebe's ears: "I expect a triumphant tour." "Or else" was unspoken but clear. The underlying message came through each time Selmabelle's voice on the phone had reminded Phoebe that the contract for The Association for Castles and Stately Homes was up for renewal.

When at last the distressing party was over, Phoebe wanted to return the jewelry to George. But he was occupied, standing by the door, talking with departing guests and with Sir Chatham, who would soon turn away from his host to push up his right sleeve, a sign to Phoebe that he was anxious to leave. Already he had told her: "The taxi is waiting." She considered handing the jewelry to a maid or taking it upstairs to Cynthia's room herself, but she would feel like an intruder entering the bedroom alone.

She had to take it upon herself, as politely as possible, to interrupt Cynthia, who was busy saying good-bye to guests. Phoebe witnessed Cynthia's sudden distress at the sight of her. With the hostess in this state, Phoebe barely mentioned the jewelry but noticed that Cynthia glanced toward the living room. Did she mean for her to leave the bracelets and necklace in that room? Phoebe, in haste, whirled about the living room, looking at the polished tables and tapestry-upholstered furniture, finally deposited the pieces in an oriental bowl on the mantel.

In the taxi, returning to the hotel, Sir Chatham was quiet. George Yorbrook Adams, as well as several of the guests, had offered to drive him back to the hotel but he had declined, insisting correctly that the driver who had brought them would return for them.

Seated beside Sir Chatham in the taxi, Phoebe reflected that usually when she was with him, she almost forgot that he was the chairman of the association and thought of him as her very special, inspiring friend. Now, faced with his silence, she felt as if she had lost her friend and he had reappeared as a formidable and criticizing Someone. Someone she felt it best not to question. Maybe he was just finally tired?

Early tomorrow morning he would see her dressed in a bright dress instead of this splattered, now-too-warm black suit. Then he would respond to her enthusiastic greeting.

In her hotel room, Phoebe searched for her suitcase. There was not even a message about it. She stamped her foot, then catching sight of herself in the dresser mirror, she was as horrified as she had been during dinner when she had excused herself to rush to the powder room at Cynthia's. The cologne she had applied then had worn off and now she detected an unpleasant odor of shrimp and tomatoes, making her hot with embarrassment again as she wiggled and stepped her way out of the skirt. Had Sir Chatham noticed the smell in the taxi? Trying to be calm, she picked up the phone only to learn that the hotel cleaners had closed at midnight and would start up service again at six in the morning, the very time that she would have to leave the hotel for the morning TV show with Sir Chatham.

She grabbed a hand towel from the bathroom and, with water, worked over the mess on her skirt. She rubbed too hard; the wool knit began to stretch. White fuzz from the towel made the skirt look worse. She laid the skirt over one of the twin beds.

She showered, then opened the kit provided by the airline and found a toothbrush, paste, and shaving equipment. Remembering that the attendant had said this was a supply for a man, she laughed it off. But climbing into bed, she missed the feel of her satin nightgown, now folded away in the missing suitcase. Having no cosmetics, she lay on her back trying to preserve the trace of makeup that remained on her face. When she and Sir Chatham would leave for the TV show the next morning, it would be too early for the drug store to have opened.

Sleep, she told herself. Instead she thought of Lawrence in the apartment with Jill. *Quit stewing*, she demanded. Had she made the right decision in depositing the turquoise and silver jewelry in the oriental bowl? "I'll telephone Selmabelle," Cynthia had said, her parting words when Phoebe had thanked her for the party. How would the news of the evening's fiasco set with America's foremost, but least tolerant hostess? Selmabelle demanded that Phoebe conduct herself in such a way as to reflect credit on Selmabelle's celebrated reputation, her distinguished clients.

Phoebe bolted upright in bed. Should she report the evening to Selmabelle, ask her advice? *No, deal with this yourself.* She had to make the rest of the trip a *triumph!*

After the TV show the next morning when Phoebe and Sir Chatham emerged from the studio, members of the audience waited outside in the eighth floor hallway. They thrust papers at Sir Chatham, asking for his autograph. When he wrote "Chatham Wigans," a girl objected. "You left out part of it. You forgot 'Sir.'"

A boy whispered to Phoebe, "Is he your grandfather?"

"I wish he were," Phoebe said.

Others asked her for her autograph too. Writing "Phoebe Stanhope," she sensed their puzzlement. A heavyset woman in a lopsided hat approached her tentatively with a paper and pencil and asked, "Are you *somebody*?"

Phoebe answered, "Everybody's somebody. Isn't that right?" The woman frowned as she studied Phoebe's signature.

Conscious of their next appointment, Phoebe whispered to Sir

Chatham that to escape more autograph seekers, they could duck out the back way. Once inside the elevator, as she congratulated him on the show, she was aware that a small man had slipped in with them. Smiling, the man stood beside Sir Chatham, saying he had enjoyed the program. He asked, "Could I have a peek at the watches, up close?"

The elevator reached the ground floor and Phoebe excused herself to run to the nearby drug store she had spotted earlier when they'd arrived by taxi. Because the elevator had landed them in the back of the building in a kind of alley, she had to dash around the corner. Hastily, she made her cosmetic selections.

She had expected Sir Chatham to wait for her where she had left him, but when she returned, she could not find him. Alarmed, she began to call his name and to run up and down the street of shops, where she looked in, thinking he must have decided to buy something himself.

She rushed back to the TV building and rang for the service elevator they had used. It seemed endlessly slow in arriving. Once inside, she was startled to see, on the floor, Sir Chatham's straw hat lying upside down. In a panic, she picked it up and held it to her pounding heart, as if pledging allegiance to him.

On the TV floor, she rushed into the rear corridor and found a commotion of TV staff people surrounding Sir Chatham. He was surprisingly seated in a chair as if someone had provided it in this unexpected place. "Knife point," she heard a young man say.

In an uncharacteristic, high strained voice, Sir Chatham said, "It was my favorite. I liked to watch it tick." He wore no coat. His shirtsleeves were empty of watches. His hair, usually so carefully groomed, stood out from his head as if it had been ruffled by an unfriendly person.

"Sir Chatham . . ." Phoebe said. She dreaded to hear him say that his watches had been stolen.

"We've called the police," said a female production assistant.

Sir Chatham looked suddenly really old, he was trembling. He seemed

to have lost his amazing agility. Why had she thought she needed cosmetics so badly? How could she explain all of this to Selmabelle?

"Barbarian!" Sir Chatham cried out in his new high-pitched voice,
to the two policemen who had just arrived. "He was a barbarian!"

Phoebe anxiously reviewed in her mind that Sir Chatham was
now due for his next publicity appointment. Should she go ahead
and represent him, try to do his interview for him? How could she
be convincing discussing Stately Homes and Castles in Britain? She'd
never even been in a castle. Or a stately home, for that matter, unless
she counted Marcia's parents' house or Selmabelle's. She had never
even been in Britain.

She had to consider Sir Chatham first. She must at least consult him.

"Sir Chatham," she said, trying to force calmness into her voice. "Do
you want to go on with the schedule? We'll have to—"

"Who are you?" asked one of the cops.

Phoebe gave her name.

"Are you related to him?"

"I'm in charge of his tour. He has an appointment with the *Chicago
Daily Herald.*"

The other policeman, younger than his partner and rosy-cheeked,
smiled at Phoebe. "What do you mean you're in charge?"

"I work for Selmabelle Flaunton. She assigned me to accompany Sir
Chatham. I'm with him, I'm his friend."

"You were with him when it happened?"

"I was in the drugstore." She glanced at Sir Chatham. Open-
mouthed, he slumped in his chair, his white hair untidy, his skin
splotchy. Phoebe said to the policeman, "He had watches up and
down both arms. They're very valuable, they're dear to him. One was
his favorite, you can see the inner workings."

The older cop was now talking to bystanders. "Did you see the assailant?" he asked. No one had. He turned to Phoebe. "You see the
assailant?"

"He got on the elevator with us."

"I thought you were in the drugstore."

Phoebe explained the sequence of events. "The man seemed friendly, he was smiling . . ."

"Had you ever seen him before?"

"No . . ." The more questions the police asked, the worse Phoebe felt and the more she wanted to talk with someone. With Lawrence. Lawrence knew both Sir Chatham and Selmabelle. In a small, crowded anteroom, a TV assistant allowed her to make a long distance call.

The abrupt voice of Mrs. Cartright, Lawrence's secretary, informed her, "Mr. Bradley's away. He's out of the office today."

"Could you tell me how I can reach him?" There was a pause on the line. "I work for Selmabelle Flaunton, I need legal advice." As soon as Phoebe had blurted this out, she wanted to take it back. Why had she said that? Selmabelle might find out about this call.

"No, I don't," Phoebe said, as if correcting herself. "I don't work for her."

"I beg your pardon," Mrs. Cartright said.

"Thank you," said Phoebe, hanging up.

Why had she made the call? No one was accusing her outright, not yet.

"If you need to talk to me," Phoebe said to the policemen, "you can reach me at The Mallard."

"You told us that," the younger policemen said.

She thought, They can tell I'm nervous.

In the taxi Sir Chatham forlornly pushed up one sleeve, then the other. Phoebe said, "I wish I'd stayed with you. I could have screamed."

"He would have killed me, he had a knife to my throat."

"Oh, Sir Chatham!"

When they arrived at the Pump Room restaurant, they were led to a table where Ray Leopold, the reporter for the *Chicago Daily Herald*, slouched, sipping a dark-colored drink. Tall, slender, and so limber that when he half-stood upon their arrival, Phoebe was reminded of a long cloth doll she'd once seen that could be tied into knots.

The reporter lowered himself back into his seat and was apparently relaxed even as Phoebe told him about the theft and the police. During lunch, Ray Leopold looked at Phoebe as if it gave him pleasure to be in her company.

She tried to turn his attention away from herself so he would concentrate fully on Sir Chatham. "Those watches," she said, "mean everything to Sir Chatham."

Like other Americans, including the media they had encountered on the trip, Ray Leopold seemed impressed by Sir Chatham's title and the houses and castles he represented. Beginning again to write in his notebook, he said, "Sir, you say he stole all your watches?"

As Sir Chatham talked about his timepieces, he looked vulnerable and his voice made Phoebe even more worried about his health. She had to hold herself back from insisting he see a doctor at once. She was in charge of the tour but did that give her the right? Should she call Selmabelle? Selmabelle had her own recent health problems.

Now as Sir Chatham described his favorite watches to the reporter, Phoebe remembered the night in Lawrence's apartment when she'd picked up his watch from the bedside table. Trying it on, she'd found it much too large; she'd turned it over to see if there was an engraving on the back: TO LAWRENCE WITH LOVE FROM JANE. She'd been so relieved and encouraged to discover no wording there.

Suddenly now, this took on new significance! She tried to guess how many people in the world wore wristwatches. How many of their watches had engravings on the back? Did anyone ever ask, "May I look at the back of your watch?"

She sat forward. "Excuse me," she heard herself interrupting.

Then her face felt hot—she had stopped the flow of the interview. "I'm sorry."

Sir Chatham looked at her. "Phoebe?"

"I wondered if there are engravings on the back of any of your watches . . ."

Sir Chatham bowed his head. "On the rectangular Patek. The one with the gold case and the enamel painted dial." His faded old eyes looked up at Phoebe. "My lady gave it to me on our fiftieth wedding anniversary. *'For our next 50 years'* she had engraved on the back."

Phoebe could not sleep that night until long after midnight. The phone in her hotel room awakened her and she realized that it was morning and she was talking with someone from the Chicago Police Department.

Phoebe sat up in bed, trying to be alert as she heard him say, ". . . Mrs. George Yorbrook Adams."

Phoebe said, "What did you say about Mrs. Adams?"

"I asked if you knew her."

"Oh, God, is this about her jewelry?" Phoebe became aware that she'd spoken her thoughts aloud; it was too early in the morning.

"Will you say that again? What's that about her jewels?"

Phoebe slid out of bed, still holding the phone. "Nothing. I didn't say anything."

There was a silence on the other end. Then: "Miss Stanhope, would it be convenient for you to come to the station house this morning? Say ten o'clock?"

After replacing the phone, Phoebe asked herself why she couldn't have been more wide-awake.

She idled around the room. Should she try to call him back, do her best to straighten things out right now? No, that might make it worse.

Still naked from sleeping without her lost nightgown, she cracked the door of her hotel room and stuck her hand out to retrieve the *Chicago Daily Herald* left in front of the door. Opening the pages, she spotted the headline: TICKING TREASURES TAKEN / TITLED BRIT OFFERS REWARD.

The reporter had devoted most of the story to the subject of the theft, barely mentioning the stately homes and castles—a promotional weakness, Phoebe realized, which would not go unnoticed by Selmabelle.

Last night before going to bed, Phoebe had seen the "titled watch man" describing the theft on the TV news. It had been an excerpt of the interview conducted earlier in the day when she herself had been standing near Sir Chatham. He also had talked about the theft during radio programs. Had Cynthia and George Yorbrook Adams been aware of the coverage? They certainly would be captured by this newspaper story.

Was Cynthia's jewelry really missing? Phoebe fervently wished now she had asked someone to witness her placing the items in the oriental bowl.

Why had the police asked if she knew Cynthia? Calm down, she told herself. Undoubtedly, the pieces were still in the bowl and no one had thought to look there.

She wished the policeman had not phoned so early . . . if only he hadn't questioned her when she was half-asleep. Oh God, why did she blurt things out? Because she felt guilty. She should never have left Sir Chatham.

It came to her that whenever she felt extremely upset or guilty, she blurted. On New Year's Eve she had been desperate. When would she ever learn? Now. She should start learning now.

But what should she *do?* She could hardly ignore the police. She'd tell Sir Chatham that something had come up and she'd be back shortly. Yet if she did this, she would be leaving him again. But if she ignored the police request, they'd come and find her. That would not calm Sir Chatham.

Phoebe rehearsed in her mind how it would be when she walked into the police station. She would enter with confidence and simply tell them the truth. It was when she deviated from the truth, tried to hide something, that she got into trouble. Warnings from her childhood still nudged her: "Phoebe, you must always tell the truth!" Or else . . . No, it wasn't always hiding the truth that got her into trouble. What was sometimes worse was when she blurted, told too much. Oh, God, there were so many things to think about—to avoid, to do.

Ready to leave for her appointment with the police, Phoebe told herself that she had better take a minute to call Cynthia, whether she wanted to or not. A maid answered, but when Phoebe gave her name, the maid said, "Mrs. Adams is not in." Was Cynthia avoiding her? Would she really be out this early in the morning? Phoebe had heard that the English were champions at the correct cold shoulder.

Phoebe hurried down the hotel corridor and paused in front of Sir Chatham's hotel room. Hanging on his doorknob was a sign: DO NOT DISTURB. He had never used such a sign before. Last night his last words to Phoebe were that he felt "dog-tired" and would have breakfast in his room. Had he already had breakfast? Or did this sign mean he had become ill in the night?

Why hadn't he phoned her? Was *he* giving her the cold shoulder too? Had Cynthia had phoned *him*? Maybe he was having second thoughts about Phoebe leaving him. Did he remember that she was the one who had suggested they take that back elevator?

A heavyset hotel maid came out into the hall from a nearby room and pushed her cart of cleaning supplies along the corridor toward Phoebe. How could Phoebe quickly explain her relationship to Sir Chatham? She said, "Excuse me, I'm very worried. My grandfather is staying in this room. Have you seen him this morning?" Phoebe pointed to the Do Not Disturb sign.

"I put," the maid said.

"You put the sign here?"

The maid frowned, as if cautious, as if Phoebe might be accusing her. "He say, 'not well.'"

"Is he *very* ill? Sick?"

The maid looked worried and appeared not to know what to reply. Phoebe pulled dollar bills from her handbag and pressed them into her hand.

She longed to be let into Sir Chatham's room. But it could startle him. He was too fragile now for her, in any way, to alarm him. He might be asleep. She would be gone no more than an hour at most. She couldn't keep the police waiting. She scribbled a note on a sheet from her small address book, slipped it under the door, then rushed for a taxi.

At the police station she was conscious that she was the center of attention of uniformed bystanders. She spoke to one of several men behind a counter. "I'm here to see Lieutenant Frazier."

She felt eyes follow her as a young policeman walked with her along a corridor past a room which had a bunch of empty chairs haphazardly set in front of a blackboard. They came to a small office where Lieutenant Frazier, who had phoned her, sat behind a cluttered desk. As she walked in alone, he rose, came around the desk, and pulled out a chair for her. He had a dark mustache, a balding head, and was older than he had sounded on the phone. He smiled in a friendly way, but she remembered that the man in the elevator had smiled too.

To the right of Phoebe's chair, a bookcase sagged under the weight of large bound books, maybe the history of criminals, she thought. Lieutenant Frazier sat looking at her.

She said, "I've never been in a police station before."

"I'm not surprised," he said. "Now, you mentioned some jewels."

"You mentioned Mrs. Adams—I wasn't sure why you were talking about her."

"She's reported missing some valuable items—I believe she lent them to you."

"Oh, but they weren't valuable."

His dark eyes looked into hers. "She says they're worth a lot."

"It was her idea for me to wear them. Anyway, it wasn't really jewels, just some old turquoise-and-silver jewelry she had in a box with a lot of old jumbled-up beads."

Lieutenant Frazier seemed to read from notes on his desk. "She says she now realizes she should have locked them up in her bank box. She'd planned to insure them but hadn't got around to it." He looked up at Phoebe. "I gather the items were of historic importance and rare. She said they should be in a museum."

Phoebe tried to appear calm as she took in this information. "I didn't take them, if that's what anybody thinks."

He smiled in a kindly way. He seemed nice after all. She had a hunch that if she were seated closer, he'd pat her hand.

Instead he crossed his arms and told Phoebe, "She said you'd been very disruptive at the dinner—"

"Oh, not on purpose. I did upset a tray but I certainly didn't do it on purpose. To tell you the truth, I'm surprised she said all that, she was all right at the party."

"You have to put yourself in the lady's shoes. She lost something that's valuable. She's mad."

"Mad?"

He studied her face.

"Oh, God," Phoebe said. "She's a friend of my boss. Well, anyway, she acted friendly toward me."

"She doesn't sound that way now."

"Her husband was friendly too, very friendly. He even took me upstairs to their bedroom—" Lieutenant Frazier's eyebrows lifted slightly.

Phoebe quickly said, "To help me look at her jewelry."

Lieutenant Frazier leaned forward, toward Phoebe. "Maybe she's jealous—"

"Oh, no, she wanted him to show me the jewelry. It was her idea and Sir Chatham's. She's a friend of Sir Chatham Wigans. I'm worried about his watches."

The lieutenant gave her a reassuring look. "We're working on that."

"I'm really worried about Sir Chatham."

Lieutenant Frazier leaned back in his chair. "As long as we're talking about that, I understand the assailant was on the elevator with you. Had you ever seen him before?"

"No."

"No acquaintance with him?"

"Of course not." Phoebe paused. "I don't understand why you're asking me that. What do you mean, do I have an acquaintance with him? I'd do anything to get Sir Chatham's watches back."

Lieutenant Frazier continued to look at her.

"And I didn't steal anything," Phoebe said. "I put Cynthia's jewelry in an oriental bowl on the mantel in her living room. I wish now I'd never gone to her party. But I had to go—I was on my job, I'm still on my job. I wish now I'd never heard of her."

Abruptly the lieutenant stood up. Had she said something wrong? "Thank you very much. You'll hear from us."

Phoebe returned to the hotel to find the Do Not Disturb sign still on Sir Chatham's door. She reviewed what the hotel maid had said. Phoebe knocked lightly on the door, then, in a panic, rushed to her own room to call him.

The phone was ringing as she entered. She hurried to answer and heard: "Phoebe!" Selmabelle's voice reverberated through the phone. "What do you think you're doing? You phoned the law firm and said you worked for me, then denied it. What kind of stunt are you trying to pull? Why were you calling Lawrence Bradley in the first place?"

Phoebe burst out, "Selmabelle, I have something to tell you. Sir Chatham's sick."

"Is this one of your stunts?"

"No, it's not a stunt. I need to get a doctor."

"What's happened? What did you—"

"Selmabelle, I have to go—I'm *very* worried."

Phoebe phoned Sir Chatham's room, but he did not answer. She tried Cynthia's number, gave the maid her name. "I'm calling for the name of a doctor."

"Mrs. Adams is not in."

"What about Mr. Adams—is he there?"

"I can leave a message for you."

"Thank you." Phoebe rushed down the corridor. The sign was still on the door. She had to get into his room. She ran through the hall in search of the maid, who must have gone off duty. Downstairs, in the hotel lobby, Phoebe found the assistant manager, explained the emergency situation.

A tall, sandy-haired man with glasses arrived: Dr. Burns. The hotel manager let him into Sir Chatham's room to examine the old man, who complained of a blinding headache as he lay in his hotel bed. Phoebe watched as the doctor took Sir Chatham's blood pressure once again, then again. He phoned for an ambulance.

As they waited for it to arrive, the doctor told Phoebe to sit down and relax. "You look pale. You might want to take it easy yourself."

"Yes," Phoebe said. "Except I can't possibly."

Twenty-one

OUR HOURS LATER PHOEBE NERVOUSLY LEFT the hospital bedside of the sleeping, medicated Sir Chatham to return briefly to the hotel. She picked up her phone messages and cringed at the sight of two from Selmabelle.

Just inside the door of her room, she saw her familiar, black, lost-by-the-airline suitcase. She had an urge to kick it. She kicked it. She hit it with both her fists before she opened it. Dragging out her evening dress, she was enraged at the thought that if the airline had not lost her luggage, she would never have borrowed Cynthia's jewelry; she would not have been without cosmetics; she'd never have left Sir Chatham in that elevator; he would not be in the hospital; and she would not be tense with worry that he might die. She wouldn't have to deal with the police, cancel the rest of Sir Chatham's appointments. In a fury she thought of the indifferent attendant at the airline's lost luggage counter who had handed her a kit for a man: "We ran out of kits for women."

And she wouldn't have phoned Lawrence's secretary. She wouldn't have to worry that Lawrence's stern father would hold him responsible for upsetting Selmabelle. Jane would hear about it, tell her aunt: "See, what did I tell you about that Phoebe? Fire her!" This time Selmabelle would say, "I already have that well in mind."

The phone rang. Should she pretend she wasn't in, the way Cynthia must be doing? She dreaded to think it might be Selmabelle calling again.

Courage, Phoebe said to herself and picked up the ringing phone.

"Honey," George Yorbrook Adams began.

"Oh, George, I needed to hear a friendly voice."

"I had a message you called."

"I asked for Cynthia but your maid said she wasn't in." Phoebe explained that Sir Chatham was now in the hospital, suffering from dangerously high blood pressure, probably brought on by the shock of the theft of his watches.

George said he was sorry. Then answering Phoebe's questions, he offered: "I tried to tell Cynthia you didn't want to borrow her jewelry—I said you were scared something would happen. That just made it worse. She just got more suspicious when I stood up for you."

"Suspicious?" Phoebe said.

"She'd be the last one to admit it, but I think there's a wide streak of jealousy—"

"But she's the one who suggested—"

"Honey, could I ask what you happened to be doing when the phone rang?"

"Unpacking my suitcase that the airline—"

"Want me to help you unpack? There's matters I don't like to discuss on the phone. My office is close to your hotel."

Phoebe said, "I'll meet you in the lobby."

"We need a drink," George Yorbrook Adams said in a way of greeting Phoebe. When she was seated across the small table from him in the hotel's dimly lit cocktail lounge, she observed the off-and-on smile on his suntanned face. She barely sipped from her glass while he downed his first drink. He took a swig of his second bourbon. "I know it was Cynthia's idea for you to borrow her jewelry," he said. "She likes to look generous and she is, don't get me wrong, but there's this other thing going along in her mind."

Phoebe said, "What thing?"

"You've heard of jealousy—"

"Oh?" Phoebe said.

"Yes, and with good reason, honey. You are mighty pretty. I couldn't deny it when she accused me of thinking that. She'd started talking about all the weight she'd gained and was kinda comparing her figure to yours." George leaned toward Phoebe. "I want to cheer you up. I don't seem to be doing it."

"I'd feel better if I knew what happened to her jewelry after I put it in that bowl."

"I can tell you what I really think about the jewelry. But we should get really comfortable first, honey, not stay here in the bar."

Phoebe chose not to answer.

"I'll never claim to know a woman's mind but I'm always trying."

"Yes, I remember you said something about that before."

"I'll say this now: I'm not sure she lost that jewelry."

"I don't understand," Phoebe said.

"You've heard about a woman's fury and scorn when her party's ruined?"

"What do you mean?"

"Honey—"

"You mean she hid the jewelry herself?"

"*You* said that, honey. We could talk a whole lot more about this and get a whole lot more comfortable up there in your room, couldn't—"

"No, I don't think we could." Phoebe stood up from the table. "I don't want anything more to do with either one of you."

George slowly rose. "I think I told you I'll be seeing Charlie Harkens in Tulsa next week. Any messages?"

"No, thank you."

"I'm sure we'll have an interesting talk," George said. "What about Selmabelle, when we call her?"

"Thanks, I'll take care of that myself."

"I guess I should tell you," George said, "just in case you get any more ideas about Cynthia—I won't take responsibility for any thoughts in your head." He smiled.

"I take full responsibility for my own thoughts," Phoebe said. "Also my actions. You better do the same."

He said, "We'll see about you."

Back in her room, Phoebe rehearsed a call to Selmabelle. She would sound positive, play things by ear. Lawrence got away with that kind of living. While pacing the floor, trying out things to say, the phone rang.

She heard Red-Jack's voice: "Wilbur told me how I could reach you. Are you sitting down? Marcia's back in the hospital. I told you I had to watch everything I said to her. I had a nurse at home, but this happened when we were at her folks' house—"

"What happened?"

"She tried to take her own life."

"Oh, no!" Phoebe closed her eyes, held the phone tightly, as Red-Jack explained that two nights before when he and Marcia had been at her folks' house, Marcia had left the dinner table, saying she had to see about the baby. Red-Jack had not paid close attention because her dad was talking to him. But when Red-Jack realized that Marcia had not come back to the table, he became suspicious, then alarmed. He leaped up the stairs and found her in her bedroom on the floor. He tried to rouse her. When he spotted the empty pill bottle, he picked her up and, praying it was not too late, carried her limp body to the car.

In the hospital they pumped her stomach and the next day—yesterday—she was in and out of sleep. But she was still so toxic, the nurses made her walk around for hours.

Marcia had found the sleeping pills in her mother's medicine cabinet. "Her mom kept saying the bottle couldn't have been full because she'd taken some of the pills herself. But when Marcia was awake—maybe I shouldn't tell you this, Pheeb—I think she did it because of you . . ."

Phoebe shifted the phone to her other ear. "Me?"

"Partly because of you anyway. When she woke up, I mean when she was saying anything, it was about the two of you."

"The two of us? What do you mean—what about?"

"That she's not a good mother. She's done everything wrong and God know this—that's why Niles was killed just when she was going to marry him. In her suicide note she wrote down that you'd make a good mother and wanted a baby, and when she's gone, you should have DeeDee."

"Oh, no, Red-Jack, oh, no. I'll be there as soon as I can. I have a crisis here, but when I can, I'll call you back."

Replacing the phone, she knew she had to think clearly. She looked again at the most recent message slip, left while she'd been in the bar with George: "Urgent, phone Selmabelle."

Phoebe warned herself: Don't call until prepared! Selmabelle would *not* fire her while she was waiting for news from her. Maybe she should return to the hospital, taking her files and phone numbers with her, and make calls from there. It was her duty to be with Sir Chatham. She wanted to be with him.

From her suitcase Phoebe lifted out the strawberry print dress. Maybe this print would cheer up Sir Chatham.

But when she arrived back in Sir Chatham's hospital room, she found that he was asleep and that the doctor had left orders for him not to be disturbed. "No one," the nurse said, "is to disturb him tonight."

Conscious of the sound of the plane's engines, Phoebe tried to relax from the rush to make the flight. She reassured herself she would be gone only overnight; she had a lot to accomplish in a short time in Harkenstown. She leaned her head against the high headrest. In her imagination she saw Marcia in her mother's elaborate bathroom, taking the bottle of sleeping pills from the medicine cabinet, turning on the water from the silver faucet, looking down at the pills in her hand before swallowing them. She envisioned Red-Jack discovering her small body lying on the white carpet in her bedroom, reflected from all angles in mirrors. Maybe she had sat on the bed, where she had not been allowed to sit as a child, to write her suicide note.

During the flight, Phoebe slumped in her seat, exhausted, but she was too on edge to sleep. How much risk was she taking by leaving Sir Chatham? She thought of calls she should have returned.

At least she had phoned Selmabelle to say Sir Chatham was resting comfortably. "What does *that* mean?" Selmabelle had demanded.

"That's what the nurse tells me," Phoebe had answered. "I'm calling from the hospital." Selmabelle did not need to know—did she?—that Phoebe had hung up, rushed back to the hotel to throw a few things in her suitcase, then grabbed a cab to the airport.

As the plane neared Wichita, Phoebe thought how strange it would seem to be in Harkenstown—how disorienting not to stay in her childhood home or the house she had shared with Niles. At least Kansas was a big state; Mother Bertha, miles away in Glennerville, need not know about this trip. The plane circled over the lights of Wichita. As it gently bumped along the ground in a landing, Phoebe experienced a mild surprise, making her realize that she'd not fully expected to arrive safely.

She followed passengers out of the plane, then she and Red-Jack hugged one another in shared anxiety. They sped in his Buick through darkened country toward Harkenstown.

She recalled that months before, when she'd prepared to leave Kansas, there had been snow on this flat land. Now light rain barely cooled the June heat. On this dark night she could not see the far-reaching wheat fields but knew that soon it would be harvest time.

Red-Jack was quiet, the radio off. Kansas winds battered the car, shaking memories loose to surround her. To the left of the highway appeared the ghostly outline of the Harkens grain elevator. After passing this rural skyscraper, she began to dread going by the Jayhawker Motel, where on the ice and in blinding snow, Niles had started to turn in from the highway and had kept turning until the collision.

As they passed The Jayhawker, Phoebe forced herself to look at the dim lights of the motel set back from the highway. Holding her breath, she tried to forget her words: "If you're going, go on, go on . . ." Then she closed her eyes, telling herself she could not escape what had already happened. She had to accept the circumstances of her life.

She opened her eyes to the sight of Main Street. It seemed wider and the sparse, nighttime traffic slower than she had remembered. At the traffic light, Red-Jack did not turn right, but continued along Main Street.

Phoebe sat up straight. "Aren't you taking me to the Harkenstown Hotel?"

Red-Jack stayed on Main Street, going by the Harkenstown Tower Building, then Farm State Implements, Inc., where Niles had worked. "I told you on the phone," Red-Jack said, "you can't stay in a hotel in your own hometown, Pheeb. Marcia's mom's expecting you."

"Please, Red-Jack—"

"It's all settled," Red-Jack said. He was speeding through a residential area. The rain became heavier as he drove past large houses in the north part of town. He turned into Cottonwood Street, slowed as he approached the drive leading into the grounds of the great gabled house of Marcia's parents. He steered the car down the front drive between the rain-soaked shrubbery, that bordered the road leading to the front entryway.

Red-Jack hurried to ring the front doorbell, setting off familiar chimes. As he and Phoebe stood at the sheltered doorway, she tried to prime herself to face Marcia's mother. She pictured her as she'd last seen her: standing at the grave site with Marcia—mother and daughter huddled together in their furs.

She hoped she wouldn't have to talk with Marcia's dad. She recalled George Yorbrook Adams saying he'd see "good old Charlie Harkens" in Tulsa.

When Mrs. Bain, the housekeeper, opened the door, Phoebe saw that she was dressed in her usual black but she looked more stooped and thinner than Phoebe had remembered. She must have been in her middle years when Phoebe had first accompanied Marcia home from first grade. "It's nice to see you again, Mrs. Bain," Phoebe said, then quickly added, "but I'm sorry about—"

"Mr. and Mrs. Harkens are playing in that bridge tournament out at the country club," Mrs. Bain said. "It's still going on." Phoebe tried to imagine Marcia's mother sitting at a bridge table when only two nights before her daughter had opened her medicine chest and swallowed her sleeping pills.

In the high-ceilinged foyer, Red-Jack appeared self-conscious as he traced the pineapple-patterned wallpaper with his finger. "I'll take Pheeb's suitcase upstairs, Mrs. Bain," he said, suddenly grasping the handle of the suitcase, which on this trip Phoebe had carried onto the plane. He accompanied Phoebe and Mrs. Bain up the floral-carpeted staircase and through the hall. After they passed Marcia's girlhood bedroom, Mrs. Bain said Phoebe was to stay in the next room.

Setting the suitcase on the luggage rack in the spacious bedroom, Red-Jack said he'd wait for Phoebe down below in the rec room. "I'll play me some pool. No," he amended his plans, "I'll see you in the morning, Pheeb. It's too late now to go to the hospital."

Phoebe hurried after him to say, "You'll remember, won't you? I absolutely *have* to get back to Chicago—"

"How many times are you going to keep telling me that?" Red-Jack said, leaping down the stairs.

Phoebe dropped her handbag onto the double bed covered by a taffeta spread, that matched the blue of the draperies at the windows. She looked down at the lights on the block-wide lawn at the front of the house where there was an abundance of shrubbery and white roses. It appeared, even from this distance, that some rose petals lay on the ground, the bushes having been damaged by the heavy rain, which by now had let up. She thought of herself and Marcia running around these grounds in the freezing—or scorching—wind while the adults stayed indoors.

Phoebe peeked down the hall toward Mr. Harkens's bedroom. Beside it was Mrs. Harkens's bedroom and adjacent dressing room. Years before Phoebe and Marcia had dressed up in Marcia's mother's furs and evening gowns and had played "movie star on location." All that play-acting, Phoebe thought, had not prepared them for real-life drama.

Phoebe saw in the dresser mirror the worried look on her face. She found Mrs. Bain, arranging towels in the linen closet. "Mrs. Bain," Phoebe said, "if it's convenient. I'd really love to see the baby now."

Phoebe tried to be calm as Mrs. Bain led the way to the pink-and-white nursery. Delia Dawn was lying in a crib dressed in a pink nightgown trimmed with lace around the wrists. Mrs. Bain had said she might be asleep. But when Mrs. Bain turned her over, here she was, awake and looking at Phoebe, as if she'd just been waiting for her. She stretched, clenched her tiny hands, and continued to look up. Phoebe, bending over, smiled, whispered, "Hello, Delia Dawn, hello, little sweetheart."

Phoebe said to Mrs. Bain, "Look at those blue eyes! Do you think she'll keep Marcia's eyes?"

"She has her dark hair," Mrs. Bain said. "I think it would be nice if she had her daddy's red hair."

Phoebe straightened. "Yes. That would be nice. I wish she did have red hair." She wondered if Mrs. Bain knew the significance of what she had said. Mrs. Bain, looking at Phoebe, seemed to consider her remarks, then bent down and picked up the baby.

"May I hold her?" Phoebe asked. When Mrs. Bain transferred the baby into her arms, Phoebe found her heavier than she had expected. This weight in her arms and the responsibility she felt made Phoebe sit down in the rocking chair while holding her. Phoebe looked down to admire her delicate features, the smooth baby skin. She smelled of baby powder together with a faint sour odor. "Oh, you're beautiful," Phoebe said. "You're absolutely darling, yes, you are."

"I'll be back," said Mrs. Bain and Phoebe, barely noticing, nodded. Phoebe had wondered if she might feel some resentment at the sight of this child. But now, holding Delia Dawn, she wanted only to protect and keep her safe. She felt an overpowering tenderness for this tiny person at the beginning of her life. Phoebe wished with all her strength that she could assure her an untroubled future. She sat rocking a long time while humming "Rockabye Baby." She realized that Delia Dawn—DeeDee—was asleep. Phoebe's own eyelids were refusing to stay open. She forced herself awake and gingerly lowered the sleeping baby into her bed. But Phoebe did not want to leave her. She pulled the rocking chair close by, and with a hand on the crib, she slowly leaned back in the chair.

Phoebe was awakened by the baby's crying. She looked up to see Mrs. Bain, who had changed into a nightgown, lifting DeeDee from her bed. "I'll take her now," Mrs. Bain said, as if dismissing Phoebe. She had told Phoebe earlier that now that she was caring for the baby, she had the room next to the nursery.

Phoebe felt offended that the baby had been taken from her; somehow tonight, this felt wrenching. It seemed a cruel and unnecessary reminder that she had lost her own baby. Why had she chanced leaving Sir Chatham to come here? Even Marcia's parents were at the country club playing bridge, as if there was no emergency. They might be home soon and Phoebe did not want to talk with them.

She changed into her nightgown quickly, slipped into bed. Marcia, two nights before, had lain unconscious in the next room, ready for death. Trying to sleep, Phoebe recalled Red-Jack's voice on the phone, "I think it was because of you . . ."

Early the next morning Phoebe dressed, crept downstairs, and found

Red-Jack, smelling faintly of whiskey and waiting for her. He was lying on a sofa in the expansive living room, familiar to her with its heavy furniture and the window seat where she and Marcia used to play with their dolls. Red-Jack sat up. "Have you had coffee?"

"No, but could we leave?" Phoebe said. "I've written a note to Mrs. Harkens to thank her."

They stopped at the Prairie Schooner and sat in Red-Jack's favorite booth. To Phoebe it seemed strange to be in this place where months before she had confirmed to Red-Jack that she would no longer live in Harkenstown. Now she told him that she had held the precious DeeDee in her arms and sung to her. Red-Jack was silent as she talked about the baby and he did not speak as he drove them to Memorial Hospital.

When he pulled into the parking lot, Phoebe caught a glimpse of the morgue where she had identified Niles's body. What had she been saying? She had lost her train of thought—her mind was playing tricks again.

"Oh, now I remember," she said and told Red-Jack that during last night when she couldn't sleep, she had tiptoed into the nursery to peek again at the baby.

Red-Jack turned off the car's engine and without looking at Phoebe, he said, "You'd like to have DeeDee, wouldn't you?" He stared down at the steering wheel. "I don't want anybody taking DeeDee. She's all I've got if Marcia dies. I know Marcia wants you to have her." Frowning, he glanced at Phoebe. "I keep thinking: before you went back east, you didn't even want to see Marcia."

"I had good reason."

"Well, you still got the same reason. And now you've seen the baby."

"Red-Jack, why did you phone me?" Phoebe opened the car door. In the morning sunlight, she ran across the graveled parking lot toward the hospital. Red-Jack caught up with her, grasping her arm. "Pheeb, you don't even know what room Marcia—"

"I guess they'll tell me at the desk."

"No, they won't. Mr. Harkens left word no one is to know where she is. And he's on the hospital board."

"Then I guess you'll tell me, Red-Jack."

"What are you going to say to her?"

"I don't know. I want to see how she is." Phoebe walked fast and Red-Jack kept up with her as she entered the lobby of the hospital. "I can call up Mrs. Harkens," Phoebe said, "and ask her the room number."

"No," Red-Jack said, guiding her toward the elevators. "I'll take you to the room."

He pulled her to the back of the large elevator away from the operator, so he could speak to her privately in a lowered voice. "The doctor—the psychiatrist—he says not to give Marcia advice, just be encouraging."

"What else?"

"Hell, he hardly speaks to me—he says he needs Marcia's permission and she won't give it." As they got off on the third floor, Red-Jack said, "These goddamned doctors care more about their goddamned rules than they care about how I feel."

At the door of 312N, Red-Jack spoke briefly with Marcia's private nurse, then nodded to Phoebe to enter. Phoebe held her breath and the door handle for a moment before she walked alone into the room, which had green painted walls and almost no furniture. Marcia was propped up on the bed, looking pale in a light blue gown, her slightly protruding teeth more prominent now, her face so thin and drawn Phoebe had to convince herself that she was in the right room.

Marcia squinted at Phoebe, then turned away: "You're here to take the baby." Phoebe could barely hear her strained voice.

"No," Phoebe said, "I'm here to see you. Red-Jack called me." She pulled the armchair closer to the bed and sat down. "I was worried about you."

Marcia was still propped up, holding her knees. Leaning her thin face against her knees, she turned to look at Phoebe, contemplating her from an angle.

"Red-Jack told me about the pills," Phoebe said. "That really scared me. I want you to feel better."

Marcia had her lips clamped.

"I'm staying at your folks' house," Phoebe said. "I keep thinking how we used to play jacks and Ping-Pong and movie star in your rec room? Remember? We had some really good old times, didn't we?"

Marcia did not answer; her head was against her hunched shoulder.

Phoebe stood up. Were there bars behind the window curtains? She noticed a vase of blue-purple irises on the dresser. Or were these artificial? With Marcia watching, Phoebe restrained herself from touching a petal or a leaf. Should she have brought flowers? Were real flowers forbidden? Phoebe stepped toward the bed, wondering how many flowers and plants were poisonous, remembering Red-Jack had said that the doctor wanted to keep everything harmful away from his suicidal patient. As Phoebe sat down again, Marcia turned her head away. "You're here to take the baby."

"I'm *not* taking the baby, Marcia. I'm here to tell you that."

Marcia made her small hands into fists and now looked at Phoebe with pleading eyes. She did not speak but feebly pounded the bed. Phoebe thought of Red-Jack quoting from her suicide note. She had said that God knew she had done everything wrong. And when she was gone, Phoebe would have the baby.

Phoebe stood up, then sat down again. "I saw the baby. She's beautiful, Marcia. She belongs to you, she needs her mother." With Marcia still silent, Phoebe said, "You've given her a lovely name: Delia Dawn . . . Ordall." Then Phoebe sat silently too, finally asked, "Do you want to tell me anything? Do you want me to go?" Marcia had her chin on her chest. Phoebe slowly pushed herself to her feet. "Want me to give you a hug?" With no reply from Marcia, Phoebe threw her a kiss instead. "I'll be thinking of you. And the baby. Together."

Red-Jack was waiting in the hall. Phoebe shook her head. He embraced her. "There aren't too many goddamned miracles around as far as I can tell," he said on the way to the car, "unless it's DeeDee."

As Red-Jack sped toward the Wichita airport, he asked again, "But how do you think she seems?"

"I can see why you'd need somebody to talk to. I hope I said the right things . . ."

"Don't worry, Pheeb."

"You worry."

"Hell, all the time. But I can't talk about it to anybody."

"What about Robert Rowley?" Phoebe said, referring to the church and TV organist.

"I don't want to gab to somebody who works where I do."

"He's wonderful with Mother Bertha. They're still in touch with each other by phone. I think he's discreet or I certainly wouldn't suggest—"

Red-Jack hit the steering wheel. "I keep trying to get it into my goddamn head that my wife had another man's baby." He glanced at Phoebe. "Sorry, Pheeb, this is hard on you too." He ran his hand over his stubby hair. "My folks are all puffed up about their grandkid. I can't tell them she's not really theirs."

"Can you talk to Marcia's folks? You said they know . . ."

"But you see how they are: they go out to the country club—everything's just fine and dandy. That's the way they act: life's exactly the way they want it—beautiful, hell. You see how her mom's acting about you. They had you stay at the house, that way you don't cause problems in the *community*—boy, the community's everything to her." Red-Jack wove in and around cars, increasing speed, causing Phoebe to hug herself, press back on the seat, but she had to make the flight.

While moving with the traffic into the airport, Red-Jack said, "Hell! Her folks don't want anybody to know Marcia's in the hospital, let alone that her doctor's a psychiatrist. It's getting me down, Pheeb. When somebody asks me a question, I have to put on an act . . ."

"Bad news makes everybody into an actor," Phoebe said, "in one way or another, sooner or later. You pretend you're feeling good when you feel terrible. You try to act like you're not preoccupied when you can't keep your mind on what you're supposed to be doing. You get sick . . ."

Phoebe's mind moved from Marcia to Sir Chatham.

In Chicago, as Phoebe stepped closer to Sir Chatham's hospital room, she confirmed to herself that she would not volunteer where she had been. On her return she had checked her suitcase downstairs. Now she lingered at Sir Chatham's door, then walked into the room. The bed was empty. Phoebe saw that the bathroom door was ajar. She called, "Sir Chatham," then rushed out to the nurses' station, where the only nurse there was studying a chart while talking on the phone. In the corridor, Phoebe stopped a nurse's aide, who had been talkative when Sir Chatham had first arrived at the hospital. "Sir Chatham Wigans . . ." Phoebe began. "He's not in his room."

"Check with the nurse. Maybe he's having more tests." The nurse's aide hiked down the hall past several patients in wheel chairs. Phoebe followed her. "Excuse me."

The aide said, "Has he finished with the lawyer?"

"The lawyer?" Phoebe hurried to keep up with her. "The lawyer you mentioned—is he from New York?"

"It's not my duty to ask visitors where they're from," the aide said, ducking into a room that bore a sign: STAFF ONLY.

Phoebe rushed on to the visitors' lounge. Sir Chatham, wearing his plaid robe, was slumped in a highback chair. His frail hands were crossed over his lap, his sleeves pulled down over his wrists—a poignant reminder of his lost treasures. His old eyes met Phoebe's.

When she approached him, the man seated next to Sir Chatham stood up and introduced himself as E.H. Trueblood and named his Chicago law firm. Short, barrel-chested, and wearing wire-rim glasses, he held papers in his hand. In sudden tension, Phoebe looked from his serious face to Sir Chatham's and back. Was a lawyer needed because of the association's contract? Was Selmabelle about to lose the account? Selmabelle would blame her. Or was he someone representing Selmabelle? Maybe Lawrence or his father had recommended him?

A large, big-bosomed nurse came into the room. "Oh, your granddaughter's here," she said cheerfully to Sir Chatham. Phoebe quickly glanced at Sir Chatham and was relieved to see him smile. He had to be better; this was the first smile she'd seen on his dear face since the robbery. The nurse gave Sir Chatham two white pills, which she had carried in a tiny paper cup, and he took them with water from a glass, sipping from a glass straw.

After the nurse had gone, Sir Chatham said to Phoebe, "They found my watches."

"Oh, God, thank God," Phoebe said.

Mr. Trueblood was looking at her. "He says it's all due to you." He sat down, placed papers into a file, then forced the file into his heavily packed briefcase. "The police will bring his watches back to him," he said and smiled at Sir Chatham, as if he were complimenting a child.

He turned his smile on Phoebe. "Sir Chatham says you're the one who asked if there were any engravings on the watches." The large reward and description of the engraving, as reported in the newspaper, had alerted pawnbrokers. So when the thief took the watches to a shop, the pawnbroker was ready for him. "Now the pawnbroker's claiming his reward."

After Mr. Trueblood left, Phoebe asked Sir Chatham, "How are you feeling?"

"I just want to go home." He looked up at Phoebe, who stood by his chair. "Will you come with me?" He glanced away as if embarrassed that in his life of accomplishments, he now, in body and spirit, was needy.

Twenty-two

O N THE PLANE TO NEW YORK, with the exception of the engraved watch, Sir Chatham did not wear his timepieces. Before their flight, he'd appeared chagrined when he'd admitted to Phoebe that because of his anxiety about his watches and his limited energy for fastening them on and off, he had them secreted in his smallest suitcase. Then he had entrusted the case to Phoebe.

Weighed down by this responsibility, she kept the tips of her shoes touching it. Even with this safeguard, she looked below the plane seat in front of her to be sure the slightly worn, but still handsome, black leather case was where she had placed it.

Sir Chatham didn't read the newspaper or his book on the history of clocks and wristwatches, but napped while Phoebe herself sat tensely upright, concerned about Selmabelle's reaction to Sir Chatham's plea that she accompany him to England. His plan, as ordered by Dr. Burns, was that they would stay in New York two days, giving him a comfortable stopover, then fly on to London together. The doctor had emphasized the necessity of travel medication; with his condition and age there was danger of a stroke. As Sir Chatham dozed in the seat beside her, Phoebe went over in her mind that he was scheduled to rest in his New York hotel room.

Arriving in the city at night, she registered him into the Waldorf. When she asked if he needed someone with him, he said. "No! I don't need a nurse or a nanny!" He's tired, Phoebe thought while riding in the taxi on the way to the apartment. Then she forced herself to accept the fact that she had to face Jill. Should she come right out and ask her for details about Lawrence's impromptu visit? Had she seen him since? It was unnerving that these were questions she would have talked over with Jill—but they would have been discussing another woman, not Jill.

Phoebe unlocked the door. "I'm back." No answer. She set down her suitcase, walked around the surprisingly neat apartment, peeked into the bathroom. She slumped, relieved. But then she realized she was a bit sorry too. She had hoped to get it over with: the initial— whatever it was going to be.

Jill's suitcase was missing from the closet. Maybe she was out of town on an interview for a new job.

Or with Lawrence? Or Gilbert? Jill had said she was interested in Gilbert. Had things worked out for her with him? She might have taken a suitcase of clothes for Gilbert to choose what she should wear for a portrait. Gilbert would realize that Jill was showing him many of the same clothes he'd seen before. He'd recognize Jill's things which Phoebe had borrowed when she'd taken her own suitcase to his studio.

I can't go to England not knowing. I HAVE to know. With such a short stay in the city, she'd better call Lawrence at home tonight. She'd never phoned him at his apartment but why wait until tomorrow to call his office and be embarrassed speaking with Mrs. Cartright again? What if Jill is in his apartment? Or Jane?

He might be home alone. They would make plans for tomorrow night for dinner where she'd sit across the table from him—maybe even beside him—in some restaurant. The Japanese restaurant? She'd smile and tell him that she had been inspired to save Sir Chatham's watches by having looked at the back of his watch.

No! She couldn't tell Lawrence that she'd first thought of such a watch engraving when he'd left her alone in his bedroom while he'd gone to the next room to talk on the phone—probably to Jane. He'd be surprised to know she had examined his watch to see if the back had an inscription from Jane.

Phoebe held her breath, dialed Lawrence's number. After two rings, his deep voice said, "Hello."

"Lawrence?"

"Phoebe!"

"I'm back," she managed. "Briefly."

"Darling . . ."

The next night Phoebe continued to roam the Fifth Avenue lobby of the Plaza Hotel. She sat down on the circular banquette in the center of the room, then stood again by the entrance. She had spent her day partly at the office defending herself against Selmabelle, and a long time at the passport office acquiring an emergency passport. Now she kept repeating to herself that she had to see Lawrence before she left for England. She must not miss him.

As she waited and waited for him, she reviewed their phone conversation. She was sure he'd said then that they would meet at seven in *this* lobby of the Plaza, not the other lobby on Fifty-ninth Street. If she left this lobby now to go to the other one, she might miss him. Finally she dashed to check the other lobby, then ran back to the original waiting area. A man standing near the door turned again to look at her; she moved away from his gaze.

She confirmed in her mind that Lawrence had said they would eat in the Plaza or a nearby restaurant, according to their mood. "Hey," he'd said, "and maybe dance." She knew she remembered correctly because the places sounded more expensive than he usually suggested. Phoebe circled the Fifth Avenue lobby and rechecked her watch, then stood on the wide steps in front of the hotel to wait for him. Her annoyance verged on anger. Now that she had waited fifty-five minutes, she would leave in five minutes. When she climbed into the taxi, she gave the driver her address, but still looked at arriving cabs for a glimpse of him.

At home she tried again to call him at his apartment, then rang the night number at his office. No answer. She replaced the phone. As she paced the room, she felt confined by the small space. She wondered again: where is Jill?

Hearing the ringing phone, she rushed to answer it.

"How are you?" Lawrence asked her.

"What happened?"

"I'm on my way."

When he arrived, as he stepped into the apartment, Phoebe interrupted his apology. "What happened?"

"Things got confused."

"Confused?" She turned away, then faced him. "You kept me waiting in that lobby for an hour—I left in an hour." Usually, she remained sweet to him when he had been undependable, but now she was enraged. "What do you mean—what the hell do you mean: '*Things* got confused'?"

"I know. You want to shoot me. I'll help you pull the trigger."

"What makes you think you can act like this?" She hurled accusations in a tirade, as accumulated frustration and fury forced her onward. "This is *not* the first time you've said you were going to do something, then didn't do it. You say good-bye at the end of an evening—you say 'I'll call you tomorrow.' And then you don't do it. *Why* do you say something," she demanded, "if you're not going to do it?" She could not stop herself, she did not want to stop herself. She was "furious, absolutely livid," she stormed. "You're—"

"I agree with you," he said, "one thousand percent." As he left the apartment he said, "Good-bye." Nothing else. She shut the door, then opened it wide, and with all her aroused strength, slammed it, then slammed it again as hard as she could.

A few minutes later, the phone rang. Phoebe let it ring and ring, finally grabbed it. "Are you still steaming?" Lawrence asked.

"Do you have another question?"

"I was wondering if I dare come back? Are you getting lonesome?"

"No, I most certainly am *not* getting lonesome!"

"You're not expecting to hear from my brother, by any chance?"

She banged down the phone, then turned while tense. She experienced a sudden painful crick in her neck. "Damn it to hell!" she yelled.

Phoebe still held her head and neck in a strained position when she boarded the transatlantic plane with Sir Chatham. The attentive stewards welcomed them to the first class section. They fussed over their titled passenger, showing they knew he was a legend in the travel world.

Phoebe turned her body, favoring her stiff neck, to look at her frail traveling companion. She thought how Selmabelle had always shown her strong awareness of his importance too. After his request for Phoebe to accompany him to England, Selmabelle seemed to be especially alert to Phoebe's actions now that she was so highly valued by the association's chairman. Yesterday Selmabelle had summoned her employee to her desk. Selmabelle eased into a conversation, then said to Phoebe with a sly smile, "Don't get the idea, my girl, you can become the head of Selmabelle Flaunton, Inc."

Now while Sir Chatham dozed beside her on the flight, Phoebe took her notebook out of her travel bag. Having packed it with plans to jot down her British travel impressions in an effort to please Selmabelle, she now found herself writing about trust and distrust, Niles and Lawrence. Why, on the phone, had Lawrence asked if she was expecting to hear from his brother if he didn't care?

Lawrence's question had inspired her, in New York, to try to call Gilbert first at his apartment, then at his studio. She'd hoped Gilbert might give her a word about Jill. Finally, she'd given up and had left a message with his answering service that she was on her way to England and supplied phone numbers where she could be reached.

She'd been cautious when phoning Jill's office for information as to her whereabouts. When pressed for the purpose of her call, Phoebe had hung up. Jill might be making up some phony excuse to be away from her job to look for a "more interesting one."

Sir Chatham shifted position in his airline seat, then slept again with his mouth open. Watching him breathe, Phoebe wondered if he dreamed and what he dreamed about. Finally she must have dozed herself for she found herself waking up to the roar of the plane, the smell of coffee, and breakfast being served by the airline stewards.

As Phoebe and Sir Chatham examined their breakfast trays, Phoebe admitted to him that she had been unable to reach his housekeeper by phone. He seemed relieved then that Phoebe had arranged for him to stay briefly in a hotel. She promised to make sure his London flat was ready for his off-schedule return.

At the busy airport in London, Phoebe walked beside a porter who pushed Sir Chatham in a wheelchair. She became aware of several men in uniform holding up signs, each bearing the name of a well-known hotel: the Savoy, the Dorchester . . .

Then she spotted the sign for The Royal Rose. Standing with the uniformed attendant from The Royal Rose Hotel was Edward Hibbard, the slender, blond Englishman she had met on the train from Kansas to New York. She recalled when he had taken her to Selmabelle's party, the night she got her job. She could see that he still displayed a red rose in his lapel, a kind of advertisement for the hotel.

"I say," Edward said, as he rushed forward to greet Sir Chatham and to kiss Phoebe on the cheek. "Welcome!" As they headed for the car, Phoebe noticed his customary tie with the row of red roses.

When they settled into the enormous black limousine—a Daimler, Edward told Phoebe—Sir Chatham appeared strained and tired. He frowned as he sat on the wide, plush seat and held on to the strap by the window. Phoebe felt it might increase his discomfort if she revealed too much worry about him. To brighten the atmosphere, she commented, "Nothing could be as luxurious as this car."

Edward's lips, below his blond mustache, moved into a smile. "It suits you—luxury. So you like this better than a train? Phoebe and I first met on a train," Edward told Sir Chatham. "Gilbert Bradley was on that train. I'm not sure if this is a coincidence—he rang up today for a reservation."

Phoebe tried not to show her surprise. But she still puzzled over Gilbert, even when she was in her spacious hotel suite at The Royal Rose.

Favoring her stiff neck, she gingerly leaned over an antique table to breathe in the scent of the red roses of welcome from Edward Hibbard, then moved to an arrangement of yellow roses and irises from Lord and Lady Petwell. She could see the influence of Sir Chatham—under his direction, she had phoned Lord Petwell from New York to let the Association for Castles and Stately Homes know that their chairman was on his way home, accompanied by Phoebe Stanhope of Selmabelle Flaunton Enterprises, Inc.

As she removed her shoes for full enjoyment of the suite's cushioned rose-patterned carpet, she again questioned why Gilbert was about to arrive. In the adjoining bedroom she ran her hands over the satin chairs and silk spread. Her stiff neck prevented a full view of the high ceiling but she strained to glimpse the border of plaster roses.

Edward gave no explanation of Gilbert's plans the next morning when he took her on a much-briefer-than-he-wanted sightseeing tour of London, ending at the residential building on Curzon Street where Sir Chatham lived. At Phoebe's suggestion, Sir Chatham was staying longer in the hotel to rest.

At the entrance to the old, well-kept building, which seemed appropriate to be the London residence of Sir Chatham, she said goodbye to Edward. Then she rode in the polished, wood-paneled elevator—the lift, she corrected herself silently—to the third floor. She felt like an intruder inserting the key into the lock of the flat but she had promised Sir Chatham.

The air in the closed-up flat smelled stale and the fabric on the bulky furniture in the sitting room seemed faded like Sir Chatham's old eyes. There were clocks in a row on the mantel and grandfather clocks standing here and there, wedged between cabinets. Phoebe knew she was in his flat even before she spotted the framed photographs on the wall. Here was Sir Chatham, seeming to charm a group of aged women seated in big, comfortable-looking chairs as he showed them his collection of watches. How women must have loved him! If she had been born closer to him in time and place, she might have been one of them. How much timing and chance had to do with life! And how appropriate that he should be devoted to timepieces and historic properties.

In the bedroom on the bedside table, she discovered the picture that she was sure had to be Florence as a bride, standing next to the young Chatham Wigans. They stood straight-spined and held hands even in this formal-looking picture. Phoebe studied Florence's plain, honest face, with her hair pulled back from her forehead. Phoebe wondered if she had followed a secret plan to keep her important husband faithful. Had he been faithful?

In one of the bookshelves lining the walls of his study, Phoebe found a row of books he had written. Then she saw that they were copies of a single title: his autobiography, *In My Time*. He had asked Phoebe to bring back a copy to the hotel for him to autograph to her. He had seemed in a hurry to give it to her.

A doorbell sounded. Phoebe tiptoed into the hallway. The bell sounded again. She inched her way. She cracked the door open. In the corridor a large man hovered, then moved toward her.

"Gilbert!" Phoebe cried.

After he stepped inside, she motioned for him to take one of the large chairs in Sir Chatham's sitting room. She sat down opposite him. He told her that he'd been encouraged, then worried by her phone message left in New York, containing phone numbers where she might be reached in England. "I realized you needed me," he said.

"Needed you?"

She rose from her chair and Gilbert trailed her to the kitchen. She felt he was watching her as she opened one cupboard after another. "I'm checking supplies," she said. "I'm here on my job."

"I'm going to be working over here too," he said. "Phoebe, you don't seem to know how I feel about you."

When she turned toward him, he took her into his arms.

"You're nice to be concerned, Gilbert, but to tell you the truth," she said, "when I phoned you in New York, I was looking for Jill." Escaping from his embrace, Phoebe again looked into the cupboards.

Gilbert strode back and forth in the kitchen. "Phoebe, sometimes I think I've caught on to understanding you—"

"I thought maybe you'd been painting Jill's portrait," Phoebe said. She began to take items off the shelves without knowing what they were.

Gilbert placed his hands on her shoulders, turned her around to face him. "You and I are always misunderstanding each other," he said.

"I guess we are."

"You don't give us a chance. I thought you'd probably heard the news about my brother."

"Your brother? No."

"You haven't heard he's taking the big step?"

"Lawrence is?" Phoebe turned back to the cupboard. "You mean marriage? Are you sure?"

"No, I'm *never* sure about my brother. But I understand he's been having a hard time at the office. I'm sure he's figured out that Dad would like this news."

She had to force her voice: "But he already told you?"

"He dropped by my studio—incidentally, it was the first time since you both were there."

"Oh?" Tears were moistening Phoebe's eyes. "And then he made his announcement to you?"

"He's not always consistent. He asked to see your portrait, by the way."

"But you didn't do a portrait."

"I've been working on a large drawing from memory."

"Oh. Did he like it?" Phoebe shrugged. "Not that it matters." She ambled into the sitting room, slipped into a chair. "Did he like the drawing?"

"He didn't say." Gilbert followed her. "But he's never looked so nervous before, but then he's never gone so far in taking the big step. He gave me the big news, then left—he said he was on his way to the Plaza."

"The Plaza! Well . . ." Phoebe stood up from her chair, then sat down again. Was that when he'd kept her waiting in the lobby? Phoebe whispered, "You didn't mention who the bride is."

"I notice you didn't say 'the lucky bride.'"

"No, I didn't."

"It's Jane," Gilbert said.

There was a silence.

"All the clocks are stopped," Gilbert said.

"Don't touch them! Sir Chatham wouldn't want them touched!"

"Phoebe, don't get so—you seem surprised about my brother. Let's get out of here—we'll have lunch. How about tea then? Why won't you let me take you to tea?"

"To begin with, this flat is dusty."

"Phoebe, you're not a maid!"

"I can't reach his cleaning woman."

"Take it easy, don't get so riled up. I'm surprised you're so surprised about Lawrence. I'd think Selmabelle would have told you. Especially since Jane depends on Selmabelle for everything. You planned Jane's party, so I thought now Selmabelle would probably assign you to plan her wedding."

Phoebe stared at Gilbert without speaking.

"All right," he said. "I'm leaving."

She shut the door after him, then charged around the flat, telling herself she had to find a way to calm down.

Gramma's advice from long ago surfaced in her mind: "Phoebe, honey, you're all upset. Take a *long warm bath*—that'll relax you and make you feel a whole lot better." Phoebe asked herself if she really should take a bath here in Sir Chatham's flat. She had to do something.

Why not? It was a lot better than throwing things, smashing up the furniture.

Now in the bathroom, Phoebe undressed as she ran the bath water, then discovered it was icy cold. She turned off the noisy water and realized someone was walking in the flat.

Naked, the bathroom door still wide open, she faced a startled, middle-aged, prominent-bosomed woman. Phoebe grabbed up a towel and held it over herself.

Quickly averting her eyes, the woman stepped back and stood half-turned away.

"Oh, excuse me," Phoebe said, "you're Mrs. Ferguson, aren't you? I told Sir Chatham I'd see about his flat when I couldn't reach you."

"Where is he, miss?"

"At The Royal Rose. I told him I'd make sure his flat was ready—"

"Oh, I'll see to it. I've taken care of it for thirty-three years, miss."

Phoebe moved into a corner of the bathroom and began to dress. "I started to take a bath but the water's cold—"

"Shall I make you a nice cup of tea? I've brought milk. And cheese and biscuits. My sister said you'd rung up. I just didn't expect—"

"You didn't expect him back so soon—I understand." Phoebe peeked at Mrs. Ferguson, who still stood turned away. "A lot's happened," Phoebe said. "I'm sure he'll tell you when he's able to. He's not well."

"Oh,—the dear man!"

"He is, isn't he?"

Mrs. Ferguson blushed again, hurried toward the kitchen.

After Mrs. Fergeson's generous tea, Phoebe returned by taxi to The Royal Rose. In the lobby, she caught a glimpse of Sir Chatham seated with several men in the lounge. She recognized the large, white-haired man with the hearty laugh as Lord Petwell.

While Phoebe lingered to watch the group, Lord Petwell stood up. Did he think she was rude for staring? Should she rush off? Wearing a pinstriped suit and walking in an awkward way, he was already coming in her direction. "So," he said in a jovial voice, "you're back in England. It's good you've come home." He escorted her toward Sir Chatham. "I was just telling Phoebe that it's a good job she's come home. She's beginning to sound American."

"But I am American," Phoebe said.

"She's been in America too long," Lord Petwell said.

As Phoebe sat down with the group, she saw that one of the men was Gilbert. Sir Chatham was saying how delightful it was to have Phoebe on "this side of the dear old Atlantic." She smiled as he introduced her as his "taskmaster."

"This young lady can charm a bird off a tree," Sir Chatham told the group. "While we journeyed in America, she insisted I go on the telly to answer questions from reporters at press conferences. And address the populace from one speaker's platform after another." Sir Chatham smiled at Phoebe. "If she makes up her mind that you have to appear on the screen or do a broadcast, it's very difficult to say 'no.'"

Listening to him now, Phoebe felt as if she and Sir Chatham were in a conspiracy; he was implying he'd tried to avoid attention and publicity. Memory told her that he'd been eager for the spotlight and always had known the purpose of his "goodwill tour." Yet, like the others listening to him now, she could feel herself responding to his charm.

Phoebe noticed that he did not mention the theft of his watches. Perhaps that was because Lord Petwell was busy saying that his wife had never forgotten her day with Phoebe at the Empire State Building. Now his wife wanted Phoebe to join her in a visit to her cousin's place.

"Splendid!" Sir Chatham said.

Phoebe was amazed by Sir Chatham's display of enthusiasm after days of misery and medicines. He still looked frail and as if he was straining to appear robust before his male colleagues.

Sir Chatham smiled as Lord Petwell outlined travel plans for Phoebe to visit Lady Petwell at Ravensleigh Castle, the home of her cousin. The name rang a bell for Phoebe—she remembered Selmabelle speaking of Lord Ravensleigh, who'd had an employee "who had become too lordly for words and one simply had to fire him."

Gilbert sat forward in his seat, "I could join Phoebe at Ravensleigh. I've promised to do a portrait."

Phoebe turned away from his gaze. She felt less enthusiastic than the others about Gilbert following her there.

But how could she protest when the association's officials seemed so pleased, even proud of themselves, that the plan was set? Their urging seemed excessive to Phoebe, until she reminded herself that the promotion of visits to houses and castles was, after all, their business. And her own too!

The arrangement was settled: Phoebe would travel alone and Gilbert would follow in one or two days' time.

Before Sir Chatham's planned move back to his flat, he and Phoebe sat close to one another in matching armchairs in his hotel suite's sitting room. "After you return from Ravensleigh," Sir Chatham said, "I'd like you to see Devon. And especially my greenhouse. I'd like to know if it's what you had in mind when you said you planned to live in one." Phoebe joined his laughter.

Then he handed her the book he had requested that she bring back from his flat: his autobiography, *In My Time*. "Would you like to take this to Ravensleigh? Perhaps you might glance at it."

Smiling, she opened it. On the flyleaf, she found his now shaky handwriting, in green ink: "To Phoebe, delightful companion, whom I'd like to adopt, and then have stay with me in Devon—at least until the orchids bloom. With the author's gratitude, affectionate greeting, and very real regard." It was signed: Chatham Wigans.

Phoebe turned to Sir Chatham. He looked at her expectantly as if awaiting approval of his kind thoughts.

Phoebe hugged the book. "Oh, thank you," she said, emphasizing the words. As she walked down the hotel corridor to her own suite, she thought he couldn't be serious about her staying in Devon, surely. She could hardly wait to show the book with its inscription to someone on her return to New York. Who? Her first thought was to show it to Jill.

If things were as they once had been with Jill and she were in England now, she could help her decide what clothes to take to the castle. *To the castle!* The phrase seemed so inflated and lofty that Phoebe's face felt hot. She half-questioned, for a moment, if she could be having delusions of grandeur.

She tried not to be impressed.

Twenty-three

BUT THAT WAS NOT EASY, for the next afternoon a Rolls-Royce, bearing the gilt crest of the Earl of Ravensleigh on the door, stood waiting in front of The Royal Rose. The hotel doorman opened the car door and took care to see that Phoebe was comfortably settled in the back seat, which smelled of the rich, red leather upholstery.

On this chilly summer day, riding through London as the lone passenger, Phoebe began to feel that the chauffeur, up front, was too far away. If she were seated beside him, she could talk about the tall, square black taxicabs, so different from the yellow cabs in New York. But she decided that to request to sit beside the chauffeur would not be the thing to do in England. The driver kept his shoulders erect. The back of his gray-haired head and black cap looked forbiddingly set in a long-standing, traditional way of doing things.

In childhood, coming out of a movie with Marcia, Phoebe had said, "Let's play like we live in England." They had assumed what they had believed were English accents and tried not to giggle when talking with adults.

Now traveling through rolling green countryside, Phoebe leaned forward to query the chauffeur, who politely answered her questions, yet introduced no conversation himself. But after they had traveled about an hour, he said, "This is Kent, miss." At last through a gap in the trees, the stone castle appeared in the distance like that in a storybook, its towers rising against the overcast sky, crenelations notched across the top.

Yet even from here, Phoebe could tell that this was a real structure firmly grounded on a hill, a vast ancient building. Catching sight of deer grazing in the meadow, she knew they were on castle property. She had seen deer in the guidebook, which described Ravensleigh as a "medieval fortress. Over the centuries it has been added to, and now has over one hundred rooms." Sir Chatham had told her: "It rivals Warwick Castle."

As they neared the castle, the sun was beginning to blink through the trees. They passed a large graveled area, a parking space which seemed reserved for tour buses and paying guests. Phoebe spotted tourists climbing out of cars, making their way in couples or groups toward the entrance.

Here and there, a man or woman, or entire parties, turned to see who was riding by in the chauffeur-driven Rolls.

Phoebe wished someone were with her; it was hard to take in all of this alone. She thought of the fun feeling she'd shared with Jill and, despite recent doubts, she now pictured Jill stifling a giggle while riding along in this car. Phoebe conceived their prank, languidly waving to tourists in a regal gesture of acknowledgment. She visualized Jill raising her hand, and with a skillful wrist movement, slowly turning her hand with its upraised fingers in a circle, a majestic waving, as though making a state visit. Then recalling the crest on the car door, Phoebe fancied they were noble persons who lived in the castle. In her imagination they waved slowly, grandly, and hoped the chauffeur did not notice their lark in his rearview mirror.

Looking out the car window, Phoebe wondered if some of those tourists who stared at her were from Kansas? They would be astonished and puzzled to know that it was just Phoebe Fields Stanhope from Harkenstown who was riding by and that she was about to enter historic Ravensleigh Castle as a guest of Lord Ravensleigh and his cousin, Lady Petwell.

Phoebe thought of her grandmother who liked people who were down-to-earth. She wished she could reach her to say that she would not get stuck up or put on airs.

In the shadow of the castle, the chauffeur stopped and opened the door of the Rolls. Phoebe stepped out onto the road beside a lawn bordered with small rocks. Her luggage was whisked away. She was greeted by a man in striped pants and a formal-looking coat. She guessed that he was the butler as he led her through an enclosed gravel-floored courtyard, finally into a vast room with a ceiling so far above, it seemed almost a substitute sky.

It was here that Phoebe confronted a group of tourists. They gazed up while the tour guide's voice echoed: "When Sir Walter Scott visited Ravensleigh Castle, he praised this room, known as The Great Hall. The marble floor you stand on overlays the original flagstones, the walls are hung with sixteenth-century Belgian tapestries . . ."

Phoebe's attention was caught by a row of suits of armor on display, as if knights-of-old stood in a receiving line to welcome her to the castle. Ahead, the butler was waiting for her and she hurried after him through chilly passageways, up stairs, down more corridors. Rushing after him, Phoebe remembered that she used to think Marcia's folks' house was big.

At last, opening a door, the butler announced that this was the Green Bedroom. She should ring when ready to see His Lordship, who was expecting her.

Phoebe silently translated: His Lordship, the Earl of Ravensleigh.

Alone, Phoebe stepped into the large bedroom, lighted even now in the afternoon by a crystal chandelier. It shone down on the wide bed, covered by a spread of sea-green silk. Atop two long chests, painted with garlands of flowers, there were magazines in English and

French, bottles of sherry, Scotch, and brandy, as well as a bowl of surprisingly small, fragrant oranges.

She lay back on the chaise lounge, cushioned with pillows of green silk, then sprang up to choose a chocolate mint from a dish on the bedside table.

When she picked up a booklet, she discovered it was a thin telephone directory, listing numbers for the castle and grounds. She noticed it was not in alphabetical order, but began with His Lordship's Study; then His Lordship's Bedroom. Next: Her Ladyship's Study and Her Ladyships's Bedroom. Phoebe wished that it said Her Ladyship's Chamber—more appropriate for a castle, even if it was a tourist attraction.

But she reminded herself that first this had been, and still was, a *real* and *historic* castle. She found listed under Bedrooms, her own Green Bedroom. So named, according to a framed notice on the dresser, because of the tapestry panels put on the wall in 1777 by the Third Earl of Ravensleigh. Phoebe marveled as she touched the ancient fabric, now a pale green (she wondered how much it had faded), depicting a garden.

She emphasized to herself that *that* Earl was the Third Earl, but the *current* Earl was the Twelfth and he was expecting her. A maid answered Phoebe's hurried ring and quickly escorted her through passages to the tall, gilded double doors of The Red Drawing Room.

Entering the enormous room alone, Phoebe looked about at the red, lacquered walls; large, dark, varnished paintings; heavy furniture upholstered in red. Suddenly she caught sight of His Lordship, the Earl of Ravensleigh, standing with one hand on the mantel of the huge fireplace, watching her. He looked graceful as a dancer and was slim and wearing tights, a black leotard bodysuit, and a red-and-black scarf.

Though as she stepped closer, she realized he had the beginning of a potbelly. Sir Chatham had told her that he was thirty-three years old, gave readings of his own poetry, and only recently had succeeded to the title of Earl, following the death of his father.

He smiled faintly and held out his hand. Before Phoebe could give him a firm handshake, he grasped her fingertips, and told her that his wife and children were in London for a series of dental appointments. "Too dreary. But my cousin is here."

Lady Petwell, with yellow curls framing her lined face and dressed in a beige tweed suit, beamed as she came into the room and rushed toward Phoebe. As Lady Petwell placed her cheek next to Phoebe's in greeting, Phoebe recognized her perfume from their day in New York.

The butler carried in a tray laden with a large gold and silver teapot, scones, lemon cake, and tiny white-bread sandwiches, which Phoebe was to learn, were filled with chicken or cucumber. Lady Petwell leaned forward in her chair and showed her large teeth in a smile to Phoebe. Speaking in her extravagant upper class accent, she confided, "I've told everyone about our visit to the Empire State Building."

Smiling back, Phoebe tried to think how Lady Petwell had described her fear of fainting on the fifty-seventh floor, their elevator rides broken up into sections.

"Oh, now I see," Lord Ravensleigh said, changing his tone to a correct coolness, which Phoebe had been told the English use when annoyed. "I didn't realize until now," he said, "that you were the one."

"The one?" Phoebe said.

"Who inspired her," said Lord Ravensleigh. He turned to frown at Lady Petwell. To the accompaniment of her giggles, he told Phoebe that his cousin had visited Ravensleigh Castle soon after her return from New York. Having experienced sightseeing in New York, his cousin had persuaded his wife that the two of them should dress as tourists with scarves on their heads and join a group touring the castle. They had chosen a tour which Lord Ravensleigh *personally* was leading. But he hadn't noticed them until his wife brought out a camera from a pocket in her coat and took aim at him.

Because cameras were strictly forbidden, the tourists who had checked theirs were furious, especially after some of the English visitors recognized his wife—The Countess of Ravensleigh, Phoebe translated. After that incident and the attendant press stories, he had experienced a wretched time trying to enforce the no-cameras rule.

"Visitors want souvenirs," he said, "and I provide a shop where they can buy postcards and trinkets and copies of my poetry books. For kleptomaniacs, we have our own writing paper here and there in the rooms—a trick I borrowed from a colleague." He named popular Petwell Castle, Warwick Castle, Beaulieu, Longleat, Woburn Abbey. "But I plan to be top dog. I plan to have more visitors than anyone."

"Good for you," Phoebe heard herself saying.

Lord Ravensleigh made it clear that he wanted help in promoting his castle to American tourists. He needed more dollars to keep up the place; he was paying death duties. Considering her own finances, Phoebe found something comical in his plea for dollars to her, of all people.

Outdoors, when Phoebe walked with Lord Ravensleigh through the rose garden, she leaned to breathe in deeply the scent of one rose after another. He told her he would have the gardener cut a rose for her.

A rose turned out to be several dozen, Phoebe found with delight when later she returned to her bedroom. She enjoyed the sight and perfume of roses of many shades, arranged in vases on the desk, the dressers, on tables throughout the large room.

With all this splendor, she half-expected a servant to say, as in novels, "May I draw your bath?" But she found that it had already been drawn, just as her clothes had been pressed and her cosmetics placed on the dressing table. It hadn't occurred to her that her suitcase would be unpacked. When she saw, on a hanger, her robe with the big safety pin still holding together the shoulder seam, she let out an embarrassed laugh. Then she told herself it was surprising that the maid hadn't taken care of that too, considering all she had done.

In the bathroom, a framed sign on the wall requested conservation of water because of plumbing in the castle. It contradicted the full tub. Phoebe dipped her finger into the water, filled to the brim of the big, claw-footed bathtub. The water was invitingly and surprisingly warm, so someone must have alerted the maid when she was about to return to her room.

A warm bath tempted her. Right now, even though it was summer, her feet were so cold in this extremely chilly weather that she remembered, during winters in Kansas, Niles used to jokingly accuse her of soaking her feet in ice water before coming to bed.

Yet Phoebe was concerned now that a bath might loosen her new, elaborate hair-set, which she'd had done this morning in the hotel's beauty shop.

But she was not in Kansas anymore. This was a once-in-a-lifetime visit to a *castle!* Despite her hairdo, she eased herself into the tub, and luxuriated in the lather of the lavender-scented soap stamped RAVENSLEIGH CASTLE. She kicked her long legs in the water—until she remembered that Lawrence had said he loved her legs.

She remembered too that Lady Petwell, just before excusing herself from the tea table, had requested with a giggle that her cousin take Phoebe and herself to a pub in the early evening. Phoebe had a hunch that Lady Petwell had never been in a pub, just as she'd never been in a taxi before her ride in New York with Phoebe to the Empire State Building.

But then, Phoebe thought, she herself hadn't visited an English pub either. She hurried to be ready to go.

As the departing car passed the castle's parking area, the late afternoon tourists had a glimpse of Lord Ravensleigh in the back seat of the Rolls with Lady Petwell. Phoebe, seated between them, was pleased that he acknowledged the visitors with a wave. Lady Petwell, giggling, leaned forward and raised her hand. Quickly while she had the chance, Phoebe waved too, though she began to wonder if she was being brash in sharing this greeting. Was she being an *upstart American?*

Yet Lord Ravensleigh seemed amiable as they neared the village of

Ravensleigh. "This road leads into the High Street," he said. "I know in America the term is 'Main Street.'"

They passed a monument of Queen Victoria in front of the Town Hall, soon stopped at the Royal Swan. After they were ushered out of the car by the chauffeur, a group of five chattering, American-looking tourists rushed to ask Lord Ravensleigh for his autograph. He quickly obliged.

"I'm used to that," he told Phoebe as they entered the noisy pub. "I like it if they want me to sign one of my books of poems." Phoebe remembered Sir Chatham had told her he was known as the Poet Earl. While they stood near the entrance to the pub, he added, "A poetry club from Boston and another from St. Louis visited the castle and made me an honorary lifetime member. I'm not sure what that entitles me to but I thought it was kind."

Inside the pub, as they moved through the rowdy voices and smells of beer and occasional sweat, Lady Petwell glanced about, wide-eyed. She said, "I don't want to stay here." She turned around and strode to the front and out the door.

Phoebe reluctantly followed her outside to the street. Here Phoebe's eyes were on a man approaching, dressed in a scarlet cutaway trimmed in gold braid, gold-colored knee breeches and stockings, buckle shoes, and a black three-cornered hat. He carried an enormous bell. And like the Pied Piper, he was followed by excited children.

Phoebe said to Lord Ravensleigh, "Wait! Who's that?"

Lord Ravensleigh summoned the man and said his guest wanted to know his identity. Phoebe could see by their easy communication that they knew one another. The man appeared highly respectful of the Earl. Yet he showed a slight smile when he said, "Is she from the colonies, melord?"

"I'm from the States, New York," Phoebe answered for herself.

"The colonies," the man said.

After Lord Ravensleigh made a hasty introduction, saying that Timothy Harvey was the Town Crier of Ravensleigh, he looked toward the car. Lady Petwell had already placed herself, with the aid of the chauffeur, in the back of the Rolls and now scowled. Lord Ravensleigh seemed anxious not to keep her waiting.

Seeing the look on Lady Petwell's face, Phoebe silently predicted an unpleasant evening ahead in the castle. At once she pulled her tape recorder from her large bag, and told Lord Ravensleigh that she thought the town crier would make a good tourist story. "I'd like to interview him."

Lord Ravensleigh, appearing relieved, climbed into the Rolls. He said, "The car will return for you." Timothy agreed he would ring the castle when they had finished.

"Do you want to see me strut my stuff?" Timothy asked Phoebe. "Isn't that what they say in the colonies?"

Phoebe silently conceded that some people probably had said that a long time ago. Aloud, she said, "I'd love to—"

But already Timothy Harvey had grasped the great bell by its ebony handle and was swinging it above his head. It caused such an enormous clanging that the giggling children clasped their hands over their ears. A small spotted dog barked at him and tourists joined the children to crowd around him. He continued to ring his clanging bell. Then he lifted his head, covered by his three-cornered hat, opened his large mouth, and bellowed, "Oh-yay . . . oh-yay . . . oh-yay." Phoebe noticed that this rhymed with "Oh, hay," and the second syllable of each word was held a long time.

Now Timothy unrolled a scroll and reading from it, he shouted, "There will be a five-shilling reward for lost spectacles." He called out an invitation to visit Ravensleigh Castle and the shops and establishments of the town of Ravensleigh, and announced events open to tourists. "May ye find increasing happiness. God bless ye all and"—then came the loudest, most impassioned plea—"GOD SAVE THE QUEEN!"

Phoebe, recording, said to him, "I thought town criers said *Hear Ye. Hear Ye.* You say: *Oh-yay.*"

"That's Norman French for *Hear Ye*," he answered as Phoebe held the microphone in front of his red face.

"How do you spell it?"

"O-Y-E-Zed. Zed, the last letter in the alphabet. I know you say Zee. You're from the colonies." This cry, he told her, had first been heard at the Battle of Hastings in 1066, when "William the Conk" arrived from France.

"There have been town criers here in Ravensleigh since the fourteenth century." As he spoke, he patted a little boy's head. "But I ain't been here that long—only seven years," he said to the child. The little boy looked up at the town crier, who added, "Seven years probably seems a long time to you, young man."

Phoebe could see that Timothy Harvey was talking into the microphone, but also to the audience gathered around him. He told a group of Americans that his bell weighed eleven pounds.

Between cries and comments to Phoebe, he showed one child, then another, his bell, his three-cornered hat, his buckled shoes. He appeared to be a perpetual politician or an extra uncle or grandfather to them, as they seemed to expect this.

One little girl hung onto his coattails and looked up at Phoebe shyly when she tried to talk to her. Phoebe longed to take her into her arms and hug her, but the child backed away.

When Timothy saw that Phoebe was about to ask more questions, he suggested that they go into "the rub-a-dub-dub" for a "pig's ear" or "a cuppa Rosy-Lee." Grinning, showing his crooked teeth, he said this was cockney rhyming slang.

Inside the pub, Phoebe and Timothy settled into a corner. Phoebe placed the tape recorder on the table. He told her that "a pig's ear" was a beer; "Rosy-Lee" was tea; and "Mother's ruin" was gin. Whiskey: "Makes-you-frisky." They sat at the "Cain-and-Able" (the table) in the "Johnny-Horner" (the corner).

"I'm a Londoner," he said, "born within the sound of Bow Bells. Then one fine day I put on my tit-for-tat." He paused.

"Your hat?" Phoebe said.

He nodded. "And came here to Ravensleigh with me trouble-and-strife."

"Is that your wife?" Phoebe said. "How does she like being called that?"

"I'm her old pot-and-pan, her old man."

"What's it like being the town crier? Do you have any occupational hazards?"

"Dogs and drunks. Me plates-of-meat, me feet—they give me trouble. And me voice. This helps that." He lifted his mug of beer and took a swig.

In answer to Phoebe's interview questions, he told her that in addition to his duties as town crier, which included attending municipal functions and selling tickets at the castle, he had another job, that of toastmaster. He explained that a toastmaster announces in a formal manner the arrival of guests at banquets. "His Excellency, the Ambassador and Lady Tiddley-Push," he called out in illustration, drawing even more attention to himself and Phoebe, who held the microphone as he talked.

"Oh, I've seen toastmasters in movies," Phoebe said in a surprised voice, "but I didn't know that's what they're called."

"An English toastmaster ain't like your joke-blokes in the colonies. I don't tell jokes—not as part of me job. Back in the good old days of King Charlie the First and Second, a toastmaster went 'round the banquet hall dropping toast into the wine or the soup plates."

A fat man, wearing a gray sweater, leaned toward Phoebe from the next table. He looked eager to speak so she held the microphone toward his round, mustached face. He took a deep breath and said in an American Midwestern voice, "I have a hobby of foods and wines. I thought you'd want to know that this toast he's talking about was a delicacy, treated with spices, rare, expensive spices. That's why the fairest and most admired lady was called 'the toast of the town.'"

Phoebe thanked the man but her mind was on Henny Tibbold and the ambassador leading the toast to "darling Jane" at her party.

"I don't on purpose drop anything into the soup or wine," Timothy said. "But I'm in the soup sometimes meself."

"That makes two of us," Phoebe said.

At her suggestion, Timothy took Phoebe on a tour of the pub. They nibbled bar food (including Timothy's favorite: sausage rolls) and talked with more and more townspeople and tourists. So, it was much later than she had anticipated when Timothy phoned for the car and the chauffeur silently drove her back to the castle.

When at last Phoebe was in bed in the Green Bedroom, she tried to unwind. But she was overtired and in such a stimulated state that she could tell she would lie annoyingly awake with a hodge-podge of anxieties and thoughts. Even the welcome hot water bottle that met her feet when she settled under the covers would not relax her enough to bring on sleep.

From the bedside table she picked up Sir Chatham's autobiography. In London, Edward had told her that Sir Chatham wrote the way he talked. "He's a 'Gold Name dropper'—that's what an American friend of mine calls him. He says, 'Sir Chatham Wigans is the only man I know personally who is on a first-name basis with God.'"

Phoebe had defended him: "But they're the people Sir Chatham knows. I'll bet he doesn't know many people who aren't famous. Except me."

Now at a late hour, propped up in bed, reading about Sir Chatham's life, Phoebe enjoyed two long chapters before she finally closed the book, and then her eyes, but for hours it seemed, she could not shut off the jumble of questions and impressions in her mind.

Twenty-four

THE NEXT MORNING, under a brightening sky, Lord Ravensleigh escorted Phoebe onto the castle grounds where a peacock strutted on the lawn, then unfurled its tail of colors. Delighted, Phoebe saw that the colors really did include peacock blue, reminding her of the evening dress she would wear that night.

Suddenly she realized that Gilbert had arrived. He strode across the grass toward them, sporting a brown suit and sweater, a contrast to the tights and red-and-black scarf worn by the Poet Earl. Smiling, the men shook hands, then Gilbert leaned to kiss Phoebe on the cheek. He spoke of his first visit, as a child, to the castle with his family and Selmabelle.

Gilbert looked at Phoebe when he added that, back then, his mother had told him that Selmabelle had been a guest in the castle on numerous occasions, beginning when she was just a toddler.

Phoebe laughed to herself imagining Selmabelle as a tiny child in the castle. A miniature Selmabelle. Had she been giving orders then too?

But quickly Phoebe realized that right now Lord Ravensleigh was talking about Gilbert as a child, telling about his first visit to the castle. Even at that early age, Gilbert had made impressive sketches of his child-host and the children who had come to play in the castle. Right then the young nobleman had decided that some day Gilbert would be the artist who would paint his portrait for the castle's Long Gallery.

Lord Ravensleigh said, "I heard Gilbert's mother tell him: 'Children say things—he may not remember it by the time he grows up.' I felt insulted as if I didn't know what I was talking about. That made me *determined* that Gilbert *would* be the artist and I've had it in mind all these years. Now is the time . . ."

So, Phoebe thought, Gilbert really did have a reason to come to England. It was not just to follow her.

As Phoebe strolled with the men in the shade of huge trees, Lord Ravensleigh asked Gilbert, "How's Brother Lawrence?"

"He's getting married."

"I say! Jane, is it?"

"She's the one."

"By Jove, they could come to Ravensleigh on their honeymoon."

"He didn't mention a honeymoon," Gilbert said.

"Maybe have the wedding here."

Phoebe pretended to examine the footpath. Had Lawrence expected Gilbert to pass along his news to her so that he wouldn't have to tell her himself?

Phoebe felt Lord Ravensleigh looking at her. Was he wondering why her face was flushed? She heard him say to her, "About the wedding— would you like to mention it to Selmabelle? I should think she'd have a hand in her niece's wedding. She did with the other niece . . ." He stopped suddenly, as if just remembering: Gilbert had been the groom.

That night, while dressing in her peacock blue chiffon gown, Phoebe lectured herself: she would not allow thoughts of Lawrence Bradley to ruin her visit. She was here on her job. She examined her hair once more, then made her way to the Long Gallery, now set up with chairs like an auditorium. She took her place on the front row beside Lady Petwell, who had changed from tweeds to gray silk and rubies.

"Good evening," Lady Petwell answered Phoebe's greeting. She showed her large teeth in a smile and raised her pale eyebrows, when she turned in her seat to look directly at Phoebe next to her. Then Lady Petwell glanced quickly about the room, as if stimulated here in familiar territory. Behind them, the castle visitors, admitted by ticket, were settling into their seats. Gilbert, on the other side of Lady Petwell, was busy with his pencil and sketchpad.

Lord Ravensleigh, the Poet Earl, entered the picture gallery and strode to the podium with the eyes of the audience and his ancestors on him. Phoebe wondered what Gilbert thought of the portraits of the nobleman's forebears lining the walls. The previous Earls of Ravensleigh, dressed in red ceremonial robes, looked out from their canvases, most with haughty disdain, in single portraits, or in family pictures with each Countess of Ravensleigh weighed down by a tiara and surrounded by children and their well-bred dogs.

Phoebe began to visualize the portrait that Gilbert had started today of the present Lord Ravensleigh. She imagined the Poet Earl standing rigid-straight, chin lifted, one hand on his hip, wearing the crimson robe.

But that was not his stance now. Lord Ravensleigh, in person, in black tie, leaned over the large wooden lectern and leafed through his book of poems in preparation for his reading. Gilbert sketched him as he raised his head and faced his audience.

When the nobleman began to speak in his now singsong voice, one hand beat the air in rhythm with his words. Between his love poems, Phoebe turned to glance at the audience, noticing looks of rapture on the faces of several women, and at least two men.

Then Phoebe became a part of the privileged group of invited guests, chatting their way into The Yellow Dining Room, rich with ornamental gold leaf on the wall panels and high ceiling, and lavishly set for eight. She wished she had brought her tape recorder with her tonight. She should have recorded at least a bit of the poetry, though maybe recording equipment wasn't allowed in the castle. Lord Ravensleigh had made it clear that cameras were "strictly forbidden." Yet he had agreed to be interviewed about the castle during her visit.

Phoebe took her place at the table between a theatrical producer and a portly member of Parliament, who spoke to her of the recent opening of the St. Lawrence Seaway. Hearing the name Lawrence, Phoebe could not stop her thoughts of him, visualizing him here on his honeymoon, sharing with Jane such dishes as this poached salmon and cucumber, then roast lamb with mint sauce. When Phoebe poured Devonshire cream over her summer pudding, which was decorated with strawberries, blackberries, and raspberries, she imagined Jane coyly smiling at Lawrence as she sampled this divine delicacy.

Now, across the table, a scrawny, black-haired woman dressed in black with pearls, was speaking. "I live—love, actually—among ghosts."

"My word," the Member of Parliament said, then asked Lord Ravensleigh if he had a resident ghost.

"I usually save that," he answered, "for the visit to the dungeon."

"Is that where he lives?" the producer asked with a laugh. "Or should I say 'dwells'?"

"Hovers," Lord Ravensleigh said. "He roams the castle, hovering in one room, then another."

"Who?" Phoebe said.

"The Third Earl of Ravensleigh," the black-haired woman answered, as if this were ordinary dinner talk.

"He was stabbed in The Great Hall," Lord Ravensleigh said, "and the body dragged to the steps leading to the dungeon. My theory is he was stabbed by his wife's lover. Some historians say 'by a manservant once beaten for misconduct.'"

The producer laughed. "Perhaps the wife's lover and the manservant were one and the same person."

Lady Petwell leaned forward in her chair as if the guests were discussing her favorite subject.

"We try to play down the idea of ghosts," a green-gowned blond woman said. "If one admits to ghosts, it's hard to keep staff, don't you agree? And the children are afraid to go up to bed."

But Phoebe was aware that ghosts were not played down here at the table. Following the final after-dinner toast, Gilbert left his seat by Lady Petwell and came around to Phoebe. Now standing up from the table, Phoebe did not tell him she was feeling a bit woozy from the champagne on top of the wines served throughout the meal.

To begin Lord Ravensleigh's private midnight castle tour, for the sake of authenticity, the electric lights were switched off in parts of the castle. The guests carried candles as they proceeded to the spot where the body of the Third Earl had been dragged.

Phoebe, holding her candle, was mesmerized by its flickering light and felt sleepy. She was cautious as she went down the worn, stone steps in the narrow dark staircase to the dungeon. In this hole the guests were crowded together and shadows danced over the dank, grimy, fourteenth-century stone walls surrounding them. Phoebe hated being in this cold, gruesome place, where in earlier centuries, prisoners had been held almost without light or ventilation, and taken out only long enough to experience the horrors of the torture chamber.

Lord Ravensleigh escorted Phoebe up another dark staircase, this one circular and in a castle tower, where he told her that the stone walls were ten feet thick. The staircase was so twisting and narrow that Phoebe could not see Gilbert on a lower step when he called up to Lord Ravensleigh asking if he remembered their childhood game of shoving each other down these stairs.

Lord Ravensleigh groaned in answer. After climbing up and up more winding stairs, and more winding stairs, he and Phoebe reached the top of the steps and faced a wooden door hung with iron fittings. "You go first," Lord Ravensleigh invited.

Phoebe cautiously and slowly opened the ancient door to discover a small office. At a desk, a woman in a dark green dress ferociously pounded a noisy typewriter. This sight and sound in this medieval tower at this hour so surprised Phoebe, she let out a laugh before she caught herself. The typist—her gray hair loosened from its hairpins—looked up at Phoebe and stopped her rhythmic clatter to sudden silence.

Then the guests, crowding in, talked all at once. Lord Ravensleigh motioned toward another door, this one to an inner room: "My office," he said. Phoebe found it hard to imagine climbing all these steps to get to work. His office door displayed a sign: GENIUS AT WORK.

As they descended the steps, Phoebe said to Lord Ravensleigh, "That's a great sign on your office door."

The lights came on at the bottom of the tower stairs and a servant collected the candles. They were now at the entrance to a part of the castle which seemed like a museum with huge display cases. It was here that Lord Ravensleigh said to Phoebe, "The sign is from your world. I bought it in New York, at a shop in Greenwich Village." He turned to Gilbert. "You were with me—you and your wife . . ."

Gilbert frowned. "I remember."

Stepping away from the men while pretending to inspect a display case of porcelain vases, Phoebe stayed close enough to eavesdrop on Gilbert's comments to Lord Ravensleigh. "Lawrence never worried about causing trouble in my marriage except for what Dad might say . . ."

Phoebe was surprised to hear Gilbert speak so openly of family secrets. Still, he had drunk plenty of toasts tonight and he and Lord Ravensleigh were a continent away from his family.

Lord Ravensleigh continued his tour spiel and pointed out items in a glass case of historic gold plates and heirloom cups. Phoebe longed to ask Gilbert how much his family had discussed the wealth represented here. She guessed these displays of treasures had sparked Lawrence's childhood ambitions and increased his stinginess. Later on, his memory of priceless heirlooms may even have inspired him to become an estates lawyer. She'd bet anything he'd at last chosen Jane because she was the favored one in her family, the sister who would inherit more, especially from her Auntie Sel.

When Lord Ravensleigh finally led the group into the bedroom named in honor of Queen Elizabeth I, Phoebe was so fatigued from last night's sleepless hours, she had the notion that she would duck under the red velvet rope and climb into the huge, high, red-canopied bed. She imagined crawling under the crimson covers, embroidered with the crown and the initials *E R*. She could almost hear Selmabelle's enraged cry: "Blasphemy!"

Phoebe stayed standing behind the velvet rope, lingering with the group looking at the bed. The producer, who had sat beside her at dinner, now teetered unsteadily at her side. "A bed is a bed is a bed," he told her in a loud drunken voice, "except when you're in it." His face and stale cigar breath were forced on her as he said, "That's where I want to be."

Phoebe ducked away. After a quick "thank you and good-night" to Lord Ravensleigh and Lady Petwell, she returned to the Green Bedroom. When she slid her body into the wide comfortable bed, where the covers had been folded back in readiness by the maid, Phoebe sighed happily.

She had the feeling now of being truly pampered in this castle as she switched off the bedside lamp.

Lying in the darkened room, she became aware of a light beyond the foot of the bed. The light was in the shape of a vertical picture, such as a portrait, but she knew it could not be on the wall—it was in the middle of the room, a rectangular glow hanging in space.

The rest of the room remained dark. She sat up to test whether she'd been asleep and dreaming but the light was still there. She found herself rubbing her eyes in disbelief. She had read of people doing this in novels, but she had never thought she'd do it herself. Recalling ghost stories at dinner, she had the feeling she was being watched in the dark.

Quickly, she leaned to her left to turn on the lamp. Her fingers fumbled among the porcelain flowers in search of the lamp pull, but in her panic, she could not find it. She slid to the far side of the bed. Stepping onto the carpet, she looked out the window at the sweep of lawn, faintly visible in the night, but she could see nothing to explain the light. In a plan to switch on the chandelier, she felt her way around furniture. Suddenly she was afraid to take another step. She crawled back across the bed, and determined, trembling, she located the lamp pull.

Now the room clearly in sight, she detected there was nothing in the space where the light had been. *I don't believe in ghosts. I've never believed in ghosts.* Now she was not so sure.

If the champagne had affected her, she'd still be seeing things, wouldn't she? As a test, she switched the lamp off, then on, and studied the room. The gold antique clock above the desk showed six minutes past two. Two entrances led into the room from the main corridor. One door was next to the bedside table, and a second door was in line with the spot where the light had been. Someone—something—had entered the second door.

She got up and brought magazines back to bed. Trying to read, she found herself still frightened and pondering. She felt reasonably sure the light had to have been earthly rather than unearthly.

Yet Lord Ravensleigh had said the resident ghost hovers in one room, then another. Where people are, she thought. She pushed the covers aside, stepped onto the carpet, and forced herself to walk slowly about the room. He'd said that the ghost moves about from one place to another. Like me, she thought: *searching.* Is that how ghost stories get started? Out of the needs of the living? No matter how you look at it, ghosts have to have more to do with the living than the dead.

Near the desk she touched the tapestry put on the wall by the Third Earl of Ravensleigh. He was dead, murdered on the floor below, and she was alive. Someday she too would be dead, a part of the whole: all those who had lived and were now dead, all those who would live and die. Gramma had said, "You die the way you live; you live the way you die. You go full circle."

How much had she helped Niles to live as well as to die? That moment in her life she most wanted to change was the one she was for-ever destined to relive: "If you're going, go on. Go on . . ." If only she could unsay her words, Niles would not be out of reach, out of life.

Quit it, she told herself, these middle-of-the-night anxieties will be gone by morning. Even the assurance itself disquieted her. Would she need to reassure herself if she had no cause for apprehension?

Looking out the window, she visualized Lawrence the boy running across the darkened lawn. As if in a dream, she saw the child holding a golden crown high above his head as he ran.

What did this mean? What was happening to her? She reviewed that when Lawrence and Gilbert had first visited the castle, Lord Ravensleigh would have been a child too. According to Sir Chatham, he had been called Lord Montcombe, before succeeding, upon the re-cent death of his father, to the title, the Earl of Ravensleigh. But Phoebe guessed that the children would have used his given name Harold.

The boys would have played in the dungeon, explored secret hiding nooks in the castle, shoved each other while trying to climb into a suit of armor, looked for peacock eggs in unlikely places—perhaps in the woods she'd passed on the way to the castle? She wondered what pea-cock eggs looked like. Big? Henry VIII must have had roasted peacock at his medieval banquets and peacock eggs for breakfast. Scrambled? Hard-boiled? Not peacock eggs, she suddenly realized: peahen eggs.

Her thoughts slightly amused her but she did not belong in this world of these people. She was just a business someone to them, someone who was supposed to help Lord Ravensleigh and Lord and Lady Petwell increase visitors to their castles. Where was her life? Where did she belong?

If she had to work to "fit in," she didn't really belong. But how many times in her life would she be a guest in a *castle!* The answer forced her to recapture the spirit of adventure. She'd pretend she had just stepped into a whiff of magic smoke, as she had pretended in childhood. She coaxed herself back to bed.

When she awoke, the lamp was still on, the clock ticked, the room glowed with daylight. While she sipped tea the maid had brought, Lord Ravensleigh phoned and asked if she had slept well.

Phoebe told him about the mystery light. "It was a trick," she said. "Wasn't it?"

"A trick?"

"A prank," she said with a little laugh. "Did you and Lady Petwell play a joke? One of you?"

"Do you think we play jokes at two o'clock in the morning?"

Phoebe had not mentioned that the light had appeared at two o'clock.

When the tall Wedgwood-decorated phone on the bedside table started ringing again, Phoebe stared at it before answering. "Phoebe?" The voice was familiar but in her present state Phoebe could not place it. "This is Barbara Hadley."

"Barbara!" At once Phoebe visualized the TV office in Harkenstown and, at the desk next to her own, heavy-set Barbara, her cowriter.

"Phoebe, I've had one hell of a time tracking you down, but now that I've got ahold of you, I'm not sure you'll want to hear this—it's bad news."

"What?" Phoebe closed her eyes. "Is it about Marcia?"

"Phoebe, brace yourself! She drowned."

"Drowned? Oh, my God! Where? How?"

"We were at the staff picnic. At Meadowlark. And you know, she'd been sick a lot. Phoebe, this was her first outing."

In memory Phoebe saw Meadowlark Lake, made large by laborers, not nature. She visualized the end of the lake—the grassy spot where the TV staff's annual picnic always had been held. Where also last Labor Day, she and Niles, Marcia and Red-Jack had stayed in cabins—Phoebe still in mourning because of her recent miscarriage. Where Niles and Marcia had just "found it happening . . ."

Now Phoebe said to Barbara, "I want to be sure I understand this. Marcia was—"

"Marcia and Red-Jack were out in the rowboat. He was rowing. I remember I looked out and I was thinking they were out quite a ways. Then I saw Marcia stand up in the boat, which made it rock, and she threw a beer bottle at him. And he fell over backwards in the boat and Marcia went overboard. Phoebe, they discovered a broken drinking glass in the boat with blood—"

"Blood?"

"Marcia's. When they found her body, they saw the damage to her wrists—"

"Oh God! What about Red-Jack?"

"I saw him stagger up in the boat, then he went headfirst into the water. He was drunk—everybody thinks he was trying to save her. They both drowned before anybody could reach them."

"They're *both* dead?" Phoebe bent over. "Oh, my God! No! What about the baby?"

"Phoebe, listen, that's what I want to tell you. Just before they went out in the boat, Marcia gave me this envelope addressed to you."

"To me?"

"I stuck it in my pocket so I had it when she drowned. I got very worried when I couldn't get you on the phone. I started to give it to the police and then to her mother. But I kept remembering what Marcia said—"

"What did she—"

"She said, 'Get this to Phoebe and don't tell anyone.' Listen, Phoebe, she looked funny, really weird, and the envelope was all twisted up. It was really strange, the way she made such a big point of it."

"What's in it? Open it!"

"I already did. There's a note in it to you. It says: 'They'll fight you—don't let them! You've got to get DeeDee away from them.'"

Phoebe reached Marcia's mother on the phone. Mrs. Harkens interrupted Phoebe's plea. Hearing her high insistent voice coming through the transatlantic wire, Phoebe felt as if she were once again in the same room with her, watching her fluff her blond hair, seeing her blue eyes darting here and there. Phoebe was again breathing in her heavy perfume, as she moved about the luxurious bedroom, pulling the telephone cord behind her over the beige carpet, her pink negligee trailing her high-heeled satin slippers.

"You know people in the community would wonder," Mrs. Harkens was saying to Phoebe now.

"But Marcia wanted me to have—"

"Charlie and I talked about it a long time. I'd told Marcia earlier: 'You can't give up your baby. What will people think?' Then, as you can imagine, what happened at the lake was spread all over the front page of the damned paper, not only in town but all over the state. Before Marcia died, I tried to get her to look at the whole thing sensibly. I always tried to instill in her the importance of appearances. You know that yourself, Phoebe."

"Yes, but that's—"

"That idiot Red-Jack ran his mouth off to that silly organist—you know, the one at the church and the TV station—Robert Rowley. Can you believe that Red-Jack told *him* that Niles was the baby's real father? Charlie and I got in touch with Robert and he claims he hasn't told Niles's mother, even though he talks to her—he says he hasn't told anyone. So he says! I just hope he won't blab to the news people. I know he's tempted, he's right there at the TV station. That makes me really nervous. Charlie and I were already fed up with Red-Jack. I told him he could *not* have the baby. We're going to keep her, raise her—we are, after all, her real grandparents. We want things to look right and that's for DeeDee's benefit as well as—"

"But *Marcia* wanted *me* to have the baby."

"No, Phoebe. Absolutely not! You can't take the baby yourself.

Red-Jack said he'd told you about the first time Marcia tried to kill herself but everything's changed now. I had a talk with Marcia before she went on that picnic. You simply can't have the baby, Phoebe. It's out of the question. You left Harkenstown of your own free will. Now it's better for everyone if you just stay away. Don't come back here. I was a good mother to you when you needed a mother. I was a good mother to Marcia, but I can't spread my mothering out any-more now except for Delia Dawn—"

"Marcia wanted me to have the baby," Phoebe said.

"I told you that's all been changed—"

"Not according to Marcia," Phoebe said. "I'll give her note to the newspaper and I'll give it to the TV station—"

"Now, listen here!" Mrs. Harkens said. There was a pause on the line, then: "You wouldn't do that—that's blackmail!"

Phoebe said, "I'll be giving them the rest of the story. I'll tell them the truth. And I can fill them in on a lot more than just the note."

"Phoebe, listen—"

"You just wait and see what I do," Phoebe said before hanging up.

When she staggered out on the lawn where she'd been yesterday morning with Lord Ravensleigh, she saw Gilbert coming toward her, ahead of a group of tourists being lectured by a guide. She rushed to Gilbert. "Have you seen Lord Ravensleigh? Or Lady Petwell? I have to tell them: I've got to leave."

Gilbert frowned. "Why?" He took her arm, and forcefully urged her toward the breakfast room. Grabbing two plates from the sideboard, he told her to sit down. She took one plate from him to place a piece of dry toast on it. He pulled out two chairs, one for her and one beside it for himself. "Sit down," he said, and took the plates back to the side-board and filled them with scrambled eggs, bacon, kippers, tomatoes.

Staring at the heaping plate he'd set before her on the table, Phoebe felt nausea rising in her.

As Gilbert studied her, he said, "What is it, Phoebe? Talk to me!

You look as though you want to cry. Cry!" Now with his arm around her, she let out tears and words about the news she'd just heard from Kansas, about New Year's Eve, about Niles and Marcia, the baby, the call to Mrs. Harkens . . .

Phoebe, leaning toward the table, placed her hands over her face, then sat up. He took her hand. He turned it to kiss the inside of her wrist. "I'll go with you to Kansas."

"That's not why I told you."

"Phoebe, when you have an emergency, I have an emergency. I'll check on trains to London . . ." Gilbert stopped speaking.

A maid had entered the room and now stood beside the table. "I beg your pardon, miss, you have a telephone call. Would you like to take it in the library?"

Gilbert stood up.

Phoebe followed the maid. When she sat down in a cold, dark leather armchair, the servant shut the door after herself. Phoebe, alone in the room, was surrounded by high walls of books that seemed ready to topple on her. On the phone, she heard the name "Katherine Ferguson." It took a moment for her to think of Sir Chatham's housekeeper.

"Miss, when I came into the flat this morning . . ." There was a long pause.

"Yes?" Phoebe said.

Mrs. Ferguson was crying as she spoke: "I found him. A massive stroke, that's what they said . . ."

"Oh, no! No, please, God. No! . . . Will he—"

"Oh, miss, he's already dead."

Twenty-five

TWO HOURS LATER PHOEBE HUNCHED into herself on the seat beside Gilbert on the train to London. One hand held tightly to the arm of the train seat as the green of the countryside flew by the window. I'm sitting in a train seat, she told herself in her need to hold onto reality. It was as if she were in a land where she did not know the language, the actuality of things.

Gradually she realized Gilbert, seated beside her, had taken hold of her other hand. She struggled to focus on what he was saying: "And I reached Lord Petwell. He said Sir Chatham always insisted he didn't want a fuss made—he just wants to lie next to his lady in the church-yard near his house in Devon. Lord Petwell said it was hard for him to believe he *really* wanted a simple service—people have made a fuss over Chatty all his life."

Phoebe bent over in her seat. "Selmabelle will say I shouldn't have left him, she'll say I should never have gone to Ravensleigh."

"You'll have to tell her he insisted you go."

"I keep wondering why he wanted me to come home to England with him. He told me he needed help, and then when we got over here, he sent me away." Phoebe straightened. "It was his damned male colleagues, he didn't want them to know he was fragile. You were there when they worked out the plans, you heard him . . ."

Slipping an arm around her, he said, "Phoebe, you can't change things now."

When they arrived at The Royal Rose, where they both were staying, Gilbert followed Phoebe to the mail desk. The clerk handed her several envelopes. Gilbert walked with her to the lift. "You sure you'll be all right?" he said, as the lift door began to close, then hid him from view.

On her floor, she approached the door to the suite Sir Chatham had occupied before moving back into his flat. She stopped in the corridor, wanting to pound in protest on the door to the suite where he'd autographed his book for her—where he'd slept, where she'd last seen him. She walked on, then beat on the door to her own suite before unlocking it. She threw her handbag onto the sofa where she sat down. The envelopes spilled around her. She recognized Jill's familiar handwriting on a blue envelope.

Hi Phoebe, We just missed each other. I was surprised by your note that you were going to England. I wasn't in the apartment because I was with Bill in the country. Yeah, he came back, contrite and swearing it would be the way I want it. Hey, gal, I hope you'll understand, but I think I'm going to need to have the apartment to myself, or rather for Bill and me until we can work things out on his divorce and everything. So I'm really sorry, I know this leaves you without a place to live. But you've always said you planned to stay here only temporarily. One other thing, I hate to admit this—Bill tore up your picture of Niles. He thought he was a boyfriend of mine and I think I've told you, he's very jealous. I'm sorry, Phoebe, but I thought I should let you know so it wouldn't be such a shock when you come into the apartment and don't see it. If you don't come back soon, should I pack up your stuff and send it to Selmabelle's or put it in storage, or what? Let me know and wish me luck! Keep your fingers crossed for me. Toes too! Write! Love, Jill."

Phoebe had a hard time folding the letter, then asked herself why she was working to push it back into its envelope. Suddenly she threw the letter and it whirled, then fell, as if wounded. She was happy for Jill but the timing felt so unfortunate.

Phoebe swallowed and forced herself to place a call to Selmabelle. "Service to the United States," the hotel operator's voice told her "is still interrupted, madam."

"Still?"

"The storm on the eastern coast of the United States—"

"I just talked to the states this morning—"

"I'm sorry, madam. We've been unable to put a call through for the past hour."

Phoebe held her head, then phoned Mrs. Ferguson. "I need to open Sir Chatham's small suitcase. I'd like to have someone with me."

In Chicago, on the way to the airport, Sir Chatham had said, "If anything happens to me while we're traveling, Phoebe, I want you to open this case." She had tried to assure him then that this would never be necessary.

Mrs. Ferguson arrived, red-eyed and dressed up in a navy blue shirtwaist dress and hat. She accompanied Phoebe to the manager's office to retrieve the case from the hotel safe where it had been kept in Phoebe's name. Back in her suite Phoebe placed it on the dresser, unlocked it, and lifted the lid.

"Oh, look, miss!" Mrs. Ferguson said.

Inside the case, the watches were arranged in tight rows. The watchbands were snugly fitted around velvet-covered forms, so that the faces of the watches were visible. "Oh, miss, he must have wanted to be able to see them, even when he wasn't wearing them. Mr. Beacon in Bond Street must have made him this case. Oh, he did like things shipshape. 'Shipshape and Bristol fashion,' he used to say."

Under the trays of watches, they discovered a large envelope addressed to Phoebe. Noting the return address, she recognized the name E. H. Trueblood, the lawyer she'd seen with Sir Chatham in the Chicago hospital. Using her nail file, Phoebe slit open the envelope to find a document, bound inside a blue cover, marked: THE LAST WILL AND TESTAMENT . . . "I, Chatham Robert Cecil William Wigans

. . . do make, publish, and declare this to be my Last Will and Testament, hereby revoking any and all Wills and Codicils by me at any time heretofore made . . ."

Phoebe ran her eyes down the beginning paragraphs, amazed that Sir Chatham had entrusted this document to her. Still, he had asked her to care for his watches. An attached letter informed her that the will also had been sent to Sir Chatham's London solicitor, Sir John Digby-Collins, and that only a small portion of the new will was different from the old will. So his old will was what had been in the bulky envelope that Sir Chatham had insisted he had to take with him in the ambulance from the Chicago hotel to the hospital!

Scanning the pages, she took in that he'd left money to five charities. Noting the names of Canadian relatives, Phoebe saw that he'd left his London flat to two great-nephews as well as the sum of fifty thousand pounds each, and to other relatives, one thousand pounds each.

"To my faithful London housekeeper, Mrs. Katherine Margaret Ferguson, ten thousand pounds . . ."

"Come and look at this," Phoebe said to Mrs. Ferguson.

Mrs. Ferguson blushed. "I don't think I should, miss."

"Look, this concerns you." Phoebe pointed out her name. Mrs. Ferguson said, "Oh, miss," then stepping away, pressed a hand over the brooch at the neck of her dress.

Quickly, Phoebe read: "To my faithful Devon gardener, Mr. Henry Homer Philburn Jones, ten thousand pounds . . .

"To my faithful Devon housekeeper, Mrs. Phyllis Louise Williamson, ten thousand pounds . . .

"To Mrs. Phoebe Stanhope of the city, county, and state of New York, U.S.A., who is like a granddaughter to me, and presently employed by Selmabelle Flaunton Enterprises, Inc., I give, devise, and bequeath all of my right, title, and interest in the Daffodil House and greenhouse and the land associated therewith of my Devon property south of the Village of Marycombe, such land described as . . ."

Phoebe's eyes rushed on to see: "I direct my Trustee for the life of the beneficiary, Mrs. Phoebe Stanhope, to pay out from the Trust, established in Paragraph Twenty-two hereunder, the sum of seven thousand pounds immediately and thereafter seven thousand pounds on or about December 10th per annum, to be used in the first instance at the sole discretion of the Trustee for the proper maintenance of the Daffodil House and the greenhouse and the land associated therewith, with the remainder to be paid to the beneficiary herself on or about December 10th every year for the remainder of her life . . ."

Astounded, Phoebe turned to Mrs. Ferguson, "The Daffodil House?"

"Oh, it's cozy, miss. Some distance from the main house but on the property—right near the greenhouse. It's not very big but it's a gem. Sir Chatham and his lady used it mostly as a guesthouse. She gave it that name because it's where the first daffodils come out in February. Everyone who stayed in the Daffodil House loved it."

Phoebe said, "Have you seen it?"

"Yes, miss. When they gave parties at the house, sometimes I'd go down to Devon to help."

Phoebe hurried to read: "To the Village of Marycombe, Devon, I give, devise, and bequeath the remainder of the land in my Devon property and all the buildings thereon, including the main house, the gatehouse, the gardener's cottage, the two storage sheds, the garage, and the land described as . . ." Phoebe skipped down to: "to be used at the discretion of the Trustee and the Marycombe Village Council for the establishment of a library, and for the use of Council meetings and civic functions, including special holiday celebrations . . . I direct that my watch collection, as described and itemized in Appendix C, be secured in a special case and be on display in the library, the hours, and occasions for display to be at the discretion of the Trustee and the Village Council . . ."

Her heart and thoughts racing, Phoebe placed the document back in the case.

"Oh, miss!" Mrs. Ferguson said. "Oh, *miss!*"

That night, while brushing her hair in preparation for an early dinner with Gilbert, Phoebe halted one debate in her busy mind. She would not tell Gilbert or anyone else at this time about the will. Gilbert might want to call Lawrence for his comments as an estates lawyer. She wondered if Lawrence knew Sir Chatham's solicitor.

Certainly he had known Sir Chatham a long time; Lawrence had been only five or six years old when they had first met. Phoebe recalled asking Sir Chatham, while at dinner one night during the tour, about Lawrence as a child. She had tried to appear nonchalant in her questions. Sir Chatham had laughed with delight, then eyed her as if he'd caught on to her interest. "Oh, Lawrence was a little rascal. Everybody's darling—the ladies couldn't get enough of him. My dear, can't you just imagine?"

Swirling the brandy in his glass, Sir Chatham had gone on to say that he himself had been a scamp sometimes in his life. Suddenly he had leaned toward her and peeked down her dress, and said with glee, "Girl!" Appearing flustered then, he had straightened, returned to his usual self.

Phoebe had been so surprised she had pretended nothing had happened. The incident was never mentioned by either of them.

But later in the tour, Phoebe had admitted her interest in Lawrence. She mentioned to Sir Chatham that Jane would be an heiress and this probably attracted Lawrence. "Shall we test him, my dear?" Sir Chatham had said. "Should we start a rumor that you're to be my sole heir?"

"Oh, no!" Phoebe had answered. "But thank you for the thought."

Had this conversation given him the idea to include her, in reality, in his will? Or was it that she had quoted her own childhood statement that she would live in a greenhouse? Or because she'd reminded him of his "lady." And she had helped in the recovery of his watches.

Now crossing the lobby of The Royal Rose on the way to the dining room, Phoebe sadly recalled Sir Chatham carrying his cane and walking briskly beside her, as he had done during the U.S. tour. Reaching the dining room, she was shown to a front table where Gilbert awaited her. He watched her, seeming concerned.

He did not seem surprised that she did not talk much. Finally, she said that she had sat at a table with Sir Chatham in many hotel dining rooms during their tour of the United States. Phoebe confessed that beneath her sadness about Sir Chatham, she was anxious about delaying her trip to Kansas. Gilbert placed his hand over hers. "Phoebe, you don't look well."

She said good-night to him and returned to her suite to try the call to Selmabelle again. She reassured herself that since it was two in the morning in New York, she had to use the number for Selmabelle's private quarters. She hoped Jane would not answer, even if she was still "visiting," still occupying a room on Auntie Sel's top floor. This time the call was going through.

"Hello," said a young-sounding, sleepy voice.

Phoebe had an urge to hang up but she said, "I'm calling from London, I'm sorry to call so late, but could I speak with Selmabelle?"

A frown was in Jane's tone: "Who is this?"

"Phoebe." There was a pause. "Phoebe Stanhope."

"You woke me up. She won't want to talk to you. She's asleep." A hang-up buzz trailed Jane's nasty voice.

Phoebe placed the call again, and this time Bessie answered. "Oh, Miss Phoebe, I miss you."

Coming on the line, Selmabelle said, "This better be important."

"Selmabelle, I hate telling you this—"

"Don't take the rest of the night," Selmabelle said in a slow, drowsy voice.

"Selmabelle, Sir Chatham died—"

"Died?" Following Phoebe's hurried explanation, Selmabelle suddenly seemed awake. "Get hold of Edward Hibbard." Phoebe grabbed a pen and a Royal Rose notepad. "Make a reservation for me. And one for Jane. Order flowers and don't be skimpy." Selmabelle barked more commands: "Order a car, make these calls . . ."

When Phoebe hung up, she tried to clear her mind, to study the list.

The next morning, after a turning, sleepless night, Phoebe took time to meet Gilbert at a corner table in The Royal Rose lounge. He had brought a stack of London newspapers, pointing out lengthy obituaries in *The Times* and the *Daily Telegraph* for Sir Chatham. Reading about his distinguished life and career, Phoebe felt her eyes fill and she blinked, trying to make out the print. She had experienced a closeness with Sir Chatham Wigans that was not included, and never could be included, in these or any other accounts of him. They had shared something special; she knew he had felt it too.

Yet, as far as anyone else would know, she had been associated with him only in business.

She had been honored to work for him. And he was the only one who genuinely had supported her professionally. Downing two aspirin with gulps of coffee, Phoebe pored over more accounts and photos in other papers, feeling proud of him and the many accomplishments, honors, and offices he had held.

It was mentioned that he was survived by Canadian relatives. No matter that Sir Chatham had said in the will that she was like a granddaughter to him, she could not be counted by the world as a relative. Would some relative, or even the village of Marycombe, contest the will, despite the warning in the will that any party which challenged it would inherit nothing? Suddenly Phoebe thought of her grandmother's old-fashioned word: "adventuress." She wondered if, even though small, her inheritance would be viewed in a negative fashion.

Phoebe's eyes stayed on a picture of Sir Chatham and former Prime Minister Winston Churchill seated on chairs in a garden at Chartwell, Churchill's country residence. Both men held cigars. Phoebe had never seen Sir Chatham smoke. Had he smoked with Churchill to show companionship? Sir Chatham had adjusted to

American ways, even to "ungodly early-morning telly." When in America . . . When with Churchill . . .

She remembered Sir Chatham saying that he and Churchill shared a love of brandy. Then she was annoyed recalling that Lawrence liked brandy too. Forget that! she told herself.

She turned to ask Gilbert for the one paper she had not yet read.

"Maybe you'll want to skip this one," Gilbert said.

Phoebe held out her hand, then saw that in describing Sir Chatham's tour of America, the tabloid had reported he'd been accompanied by "a mysterious auburn-haired beauty." She threw down the paper, feeling this tabloid had cheapened the reports about Sir Chatham—and herself too, even though she had not been named. At this moment she did not want to speak. Gilbert was silent too.

When Phoebe witnessed Selmabelle making a grand entrance on arrival at The Royal Rose, followed not only by Jane but by Lawrence, she ducked behind a marble pillar. She peeked out to see Edward Hibbard escorting them into the lift.

She had not expected to see Lawrence! As the lift doors closed on the arrival party, she made an about-face. Her impulse was to check herself out of The Royal Rose, leaving no forwarding address, just a note for Selmabelle: "I hope you had a comfortable trip . . ."

She could move to The Savoy, registering as Phoebe Fields. Handing over her passport, which would identify her as Phoebe Fields Stanhope, she'd say, "I'd like to use Fields—my maiden name—for the moment."

Yet here at The Royal Rose, as Selmabelle's employee, she was a guest and on Selmabelle's expense account. She would need every penny in her pursuit and care of DeeDee. She had to stay put. She would leave a note for Selmabelle saying, "I've taken care of your requests."

She would avoid Gilbert so not to be brought into his brother's orbit.

Entering her suite, she found a message from Sir Chatham's solicitor.

For the funeral, Phoebe did not wear black. She chose to honor Sir Chatham in her own way by dressing in the strawberry print he had liked, and adding a dark veil hastily purchased at Debenham's. Under a giant oak, in the churchyard in the village of Marycombe near Sir Chatham's property, she stood with Lord and Lady Petwell and Sir Chatham's solicitor, Sir John Digby-Collins, and his wife.

The press had tracked Phoebe to The Royal Rose when it had come out in the tabloid that the "mystery beauty"—newly identified—had accompanied Sir Chatham not only on his American tour but on his return trip to England as well. She had stopped using the main entrance to the hotel and started wearing a tam pulled down on her head to hide her hair.

In the newspapers, it had been reported that the funeral was to be a private service but now, in the churchyard, she spotted a bald-headed man with a camera which looked suspiciously professional. She became aware of the press lurking about with cameras, microphones, and notebooks. She peeked behind her, where Mrs. Ferguson stood with the villagers who cared for Sir Chatham's Devon property, including the Daffodil House and greenhouse. Phoebe and Mrs. Ferguson had spoken briefly on arrival at the churchyard.

Selmabelle and Jane moved into place at the gravesite, both dressed in black, and flanked by Gilbert and Lawrence. In a glance, Phoebe could see by Gilbert's alert posture that, despite her veil, he recognized her. She guessed that Selmabelle also had penetrated her disguise, for she looked several times in Phoebe's direction with a brooding face, then glanced away apparently as soon as she realized she had Phoebe's attention.

Jane's eyes were on Lawrence, who stood at her side. His head slightly bowed, Lawrence frowned, which was to Phoebe an unfamiliar expression for him. She realized now she'd known only the light-hearted, social side of his personality. It came to her that she'd learned more about Lawrence from Gilbert than she had ever learned from Lawrence himself.

When the service was over, Sir John Digby-Collins lifted his large, white-haired head. Looking off in the distance, rather than at Phoebe or anyone in particular, he said, "I think that was the right farewell. Sir Chatham would have approved."

Phoebe had first heard Sir John's English voice on the phone when he'd offered his condolences, adding that Sir Chatham had written to him privately about her. The solicitor then had referred to her as a principal heir and to Sir Chatham as a public figure. He made it clear that it had long been known in certain circles that he represented Sir Chatham Wigans. He and a principal heir had numerous details to discuss. Would she like to come to his office—he would send a car—or would she prefer that he and his secretary come to the second-floor meeting rooms in The Royal Rose? They had met at the hotel.

Now in the churchyard Phoebe walked with Sir John and his wife to his car but Gilbert caught up with them. "Phoebe, I've been trying to find you. I've left messages—"

"I'll find you," Phoebe said, as Sir John's chauffeur held open the car door.

Gilbert lifted her veil and kissed her.

That was the picture that appeared in the papers. The tabloid headlined the story: MYSTERY BEAUTY UNVEILED.

Phoebe was surprised that the press story had preceded her to Kansas. As she got off the plane in Wichita and was met by Robert Rowley, he had with him a copy of the *Harkenstown News*. There on the front page was her picture from the high school yearbook: HARKENSTOWNER HEIRESS TO BRITISH KNIGHT.

Phoebe introduced Gilbert to Robert Rowley and the two men shook hands. Quickly Phoebe scanned the local newspaper's account. *This is ridiculous,* she thought. *They're trying to make this into some kind of fairy tale. And it's my life.* This small inheritance was not going to make her rich, nice as it was. "They're stretching the truth," she said aloud.

In London, the press had not given full details of her legacy, only that she was a "principal heir," which seemed to her a stretch of the truth too, but maybe not, since Sir John also had used these words. Phoebe had told Sir John that for a few days she would like only limited information to be provided about her inheritance. The Harkenstown paper had more details so the story was out now.

Robert appeared to be puzzled that a man had accompanied Phoebe to her hometown. She had expected this reaction from Robert, the church organist and her former TV colleague—just as she had expected to hear from Lawrence while she was still in London. Then she had guessed Lawrence would phone her as soon as he saw the story in the British papers, listing her as an heir.

"Well, you're a deep one!" Lawrence had teased when they had run into one another in a lift at The Royal Rose. "I just phoned your room," he said. "You didn't let me know you were in London. You obviously let my brother know—"

"And he let me know about your engagement," she answered without looking at him. "Congratulations!"

"That's questionable."

"Is it? That's interesting," she said, then silently congratulated *herself* for having guessed his reaction. Standing so close beside him in the lift, she could feel her heart reacting but she would *not* slip back into the pressure of uncertainty, all the games he dealt in. She had to choose between him and herself, her own sanity. "I really can't talk now," she said, rushing off the lift, hurrying toward the back of the lobby.

"Are you meeting my brother?" he said, following her.

"Yes," Phoebe said, her voice strong as she strode toward a side exit, wanting him to know she would offer no apology for leaving him, as if in favor of his brother.

Suddenly she whirled around and faced Lawrence. He smiled and held open his arms as if he expected her to run into them. She said, "You bastard."

His face was serious now and puzzled. "Darling . . ."

"Honesty isn't even in your *vocabulary*, is it?" She turned, leaving him, and walked deliberately to the exit.

Then strengthened by this encounter and wearing a tam and dark glasses, she strolled in Hyde Park with Gilbert. She told him that instead of traveling with her to Kansas, he should stay in England to finish Lord Ravensleigh's portrait.

"I've already arranged to finish it when we come back to England together."

"Together?"

"Yes." Gilbert stopped her in the path. "And you need me to go with you to Kansas, Phoebe. I'm staying in your life and you're staying in mine." She did not answer him. They were silent as they walked on, under the trees in the park. "Phoebe, maybe I didn't say that right. I can see on your face—"

"I didn't expect you to say that. I have to think about this, Gilbert. For one thing, don't get me wrong, but most people don't make long trips like this just . . ."

Her voice trailed off as he took her hands. He said, "I might as well say it: what I really want, what I mean is, Phoebe, I'm talking about . . . about a lifetime together."

Lifetime? she said silently.

"Phoebe," Gilbert said. "I'm not sure whether to say more now about what I have in mind . . . but I guess you know what I mean— I'm talking about marriage."

Listening, she began to think what it would be like to spend her life with Gilbert. If they married, she would have Lawrence as her brother-in-law! Suddenly she envisioned the first family dinner; she and Gilbert seated at the table with Lawrence and Jane.

Well, she would not cave in! She might even enjoy it, in some perverse way. She would *not* let Lawrence influence her decision.

By this time she had to live with her hunch that she'd seen through

Lawrence earlier than she'd ever wanted to admit to herself. So help me, she thought, she would never again be hooked by his voice, his charm and wit, his ability to make her laugh. She'd close herself off from his flattery, his flashes of desire, his stinginess, his total unreliability. Why had she ever thought that Lawrence, of all people, could fulfill her need brought on by the multiple shocks of New Year's Eve?

Again, she heard her college English teacher, Miss Thompson, quoting Henry James: "Never say you know the last word about any human heart."

Certainly Gilbert had been right when he'd said, "You don't let us know each other." He'd told her one reason he wanted to paint her portrait was to study her, to know her better.

He was watching her now as they walked in the park. Phoebe looked into his expectant face. Suddenly he clutched her shoulders. "Phoebe, I love you."

She hesitated, then said, "I'm glad you told me that."

Yet she felt rushed. She knew she wanted a life she made herself. She didn't want anyone giving her a ready-made life. Nothing "off the peg."

"Gilbert," Phoebe said. "I haven't made up my mind about any of this."

"I know you haven't."

"But you've touched me. I'm thinking about it. I remember everything you've said to me." Then she emphasized: "And *I know you mean what you say.*"

As they walked on, she began to consider that maybe she should let him go with her to Kansas. It would be a chance to know him better. And what would she gain by leaving him behind?

It seemed natural then as she sat, drifting into sleep, beside Gilbert on the transatlantic flight. The first-class seat that Gilbert had insisted on providing felt so roomy and luxurious. They changed planes, flying out of New York, then Kansas City, and on every flight he sketched her. Over Kansas, he said, "You know what I'd like to see?"

"What?"

"A tumbling tumbleweed."

"Really?" Phoebe smiled. "Gilbert, you have a way of surprising me. I've only seen a few in my whole life."

At the airport Phoebe excused herself to make a phone call. "I'm in the Wichita airport," she told Mrs. Harkens, Marcia's mother, when she reached her.

"I thought you were in England."

"I'm here in Wichita now. So you can tell I wasn't making idle talk. Robert Rowley is with me and he's about to drive me to Harkenstown. We plan to show Marcia's note to the TV station so the story can be on tonight's evening news. And we're about to take Marcia's note to the newspaper—"

"Phoebe, wait! I've talked to Charlie. We want to talk about this and work things out. Phoebe, come and stay here with us. Stay here!"

Phoebe said, "I'm not sure."

"This has always been your second home."

"All right, I guess, while I'm in town. I'll see DeeDee sooner that way, thank you. But I have someone with me."

"We have plenty of room," Mrs. Harkens said in an anxious voice. "You know that, Phoebe."

"I'll see you then," Phoebe said, and rejoined Gilbert and Robert Rowley.

As the trio walked in the hot Kansas wind to Robert's car, Phoebe watched Gilbert. His searching eyes looked out beyond the large parking lot toward the distant horizon. Squinting, he said, "It is flat." He put on his dark glasses against the glare of the early afternoon sun.

In the car Phoebe sat in the front seat beside Robert, and Gilbert heaved himself into the back. As they headed out on the highway to Harkenstown, Robert called back to Gilbert, "Did Phoebe tell you that her mother was my first piano teacher?"

"She might have mentioned it," Gilbert said. "I'd like to hear more, I'm interested in everything about Phoebe."

"I've been taking care of her piano," Robert said.

"I want you to keep it for helping me," Phoebe said. "Robert has been very helpful," she commented, turning to glance back at Gilbert. "He's stayed in touch with Niles's mother for me. She lives in Glennerville and they talk long distance."

"Usually on Sunday afternoon," Robert said as he steered the car past a red truck. "She wants to know what hymns I played in church. Phoebe, one of her neighbors showed her the write-up about you in the *Harkenstown News.*"

"I'm sure she called you about *that!*"

"I tried to play it down."

"Thank you, oh, thank you, Robert. Right now, I'm bracing myself for the maneuvering with Marcia's folks. You and Gilbert both know the real story. I'm *really* grateful to both of you. When we get to Harkenstown, instead of the hotel, Robert, could you drive us to Marcia's parents' house? And, please, if you don't mind, I'd really like for you to come into the house with us, Robert, so Mrs. Harkens can see you're with me. I think that'll convince her that you know the whole story and you're ready to tell it, along with me."

"I told you I'd help you, Phoebe," Robert said.

"Appearances are everything to Mrs. Harkens—"

"I've been giving hints to your mother-in-law," Robert said. "I mentioned DeeDee enough and by now I think she's caught on. She's full of questions. In fact, she's beginning to hound me."

"I'll call her when I can give her some real news."

"We're all full of questions," Gilbert said from the back seat. "I'm especially waiting for one answer. Or I was." Phoebe felt Gilbert touch her shoulder, then stroke her hair. "Now I've decided I'll answer the question for you myself."

Phoebe turned and smiled at Gilbert. "No, you won't,"

"Hold it! Hold that position a minute," Gilbert said. "I want to remember it, I want to sketch you like this."

As the car finally turned into the driveway of the Harkens house, Robert suddenly pressed the brakes, throwing Phoebe forward toward the windshield.

"Phoebe!" She heard the shouting before she spotted the stout woman, dressed in black, struggling to run toward the car from the grape arbor. "I thought you were never going to get here," Mother Bertha cried out. "I was just about ready to go into the house by myself. Now, let's hurry, so we can all go in together to claim my grandbaby. That poor darling orphan needs two grandmas, not just one uppity one."

Phoebe hurried out of the car to hug her mother-in-law. "Mother Bertha, I'm surprised to see you."

"Why? I'm not surprised to see you."

Mother Bertha stopped to watch Robert drive on toward the house. Gilbert was looking back at them from the rear seat. Robert followed the driveway, and brought the car to a stop nearer the entrance of the house.

"I parked my car out there in the street," Mother Bertha told Phoebe, "and then to get out of this sun, I sneaked into that grape arbor to wait. Nobody came from the house to shoo me off. If they had, I'd have told them what for."

Phoebe took her arm. "I'm glad you're able to drive again."

As they walked toward the house, Mother Bertha said, "I had to be strong for my boy and my grandbaby. I drove all the way here to Harkenstown from Glennerville yesterday. Then last night I slept in the car out in the cemetery. First, I walked around and around my boy's grave in the moonlight and car lights. I promised him I'd take care of his little girl. He told me he knew I'd never turn away from my own flesh and blood. Phoebe, you can visit my grandbaby, but she's going home with me to Glennerville."

"I see." Phoebe felt herself stiffen and asked silently if she was being selfish. What would DeeDee feel when she later learned she had been taken from her two grandmas, three if Red-Jack's mother were counted? How could Phoebe know that she was offering DeeDee a better life?

She'd felt these questions tugging at her before, but now, in the bright sunlight, the future and Phoebe were staring at each other. *Could* she assure DeeDee a happy life? How could anyone do that? Was what she had to offer really superior to that provided by Mrs. Harkens, aided by Mrs. Bain? Or even by Mother Bertha with her passion for a grandbaby? Would Phoebe deprive DeeDee of some of her roots, the warmth of knowing of her real Kansas ancestors, such as Marcia's pioneer great grandfather, who had founded Harkens-town? Yet, some of Phoebe's forebears had been pioneers too. Had her forefathers and Marcia's known each other? How much did any of that matter now? Phoebe's mother had said, "We're not ancestor worshipers."

There's only a limited number of solutions, Phoebe told herself. Marcia had been in a better position than anyone else to judge what Mrs. Harkens offered as a mother and she fervently had wanted Phoebe to have DeeDee. She must rely on that.

Could the wish Marcia had expressed in her note even be honored? Can you will a baby the way you can will a piano? Phoebe sensed legal combat ahead. She could do battle. And she would be a good mother to DeeDee—she would love her. She loved her already. She had to be responsible. The baby could hardly choose at this moment.

Phoebe continued to walk toward the house with Niles's mother. "Mother Bertha, I think I should tell you: Marcia wanted me to have the baby."

Mother Bertha pulled Phoebe to a halt. "She just didn't think of me. If she did, she probably thought I'd be like her mother and worry about what the neighbors think. I admit that once I might have given that some thought, Phoebe, but what the neighbors think won't bring back my boy or give me my grandbaby."

"That's right, Mother Bertha," Phoebe said. "You're DeeDee's grandmother. And you'll still be her grandmother when I take her."

"What do you mean by that?"

"I plan to take her back to England to stay. At least until the orchids bloom."

"You got orchids there?"

"In my greenhouse. You'll have to come and see."

Mother Bertha, hobbling beside Phoebe, answered, "Sometime, but first—"

"I'll let you know the best time." Phoebe turned to face Mother Bertha directly. Out of the corner of her eye, she could see Gilbert coming toward them, then felt him take her hand. She squeezed his hand. "As Mrs. Harkens says," Phoebe said, "we'll work it out."

The End